'If you're in the market for a stellar read, put these three angels at the top of your shopping list' *Daily Record*

'A comic and poignant tale' *Sunday Express*

'Always original and laugh-out-loud funny, Kate Harrison's wonderful novels deserve a place on every bookshelf'
Chris Manby

'Fabulous premise, great characters and a few surprises . . . scarily addictive' *Daily Record*

'A poignant, very funny story, full of warmth and insight'
Sophie Kinsella

'A fun, light read for the girls' *Heat*

'You are just transported into the world of secret shopping and the lives of the three women . . . *The Secret Shopper's Revenge* is brilliant, well written and captivating entertainment . . . 5/5' www.trashionista.com

'Fresh, feisty and fun' *Company*

'Classic chick lit . . . deeply moving' *Daily Telegraph*

D1151185

Kate Harrison gained hands-on retail experience as a Saturday girl in a hardware store, a shelf-stacker, and undercover consumer journalist and, of course, as a mystery shopper. She now writes full-time, and her six previous novels, including the bestselling *The Secret Shopper's Revenge*, are available from Orion. Kate lives in Brighton. To learn more about Kate and her novels visit her website at www.kate-harrison.com

By Kate Harrison

Old School Ties
The Starter Marriage
Brown Owl's Guide to Life
The Self-Preservation Society
The Secret Shopper's Revenge
The Secret Shopper Unwrapped
The Secret Shopper Affair

THE SECRET
SHOPPER AFFAIR

Kate Harrison

An Orion paperback

First published in Great Britain in 2011
by Orion
This paperback edition published in 2011
by Orion Books Ltd,
Orion House, 5 Upper St Martin's Lane,
London WC2H 9EA

An Hachette UK company

A CIP catalogue record for this book
is available from the British Library.

Typeset at The Spartan Press Ltd,
Lymington, Hants

Printed and bound in Great Britain by
Clays Ltd, St Ives plc

The Orion Publishing Group's policy is to use papers
that are natural, renewable and recyclable products and
made from wood grown in sustainable forests. The logging
and manufacturing processes are expected to conform to
the environmental regulations of the country of origin.

www.orionbooks.co.uk

'Friendship is a sheltering tree.' SAMUEL COLERIDGE

'A true friend stabs you in the front.' OSCAR WILDE

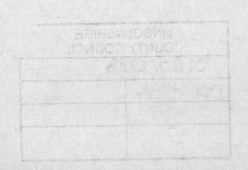

March

Mothering Sunday

CHAPTER 1

Sandie

Once upon a time, there was a girl who grew up not believing in fairy tales.

I knew from the beginning that handsome princes did *not* exist, and neither did turreted castles nor fairy god-mothers. Instead of wishing on a star, I put my faith in elbow grease and GCSEs, and I worked my way up, from the basement stockroom of Garnett's, the best department store in the world, towards the oak-panelled glory of the management floor. Unlike Cinders, I did it the hard way.

Which is why, when I somehow scored the fairy-tale hat trick – handsome prince, castle with its very own turret, plus two best friends who would make perfect godmothers – it all seemed too good to be true.

Guess what? It was.

'Oh, my word. Sandra, there is no way that this house is going to be anywhere near ready in time for the baby!'

My gramma raised me, so perhaps it's not surprising we're both pessimists.

My mother Marnie, meanwhile, always thinks her wine glass is half full. 'Ah, but look at the potential. It is the most amazing house I've ever seen. That tower is perfect, and this street is like millionaire's row. I bet your neighbours are actors and rock stars! It just needs a lick of paint.'

'Not to mention windows, doors and walls,' I say, shivering uncontrollably. We're in the basement of the new house, Gramma, Mum and me in hard hats and fluorescent jackets, standing closer together than we normally do, like cavemen huddling together for warmth. I don't think there can be anywhere in London that's colder than this.

I blame the architect. His computer model was so advanced that until now, I almost believed I'd already walked around the cream and ochre kitchen with the hand-painted bronze range, and laid a table for sixteen in the dramatic dining room. I'd gazed out of the floor-to-ceiling windows that beckon you up the chunky limestone steps and into the lush tropical-style garden. I'd imagined our sleeping baby in its Beatrix Potter-themed nursery, in the turret that the original Victorian owners had added as a mad, but madly enchanting, act of building folly.

But ten minutes here, and the fantasy is gone, as ridiculous as a pumpkin carriage. I try to smile. 'The contractors said they'll definitely get it done before July, Gramma. That's why we're paying them top rates. To work round the clock.'

She looks around her and tuts. 'So I see.'

My future dream home echoes with emptiness. No drilling, no hammering, no concrete mixer. Only the rapid tapping of four paws against tiles . . .

Monty races around the corner, his legs splaying out to the sides as he tries and fails to get a grip on the glassy red tiles of the kitchen floor. I feel bad about the tiles. We're having to rip them up, to install the baby-friendly and up-to-the-minute rubber flooring the architect recommended, but it does feel like we're ripping out a century's worth of footsteps too. Babies will have been born – and possibly conceived – on those tiles. Soldiers' boots will have marched across them during two world wars.

It must be my hormones making me so emotional. I'm normally Ms Practical, but the pregnant bit of me – well, all of me is pregnant, let's face it, however hard I try to pretend it's not – is as soft as cashmere.

Emily warned me it'd happen. Though I'm pretty sure Emily was a big softie even before she gave birth to Freddie.

There I go again. Thinking about Emily – potential God-mother Number One – makes me feel bad, too, because I know I should be with her today, supporting her latest store launch. We've been mates for three years now, and even though we don't do our undercover shopping missions to-gether any more, we're always there for each other. Except today . . .

But what do I do? Right now every minute of my life is accounted for: settling the insurance claim on our burnt-out flat, organising this refurb, keeping Mum and Gramma happy, trying to convince my clients that it's business as usual, despite the fire and my bump and the sleepiness that strikes when I least expect it.

Toby appears in the doorway. Lush, long strands of blond hair spring out from under his blue plastic hard hat. Bob the Builder he is not. 'Whatever you chaps do, don't try to go above ground level.'

'How come?'

'They've taken the old first floor out, but as yet they've neglected to put a new one in. Monty almost fell into the gap, never to be seen again.'

Hearing his name, the dog whimpers, then rolls onto his back to have his belly scratched. For once, Toby ignores him.

'We're missing a floor?'

'I'm sure it's only temporary,' says Toby, but his face tells a different story. 'That's the thing with building work, it—'

'—has to get worse before it gets better.' I finish the sentence that is our new mantra. I just never expected it to get *this* much worse. When we got the keys for the house a fortnight ago, the refurb seemed daunting but *doable*. For the first time since the fire destroyed Toby's penthouse, I could imagine calling somewhere home again. And, actually, this was much more my idea of a home than his Chelsea apartment. That was glossy and glam, whereas the new house is solid and sturdy and ever so slightly stuffy, on a leafy avenue not far from Chiswick High Road.

Choosing this place was the least logical thing I've ever done. Despite the estate agent's nonsense – 'this stunning house has stayed in one family since it was first built and offers unlimited potential for the discerning buyer, blah, blah' – Toby and I both knew that 'potential' is Rupert-speak for 'total wreck'.

And when we arrived at dusk on a bitter and overcast January day, it looked more like the Addams Family mansion than 'the perfect for ever home'. The turret didn't help: it gave the whole building the look of Dracula's castle.

Toby hated it, and anyway there was so much more to see, thanks to the credit crunch: the townhouse in Bloomsbury, the villa in Putney. Before I got together with Toby, I couldn't have afforded a lock-up garage in Leytonstone. I'm no gold-digger, whatever Toby's mother thinks, but I am lucky in love. Who'd have thought it?

Why was number ten, with its damp smell and the forest of saplings growing out of the tacked-on tower, the first house I thought of when I woke up the next day? Hormones again, it has to be.

'Shall we take a look outside, where it's warmer?' Toby suggests.

Even Marnie's perma-grin is fading, as we manoeuvre up the narrow staircase. Her denim-covered hips block the light as she walks ahead of me.

'Sandie, you won't be spending much time in the kitchen for a while,' she says between puffs. 'Give it another month and you'll be so big that you'll have to call the fire brigade to get you out.'

I look at the staircase. 'I won't get *that* big, will I?'

Marnie giggles. 'We Barrow women make big babies, eh, Ma?'

Gramma sniffs. We *never* discussed bodily functions when I was growing up.

'Come on, Ma,' says Marnie. 'I've seen the photos of when you fell with me. You looked like a hippo. It's the Barrow curse, eh?'

I stroke my bump, which is still neat. I'm twenty-two weeks, so of course I'll get a lot bigger and there's nothing I can do about it. My body is no longer my own. I was never one of those women who dreamed of babies, and at first it freaked me out, but now . . . I do feel secretly excited that I'm doing this incredible thing.

I feel Gramma's eyes on me, and I wait to be told off for considering moving into a wrecked house with a baby, or for refusing to marry the man who has asked me at least a dozen times since Christmas.

But then she walks across to me, and places her hand on my stomach, tentatively at first, until I smile and she lets it rest. I can't remember the last time she reached out to me – she's never been a touchy-feely woman. Her hands are lined and light brown, her coffee skin fading to latte with age.

Gramma moves back, surprised at herself. 'You're bonny already. But, yes, it's easy to put on a few extra pounds.' Then she whispers, 'I've got a callisthenics book you can have, afterwards. Keep your figure and you keep your man.'

Toby coughs. 'Ladies, shall we move on? We have out-buildings to inspect.'

Gramma steps away and in a final freaky moment, she *winks* at me. I didn't even know my grandmother could wink.

Yes, pregnancy has the weirdest side-effects, and they don't only affect the mum-to-be.

'Wakey, wakey, sleeping beauty!'

I jump as Toby comes into the living room. Some of my papers have fallen on the floor. 'I wasn't asleep!'

'No? And I suppose you weren't snoring like a tramp on a park bench either?'

I tut. 'So do you think they liked the house?'

'They bloody *loved* it, Brains. Your mother would move in with us given half a chance, and your gramma thinks there's no way we can stay living in sin in such a respectable neighbourhood.'

I refuse to look at him in case he proposes again. He puts a tray down on the coffee table and sits next to me on the pink damask sofa. 'So, madam, here we have chicken salad, toast, Marmite, scones, cream, jam, fruit and freshly drawn tea. A nutritious feast for my fertility goddess. Where would you like to start?'

I remember Gramma's whispered warnings about getting fat, and I shake my head. 'It's a myth, about eating for two. You'll go off me if I run to fat.'

He butters the toast thickly, adding the thinnest scrape of Marmite, and then cuts it into four fingers. 'Like I always say, the more there is of you, the better for me.'

We are a textbook case of opposites attracting: Toby is a blond bombshell, with twinkling naughty schoolboy eyes, and a body built for track and field. I am descended from hardy Jamaican stock, with hair that takes care of itself, and a strong body built for long distances. Sometimes we trace fingers over each other's skin like explorers who've struck gold.

Lord knows what our baby will look like . . .

Monty waits patiently at our feet. He always gets our leftovers now, even though he leaves crumbs all over the laminate. Since everything we owned went up in flames, thanks to my business rival and my treacherous ex-PA, we've been less house-proud. When the insurers offered us this matchbox terrace, Toby said we could afford somewhere much swankier. But I thought the cramped rooms would give us an incentive to get a move on and find our own house.

Yet, weirdly, we've ended up feeling *very* comfortable here. I never had a doll's house, but this has the same shoebox rooms, perfectly square windows and a postbox-red front door. We needed a cleaner at the penthouse, but here you can stand in the centre of every room and still reach all the corners with a duster. No one's been more surprised than Toby to find that he actually enjoys keeping house. He awards himself points every time he takes the rubbish out or scrubs the bath. He says that's 'what we did at school'. Sometimes I think a public school education is underrated.

Though will he expect the same for our baby? I give my bump a protective stroke.

'Penny for them, Brains?'

'Thinking about the house,' I fib.

'It was rather terrifying to see the old lady stripped down like that, wasn't it?' Toby decided a while back that number ten is a woman. He puts one arm around me, and rests his hand on mine, on top of the bump. The first time he did that, I felt self-conscious, because it seemed like the sort of thing people did at the end of romantic comedies. But now it makes me feel warm. *Protected.*

'I don't see how they'll do it.'

'Ah, I will make it happen. Can't have the son and heir coming home to a building site. I'll tell them we won't stand for it!'

I suspect the burly blokes who run Blues Brothers Building Services might not take Toby as seriously as he takes himself. 'While you're doing magic tricks, maybe you can finish my pitch for that wedding-planner woman who wants a store makeover. My mind's a blank.'

'You've just got to say the word and I'll give you all the experience you need of being a bride.'

9

I shake my head. 'Oh yes, because planning a wedding is what we need on top of everything else.' But then he looks hurt, and I kiss him on the forehead. 'I'll think about it. I promise. But right now I've got other things to panic about.'

'You and me both. I'm meant to have read this before tomorrow's meeting.' He leans down to pick up his briefcase from the floor. 'I haven't got past page four.'

'Give it here.'

'No. No, you're under enough pressure.'

'Rubbish. I might be pregnant, but I'm not mentally incapacitated.' I reach over to take it. 'Oof. Is this the report or the complete works of Shakespeare?' When I unzip the case, there's a full ream of paper inside.

'That's why I haven't been in the mood.'

'You're never in the mood for *spreadsheets*, let's face it, party boy.'

Toby and I became friends over Garnett's accounts. He was the playboy heir to the store, and I was the trainee from the sticks, but I could always run rings around him when it came to Excel. Although back then, the quarterly reports were a dozen pages long at the most.

'Shall I butter you a scone?'

I smile. 'In the old days, you used to buy me lunch at Claridge's. I hope you're not taking advantage of me, master.'

'I think it's a bit late for that, wench,' he says, kissing my bump through my sweater.

'What about Tyson?'

'Hmmm?' I look up from the report to the clock on the mantelpiece, and I realise it's been an hour since I picked it up. Somehow I've polished off all the scones and the toast. Monty is lying by the living flame fire, his belly full of crumbs, and Toby is leafing through a book of baby names.

'I said, what about Tyson Garnett?'

I can't tell whether he's joking. 'As in Mike Tyson?'

'Hmm. It's very modern. And no one would ever take him on with a name like that.'

'Your mother would definitely cut you out of the will.'

'I can cope with hardship, so long as we're together.'

'Well, looking at these figures, we might have to get used to hardship sooner than you're expecting.'

Toby frowns. 'I didn't get far, but the bit I read said the store's doing OK.'

I sigh. 'Yes. That's what the *words* say. But the figures say something different. The ten weeks since Christmas have been a total disaster.'

He sits upright. 'So why does Edgar's summary say everything's fine and dandy?'

'No idea. If I didn't know him better, I'd say your store manager was deliberately using the New Year sales figures to mask the meltdown. But he's not the type. Why would he do that?'

Toby thinks about this. 'Mum's been giving him a bit of a hard time lately, since we lost the Peerless Serums contract and she has to go to Harrods instead.'

'Hmm.' I bite my lip. Laetitia Garnett helps herself to whatever she fancies from the Garnett's shelves, like an authorised shoplifter. 'Take a look.'

He scans the pages I've highlighted and then shakes his head. 'I don't know what I'm meant to be seeing.' He folds his arms across his chest, and I know I've lost him.

'This is important, Toby. The way I'm reading this, Garnett's is in big trouble.'

'Ah, she's got plenty of life in her yet.'

I hesitate. I don't want to interfere, but I can't ignore what I've seen. 'That's not what the figures say,' I whisper.

He frowns. 'It's that bad?'

'That depends on how much leeway the banks will give you. But if I were a banker, I wouldn't be buying Garnett's gift tokens for next Christmas.'

'Because we might not *be* there?' His voice is small.

I nod.

He gulps. 'But that *can't* happen.'

When I first knew Toby, I thought he was like all his rich chums, spending the family money on cocktails and sports cars. But actually, Garnett's means so much more to him than most people realise: not least because his father died from the stress of trying to keep the place afloat.

'I might be wrong. But you definitely need to ask Edgar some tough questions.'

Toby gives me that look.

'No,' I say. 'I can't go back there. Please don't ask me to.'

He sighs. 'You know I wouldn't ask if I didn't need you. Even dull old Edgar could run rings round me with figures, but he wouldn't dare if you're there. Please?'

It's *so* not my job to save Garnett's. This is the store that sacked me without even questioning the flimsiest evidence that I'd stolen from them. It took Grazia, my other Fairy Godmother, to prove I'd been fitted up by my deputy, and by then I didn't want to go back to work with people who'd been so willing to believe I was a crook.

Yet despite all that, I know I can't turn my back on it. Garnett's was my first true love.

'You're on.'

He hugs me, and I try to focus on that, and the knowledge that I'm doing the right thing, instead of the nauseous feeling that envelops me when I imagine coming face to face with his cow of a mother across the boardroom table.

CHAPTER 2

Emily

It's coming up to ten past one when craft guerrilla warfare breaks out in Heartsease Common.

The love of my life is on the front line.

'Emily? Emily, where are you?' Will sounds desperate.

'In the stockroom, looking for embroidery needles.'

'Can you come out, please? World War Three's kicking off between the knitters and the crocheters. They both claim that you promised them exclusive use of the lounge bar at the Rose and Crown. You didn't, did you?'

The love of my life doesn't always have complete faith in my organisational abilities.

'No, Will,' I call out, 'I'm not completely *insane*.'

Or am I? Would a sane woman even attempt what we're doing today?

I race into the shop, where Will is trying to broker a peace agreement between the leaders of the two factions. The Emporium isn't the ideal setting for a battle. The store is on the poky side of petite, and though we've used all the decorator's tricks to open it up – dairy cream and sage paintwork, and ceiling-height ironwork bakers' shelves loaded with locally made bread – you'd struggle to throw a punch without your fist landing in the artisan soft cheese.

'. . . but is there no way you can share the space?' he's suggesting. 'After all, the Craftathon is about cross-pollination? Sharing traditional skills.'

The two women look at each other with contempt.

'Personally, I wouldn't call knitting a *skill*,' says the thinner woman, who grips a crochet hook in her fist, her knuckles white with tension. She's dug in between the organic root veg and the elderflower wine.

The plumper woman tuts from her forward position by the pickles. Her wooden needles are tucked away under her left arm, the sharp ends poking out past her substantial Fair-Isled bosom. 'There's a reason why women who crochet are known as *hookers.*'

A mother who's just reaching out for one of our irresistible choc-and-cherry whoopee pies tuts loudly, and ushers her young daughter out of the shop without buying so much as a jam tart. *Great.* The point of the Craftathon was to increase sales as well as promote community spirit. Right now, it's doing neither.

'Ladies, *please*,' Will says, smiling his most soothing smile. 'There's hardly any difference between the lounge and the saloon, is there?'

Knitter shrugs. 'It's all about reputations. And we're in the right. Jean said we could have the lounge bar.'

I glance pointedly at Will. I should have known that Jean would be behind this. She's pushing eighty, a twinset-and-pearls firebrand who came with the fixtures and fittings of the Emporium. We don't pay her, but she minds the shop, minds Freddie and *never* minds her own business.

'Well, we know all about *Jean's* reputation, don't we?' Miss Crochety is hitting back with rumours about Jean and Bob the estate agent. But my attention is drifting towards the common. One glimpse is all it takes to tempt me outside.

I brush past the warring wool fans, and out onto the grass. I can't resist. It's early yet, so the marquee workshops are still empty and the PA system hasn't yet started playing the Mother's Day playlist that Will downloaded from iTunes. But with a bit of luck and a lot of fairy dust, by two, thousands of people will descend on Heartsease to fulfil their creative selves, fill their faces, and spend loads of lovely dosh.

That's *if* we can pull it off again. Back in January, I had no doubts. The lease on the empty chemist next door to the Emporium was cheap as chips, and the perfect location for our Heartsease Handmade craft centre, my latest genius idea. But setting up the store wasn't enough of a challenge for me. Oh, no. Trivial stuff like buying half a dozen sewing machines off eBay, filling the pharmacy shelves with cheerful fabrics and patterns, or finding tutors who could pass on the secrets of French knots and silver filigree was too easy. I decided we *had* to launch the store with a bang, or rather, with a Mothering Sunday guerrilla craft extravaganza. We'd bring income into our village *and* save the world from ecological disaster, not to mention save my relationship with Will from more everyday domestic squabbles by proving I am superwoman.

Maybe my aims were a little ambitious. I'd pictured a sunny spring day, a gaggle of celebrity crafters, thousands of families sitting on a community quilt so big it'd get into the *Guinness Book of Records*, and be visible from outer space. Like Heartsease's answer to the Great Wall of China.

It's not quite turned out like that. The bitter wind blowing across the common means you'd get frostbite if you attempted a picnic. The guerrilla crafters couldn't agree on the design, so there's no Great Quilt of Berkshire. And the first twenty-nine celebrity crafters we tried had prior engagements, so our star attraction is a former radio presenter who was kicked out of *I'm a Celebrity* without having to do a Bushtucker Trial because no one recognised her.

Still. Every journey begins with a single step. Or, in the case of the Heartsease Handmade Happiness Day, with a single stitch.

'Mummy, I got treat for you . . .'

Freddie's hiding something behind his back. His face is flushed with excitement, but his idea of what counts as a top treat varies alarmingly. I've been presented with a buttercup, the hairiest dead spider I've ever seen, a mud pie, a vintage mince pie (excavated only last week from the depths of the sofa), a catnip mouse still damp from the jaws of the moggy next door, a chocolate crispy cake made at playgroup (my favourite gift so far), and the unwelcome evidence that the potty-training we'd been working on for months had finally borne fruit.

My ex-husband had no sympathy when I told him. 'If you will celebrate every wee as though he's discovered a cure for cancer, then you shouldn't be surprised when he thinks a turd is a reason to crack open the champagne.'

And this from a man who used to expect a standing ovation for stacking the dishwasher, but believed that only women had the special skills required to put the plates away afterwards . . . Though I was the one who let him get away with it, something I am determined not to do with Freddie. One day, my son will make someone the perfect husband.

'Is it a surprise, Freddie?'

'Um, yes.'

'Brilliant!' Freddie's excitement is every bit as infectious as the tummy bugs he brings home every day from Tiny Tykes. A three-and-a-half-year-old is much better than Prozac. Not that I need Prozac, of course. I'm one of the world's born optimists!

'Hold out your hands and close your eyes, Mummy!'

Would a born optimist feel dread? But I do as I'm told, hold out my palms and wait for something unpleasant – slime or sludge or prickles – but instead I feel tickly softness.

'Can I open my eyes now?'

'No! Guess!' He's giggling.

'Is it a mouse?'

'Ha! Ha! Ha!'

'It can't be a mouse because it isn't moving. I hope it isn't a *dead* mouse.'

The giggles grow louder. 'You're *stupid*, Mummy. Guess NOW!'

I'm not sure I like the bossy side of Freddie's character that's emerged in the last month or two. I know he doesn't get it from me, so it must be from Duncan. Maybe my quest to turn my son into a New Man is going to be trickier than I thought.

'OK, er, is it a chicken?'

'No!'

I turn the thing over in my hand. It's *knobbly*. 'A teddy bear? A bare teddy?'

'Hahahahahahahahahahaha!'

'I give up.'

'OK, dummy Mummy! Open your eyes.'

When I do open them, the irritation fades away. In my hand is a misshapen piece of multicoloured pink and red wool. I try to use my mummy-instincts to guess what it is.

'A . . . flower!' The petals are wonky and the green felt leaf is hanging on by the thinnest strand of cotton. But Freddie made it, which makes it more precious than a hundred red roses.

His face lights up. 'Happy birthday, Mummy!'

'Um, it's not . . .' and then I decide now is probably not the time to explain that today is a day for *all* mummies, because he'll want to know when Freddie's Day is. 'Thank you, Fredster. You're my best boy!'

I kiss him and, for the first time ever, he reels backwards and says, '*Mummy, don't!* Someone might see,' and I swear my heart is in a vice. It leaves me breathless; I know that tonight he'll be as cuddly as ever at bedtime, but I also realise this is a landmark moment, the minute I understand that I can't pretend Freddie is my baby any more.

And the minute my longing for another baby hits me all over again.

An hour later, and Heartsease has been invaded by alien creatures from the Planet Pregnant.

Neat bumps, plump bumps, bumps so huge that they defy gravity and logic. They're in the Rose and Crown, where their owners are learning crochet in the lounge bar (Miss Crotchety won the toss) and knitting in the saloon. The invaders are cursing their way through French knots in the embroidery tent, quilting in the supermarket, and candle-making in the charity shop.

You could say they're getting on my wick . . .

It shouldn't be a surprise. The whole point of choosing Mothering Sunday for the launch of Heartsease Handmade was to attract the mummy mafia from the Next Village Along. The one with the Michelin-starred gastropub and the prize-winning branch of the Women's Institute that was now run by the City-pioneers-turned-super-mums.

No one ever lives in Heartsease if they can afford the Next Village Along. Ours is an ugly duckling place, in a county full of swans. However hard the estate agents try to sell it as up-and-coming, Heartsease looks better on paper than in reality. The 'common' is a patchy strip of grass scarcely large enough for a neglected cricket pitch. The rows of old workers' cottages squaring up to each other on either side of the grass slump like teenagers with bad posture. Refugees from the city come here, hoping for community spirit and neighbours who didn't deal drugs. But though the locals aren't hostile, neither do they bake a welcome cake every time they see yet another removal van struggle through Heartsease's cramped streets.

I like to think that Will and I are changing that, just a little, with our shop and events like this. But we haven't affected the birth rate yet, while in the Next Village Along, there's a mid-wifery crisis. Findlebury Common is such an idyll that they're

18

breeding like organically fed rabbits. In all the mad whirl of preparing for today's event, I hadn't realised how crap it would make me feel to be surrounded by so many smugly expectant mothers. I know pregnancy isn't much to be smug about, what with morning sickness and varicose veins and neuroses, but I'd take all of the discomfort to have what they have. I want to be pregnant again.

Want is too weak a word. Crave, need, desire are closer. All the other things I want – a successful Craftathon, a healthy profit in the shops, a bigger flat – I'd swap in a heartbeat for a bun in the oven. A son like Will, with a Beatles-style mop of dark hair and those mercurial blue-green eyes. Or a little girl who inherits his height, and a blonder, straighter version of my temperamental hair.

Wendy, who runs Tiny Tykes, appears at my side. 'Lovely to see mums-to-be in the village,' she says, with a pointed glance at my not-flat-but-not-pregnant-either belly. 'Such a shame none of them live here.'

Wendy wants to extend her empire by forcing the council to open a primary school here and there's nothing I want more than to add a new baby's name to her petition, but Will refuses to play ball. We almost split up over it last year. I'm trying to count my blessings – lovely boyfriend, healthy son, new business – but the bumps are making it harder.

'I'm working on it,' I say. Well, it's half-true. I am working on Will. Just not in the way she probably thinks I am.

'How long did it take you to fall with Freddie?' She tries hard to keep the edge out of her voice as she says my son's name. He's not her favourite 'tyke'. All the things that make him so lovable to me – his passions for shoes and shopping, his talent for knitting, his insatiable curiosity – make her uncomfortable.

'Oh, no time at all,' I say and then, to embarrass her, I add, 'but of course, that was with my ex-husband. Not with Will.'

'Oh? Oh!' She looks stricken. 'I mean, you wouldn't know

it to look at him, would you? So virile-looking. Tall, dark *and* handsome. Still, you never can tell till you try.'

It takes me a second to realise that she isn't referring to my ex, who, at five foot four, could hardly be described as tall. She's talking about Will. And now she thinks he has a problem with his *sperm*, but I can't tell her the truth, that Will says he doesn't want a baby because we're too broke and that the planet is populated enough already. And I definitely can't tell her that, in my darker moments, I'm sure that what he really means is he doesn't want a baby with *me*.

'EMILY! Emily, my dear, this is splendid!'

That espresso voice – Italian with a hint of the Queen's English – perks me up as much as a double latte. Grazia comes to the rescue, and not for the first time. I turn and she gives me a huge hug, and I hear a distinct tut from Wendy. Whether that's because she's had her interrogation interrupted, or because she disapproves of Grazia, I don't know.

'Was it awful, Grazia? And were you brave?'

She sighs. 'He almost cried, Emily.'

'Blimey. But you didn't?'

'It is undignified to cry in public.' She looks perfectly composed, from her unsmudged mascara and her luscious scarlet lips, to her matching velvet Russian-style trouser suit and shiny Cossack boots. She certainly doesn't look like a woman who has just packed her toyboy off to Hong Kong.

'But . . .'

'I will miss Nigel, Emily, I do not have a heart of stone. But facts must be faced. Long-distance relationships never work.'

I feel close to tears. 'You love him, Grazia.'

Her eyes seem to go misty, momentarily, but then she smiles. 'There are as many ways to love as there are men in the world, and sometimes the intensity of a brief affair is so much more *piquant* than keeping a relationship on life support, no?'

'Life isn't all *Brief Encounter*, Grazia—'

But she holds up her hand. 'Let that be the last we will say on this matter.' She looks around her. 'Another marvellous show here. You will see I picked my outfit in honour of your craft theme.'

'It's so cute.' Although only Grazia could get away with the gaudiness of the black and gold embroidered cavalry marching up her sleeves and down her chest. Actually, has she had a boob job? Her bust seems to be heaving under that boxy jacket.

'Cute? No one has ever called me cute before. But it is good here. So many people.'

'Hmm. And so many *pregnant* people.'

She raises her eyebrows, something she's only been able to do since the Botox wore off – Grazia without her scowl was not right at all. 'I had not noticed.'

'No?' I shrug. 'They're everywhere.'

'If you say so.' She looks again, shakes her head. 'But where is our favourite pregnant person?'

I try not to pull a face. 'Sandie? She sends her apologies. Says she's snowed under with work, and has to go and intimidate the builders into working harder.'

The eyebrows shoot up again. 'But she should be here. The shopping angels always celebrate each other's triumphs.'

'Yes.' Though I can't say I've felt much like celebrating Sandie's triumphs lately. When we got together, we were all in the same leaky boat: I was a single mum with no cash, Sandie was a sacked shop manager with no prospects, and Grazia was a widow with no hope. Somehow, our crappy job filming rubbish customer service on hidden cameras brought us together, and made things better.

But it's different now: Sandie's luck has definitely changed for the better. There's the unplanned, unwelcome pregnancy that's turned into the most heralded event since Mary and Joseph got their big news. The fabulous, knock-down-priced villa Sandie and Toby have bought in Chiswick. The

21

wonderful architect who is going to transform it. The way Toby proposes to her on a weekly basis.

Of course, she deserves all of it, but I'm finding it hard to be pleased for her, which I guess makes me a truly shitty friend.

Grazia gives me a curious look. 'Emily?'

'Hmm? Sorry. I was miles away.'

'Might I suggest a little . . . sharpener in the Rose and Crown?'

'I don't have time. The cupcakes for the decorating workshop have got lost somewhere, and I haven't a bloody clue where my celebrity knitter is . . .'

She takes my hand. 'All the more reason for a moment of "me" time.' She reaches into the lining of her jacket and pulls out two miniature bottles of Lanson. 'And besides, we have absent friends to toast.' Grazia pops the mini-champagnes open with well-practised flicks of the wrist, and hands me mine.

'To Sandie,' declares Grazia.

'And to Nigel!' I reply.

Grazia smiles wistfully. 'Somewhere between here and the South China Sea.'

And as I clink, I see my lovely Will on the other side of the common, carrying four trays of missing cupcakes. The wind whips up his curly black hair and it's lashing his face, making him look a bit like a very tall, very well-brought-up Heathcliff. He doesn't dare let go of the cupcakes to flick the curls away, so by the time he gets to me, his big blue-green eyes are teary from the north-westerly gale. But he still gives me the broadest of smiles as he passes.

He knows how much this means to me and to Heartsease, and he'll do anything he can to make it the best it can be.

I hope I can live up to everyone's expectations. But especially his.

CHAPTER 3

Grazia

Somewhere between the Fabulous Felting tent and the Beading for Beginners marquee, the loss of Nigel hits me.

I will not cry – I never cry – but I do feel dizzy, and also surprised, since I am no stranger to being on my own. After my husband died, I was lost in grief, and even when he was alive, I was often alone. 'Our' friends were actually Leon's, and the things we did together were always based on his moods or whims. I was loved, but not always noticed.

After two years of widowhood that felt like deepest winter, I met Sandie and Emily through our secret shopping work, and they tempted me out of hibernation. Nigel was the one who thawed me out completely. But always I knew our relationship was like an Indian summer, that sooner or later he would find a girl his age or I would tire of the toyboy charm.

So why do I feel so empty? I catch a glimpse of myself in a mirror next to the découpage stall, and I look older than I have in my entire six months with Nigel. Perhaps he took my vitality along with his BlackBerry to Asia.

'You look like a lady who has an inner yearning to decorate a cupcake!'

A soft-faced woman with floury hands intercepts me. I have

no energy to put up much of a fight as she sits me down at the last empty seat of the trestle table.

I realise I am the only adult without a child escort. The Cutest Cupcakes class has begun, and the mothers and daughters have chosen their shade of pre-made buttercream, so the only colour left is a bilious green. I watch the tutor – that is icing sugar, not flour, on her girlish hands – and as she smoothes the cream onto her cake, I try to copy. Her topping has tiny peaks, and glistens like freshly fallen snow on exclusive French slopes. Mine is choppy, and the sickly colour makes it look uniquely unappetising.

'Now let's cut out some fabulous shapes!'

Again the other women have chosen their paper templates and coloured royal icing, leaving a sheet of orange icing and a set of cutters for Halloween broomsticks and cauldrons. I suppose that as a spinster of a certain age, I could qualify as a witch.

The mothers and children sit with heads close together, cutting around the shapes with blunt plastic knives. I look down at my stencil and feel a powerful urge to rip it into pieces, but today is Emily's big day and I will not cause a scene. Instead, I push my orange cauldron shapes onto the top of my cupcake. There are thumb prints all over it, but I have no intention of eating it, and no one to share it with. Or should I say, inflict it on.

'And now the finishing touch, a generous handful of sparkly sprinkles!'

One of the little girls upsets the entire pot of sparkly sprinkles, and the mothers chirrup 'never mind', and I cannot be bothered with this any more. I reach into my clutch bag for the ten-pound workshop fee, post it into the metal cash box, and walk away. Icing will not mend my hairline-fractured heart.

'You've left your cupcake!' The sweet-smiley woman runs

after me, cradling the cake in her hands like a baby animal. I take it, so as not to hurt her feelings.

I can always feed it to the birds . . .

I leave the marquee, and walk across the common, towards Bell's Emporium. I must find Emily, explain I am tired, say goodbye. She will understand. It is not as though I have not already done my bit to help the new Heartsease Handmade store, in the form of yet another loan I do not want to be repaid . . .

It is good to be in a position to be generous. After Leon, I was flat broke, but selling his paintings has bought me freedom to do as I wish, if only I knew what that was. It would have been so simple to book a first-class seat next to Nigel and live with him in Hong Kong. But I spent too many years as an adjunct to a man. I must find my own purpose in life. Then, if by some fluke I still want to be with Nigel, and he still wants to be with me, we can be together as equals.

I am not short of offers of 'purpose'. Not a day goes by without a gilt-edged invitation to an exhibition opening, or charity dinner. So very different from the dead quiet months immediately after Leon's heart attack. Every invitation comes with an expectation that I, the merry widow, might wish to donate to this good cause, or that. But however welcome my money is to zoo animals in war-torn countries, or struggling artists, writing out a cheque is not a *purpose*. And while I adore the British way of life, I cannot abide the idea of volunteering for one of her *committees*.

I put my head around the door of the light, bright Emporium, which is full of customers buying chutney and cheese and organic baby food from straw-lined wooden packing cases. The handsome Will is talking to a man with a goatee beard as they both gaze adoringly at a heavy-looking slab of wholemeal bread. Will has found his purpose, now, and so has the Emporium which, until last Christmas, was a hotchpotch shop full of pretty junk no one needed. The move into sustainable, local produce is a good one – I understand they may finally be edging towards the black – but do they really have to take it all so seriously? The eco light bulbs sit on their own little podium, even though they are barely bright enough to read by, and the worm composter has a 'SOLD OUT, NEW WRIGGLERS DUE SOON' sign next to it.

He spots me. 'Grazia! Come over! You must taste our new spelt ciabatta, see whether it tastes authentically Italian.' He lifts up a long slipper of a loaf that is the right *shape* for ciabatta, but is the grey colour of putty.

'It looks marvellous! But alas I am full of organic cupcake. Do you know where Emily is?'

'Next door, I think.'

I leave him and his customer to pay their earnest homage to the bread. The Emporium has a clear clientele, but I am less convinced by Heartsease Handmade. Why would grown women with too much to do want to knit their own clothes, when they can buy them more cheaply? But Emily was so enthusiastic – enthusiasm is Emily's essential quality – that it was easier to reach for my chequebook than to argue.

The store is half-shop, half-workshop. It's surprisingly airy, decorated in the soft colours of sugared almonds, and the craft items are displayed with the same awe as the bread next door. Candy-striped knitting needles are suspended from the ceiling; a treasure chest overflows with jewel-coloured glass beads which sparkle under the spotlight. Balls of wool in baby shades are packed into a wicker basket, and before I realise what I am doing, I have reached out to touch them. They are deliciously soft.

Maybe Emily knows what she is doing after all . . .

There is a workshop under way at the back of the store. Four women under forty are sitting around a table, each holding a wooden embroidery hoop. A stern girl in her twenties is circling, pointing out their errors and making suggestions.

From the clumsy way they are wielding their needles, I would say they are beginners.

The stern girl looks up. 'Oh, I knew we were expecting one more. Come on, you'll catch up in no time,' and she gestures to the empty chair.

'No, you misunderstand, I am looking for Emily, the owner . . .'

She smiles encouragingly. 'Emily's gone to get some sparkly floss for us, though she had to go and deal with a punch-up in the pub on her way. But why don't you have a try, while you wait? I can tell you're an embroidery fan, from your jacket.'

And I look down at my Cossack outfit, with its ornate pattern, and before I know what is happening, she has sat me down and thrust a spare hoop in my hands. These crafts-women are so *forceful*. She tells me to take a pattern from the pile in the centre of the table, but they are nothing like the patterns I remember our English neighbour working on: no ugly dog roses or cross-stitched clowns. Instead the images are jokey or cutesy: there's a template showing a curvy burlesque artist, another with skulls and body parts, and even a tasteless Bart Simpson with his trousers down.

She sees my shocked expression. 'Or you could go freeform, if you like. Sketch something onto the fabric,' she hands me a pencil, 'and then I can show you the basic stitches.'

What is it with these women and their boundless energy? I sense it will take more energy to resist her than it would to protest and there is no sign of Emily yet.

I look down at the creamy fabric, stretched tight between the two wooden circles. A blank canvas. The very words could provoke a week's worth of rage in my late husband, because he found starting work the most stressful part of all.

Yet as I look at the cloth, it seems anything but threatening. In fact, it seems curiously inviting, like a cool lake on a hot day. The hoop feels weightless in my hands and I put the pencil down, and reach forward to where the skeins of embroidery thread are piled high like a linguine rainbow. I pick up a periwinkle blue, then consider a deep ivy green, before choosing a silvery grey. I swear the shades are ten times as beautiful as those Leon chose for his canvases. The floss almost threads itself and seems to know exactly where it's entering the fabric for the first stitch . . .

'Ladies, ladies. Time to put those needles down and look at what we've got!'

It takes me a moment or two to remember where I am, and who the bossy voice belongs to.

'Let's collect up your hoops.' And before I can stop her, the embroidery teacher has snatched away my work. I catch a glimpse of outside and, to my astonishment, it is completely dark. I check my watch. Five o'clock. I have been here for an hour.

'Now then, who does *this* belong to?' asks the teacher, holding up a hoop. Despite the ring holding the fabric taut, the sewer has managed to bunch up her work with the ugliest stitches I've ever seen, in livid red thread.

A very young girl puts her hand up, and I regret my bad thoughts. 'Good first effort,' says the teacher, 'with a brave attempt at French knots. You might want to watch your tension next time though.'

'Yes, well, I've got a very stressful job *and* high blood pressure,' says the girl. 'I thought needlework might relax me, but—'

'No, I meant . . .' and then the teacher decides against trying to explain any further. She hands the girl her work back, and then goes through the rest of her pile: an accomplished, if twee, outline of a kitten in mauve and powder blue; an unfinished bouquet of flowers, stitched with a spark of originality in black; a sampler of well-done stitches from the rather cross-looking woman to my right; and then the oddest, yet most pleasing design of a heart split in two, with blood pooling beneath it, spelling out the world *broken* (though the *n* is not quite finished) in perfect satin stitch. Grey heart, grey blood, grey letters.

'And this must be *yours*?' says the teacher in an astonished voice.

'It must be,' I say, taking the hoop from her and staring at it in disbelief.

'This was intended to be a beginners' workshop, you know.'

'I . . .' I am too surprised to argue. 'I learned when I was a girl. There was a widow in our village, from England. She tried to teach me. I was terrible. More interested in boys than needlework.'

'You've improved since then,' she says, somewhat archly. She hands my piece around the table. 'Now, girls, you might not like the subject matter, but the stitching is accomplished.' The other women nod approvingly, and I touch the thread and I realise it sums up perfectly how I am feeling.

No. That is wrong. It sums up perfectly how I *felt*, because now that the piece is almost done, I feel a little better, as though some of my sadness has been stitched into the fabric.

The bell on the shop door rings, and Emily rushes into the room, holding up a handful of Day-Glo embroidery floss. 'Am I too late?' she says. 'Sorry. It was like Beirut in the pub. Those knitters, honestly . . .' Then she notices me. 'Grazia, I thought I'd missed you. And you've been sewing. Wow! I never saw you as the crafty type . . .'

She looks at my work, and then at me, and she leans forward to envelop me in the kind of hug that usually makes me uncomfortable but, right now, makes me feel cared for.

'There, there, Grazia. I promise you, everything is going to be fine.'

And I let her keep holding me, though there is a twitch in the thumb and index finger of my right hand, as I fight the urge to finish off the *n* in *broken*.

CHAPTER 4

Sandie

I step out of the taxi and look up, and then I feel it: the familiarity, the buzz, the memories.

There's no place like home.

I love everything about Garnett's. Well, everything except Laetitia. It doesn't seem possible that this store could ever fail: its limestone wedding cake, with six glorious tiers, has dominated Oxford Street for almost a century. But the figures I read last night told a different story . . .

'You ready, Brains?' asks Toby, taking my hand and giving it a little squeeze. 'I love you for doing this for me.'

Am I doing it for him, or for Garnett's? Or even my own ego? I suppose it doesn't matter, so long as I speak the truth, like the boy in *The Emperor's New Clothes*.

Though the little boy had nothing to lose . . .

We step into the store, the ground floor alone the size of four cathedrals. It's dazzlingly bright after the greyness outside, and the air is heavy with a hundred designer fragrances. At least I can bear the smell again. For the first few months of my pregnancy even my favourite perfumes made me sick. Now I can don my scented armour again. Today it's Mitsouko, Margaret Thatcher's favourite. A perfume to wear into battle . . .

I scan the beauty department. The shop floor is almost empty of browsers, but then it is a Monday morning in March. More worrying is the lack of staff. There are a couple of girls I don't recognise behind the cosmetics counters, but instead of standing to attention when they spot us, the assistants stare into space, like retail zombies. Edgar has never been the most dynamic of managers, preferring the safety of his office to the store itself, but the threat of a summons to the top floor was enough to keep us on our toes. If you had no customers to attend to, you'd be primping and polishing.

Toby is behind me, but I don't want anyone to see me with one of the bosses. 'You go up,' I whisper. He nods and he's gone.

'Good morning,' I say to the girl slumped against the till behind the Desired counter. She must be new, because in my seven years here I worked hard to learn everyone's name.

'Hi,' she says. There's a half-smile, but her limp posture doesn't change.

I read her name badge. *Clair.* Without an e. She straightens up a little as she notices me clocking it. 'Looking for anything in particular?'

The display is untidy, with a sprinkling of face powder on the glossy black surface, and gaps where tester lipsticks should be. 'Not sure. Perhaps something to pep up my look?'

She smiles half-heartedly, then spots my bump. 'Ooh. When's the baby due?'

'July.'

'I wouldn't normally say anything to a customer in case they've just got a big tummy, but you've got such a nice figure that I *knew* you were expecting. Our new organic range is fabulous, and my pregnant ladies want to use the very purest products.'

And she's off, talking me through the range and the ways that it can improve my appearance and my life. But I'm more interested in *her* transformation. She pulls out the stool for me

– oh, *that's* better – and gives me a hand massage with a creamy balm that smells of bergamot and almonds. She's good.

'Seems quiet in here today,' I say.

'Hmm. Today and every day. Been like this since Christmas.'

'Really? I suppose it's the recession.'

She looks at me, weighing me up. 'I dunno. Scary times. I come in every Monday not sure if I'll have a job by Friday.'

'They're getting rid of people?' *Edgar's report never mentioned job losses.*

'Not officially and I haven't been here long enough to be sure, but it feels like there are less of us than there used to be at tea breaks.'

In my day, the staff canteen was always packed, and a hotbed of gossip and scandalmongering. 'What do your colleagues think?'

Clair shrugs. 'We don't really talk to each other. Everyone's too nervous. Divide and rule, my boyfriend Ray calls it, so we won't step out of line . . .'

'It's that bad? And the footfall is down too, is it?'

She gives me a strange look. Damn. I shouldn't have used that word. 'Oh, I'm probably fussing about nothing; Ray always says I'm a worrier. So, what do you think of the balm?'

'Lovely. I'll take it.'

I pay and she throws in a couple of free samples but her hands are trembling.

'Thank you, Clair. Can you tell me again which floor nursery goods are on?' I try to look dumb.

'Second,' she says, 'and maternity's on the first.' But I'm sure she knows something's up. I feel her eyes on me as I walk to the lifts.

I was planning to speed up to the management floor, but I think I need a tiny bit more research. Plus, the thought of

Laetitia is making my knees shake. I reach out and touch the brass button for the first floor.

Anything to postpone my date with destiny . . .

The lift goes up and I grab my voice recorder from my bag and clip it to my lapel, so I can record my thoughts for later without having to get out a notebook.

'*Lift B. Significant scuffing to mahogany panelling. Brass dull and smeared with marks.*'

There's a moment's pause before the doors slide open, like the curtains on opening night.

Maybe my nerves are stage fright. Or maybe now that I work for myself as a sole trader – or, as Toby calls it, a 'lone ranger' – I'm too independent to get involved with management structures again. In my business, people hire me for my straight talking, which is why I love the job. But here . . . well, I never remember Edgar as a man who values constructive criticism.

'First floor for trend, style, classics, suiting, lingerie, nightwear, bridal, maternity, and ladies' shoes.' The voice is almost as old as the store itself. I used to think it was quaint but now it sounds stuffy.

I step out of the lift onto the shop floor. Or should that be *shock* floor.

Ugh.

'*First floor,*' I whisper. '*Wall to wall sickly pastel. Pink. Lemon. Violet.*'

It's so bland that I have trouble finding anything to focus on. All the signs have had sprigs of fake flowers twined around them. I guess it was meant to look fresh and cute, but it doesn't. It looks desperate.

This is the only floor that never held any allure for me – I've never been a fashionista – but I know that it matters more than any other in the store. I spent six months here as a trainee, back in the days when the New Year sales actually started in January. I remember the TV crews outside and the soup and tea that the canteen ladies always prepared for the overnight queuers. Our section head, Maureen, was waiting for me that morning . . . what, *nine* years ago, now? Doesn't seem possible.

'Took my advice, I hope, Barrow?' she barked. Maureen was in her fifties, a perfect size sixteen, with startling Monroe-style curves. But she believed that to be taken seriously a woman had to dress like a man, and in her olive-green suit she looked like a prison governor. The effect was intensified by her habit of calling us by our surnames.

'Advice?'

She reached behind the counter and pulled out a small brown bottle. 'Arnica. For bruises.' She tipped a couple of tiny white pills into the lid and handed it over. 'It's not too late. Down them in one.'

As I swallowed, the bell rang to let us know the doors were about to open. When they did, the noise was incredible, an animalistic roar, as the stampede began. Until that moment, I'd never realised determination could look so *threatening*. They came up the escalators, three abreast, and up the stairs, pushing so hard at the double doors that they almost fell underneath the boots and heels, and then out of the lifts, which strained under their weight.

I left the store twelve hours later, dazed and in no doubt that the Fashion Floor was the engine room of Garnett's sales, the ultimate attraction for our customers.

So where have they all gone?

I walk along the wide 'path' that is designed to guide the unfocused shopper right round the floor, to tempt them with the very best that the store has to offer. But is this *really* the best the store has to offer?

'*Hotchpotch of random garments on overcrowded rails. No signposting to fashion highlights, unless those faded dresses are*

*new season. Mismatched hangers. Has the aura of a down-at-heel
charity shop. Staff notable by apparent absence.'*

Every now and then I catch a glimpse of the top of someone's head, but I sense them retreating like wild deer as soon
as they spot me. I keep walking, and talking.

'Flooring grubby. Lingerie department uninviting.'

Actually, with all the bras and knickers strewn around, it's
like the morning after in a bordello. How did Toby not notice
things had slipped this far – and what on earth is Edgar playing at, letting things go?

At last I see a fellow human – another girl I don't recognise,
fiddling about with the control pants.

'Staff member in lingerie. I wait for advice on maternity bras.'

Actually, I really do need advice. The engineering of these
things looks more complicated than the Severn Bridge. But
Miss Control Pants isn't interested.

*'No response, despite catching her eye. Most shoppers would
have given up and gone to John Lewis by now.'*

I keep going, though it feels like an effort.

'Maternity wear. Oh dear.'

I might not have studied developments in maternity wear
in any detail until now, but even I realised that Demi Moore
made bumps cool all those years ago, and the pregnant-girl-
about-town has been happily parading her belly in Lycra or
decidedly unfrumpy jeans and frocks ever since.

But progress hasn't reached the first floor of Garnett's.

*'Limited range of flowery tents and dark trousers that would
only be worn by darts players with beer bellies.'*

I want to cry, not only with sadness, but with rage. I've
never seen Garnett's like this. It's only when I approach the
bridal section that things pick up. The department has always
been set back from the rest of the floor, with soft carpeting
and subtle lighting that makes complexions glow. The two
mannequins at the entrance are dressed in contrasting styles –
one classic gown with a pearled bodice, and a more modern

shift with tiny straps and a cutaway back. For the first time, there's a sign someone might still care. *Someone I think I know.*

I step inside, and, yes, my hunch was right.

'Babs?'

She turns in surprise and then leaps forward to hug me. She's only five years or so older than me, but she looks worn out. Her hair is cropped short, but she's not bothering to cover the grey. 'Always the Bridesmaid' Babs – forever the subject of bitchy gossip on the bitchiest floor of the store – looks worn down by life.

'Oh my word! Sandra Barrow! I don't believe it's you!' She steps back, noticing my bump. 'And oh, golly! I thought you were a dedicated spinster!' And her smile slips, as though I've let the side down.

'An accident,' I say.

'But no ring! Are you getting married?'

'No, no marriage plans at all. Though I am *with* the dad.' I wait for her to say something about Toby, but she doesn't. Poor Babs never was one for rumours. I'd hate her to find out from someone else – but if I tell her my connection to the boss, she'll clam up. I have to think of the greater good.

'So what are you doing here, then? We do do maternity bridal gowns. Things have changed since we started, eh, Sandie?'

'Yes. They seem to have done.' I pull a face. 'I came in for a browse but . . . everything seems to have lost its sparkle.'

She gives me a defensive look. 'In what way?'

'The store doesn't seem quite so *cared* for.'

Again, she's weighing me up. Then she sighs. 'I know. Some days I walk in here and I feel I'm the only one who gives a shit.'

'Oh, Babs,' I say, because her face looks so sad. 'I'm sure it's not that bad.'

'Look around you, Sandie. I haven't seen Edgar for months—'

36

'He was like that when I was here.'

'This is different. Every Tuesday morning, after my day off, I think it'll be better, but then I arrive and the place . . . it's almost like it stinks.'

I sniff. 'Really? Pregnancy's affected my sense of smell.'

She shakes her head. 'There's something in the air. Dust. Or neglect. Anyway,' she leans forward, 'I think they're running it down on purpose. Maybe the Russians want to buy us. Or the Chinese. You read about it in the papers.'

I smile. Babs has always had a tendency towards the paranoid, but I can't reassure her because I'd have to tell her about Toby. 'I'm sure people do care. *I* care. Where's everyone else?'

'Look around you. Lots of people left, after Christmas.'

I think of what the girl said downstairs. 'Sacked?'

She shakes her head. 'Most people get fed up, hand in their notice. I miss them. Even the evil ones. Now half the girls are temps from Eastern Europe. Huddle together at tea break. I don't understand a word.'

I look at my watch. *I'm so late.* 'Babs, I have to get going. But . . . try to keep cheerful, eh?'

And I hug her briefly, and then march off towards the stairs, noting the vinegary aroma in the shoe department and the empty gaps in the hosiery racks. I'll race around the other floors on my way to the meeting, though I already know that only a fool would want to take this makeover on.

So why are my fingers itching with anticipation?

Toby is hanging round in the grubby stairwell when I finally get to the management floor.

'Jesus, Sandie, I was about to send out the search party. I thought something had, you know, *happened* to you.' He takes me in his arms.

I wriggle out. 'Don't be silly. What could have happened?'

He gives me a look. We both know how close we came to disaster when the flat burnt down. 'Ready for the off, Brains?'

I nod.

He enters the code into the ancient keypad, then marches down the corridor towards the boardroom. If the rest of the store is suffering from faded grandeur, then behind the scenes the Garnett's glow has been snuffed out completely.

This hallowed floor, my ultimate destination when I started here, always used to feel plusher and posher than the tired staffrooms or cramped canteen. It had panache, like a seventies Cinzano ad: there were standards to be maintained.

Now that the smoking ban has softened the pipe tobacco smell, there's another even less wholesome pong, of egg sandwiches and floral air freshener.

'Ladies first,' he says, as we approach the door.

I shake my head. 'Not today. I want it to be clear that you invited me.'

He smiles and goes in ahead of me. I hear laughs and pats on backs, the sounds of a gentleman's club to which I will never belong for so many reasons: I'm not white, not male, not posh. Toby says something I can't hear, and he returns to the doorway and pulls me in, and the silence is complete.

I've only ever been in here once before and that time . . .

The first person I see in the boardroom is Edgar Murray. He blinks behind his large glasses and an odd expression passes across his face. Was that fear?

Surely Edgar must recognise me – I was a senior section head, and on his 'special projects' team – but I can tell he's struggling to remember my name.

'Sandra Barrow worked with us at Garnett's,' says Toby patiently, 'but has since gone on to set up an exclusive retail consultancy, specialising in customer focus and trouble-shooting. Her expertise is in demand across the UK, and internationally.'

'Ah, Miss Barrow!' says Edgar, his eyes drawn to my bump, which he now addresses. 'A pleasure to make your reacquaintance, I'm sure. Don't you look . . . um, *bonny*.'

'Good to see you, too, Mr Murray.' I take a few more steps into the room: the dark-stained wood panels make the space seem smaller than it is, and my silent steps on the deep-pile, garnet-red carpet increase the feeling of disconnection from the outside world.

I scan the boardroom for Laetitia, but unless she's hiding behind the antler coat rack – quite possible, given her emaciated frame – she's not here. Instead I am scrutinised by half a dozen men we nicknamed the Muppets. They're all dressed in the same greeny-brown countryside 'togs', and I'm certain none of them has bought anything from Garnett's in decades. I wouldn't trust them to run a tuck shop, yet the expressions of contempt on their faces suggest that they think *I'm* the one who shouldn't be here.

I'd forgotten how snobby this place could be. The idea that a shop girl from Birmingham could ever have a place in this boardroom must shock them to the core.

'Morning, gentlemen,' I say, hoping the crack in my voice is only obvious to me. 'Mr Garnett asked me to attend, I do hope that's not a problem.'

They whisper like plotting schoolboys, without acknowledging my greeting or smiling back.

Toby pulls out a maroon-leather upholstered chair and gestures for me to sit down. The seat creaks as I lower myself.

'Gentlemen, Miss Barrow has kindly offered us her valuable time. I would hate it if she left with the impression that old-fashioned courtesy has gone out of fashion at Garnett's.'

The Muppets look at one another – is it my imagination, or do they look a little shamefaced? – and mumble their good mornings before taking their seats. Toby is smart: none of this lot want to be lectured on manners by some young upstart. He's at least three decades their junior, and the only person not to look faded and jaded.

He smiles at them, then pours me a glass of water from the crystal carafe before sitting down himself.

Edgar looks at the old clock at the end of the boardroom. 'Are we expecting Mrs Garnett?' he asks Toby.

Toby shrugs. 'She hasn't said otherwise. But you know what my mother's schedule is like.'

Edgar nods. 'A prior charitable commitment, perhaps.'

I manage not to snort.

'To business, then.' He leans forward to press a button on the ancient intercom system. 'Hilary, we're ready to begin.'

Hilary bustles in, holding her shorthand notebook. She gives me the first genuine smile I've seen since I got in here. How does she stand working for Edgar and the Muppets?

'Quarterly strategic meeting of Garnett's board, apology for absence received from Francis Dobbs due to gout. Any comments on the last minutes?'

Silence.

'So,' says Edgar, 'our main task today is to approve the summary and financial projections outlined in the quarterly report. Any issues, gentlemen?'

'Bit bloody long, Murray,' says a man with a pocket watch on a chain. 'I have better things to do with my time than wade through all that rubbish.'

The others nod in agreement. Toby raises his eyebrows at me: he doesn't rate Edgar any more than I do, but he has an instinctive desire to stick up for the underdog. Not today, though. Today we have to focus on rescuing Garnett's, which I've realised this morning is the underdog of Oxford Street.

'Apologies for that, Mr Stoddart, it's our new system, it means that each sub-department—'

'Spare me the details,' interrupts Mr Stoddart, 'but keep it snappier next time.'

'Never could abide bean counters,' adds the 'chap' next to him.

The room erupts into scornful giggles. I don't know what I'd expected, but the rudeness astonishes me and, for the first time, I feel a bit sorry for boring old Edgar.

'To return to the *content* of the report,' says Edgar wearily, 'are we happy with the projections and the current strategy? Could I ask for a show of hands?'

There's a half-hearted response. I look at Toby and he shuffles his papers, then gives me the thumbs-up, under the table. 'Um. Actually, chaps, there is something. Miss Barrow has been looking at the report and there were a few, how shall I put it . . .'

The sentence hangs in the air.

I decide to finish it for him. 'Anomalies.'

Edgar's jaw hangs open for so long that I want to lean forward and pop it closed. At last he remembers to do it himself. 'What kind of anomalies?'

They're all gawping at me now and I freeze. Toby's hand is on my knee and he squeezes in a gesture of solidarity. I decide that the only way to do this is *not* to look at anyone.

'There seems to be a difference between what the figures are saying, and what the commentary is saying.'

The silence goes on for so long that I have to look up.

Edgar's pale face now sports an angry red circle on each cheek. Guilt, or outrage? 'I think you must be mistaken, Miss Barrow.'

'I don't believe I am. The commentary is optimistic, but the figures' – Toby squeezes my knee again – 'the figures are awful. I mean, beyond terrible. My reading of them is that Garnett's will struggle to stay afloat unless something radical is done.'

The Muppets mumble. Moustache Man gives me an intimidating stare, but the effect is reduced when I realise one of his eyes is glass. 'Why would we believe a girl we've never seen before, over our trusted store manager?'

The Barrow rage rumbles inside me. My gramma used to warn me about the grizzly-bear-like anger that runs in our family, but in the last few months, pregnancy hormones have dampened it down. Until now. The way he talks to me is like white spirit on embers.

'Because I used to work here, too. For almost as many years as Mr Murray, in fact, and I know what actually goes on, you know, *down there.*'

The men look alarmed, and I realise they think that I'm talking about 'women's problems'.

'On the shop floor,' I clarify. 'Have any of you ventured onto the shop floor lately?'

They look even more horrified. Perhaps that's another euphemism . . .

'I'll take that as a no, then. But I have. I walked the store ten minutes ago, and you know what, it's a *mess.* The place looks dirty and uncared for.'

'I refute that utterly,' says Edgar, short of breath now. 'It's a subjective opinion and one, if I may say so, almost certainly influenced by . . . I don't know what. Spite, perhaps? I did not want to bring this up, but Miss Barrow originally became a "consultant" after she was sacked for allegations of misconduct.'

Toby is on his feet. 'Which were unconditionally retracted when Miss Barrow was proven to be entirely blameless. She was offered compensation and reinstatement, as you well know. Apologise this instant.'

'Hmm. Yes. OK. I apologise,' says Edgar, though I'm sure he really wants to say *there's no smoke without fire.*

Toby looks at me and I nod. He sits down again, though his hands are in loose fists, ready to defend me again. But he doesn't realise I'm pleased about what's just happened. If I was cross before, now I feel liberated. No need to stay loyal to Edgar any more.

'Well, if Mr Murray thinks dirty floors and fingermarks all over the glass and brass work is acceptable, then I suppose that's up to him. But it's not the only issue I noted.'

Edgar tuts and crosses his arms across his pigeon chest.

'I also observed a severe shortage of staff. Hideous off-season stock in menswear. The baby-changing facilities are a health hazard, and the display kitchens on the fourth floor look like the "before" footage from a makeover show. No one was at the travel desk, the returns desk or the finance desk, and I know we're all for being ecologically friendly, but I don't think the way to achieve that is to leave half of the plasma screen TVs in electronics on stand-by.'

Toby is trying not to smile, but he gives me another discreet thumbs-up. Whereas Edgar looks as though he'd like to scratch my eyes out.

'I . . .' he tries to regain control of himself, 'I assure you the moment the meeting is over, I will check these . . . claims. But I cannot keep tabs on every tiny detail.'

'Two more things before I leave,' I say, bold now. 'First, in my entire tour, I didn't see a single item that made me want to open my purse. I know that's anecdotal, so if you prefer, I can show you figures.'

I pull out the pages I highlighted last night, the first showing a nightmarish loss in women's fashions, and the second with a summary boasting of *significant progress in establishing the store as a destination for those seeking both cutting-edge and classic apparel.* 'Can I invite you to compare and contrast the second paragraph on page seven with the spreadsheets on page ninety-three, showing net receipts since the sales period ended.'

There's a flurry of activity as they rifle through the pages. I hope at least one of these dinosaurs can read a spreadsheet, but perhaps it no longer matters. I have said my bit. They've listened. It's up to them.

'Now, now, chaps, what *have* I missed?'

I turn to see Laetitia sweeping through the door, her dove-grey coat billowing behind her like a witch's haute couture cape. Then she sees me, and that pinched but still pretty face of hers contorts into a mask of utter contempt.

'What is that little *tart* doing here?'

Toby's on his feet again and his face is twisted like a gargoyle's. 'Mother. Either you take that back, or I am walking out this moment and I promise you I will never return to this store and certainly never, ever speak to you again.'

She must be able to tell it's no empty threat. Toby hates to shout when women are present, but his sense of honour means he can't let it lie.

Edgar is on his feet too. 'I didn't want her here, but Mr Garnett insisted.'

All the Muppets except Pocket Watch are staring as Laetitia heads towards me and Toby, her face rearranged from sour to wronged. She makes me feel sick and sore inside, as though I've been forced to drink a pint of salt water.

'Mother?' Toby pulls on his jacket, and removes his Garnett's staff pass from his wallet. 'Make a decision.'

Edgar shifts from one foot to another, like a child who needs the toilet. 'Perhaps we should adjourn . . .'

Mrs Garnett skirts past the two of us, and stands at the head of the table. Her tiny figure is dwarfed by the chair and the portrait of her dramatically blond late husband staring down adoringly from the wall behind her. 'OK, Toby. You win. *So* sorry for calling you names, Sandra. Now, shall we continue? I'd hate to cut our shop girl off in her prime.'

'I've finished now. It's all there in Edgar's figures, if any of you can be bothered to read them. Put your fingers in your ears if you want, but don't say I didn't warn you.'

Laetitia smiles, baring her tiny white teeth, while she thinks up a killer putdown.

I've had enough. Done enough. I feel light-headed and hungry and grumpy: if they want to let the shop go to rack and ruin in Edgar's incapable hands, that's up to them. I stand up and head for the door, hoping I'll get there before my strength runs out, but when I grasp the handle I can hardly move it.

'Here.'

I turn, expecting to see Toby, but old Pocket Watch is quicker on his feet and is touching my arm. I smile at him, pleased that chivalry is not dead, even when it comes to common shop girls, but instead of helping me with the handle, he smiles down at me. 'I don't think we've quite finished with Miss Barrow yet.'

Toby is on standby to protect my reputation for the third time this morning, but Pocket Watch is smiling. 'Much as I hate to be proved wrong by a female, a cursory reading of these figures suggests the girl might actually have a point.'

Laetitia's face hits warp factor twenty again. The rest of the old boys stare at me: they couldn't look more astonished if their gundogs had begun reciting *Paradise Lost*.

Toby smiles. 'And that, ladies and gentlemen, is why Sandra Barrow is the best thing that has ever happened to me and could yet prove the best thing to happen to our little corner shop here. May I suggest a short tea break before we consider how best we might use her considerable abilities?'

April

CHAPTER 5

Emily

I know it's ungrateful of me, but there are times when the love of my life really, truly gets on my tits.

What's worse is the fact that he annoys me *most* when he's talking about saving the planet. I am as fond of the planet as the next woman, but I was very fond of the old Will, too, the one who had a sense of fun as well as a sense of responsibility, the man who didn't fret endlessly about his carbon footprint.

'The compost toilets were completely amazing, Em. Honestly, not pongy at all.'

'*Fascinating*.'

'He does a road show, I was thinking of inviting him and his Green Bog to Heartsease next time there's an event. I'm sure it'd go down a storm.'

'Right. Exactly what the village needs.' I take the soup off the bedsit-style hob, and twist my body round to pour it into bowls without knocking my elbows against the cupboards or fridge. Our flat above the shop has taught me all I never wanted to know about small-space living.

I hand him his soup, and settle down on the threadbare brown sofa with my own bowl. 'Oof. My feet are killing me. It's been the busiest Saturday since before Christmas.

Everyone's stocking up for Easter, I guess. We took four dozen orders for the Big Barbie Bangers from Moor Farm.'

'Brilliant. Well done you.' Will sniffs the soup. 'Is this organic?'

'No. It's normal Heinz.'

He recoils slightly. 'Hardly setting an example, are we?'

I look around me, at the empty, gloomy room. 'Who are we meant to be setting an example to? Freddie's with his dad and even if he weren't, I don't want him to grow up into a joyless adult who regards a comforting bowl of tomato soup as a crime against humanity.'

'Yes, but—'

'Or maybe you want me to try to whip up homemade soup in *here*?'

We both look at the student-style kitchenette, where making fish fingers and oven chips is as complex as a state banquet, and more often than not trips the electrics to the whole flat. On the upside, having the mini-oven in our living room does cut back on our central heating bills.

'Of course not. You're a busy working mother, Emily. But we're specialists in convenience food that won't inconvenience the planet,' he says, parroting one of his less memorable eco-slogans.

'Well, the beetroot and horseradish soup in the fridge has a toxic-looking green slick on the top. At least you know where you are with preservatives.'

He looks at the soup, then me, then the soup again. Hunger trumps social conscience and he eats. 'Hmm. I'm sure the green film wouldn't have killed us. It's all natural.'

'Kidney beans are natural. Deadly nightshade is natural. Black widow spiders are *natural*.'

Will frowns. 'If I'd known you were going to be in a mood, I wouldn't have gone. Or come back.'

'What makes you think I'm in a mood?'

'The way you're holding that spoon as though you'd like to

use it to scoop my brains out and then eat them, like the monkeys in *Indiana Jones . . .*'

'Ugh!' I giggle, despite my bad mood. 'It's been a long day. It's not the same when you're away.'

He smiles back. 'I know. And it was super, super lovely of you to let me go.'

'Go on, then. Tell me more about the conference. Did you make some good contacts?'

'Yes. Great guy there from the transition town movement. You know, making sure that we're ready for peak oil?'

I *don't* know, even though I'm sure he's explained it before. I think it has something to do with the lights going out and all the 4x4s in the Next Village Along running out of petrol. 'Wow.'

Will leans forward to rifle through the pile of leaflets and brochures on the coffee table. 'And you must read this, it's so clear that we need a Heartsease Pound.' He hands me a leaflet labelled 'Local Currencies for Local People'.

'Looks like a real page-turner. Though I don't see how printing all of this bumf is going to help the environment.'

'It's all on recycled paper,' he says, slightly defensively.

I put down my soup and look at the flyers. The print's tiny, and I struggle to read in the dim light cast by the low-energy light bulb hanging from the cracked ceiling rose. There's a guide to 'Winning the Waste War' and a campaign leaflet called 'Get Stuffed to GM'. Then there's a proper paperback called *The Pill Can Save the Planet.* I bet he'll keep that beside our bed, ready to trot out statistics next time I mention how broody I'm still feeling.

I return to my dinner. 'The language is so aggressive. All weapons and frontlines and barricades. Isn't it better to try to persuade people, rather than bully them into changing their behaviour?'

'We don't have time for the gentle approach, Emily.' The worry lines on his forehead are deepening, and his sincerity makes me feel even more of a lightweight. I *do* care, but it's a struggle to see my choice of soup as a big deal.

'Why don't I run you a bath? You've had a tough day . . .'

'A bath?' He couldn't look more shocked if I'd suggested wife-swapping. I bet he's about to mention the millions of gallons wasted by selfish bathers every day.

But this time I have my argument ready. 'Before you tell me off, number one, I promise to use the grey water on our herb tub afterwards, number two, I'll add organic sulphate-free aromatherapy oils and number three . . .' I wink at him, 'surely a bath is far less indulgent if you share it with someone else?'

'Oh, *Matron*.'

I think I might have won that argument.

After our bath (*and* what followed), I've been reminded of Will's many good qualities. We lie in each other's arms on the sofa and I don't even mind when he picks up his leaflets again and begins to read out bits about . . . well, I don't know what they're about, because the sound of his voice is so soothing and so gorgeous, whatever the words. One day, maybe, he'll sing our baby to sleep with that lilt.

'. . . so what do you think?'

'Eh?'

'I know the timing's tight, but we're closed on Monday anyway. I think you should do it, Em.'

I don't move. I *should* admit that I wasn't listening properly, but at Christmas when we had a meltdown, I begged him to be honest about the business. In return, I promised to pay attention at all times, rather than drift off into daydreams. I want to prove I can be *adult*.

'Well, um. I don't know. What makes you think I'm up to . . . it?' *Shit*. What if he's suggesting a marathon, or three months helping tribeswomen in the Sahara for Comic Relief?

'Oh, Emily. You need to have more faith in your abilities.

You're a very talented,' he strokes the inside of my wrist, 'and very gorgeous entrepreneur. I don't want to hear any more self-doubt.'

Entrepreneur? 'OK.'

'So you'll do it, then?'

I nod because, well, what else can I do?

'That's my girl. Now, let me go and get us some wine, so we can toast your future and then knock up your manifesto.'

And that is how I find myself sitting in the Snowvan (so-called because it leaves a scattering of white paint flakes wherever it goes), in the car park of a conference centre in the shadow of the gigantic Madejski football stadium in Reading.

I could go into the centre – the flyer says there's *Coffee and Networking* between 9.30 and 10 – but I've never networked in my life, so instead I'm redoing my make-up for the fifth time in the cruel rear-view mirror. Even Grazia's favourite Touche Éclat can't conceal the lingering look of terror in my eyes.

Sandie would have been the ideal person to give me a pep talk, but I can never get hold of her on the phone these days. Actually, I didn't try that hard. There's something tricky about taking advice from someone who has managed to get all the things you want – a baby, a house, an adoring man – without really trying.

OK. Gotta go. I check in the side mirror that the coast is clear, and then dash out of the van. Being seen next to this fuel-guzzling, mood-sapping rust bucket would do nothing for my prospects of being named UK Green Goddess Eco-Entrepreneur of the Year.

Ha ha ha ha ha.

Like I have any prospects.

My feet are unsteady in these heels, because I live in trainers. But when I tried my Converses on with my suit this morning, I looked like a munchkin from *The Wizard of Oz*.

Already I can hear the networking, a high-pitched hum

with a rustly undercurrent as business cards are exchanged. I don't have to do this, do I? I could pick up the application forms, then hotfoot it into town for coffee and a cream cake in John Lewis. I can even justify that as research if I go via haberdashery, picking up product and design ideas for Heartsease Homemade. Will doesn't need to know . . .

It's *so* tempting.

'Excuse me?'

I turn round to see a blonde woman sporting a pregnant belly so huge that she can't get past me through the door. These fertile types really *are* everywhere.

'Oh, I'm sorry, I was . . .'

She looks at me carefully, as though she's weighing something up. She's my age, maybe slightly older, and very attractive in a way I could never be – a hint of Grace Kelly in her blue eyes and pale, lipsticked mouth. She narrowly misses out on beautiful because her nose is slightly crooked.

'I hate these dos, don't you? So intimidating to walk into a room full of people you've never met. Especially women. You know they'll be sizing you up the moment they see you, making judgements about you because of your shoes, your clothes, your hair, even your handbag . . .'

I gulp. It hadn't occurred to me to worry about my handbag until she said that. It's a humongous plasticky one from a supermarket own-brand fashion range. Will calls it my shoulder-skip because it's so full of crap. 'Oh.'

'But you know the only way to deal with it?'

'Um. No. Unless it's to imagine them all naked?'

She laughs a sweet laugh that stops quite abruptly, like my sister's doll used to. 'No, no, you need a mantra you can repeat under your breath to yourself.'

'A mantra. Like ommmm?' I hum, hippie-style. She doesn't smile, but looks rather worried. Great. Now she thinks I'm nuts.

'No. More of a *power phrase* . . .' She looks at her watch, which I suspect is worth twice as much as our van. 'I don't have time to explain right now, we can't arrive late.' She leans forward conspiratorially. 'But my mantra is, *where there's a will, there's Abby's way.*'

It's my turn to look nonplussed. 'Right. Lovely.'

She was obviously expecting a warmer reaction, but then she tuts to herself. 'Which *obviously* makes an awful lot more sense once you know my name is Abby.' She thrusts out her hand. 'Abby Capper.'

'Oh. Yes. Abby's way. Of course. I'm Emily Turn . . . I mean, Cheney. Would you believe it's been two years since my divorce, and I still keep wanting to use my married name, it's so silly, I—'

She withdraws her hand and I take that as a signal to stop gabbling. 'Well, Emily Cheney, let's see if by the end of what I'm sure will be a riveting day, we can come up with a mantra that will help you face the world as the woman you are, not the wife you used to be!'

We're definitely the stragglers. The harassed-looking staff give us name badges, then offer us bad coffee and good croissants which are whisked away again thirty seconds later. 'You can't take them into the conference space in case of spills.'

The hall is airless and completely packed with would-be Green Goddesses. I'd usually hide at the back, but Abby strides down the centre aisle.

'There are always prime seats at the front,' she tells me, and sure enough, there's an almost empty row right underneath the dais. When the lead speaker steps up to begin her introduction, I can even count the unplucked brow hairs that give her a Neanderthal look.

Then that reminds me that I haven't tackled my own eyebrows since last summer, and I'm glad that they've dimmed the house lights.

'Welcome, friends. Today is the beginning, we hope, of a

new era in community development, spearheaded by the female talent in this room.' The heavily browed woman begins to clap and she gestures to us to join in. 'Take a moment to celebrate the power of women. To celebrate yourselves.'

Abby joins in without hesitation, and so do I, though it feels cringeworthy. She leans across to whisper, 'I thought that sisterhood-is-global stuff went out after Maggie Thatcher got in.' But when I look at her face, she's smiling with utter sincerity.

The applause dies out, and eyebrow lady resumes her speech. 'Today will be inspiring. We have a keynote address from the woman who needs no introduction.' The speaker gestures to a plump woman whose red hair has been coerced into stringy African-style beads, revealing her pale scalp.

'Well, I need an introduction,' I say to Abby. 'Who is she?'

'Maeve Topping. She's behind that chain of eco-housewares, you know. Change the World One Speck of Dust at a Time. My cleaner raves about her stuff.'

'. . . then we have a lecture on village life in the twenty-first century, on sustainable communities.'

Abby mimes a huge yawn behind her hand.

'And before our delicious vegan lunch, we'll have a Power-Point on the criteria for EU funding.'

'That's typical,' whispers Abby, 'making us wait for the only reason we're here.'

'After lunch, we'll have break-out groups and pitching workshops to help you refine your ideas.'

'As if we're going to share ideas with this bunch of back-stabbers,' Abby says.

I turn my head to look at the other women. They're mainly in their thirties and forties: some as glamorous and stream-lined as Abby, some more homely, but all with the same determined expressions. It was a bit naive of me to imagine that being eco would also make them jolly, caring-sharing types. Caring-sharing goes out the window when there's a two hundred thousand euro grant at stake . . .

I can't do this, can I? I'm kidding myself. This lot would sell their own kids for a share of the EU gravy train. Whereas I'm the girl from the sticks who worked in a bank for eight years but still thought ISAs were a Japanese fashion designer.

'. . . so without further delay, I would like to ask Maeve to take the floor to explain how she's combined her eco principles with a brain for business.'

Maeve steps up to the podium, her bluey-white skin glowing ever more brightly in the spotlight.

'Thank you, Frances. I'm always asked more or less the same question whenever I get out of the jeep at one of the tiny, often completely desolate villages where I'm considering setting up a micro-factory.' Maeve pauses. 'It's: *what's a grossly fat, ridiculously white woman like you doing in a place like this?*'

The women in the room laugh nervously.

'It's OK. That's what I like about Africa. The directness. And a question like that deserves a direct answer. So I always tell them: *I'm here to make money. And I hope you are too. You certainly look like you need some.*'

The audience laughs again. I find myself warming to Maeve and her strange hair.

'Because however much we might like to tell ourselves that we're motivated by a desire to change the world, there's one person who always comes first.' She taps the lapel of her batik jacket. 'We're all selfish, but so long as we recognise that in ourselves, then selfishness can be a strength, not a weakness . . .'

The strangest thing happens to me after lunch, when we're randomly allocated to 'break-out groups'. Abby is led away by a woman with the saintly air of an infant teacher. I'm luckier: I get to stay in the hall with feisty Maeve.

I'm feeling drowsy from the heavy tofu rissoles, and from

the heavy mental effort of trying to hold my own amongst the power women. I haven't found my mantra yet, though I have fallen back on the nervous person's standby of asking lots of questions. None of these women has any trouble talking about herself . . .

Which is why when Maeve asks us to introduce ourselves and explain a little about our plans to dominate the eco-universe, my heart sinks. The four women who go before me all go over their allocated time waffling about recycling projects and baby food empires and ideas I've heard a thousand times before. The other delegates aren't supportive: they stare at their notebooks or pick specks of dust off their designer jeans, and they don't ask any questions.

So much for sisterhood.

Then it's my turn.

'Um. Hi. I'm Emily. I must admit I'm not quite sure what I'm doing here today, except my partner saw the flyer and persuaded me to come.'

'Good for her!' says Maeve, and I blush.

'Him, actually. Will, his name is. Uh, and I also have a little boy, Freddie, who'll be four in the summer, and I run a shop in Heartsease Common, about fifteen miles from here. Two shops, now, actually. Sorry. Keep forgetting. The first store sells locally produced food and drink plus green housewares, and then the new store is a kind of craft place where you can try out different skills and—'

The baby food woman looks up from collating her newly collected business cards. 'It's Heartsease Handmade, isn't it? Wow! I've heard about you. I've been thinking of getting a group of the girls to come over for a knitting class. You do one on making couture-style clothes, don't you?'

'Yes, that's our Catwalk Copycats session!'

'I dropped in there the other day,' says another girl, the youngest, who is something to do with natural cosmetics and gives off a potent herby smell. 'Lovely place. I'd never even heard of the village before, but it was worth the trip.'

I try to look bashful, but my smile is too broad. 'Really? That's so nice of you. Next time you drop by, ask for me—'

Maeve holds up her hand. 'Far be it from me to get in the way of commerce, but you haven't explained how running your shops might qualify you for the funding.'

I nod. 'Sorry. Um. Heartsease is a bit of a nondescript place. It doesn't even have its own station. So we thought the handmade thing might help give the village an identity. Bring the community together, all that jazz. There's such a buzz around traditional crafts and simple pleasures at the moment, with the recession. Will has been looking into organising a LETS scheme, you know, local currency, so that's—'

Maeve holds up her hand again.

'Sorry, have I gone over my time?'

'Almost. But a word to the wise, sweetheart. Don't bring the man into it, especially not here. This is a prize for *female* entrepreneurs.'

'But it was his idea.'

She grins. 'Let's face it, men haven't been shy in taking credit for our ideas for, what, about two millennia. Maybe you should see redressing the balance as the ultimate in female empowerment?'

The other women laugh, and I join in, even though it doesn't seem quite fair to Will. But I guess that for two hundred thousand euros, he wouldn't mind me taking centre stage.

At the final tea break, I'm suddenly surrounded by women who've heard who I am, and who are angling for a discount. Even when the speakers call us in for the last session, I'm still being mobbed like a rock star. For the first time, I wonder whether – stupid, really, I dismiss the idea almost before I think it – but whether I might have something to offer.

Abby barges through the crowd – that woman uses her bump as a weapon – and grabs a card from my hand.

'My, my, we're popular, aren't we, Emily? What are you selling? Potions to transform husbands into George Clooney? Knock-out drops for toddlers?' She reads the card. 'Heartsease Handmade?' Her voice sounds odd. Perhaps she hadn't expected me to be capable of having a good idea.

I begin to walk back towards the hall, and the other women drift away, but she stops me in the doorway.

'This store of yours, it wouldn't happen to be in the old Bells and Whistles hardware shop, would it?'

'Yes, that's the one. Do you live locally?' Even before she answers, I have a bad feeling about her tone of voice.

'I do,' she says. 'In Upper Findlebury.'

The Village Next Door. I knew it. 'How . . . *lovely.*' I hate her already.

'But that's not why I know it. It's just that I used to have . . . dealings with the store. Tell me, did you come across a Will Powell when you took the store over?'

'Yes. He's my partner.'

Her eyes widen. '*Business* partner?'

'Well, yes. But partner-partner, too. Boyfriend. Whatever. It seems a bit daft to say boyfriend now we're in our thirties.' Abby is staring at me. 'Why, do you know him?'

'You could say that,' she says, and her voice is quite different now that the charm has evaporated. She sounds almost . . . bitter. 'We were engaged. I'm sure he's mentioned me.'

I gawp back. Abby. *Abby.* Yes, you could say he's mentioned her. But only once, because I didn't want to hear any more about her. And I never expected to come face to face with her . . .

'I must say, Emily, I'd never have expected *him* and *you*. I mean, you're an absolute butterball of loveliness but you don't seem his type. Still, he was very upset when we split. I suppose he might have wanted someone *different.*' Her voice is all sweetness again. 'Such a cute little idea, your store. Now that I know he's still involved, I must pop in and see you soon, eh? Let him know the news about the twins and everything.' She pats her bump.

Twins? 'Twins? Gosh, congratulations.'

'It is good news, isn't it? A boy and a girl, the scan says. The instant family. I really am so terribly lucky,' she says, as though luck actually has nothing to do with it at all.

And she air-kisses me before turning to walk away, and I watch the perfectly pregnant figure of *'where there's a will, there's Abby'* slink back into the hall, and I feel a horrible sense that doom is stalking me in Louboutin heels.

CHAPTER 6

Grazia

Skype is the evil invention of a young person with supermodel cheekbones.

Or perhaps one should not blame the messenger. My irritation is not really with the miraculous world wide web, but with the tiresomeness of having to apply full make-up before sitting down to check emails, in case the delightful Nigel – who needs no artificial aid in front of the web cam – happens to 'Skype' me.

Luckily this evening he manages to catch me on my way out, when I am already dolled up. My warpaint is anything but subtle, and the soft lighting in my apartment works a kind of magic, trimming off a decade at least.

'Wow, Grazia, you're looking even more amazing than usual,' he says. Strange to see him so clearly, even though he is literally halfway around the world. 'Who's the lucky man?'

'No one you know.'

'Is that good or bad?' His voice is slightly slurred, although it might be the connection.

'What time is it?'

'Late,' he says. 'Or early, I guess. Depends which way you look at it. Just got in from a tedious works do with clients. Dinner, then a bar crawl.'

'Girly bars?'

He shrugs. 'No girlies there as gorgeous as you.'

I smile. 'Fibber.'

'Don't be like that.'

He looks hurt. Even face to virtual face, conducting a friendship via the Internet is fraught with complications. 'It was a joke,' I say. 'Forgive me.'

He smiles again. 'Always. So where are you off to tonight?'

'Charity reception at the Victoria and Albert Museum. They want my money, of course, though if they can afford a party at the V&A, then they need nothing from me, do they?'

Nigel laughs. 'Don't keep them waiting, then, eh?' He pauses. 'You know, Grazia. Whatever happens . . . I do miss you.'

'And I you, Nigel.'

He leans forward to kiss the screen and I blow a kiss back.

As I step out into the London night, I feel warmer for having spoken to him. He was – he *is* – an adorable boy, but in the five months we were 'together' I always held back some of myself. I could not quite allow myself to believe that a handsome, clever bachelor like Nigel would stick around a woman fifteen years his senior. And not simply an older woman, but one whose spinsterly instincts have finally revealed themselves.

No more secret shopper. Now I am more of a secret stitcher.

It is entirely unexpected, but since the craft event in Heartsease a month ago, I have become addicted to needlework. It is the most bizarre compulsion. Whenever I am restless, I feel this urge to pick up an embroidery hoop. Sometimes I wake from a dream or nightmare, and scrabble for it in the half-light, spotting my latest piece thanks to the glow-in-the-dark thread.

Now my immaculate apartment is scattered with stitched doodles and skeins of fine-coloured floss. Some designs are abstract, others plain strange, a couple are almost beautiful. I dread to think what they would tell an analyst about my ego or my id.

If Nigel were likely to drop by, as he often did before he left London, I would have to keep my new vice concealed. Traditional handicrafts are not a turn-on to toyboys, except perhaps those who wish to be reminded of their grand-mothers . . .

I intended to walk to the museum, but the rain outside is torrential. Is this my get-out clause? I will admit to feeling slightly weary at the prospect of another evening of chit-chat and canapés. I could turn around right now, take off my make-up, spend the evening French-knotting away my doubts and insecurities.

No! Before I permit myself more weak thoughts, I march out of the block and hail a taxi. I take out the invitation to remind myself what the fund-raiser is about. An art therapy charity for children who have escaped trauma. Certainly a worthy cause but is it the one for me?

The dramatic beauty of the hall and of the central blown-glass chandelier silences me for a moment, even though I have seen it many times before. I wish I could stay here at the entrance all evening. But that is not why I am here. I *must* socialise.

Across the room, I spot a group of Leon's old friends, who used to come to wild dinners at our house in the country. The same people later sent tasteful condolence cards but refused to attend the funeral because death was the only taboo in our circles. They never contacted me again. I am not resentful, because really they were not my friends. I only ever had eyes for my husband, and so did they.

But now one must make the effort. I take a breath, and a glass of Laurent Perrier (for the cost of each bottle, one could buy a thousand colouring pencils), and I launch myself into the crowd. Like jumping into Lake Como in winter, it may be painful at first, but the more one perseveres, the more one's endurance grows.

Two hours pass in a whirl of rumour and air kisses and fizz. The nibbles are less substantial than the conversation. My feet are sore but my head is light and I have decided to give everyone here the benefit of the doubt. Of course they are shallow, but they have come out on a miserable night to support a good cause. Who am I to judge?

'We're heading off to supper now, Grazia. I'm sure we can squeeze one more in, how about it?' Pierre, a soigné sculptor who wants to be my new Gay Best Friend, takes my hand to lead me away.

'I will cramp your style, surely?' But even as I phrase my question, I know I want him to insist and, sure enough, a few minutes later, we are tearing through the waterlogged streets in another taxi.

The restaurant is loud and brightly lit, and we sit on a raised podium, so others see us. Pierre has ordered more champagne – 'I never mix my drinks. Or drugs. Well, unless it's a month with an R in it' – and when it arrives he insists on opening it in a showy way which I would normally regard as vulgar, and yet tonight I find charming.

There are a dozen people at our table, though we're making as much noise as twice as many. Why do I feel more comfortable with these people than I ever did with Leon's contemporaries? They are not so different. The group, like Leon's, is composed of attractive people, some straight, some gay, all so pleased with themselves and so mocking of the too-cool waiters and the pompous maitre d'. But they also mock themselves. It is the single English quality that I find most attractive – self-deprecation.

'And then he told me to bugger off, and to take the dog with me. I wouldn't have minded, but the dog wasn't even mine.'

Everyone laughs. Pierre puts his arm around me. 'Are you pleased you came?'

'Certainly more fun than sitting in on my own.'

'You looked a bit sad when we were first introduced tonight.'

I am surprised by his directness. 'Man trouble. Not worth thinking about.'

'Any man who would cause you trouble certainly is not worth thinking about, Grazia.'

'Ah, you *flatterer*.' But I still smile. Perhaps that is it. The reason I feel good around these people is because Pierre invited me for who I am, not who I was married to.

When the man walks into the dining room, drenched and disorientated, at first I think he must be a homeless guy who has somehow given the doorman the slip.

'Oi! Joel, over here,' Pierre calls out. 'What happened to you? Did you go for a dip in the Thames to work up an appetite or something?'

As the man walks towards our table, he is still dripping rain onto the oak floor, a waitress following discreetly behind with a cloth. He must be my age, at least, but the way his suit clings to his slim body, he looks boyish. And vulnerable.

Even before I see him properly, I *know* him. Well, I have never met this *Joel* in my life before, but I know *what* he is: his weaknesses and his strengths and my own weakness for his kind. I feel a familiar pull: I want to look after him. And look how much trouble that got me into with Leon.

Leon? Joel? Is history repeating itself?

I turn away, but not quickly enough to avoid his smile.

Now we are thirteen at the table. Unlucky for me?

'Joel. Come, come,' says Pierre, pulling over a chair from the next table and squeezing it in between mine and his own. 'Meet my friend Grazia. I know you're going to love her every bit as much as I do.'

'Don't you hate it when people say that?' asks Joel, though

66

he sits down anyway. 'Talk about raised expectations. It's like when someone thrusts a book onto you that they also "know you're going to love" and then you read it and you think, shit, I don't know this person at all.'

'On the other hand, perhaps it is fun to meet new people and encounter new books?' I suggest. 'Or, at least, perhaps it is better to see what you think yourself?'

'About books or about people?'

'Both can be surprising,' I say. Although actually, I do not expect to be surprised by Joel because I already sense exactly who he is.

For the next two hours it is as though the other people at our table have gone home, or simply disappeared.

I am focused only on trying to find something that surprises me about Joel. I discover facts – he is two years older, divorced, a self-made man with multiple careers behind him, and now 'a very independent freelance. I like to reinvent myself at least once every ten years. Staying the same doesn't interest me at all.'

We talk about England, about the Med, about Italy. He is not the kind of man who thinks of my country as a Chianti-and-olive-themed amusement park for expats, and he has smart and biting things to say about politics there. As well as about religion and music and art and all the other important subjects. He is as sharp as Nigel is nice, and I realise suddenly what has been missing.

When the waiter comes to take our plates, our main courses are untouched.

Joel leans forward. 'I felt ravenous when I came in here,' he says, as the waiter walks away, 'which is weird, because food's never been that important to me; I'm hungrier for experiences.'

I use his statement as an excuse to look at him closely. I have reassessed my first opinion of him as boyish. In fact, his frame is slender but powerful. His forearms are bronzed, the tan of a man who spends his time outdoors. 'You are not interested in food? How can you say such a thing in the presence of a red-blooded Italian woman?'

'Perhaps it's that I haven't tasted the right food yet . . .' He opens his wide, wonderful dark brown eyes at me. 'Or the right woman?'

'You know, Joel, there is a fine line between charm and smarm.'

'If I fall on the wrong side of the line, you have my permission to tell me. I have been known to let my enthusiasm run away with me.'

So many things about him enchant and surprise me, even though I feel as if I have known him for ever. I am astonished at how quickly I realise that I plan to go home with him tonight.

We are still there for coffee – also untouched – long after the rest of the group has vanished into the night. He pays the bill, then waits while the cloakroom girl finds my coat.

'Shall we walk?' I say.

The rain is so hard that it keeps triggering the glass doors. He laughs. 'Where to?'

'I thought . . .'

'The trouble is, that, well, when I go out with Pierre and the gang usually we don't go to bed till dawn, so I don't have a hotel booked. We could try to find one.'

So he knows it too.

'Or you could come back to mine . . .'

'Or we could keep going until dawn.'

'I think I may be past all that, now, Joel.' For the first time, I feel uncertain. Does he have no place of his own? Is the 'freelance' label simply a poor excuse for perpetual irresponsibility? It would not be the first time I have fallen for someone like that.

'You can sleep on the plane.'

'Plane?'

'Hmm. Because unfortunately that's the only way I know of being in Barcelona in time for breakfast.'

CHAPTER 7

Sandie

'Oh my God, Brains, are you certain the father isn't an *alien?*'

'Not an alien, but definitely not a gentleman either,' I mumble. I'd be more than justified in punching Toby in the face, but as I am lying flat out on a white leather medical couch, my lower half covered in cold jelly, my options are limited. 'This was your idea, don't forget, and calling our baby an extra-terrestrial isn't my idea of being supportive.'

Toby pulls a face. 'Sorry, that was a bit below the belt. It's just that this is . . . not *quite* what I expected.'

The sonographer, a pretty young thing who probably always makes dads-to-be smile wistfully over the expanded tummies of their pregnant partners, gives him a disapproving look. 'It's the lack of space. A bit like when you squash your face against a window pane when you're a kid.'

I look back up at the large flat-screen telly on the wall opposite. As soon as Toby got to hear about 4D baby scanning, he made an appointment without consulting me. He's already got a whole suite of apps on his iPhone to tell us the size, weight and predicted shoe size of our baby at any given moment.

Apparently the idea of these scans is to increase *bonding*, and as I refused to acknowledge that I was having a baby for the first few months, I guess I might need a helping hand. It's not that I don't care about the baby, not at all, but despite the increasingly vigorous kicks and shimmies inside me, I can't quite make the mental leap and accept that there's a person in there.

Frankly, what I am seeing on the screen is not helping. The image is a sickly sepia colour, instead of the no-nonsense black and white of the NHS scan. At first, all we could see was a random collection of body parts – an elbow . . . or a knee? The amniotic fluid made the skin ripple, so the baby seemed to have the worst cellulite ever. Finally the sonographer found the face and at least we knew what we were seeing.

Closed eyes, a flat nose, a delicate little chin, all in that same sandy colour.

I wonder what colour skin the baby will have?

It's all very clever, but I felt more emotional when we went to the local hospital for the twenty-week scan. I treasure that tiny, unsophisticated image of our baby lying on its side, its brand-new spine clearly visible. Whereas this . . .

Toby takes my hand. 'It's . . . amazing, isn't it, Sandie?' But I can tell that he can't wait to get out of here either.

'And you definitely don't want to know Baby's sex?' says the girl.

I bite my tongue. I can't bear how everyone in the pregnancy *industry* refers to *the* baby as Baby. It makes me feel like a six-year-old.

Toby *does* want to know whether the baby takes after him in the trouser department but I am not compromising on this one. It's the exception to my rule about avoiding any kind of surprise in life.

'We'd rather not know.'

'Right,' says the girl. 'Did you bring the fizzy water and the chocolate with you? If you take a few sips, it might wake Baby up a bit more. See if we can get him or her to say hello!'

Toby takes them out of the backpack he's already

designated as my hospital bag. I drink some water, and let a square of chocolate melt on my tongue. It's true that the baby often seems to wake when I eat, and it jiggles about when Toby switches his music on. I keep wondering what it sounds like, in there. And what the baby is feeling or thinking, though perhaps he or she is too busy growing to think . . .

The girl stays focused on the face, while I look at the clock. Only five minutes to go before we can get out of here and return to the real world. I feel restless, aware that I had to turn off my BlackBerry and knowing it will be chock-full of incredibly urgent Garnett's business by the time I switch it on again. I could hardly say no when they asked for a consultancy report on a potential revamp, but their deadline is crazy. I swear I can hear a clock ticking inside my head.

And then I feel desperately guilty, because this should be such a moving moment and I don't want to be one of those mothers who cares more about business meetings than bedtime stories.

Of course, seven months ago, I never wanted to be a mother at all.

'Come on now, Baby,' says the sonographer. 'We're all watching.'

Toby tightens his grip on my hand. 'Wave for Daddy, please!'

Then it happens. The baby's lips begin to move apart as though he or she is about to say something, and then we realise it's a huge yawn. It's over in a moment, but then as the mouth closes, the baby seems to be smiling.

I can't quite speak, and neither can Toby. Then the baby moves again, as if to say, *that's your lot for today, Mum and Dad.*

The sonographer smiles. 'Definitely one for the family album!'

*

In the waiting room, as they burn our DVD, I feel half-euphoric, half-terrified.

'It's really happening, isn't it?'

He nods. 'Yup.'

'What if we get it wrong?'

Until now, I've avoided being neurotic. Because I got pregnant by accident, there'd been no tortuous pre-conception regime of organic wheatgrass for me and free-flowing underpants for Toby. OK, I had a close brush with chicken pox early on and that scared me half to death, but I've tried to be sensible. Women have had babies for millennia, barely pausing between cave-cleaning or rock-breaking. Why couldn't I be like that: strong, powerful, Amazonian?

But right now I don't feel at all Amazonian. 'What if we're not up to it, Toby?'

'I've got it all under control, Brains. I've researched push-chairs and baby slings and nappies, even though, of course, we won't be doing much changing.'

'Won't we?'

'I've no objection to being a new man and all that, but we both work, so obviously we're going to have a nanny.'

I stare at him. 'Are we?'

Suddenly he looks nervous himself. 'Aren't we?'

'I'm not saying I don't think a nanny's a good idea, it's just . . .' It's just that if he's making all these assumptions about the first few weeks, then what else has he got planned? Name down for Eton as soon as the baby emerges? Hunting, shooting and fishing instruction as soon as he's walking? 'We should talk about things like this before making decisions.'

'Yeah, right.'

'What's that supposed to mean?'

'Every time I try to talk to you seriously about the baby, you change the subject. Like you do when I ask you to marry me.'

'Rubbish.'

'I'll prove it. My darling, can I make an honest woman of you?'

I sigh. 'Oh, don't start that again. Not here. We've got so much else to think about.'

'I know. I know. All you think about is Garnett's or the builders.'

'Only because they're more urgent right now. The baby . . .' I touch my stomach. 'The baby is getting on quite nicely on her own.'

'*Her*? Did the scanning woman let something slip?'

'His, her, whatever.' Funny. I hadn't even realised that I'd decided she was a girl.

Toby says nothing, but looks rather grumpy. He really does want a boy.

'OK, OK,' I say. 'Let's talk. What shall we talk about? The colour of the nursery? Whether we're even going to have a nursery. Or a roof?' Last time I checked in with the builders, they were mumbling about inadequate rafters, and I stopped listening.

'Better steer clear of that one for now, Brains.'

'Right. What about school? I suppose you want to send our baby to boarding school at the age of five or something?' Though maybe that's not such a bad idea if I'm going to be bad at this whole parenthood thing . . .

He smiles. 'I know it might not have done me any harm—'

'Debatable . . .'

'But, you know, now we've seen his squashed little face . . . Or hers. Well, I never want to send our baby away, not after all this waiting.'

I look at him and I see the longing there. It makes me feel inadequate so I plough on with practicalities. 'What about discipline? We have to be consistent. Decide where we stand on spanking.'

He can't help himself. He winks naughtily, and I send back a warning scowl. 'Be serious, Toby.'

'Um. Actually, I think corporal punishment is rotten. What kind of person gets so angry with a baby that they'd want to hurt them?'

He reaches for my hand, and his long fingers close over mine and then he lifts them together onto the bump. 'Is she moving right now?'

'No,' I say, smiling at his deliberate use of *she*. 'Maybe acting for the camera has tired *him* out. You know what boys are like! But he knows how much we're looking forward to meeting him properly.'

And even though it's the kind of sentimental notion I'd normally dismiss, I do have the weirdest sense that he or she *might* understand.

The three of us are in it together, after all.

If I had my way, I'd be heading back to Garnett's for a meeting about toilet ventilation upgrades – the glamour! – but I have to get my new deputy, Babs, to step in. I'm due for tea in Heartsease and I've already cancelled too many times to get away with another no-show.

Emily's texted me to say I'll find her in the craft store stockroom. I sneak through the shop, where a crochet class is under way, and I knock on the door.

'Em? It's Sandie.'

She pulls me in. 'I'm in hiding.'

'Who from?'

She opens the storeroom door a few centimetres. 'See that bloody woman out there? In the purple wrap dress?'

'What's she done?'

Emily lets the door close again. Her blondish hair is covered in dust, and the peaches and cream complexion that always made her look like a true country girl is duller than before. She's still curvy – the flowery craft apron is tight around her waist – but her face looks pinched, almost sour. 'She wanted to know the carbon footprint of the stuffing for the amigurumi. Oh, and whether it's organic.'

'Sorry. You lost me at amigo . . . whatever.'

She reaches into the apron pocket and pulls out a pink woollen rabbit. 'Amigurumi. They're Japanese crochet animals. If it's any consolation, I didn't know what they were either before I opened the shop.'

I take the toy. It's about the same size as Toby's iPhone, which he says is also the size of the baby right now, according to his dad-to-be pregnancy app. It sits in my hand, fragile but strong at the same time. I haven't mentioned the scan to Emily. It feels like yet another thing I can't talk to her about, for fear of rubbing in my good fortune.

'Keep it. Our tutor made it, as a sample.'

'It's sweet.'

'Sweet, and selling like red velvet cupcakes. You know, we have waiting lists for these classes. High-flying women across the Thames Valley are clamouring to make and stuff their own knitted bunnies.'

'So long as it's with organic stuffing,' I say, deadpan, and she stares at me for a second before bursting out laughing.

'Sandra Barrow, I do believe you made a joke. And they say pregnancy doesn't change people.' She checks her watch. 'OK, only a few minutes till the class ends. I daren't leave in case they ask me whether the toy dolphins are tuna-friendly.'

I don't tell her that it's the tuna that are supposed to be dolphin friendly. 'Is there anything we can do while we wait? It's a bit of a mess in here.'

'But . . .' She gestures towards my bump, the first time she's acknowledged it.

'But nothing. Toby's already treating me like an invalid, which I'm not. I enjoy hard work.' I reach into my handbag. 'And I have fruit pastilles to keep us going.'

'Yum. I didn't know you had a sweet tooth.'

'I don't. They're for when I get dizzy.'

'Oh. I got dizzy spells too! Have you got indigestion yet? Or piles? Or varicose veins?'

'Not yet. But which of those counts as the amazing, life-changing experience you told me about when I first got pregnant?'

She takes another fruit pastille and chews thoughtfully. 'Ah, you'll be fine. I didn't get piles, though I did get acid reflux. Yuk. But I'd do it all again like a shot, if I was allowed to.'

There's nothing I can say to that. 'So where shall we start?'

She looks around the room, at the open wooden shelves, which are piled with yarns and papers and fabrics and trimmings. Then she shrugs.

I swallow my irritation. 'Let's take everything off the left-hand shelves, and then sort the items by category into boxes – fabrics and packages here, trims and yarns in here, miscellaneous in this one.' I show her. The balls of wool bounce excitedly. A disturbing bagful of orange plastic teddy bear eyes goes into miscellaneous. 'Once we know what we've got, we can work out a system!'

She gawps. 'How do you know how to do that?'

'You know me, I love order.'

Emily shakes her head. 'Oh, boy, you've got some changes ahead . . .' She smiles at my belly, then picks up a reel of ribbon and tosses it into the box, winking at me.

'Is this a race, then, now?' I say and she giggles. We pick up pace and soon floss and cotton lawn are flying across the room, like a haberdashery hurricane. It's easy to get carried away, and we do.

'We're mates, still, aren't we, Sandie?'

'Yes. Of course.'

'I was worried the baby . . . was coming between us. You know, we hardly ever see each other any more, and I know it's probably my fault, because I'm such a jealous person, but—'

'Forget it,' I say. 'It's not a problem. *Oof.*'

'Was that a kick?'

I nod.

'That's a good omen for our friendship!' She opens the door a crack, and claps her hands. 'Hooray. They've gone! The coast is clear . . .'

We head to the shop, where Will is arranging a display of toxically smelly cheese. The hessian overall and wild hair give him the aura of a mad eco-professor.

'Hello, Sandie. Wow, you've hit the blooming stage, I see.'

'Well, it's that or the bucket of red wine I had at lunch-time.'

He gives me a nervous look. 'Really? You know that's not recommended.'

'It's all change round here,' says Emily. 'Will's lost his sense of humour since he went on an all-organic diet, and Sandie's hormones have turned her into a comedienne.' She gives him a peck on the cheek as she swipes a cake from the shelf behind him. He scowls.

I smile, and follow her upstairs. 'Is he OK?'

'Worrying about the planet. You're lucky you didn't get a lecture on how many forests will be chopped down to make up for the nappies your baby's going to use.'

I feel braver, now that we've hugged each other. 'I take it that means there's no budging on your own campaign for baby number two?'

'No. He's obsessed with the eco stuff, plus Freddie's playing up so much it's enough to put us both off for life. I mean, Will's probably right. It's not the time. Maybe I'm not brave enough for terry nappies and whale birthing. He'd insist on bringing up the baby the green way.'

'Maybe.'

She unravels the cake. 'Beetroot. Funny colour, but it tastes OK if you shut your eyes.'

'Is Grazia running late?'

Her face brightens. 'No! No, she's not. She called me this morning. You'll *never* guess where she is.'

'Probably not.' Wherever it is, I feel irritated. I have thousands of things I should be doing on my report, but *I* made it. What's *Grazia's* excuse?

'Barcelona!'

'I thought she hated Europe.'

She sits down. 'Put it this way, I don't think she's spending a lot of time on an open-top bus tour. Though she might be spending time with her top open!'

The penny drops. 'She's gone there with a *man*?'

'With a man she met *last night*!'

I join her on the mean little sofa, and our legs touch. 'Oh my God, is she OK?'

Emily laughs. 'I'd say she sounded pretty OK when she rang me from his limo at the airport. She went to a charity do last night, met him at dinner, and within four hours she was sipping champagne in the VIP lounge at Heathrow before "hopping over" to Spain.'

'Different world, isn't it?'

We look around Emily's dingy kitchen-cum-dining room. She frowns. 'At least you've got your huge pile in Chiswick.'

'Pile of *rubble*, yes. There's no way it's going to be done in time.'

'You're going to have the baby at the Sanctum, right?'

I shrug. 'That's what Toby wants. I'm inclined to stick to the local hospital. The midwives seem nice.'

She shakes her head. 'Have it at the Sanctum, you silly moo. Then stay there until the house is finished. Private hospitals are like hotels, aren't they? Room service, satellite TV.'

'We'll see.' I smile back, trying to ignore the edge in her voice. 'What else is new in Heartsease apart from the crochet craze?'

'The real news isn't from bloody Heartsease, but from Upper Bloody Findlebury.'

'The next village along?' Emily is paranoid about what always looks like a perfectly pleasant place to me. Is it another sign that we're growing apart?

'Yep. Guess who's showed up there?'

I sigh. 'You know I'm rubbish at guessing. The Pope? Santa?'

'No. Will's ex, Abby. The one that got away. You know, the one who made sure he ended up managing the useless Heartsease store after he dumped her.'

'What's she doing in Findlebury, then?'

'According to her, she's busy nesting before she has twins. But I met her at this Green Goddess competition thing Will talked me into. She's got her eyes on the two hundred grand for rural regeneration. I mean, does Findlebury look like it needs regenerating?'

I think about the hair and beauty salons, the boutiques and the packed coffee shops. 'Nope. It'd definitely go a lot further here. You are still entering?'

Emily shrugs. 'I dunno. I guess I'd like to, but it's not for people like me, is it? Plus, I have no desire to see that woman again in a hurry, and I certainly don't want *Will* to see her again.'

'But he left *her*, didn't he?'

'I saw this glint in her eye when she found out who I was. I think she's the sort who likes a challenge, whether that's getting hold of a pot of euro-cash, or getting back at the bloke who dumped her.' She shudders.

I suddenly feel very tired, and a bit impatient. Everything's a drama for Emily, which makes her exhausting to be with.

She smiles. 'Anyway, enough about me. You wanted to brainstorm something?'

'Yes. The board want me to come up with a master plan to save Garnett's. I mean, it's a huge honour. Something I never dreamed I'd get chance to do. And I know exactly what's *wrong*, but right now I can't think of how to put it right. I never used to be like this. So . . . empty-headed.'

'Pregnancy turns your brain into porridge. In my case, it stayed that way.'

'Rubbish. You saw the craft revival coming. Now, if you can think of something half as clever for Garnett's, then I can put my feet up and spend the rest of my pregnancy learning to knit bootees and eating cake.' I bite into a slice. 'Eurgh. Oh dear, I'm sorry, but that is revolting.'

'I don't think root vegetable cake is going to save Garnett's. So what is wrong with the place?'

'It feels neglected. Boring. Dowdy. But gaudy, too, some-how, like a WAG or banker's wife who's seen better days. And let's face it, even bankers aren't admitting that they're bankers in public any more.'

'So how long have you got?'

'They've given me a month to put together a report. Then if they approve it at the next board meeting, I guess it's all systems go.' Though secretly I have my doubts that Edgar has it in him to make any of my ideas happen. 'And if they don't approve?'

'Or if I can't think anything up? Well, I don't think the bank's patience will last much beyond October.'

'Shit.' Emily swigs almost the whole cup of tea down in one. 'You know when we first met?'

I remember it *very* well. Emily was a frazzled new mum – I won't get *that* tired, will I? – and I rescued her from the clutches of my heinous assistant Marsha, who was trying to press-gang her into buying over-priced pyjamas. One hour later, Marsha got me sacked by planting money in my locker.

'Yup. Quite a day.'

'Garnett's was my fantasy, even though I couldn't afford it. Walking out onto Oxford Street with my red glossy bag, I felt . . . insulated against the cold and the horribleness of my life. Garnett's sold dreams. You need to do that again. Simple!'

I feel momentarily irritated. If it was really that simple, we'd be doing it already. 'But people's dreams have changed, haven't they?'

'Mine are the same as they ever were,' she says, looking meaningfully at my belly.

'Sorry to snap. But I feel so responsible. Not just for the store, but for all the people who work there, for the history, the name, you know? And I'll feel so guilty if I can't save the place.'

'Yes, well, better get used to it. Guilt is one of those emotions I know all about. Welcome to the wonderful world of maternal guilt!'

I'm too exhausted to drag myself back to Garnett's, so instead I go home. Toby's still at the store – he's putting the hours in, too, doing all the schmoozing I loathe so much.

I sit in the box room on the first floor, looking at the handful of nursery things we've allowed ourselves to buy now that I'm twenty-eight weeks gone: a Peter Rabbit wall frieze, a collection of organic cotton soft toys, a down comforter. I try to zone out of baby things, and stare at my notebook. I write down some of the things Emily said:

Garnett's sold dreams.

It made me feel insulated against the cold and horribleness of my life.

I know that I have the answer somewhere in my head. I lived and I breathed and dreamed the place for so long. I've saved countless other businesses: the men's grooming store, the downmarket toyshop, and even Bell's Emporium. So why can't I do it for the business that matters most?

I lay my head on the baby's comforter, desperate for sleep, but unable to find it because I have this awful feeling I am missing something.

CHAPTER 8

Grazia

'Oh, Grazia. Much as I adore every moment I spend with you, I'm afraid you are a big, big problem.'

So this is it. Somehow, I knew, even as I boarded the plane to Spain, that this was too good to be true. What is Joel's problem? I wonder. Marriage? Addiction? Terminal illness?

I keep my eyes closed and I savour the last few moments of sun on my face and I wait.

'Yes. I really don't know where to start.'

I hear the voices of children, and the barking of dogs. 'Please, say what you have to say.'

I intend to sound businesslike, even fierce, but my voice is soft and golden, like the olive oil we poured on the *pan con tomate* we devoured this lunchtime after leaving Joel's apartment for the first time in two and a half days.

'My problem is, which part of Grazia do I adore the most?'

Despite my desire to stay cool, I feel a smile spreading across my face. 'Ah. I see.'

'Because, it goes without saying, that your body is sheer bloody heaven. A pleasure park. The most thrilling route to oblivion I have yet experienced . . .'

I laugh. 'A compliment, indeed, coming from you.' Over the last three days we have laid ourselves bare and I know that

Joel has pursued oblivion in ways that even Leon's most 'artistic' friends had not explored. The hardest of hard drugs, the wildest of sexual encounters, the most extreme of excesses. If someone had described this man to me before I met him, I would have been horrified.

Yet the connection with him is something I have waited a lifetime to experience.

'But there's seriously strong competition coming from your face. Apart from being strikingly beautiful and strikingly strokeable, it's . . . wise.'

'Is that a polite way of saying old? Because you are not exactly free of . . . wisdom yourself.'

I open my eyes. Joel is smiling, and although I know he is forty-eight, I see an ageless man. Not young the way Nigel is, all bright eyes and glossy hair, like a puppy. Joel's face is angular, with lines on his forehead and around his mouth. But he seems ageless because he is *ravenous* for life. He has explored numerous continents, careers, lifestyles, yet still wants more.

And for a hungry man, this city is the place to be. When I can drag my gaze away from his face I see life, everywhere. A group of teenagers in tie-dye clothes play guitars, their dreadlocks bouncing along in time to the rhythm. A couple in their eighties take careful steps together along the path, and the bicycles tearing past give them a respectfully wide berth. A circle of toned South Americans beat a drum as two figures half-dance, half-fight with an elegance that leaves me breathless. A young guy crawls around the grass mound near us, and I realise the animal he is playing with is not a dog but a plump white house rabbit.

I can imagine being happy to embroider here, in public, without feeling like a freak. Though, despite the revelations I have shared with Joel these last few days, that is one confession I have no intention of letting slip.

'Of course, your lips are the most exquisite colour in the world.'

'Lipstick.'

He shakes his head. 'No. Remember, I've seen them after the lipstick has been kissed away, and believe me, they are better without. I thought I had seen every shade of red, but yours is unique. Your eyes, however, are the exact colour of the best chocolate I have ever tasted, when I harvested cacao in South America. And your skin . . . well, the colour is wonderful, but it's the feel of your skin that I love the most.'

'Oh.' I cannot think of a wisecrack.

'Actually, I know my favourite part of you. It's your mind.'

I pause for a second, wondering whether it is really a compliment to be adored for something invisible. But then it strikes me. 'That *is* a coincidence. Because your brain is my favourite thing about you, too.'

He pulls a face. 'Are you *quite* sure about that? Because some men might find that a little . . . insulting to their masculinity.'

I pretend to reconsider. 'Well, there is another part offering strong competition.'

Joel growls, and then buries his face in my neck. 'I think we've had enough sunshine now, haven't we? How about we go back to the *ático* for a little reminder of our . . . less cerebral qualities?'

He pulls me to my feet – he is astonishingly strong, despite his slim frame – and we are on our way, arms round each other, stopping every few metres to kiss again, and no one bats an eyelid.

Perhaps it is time for me to reconsider my view that continental Europe is a backwater compared to urbane London.

We surface again minutes before midnight, after a supreme effort to get out of bed.

'It seems mad to let you go home without seeing the city at night,' he says, as he opens yet another bottle of cava.

'I *have* seen the city.' I look out of the windows, and the lights draw me once again onto the terrace. Joel's apartment is on the top floor of a block without a lift. When he led me up the stairwell less than three days ago – is it really so little time? – I felt claustrophobic. Outside, the sun was dazzling, but the hallway was dark and smelled of damp. The steps became narrower with every landing, until I lost count of the number of floors, and began to despair of this entire adventure. I'd accepted that Joel was bohemian but by then I was picturing a squat, complete with overflowing ashtrays and peeling wallpaper. I was wondering what excuses I could use to make my escape . . .

We reached the final landing, and as I looked down blood rushed to my head because we were so high up. The door had four different locks, and he was struggling with the last one, the keys in a huge bunch chained to his belt. 'Sorry about this,' he said, and I wondered whether he even lived here, or was borrowing a friend's flat.

And then finally the door gave way and I felt as one imagines it would feel when one is admitted to heaven for the first time (I do not *believe*, but an Italian Catholic upbringing is hard to shake). White light blinded me, and then I felt the warmth of sunshine and of his hand as he led me into the apartment.

I knew at once that it *was* his place. It was an astonishing space, at least as big as the lounge in the house Leon and I had built, but oh, so different from that blank, contemporary canvas. In our home, the white walls and spiky furniture were a challenge to our guests to perform – go on, prove how interesting you are, stake your claim, take centre stage.

This was different. Where our house was empty of anything that might define us or give anything away, Joel's apartment was like an extension of himself. The space itself had character, from the high-vaulted ceilings, to the cool tiled floors. But what I noticed first was the *stuff*. Floor-to-ceiling bookshelves were filled with travel guides, leather-bound notebooks and magazines. Bright paintings and photographs full of people covered the walls, rugs dotted the floor, and in the far corner there were drums, a banjo and a Spanish guitar . . .

The living room alone seemed to hold at least six lifetimes' worth of possessions and discoveries.

'Penny for them?' Joel has joined me on the terrace, one of thousands of unpretentious skyline gardens that stretch out across the city. During the day, you see hundreds of lines of washing, and forests of TV aerials, and the tips of spectacular churches and monuments. At night, the effect is magical, as the lights dot the city, each *barrio* with its own constellation.

Not for the first time since I arrived here, I feel my fingers twitching, almost grasping at the air for a needle and thread, wanting to reflect this city on canvas. Bizarre. Even the kind of erotic charge I have not felt since I met my late husband – or, perhaps, did not even feel back then – cannot dampen my desire to embroider.

'It's nothing,' I lie. Even though Joel is as open-minded as anyone I have met, I feel reluctant to admit to my secret vice.

'Go on. There's something on your mind, I can tell.' He hands me a crystal glass full of the bubbliest cava.

I turn to him. The last few days have been so perfect but perhaps they are simply a chink in time, an unrepeatable moment. I have told so many fibs about who I am in my life. Perhaps honesty will feel different. 'You will laugh at me.'

'Never! And anyway, with the things you know about me, I am hardly in a position to laugh, am I?'

'Are you talking about the naked romp in the fountains in Rome? Or the weeks down and out in Beverly Hills?'

He shrugs. 'Take your pick. So, share the thought.'

'I was thinking that I should love to sew the city.'

'Sew it?'

'It is a temporary craze. A childhood hobby that I redis-covered lately, for stitching. Silly, really.' I lean over to kiss him, but he ducks away.

'No, no. Why shouldn't you sew the city? Don't you dare apologise for who you are, Grazia. As I said before, I find everything about you *enchanting*, and this is no exception.'

I imagine what Leon would have said about my new pastime. Hmm. I smile. 'So you do not think it makes me seem . . . like a *grandmother*? Or an old maid?'

'I cannot think of anyone less like an old maid. Now, drain that drink. We have embroidery thread to buy! And needles.'

I laugh. 'It is past midnight.'

He shrugs. 'Barcelona is a twenty-four-hour city.'

We march across the city, and, yet again, its beauty disarms me. The view from the terrace is all streetlights and icons, but down here night transforms the alleyways of the Gothic Quarter into places that feel at once more edgy and less like a museum. Fancy boutiques and hair salons have their shutters down, but to compensate, the bars and restaurants have raised theirs, and even the tiniest side street has a choice of three or four places to match any mood: grungy, funky, chic or cheap. So many different people, too, mingling and jostling without the beer-fuelled ugliness that can afflict London's streets.

'Where are we going?'

But Joel says nothing as he pulls me past the snuggest clubs and the sweetest *coctelerias*. We do not stop. We cross over Las Ramblas. Yes, there is a little more tackiness here, in the shape of six-foot prostitutes and gaudy living statues and fat tourists eyeing up both tarts and performers and struggling to tell the two apart. Somehow, though, Joel has infected me with his *joie de vivre*. I think my favourite thing about *him* is that although he has intelligent, sensual tastes, he refuses to pass judgement. It is a quality that becomes increasingly rare as one ages. I myself was judging people harshly, oh, almost before I was out of nappies.

'You might want to watch your bag,' he says, as we take a right, up through the throng surrounding the man dressed as Pelé who is doing clever things with a football, and then alongside a group who gawp at a silver-painted fairy who perches on a lily pad, so still that she barely seems to be breathing.

Only after we have passed her do I hear a collective cry from the people, and when I look back, I see that the fairy has opened her eyes.

Joel leads me up a narrow street past the Boqueria market. It is still busy behind there, but the shops are different – juice bars, kebab take-aways, clubs with intimidating bouncers standing guard. Men of all races hang out on the street, as the tourists go by. Not threatening, but watchful. I wonder where their women are . . .

'Almost there,' Joel tells me, before stopping to kiss me in a doorway.

The street narrows further and all I can see now are shutters and apartment buildings. No more lanterns or chalked-up signs for the Cocktail of the Day. But when he pauses outside a closed-up shop, I can hear voices and music. He presses the buzzer and when there is no answer, he kicks the shutter and the clanging reverberates.

'Elena! ELENA!' he shouts, and then something in that strange strangled language that I now know is Catalan. There are few things more sexy than a man speaking words one does not understand.

Finally the light comes on in the hallway and the reinforced ironwork door – a beautiful door, now I notice it, with floral patterns I try to memorise – opens a few centimetres. The face that appears in the gap is pixie-like, though the woman it belongs to is my age. Spanish women age better than gone-to-seed

Britons, and even than run-to-fat Italians. *Jamón* is clearly better for the skin than pasta.

'Joel,' she says, and then more Catalan, before she opens the door wider and kisses him three, four times, with such passion that I feel a certain jealousy, momentarily, before I dismiss it forcefully.

'Elena, this is my friend, Grazia,' he says, in English. 'We'd love to join the party.'

She looks at me, and I feel her scrutiny for a split second, that once-over that women give each other: is she a threat? Prettier? Wrinklier? Sexier? Elena shrugs, a gesture which could mean defeat or indifference, and opens the door.

We walk along the hall, which is identical to Joel's: postboxes along the wall, bicycles to trip over, a sour smell of damp, and then Elena opens the door and jazz hits me, a cold shower of notes. I realise it is not a recording: there is a guy with a sax and another with a clarinet, and a slim girl in jeans who is singing words I do not recognise in a bluesy voice that should come from a woman three times her size.

There are twenty people crammed into the space, some kind of toy store. Dolls stare down from the shelves and the cabinets, and in the low candlelight they give the space a horror-movie feel. There is a table with booze on it, and a door towards the back of the store where I can see firefly glows of cigarettes and – judging from the herby smell – joints, too.

I smile at Joel. 'Thank you for bringing me here.'

There is a laid-back vibe, a sense that the night will last into morning, until the songs or the drink or the moment runs out. It is wonderfully, authentically *Barcelona*, though I think, right now, I would rather spend my last night in bed with Joel.

But he takes my hand and, as we pass the drinks table, he picks up two bottles of beer in his other hand, and leads me behind the jazz group, through a door on the right. 'It's fun out there, but in here is why I really brought you.'

It is dark, and the space is colder than before with a smell of . . . what? Glue? And he fumbles for the light switch, and then I see.

It is a small, cluttered workshop. Half-finished dolls and animals stare with glass eyes or pout with fresh-painted lips. A large table is crammed into the corner, and an old-fashioned coffee machine sits alongside tools and paints and a sewing machine.

'Now where does she keep . . .' He pulls out drawer after drawer of an old dresser in the other corner. 'Ah!'

And he waves, proud as a child, at what he has found for me: a deep drawer full of fabric and thread in a hundred different colours. 'Now you can sew the city!'

I reach out: so many shades of Barcelona. The terracottas of the roof terraces, the blues and golds and greens of Gaudi's crazy buildings, the silvers and oranges of streetlamps reflected on slippery paving stones. I feel as Leon must have felt when he discovered painting, when canvas and oils still felt like a compulsion rather than an obligation.

'But not now, surely? What will you do?'

He kisses me, then sits down at the work table, unscrews the top of both beers and sets them down. 'I will watch you sewing, *chica*. And then, when we tire of that, we will try to think of something else to do with our hands . . .'

May

♥

CHAPTER 9

Emily

Maybe this wasn't the *best* idea I've ever had.

Correction. There's no maybe about it. I have drastically overestimated my undercover skills, and am now at high risk of being spotted behind enemy lines. My camouflage is hopeless. No one round here is going be fooled by my own-brand jeans, or the four coatings of mascara I've applied in place of the compulsory Upper Findlebury eyelash extensions.

It started at breakfast.

'How's the application coming along?'

It took me a few moments to realise that Will was talking about the Green Goddess competition. The one I hoped he'd forgotten about.

'Oh. Um. Well, obviously I've made a start, but I don't have time to do it properly, not when we need to be giving priority to the craft centre and the shop. The closing date's coming up, anyway.'

That was where I'd planned to leave it. OK, so now and again the idea of coming home to Heartsease with a cheque for two hundred thousand euros did cross my mind. I imagined being carried on the shoulders by a crowd of villagers (the ones young enough to risk the damage to their backs). Oh, and being on the front page of the local rag, which I'd leave lying round casually when Duncan came to pick up Freddie, to prove that his 'Chubster' has more to her than he ever guessed . . .

'Not till the end of the month, though, is it?' Will chewed thoughtfully on his flax bread (which never sells, and so we're allowed to 'treat ourselves' to the out-of-date loaves. It's so tough that Freddie calls it 'mattress bread' and I think it'll turn out to be a false economy when one of us breaks a molar.). 'I hate the idea that I'm holding you back, Em. How about you take today off to work on the proposal?'

'No, that's not fair on you. The meat delivery's due, and the workshop looks like a bomb's hit it after the papier mâché class last night.'

'We're a team, aren't we? And I know this matters to you, so clearing up a few pieces of soggy newspaper is the least I can do. Take off somewhere, find a bit of peace and quiet. We'll manage fine!'

I smiled as graciously as I could. It's so much easier not to try than to fail with dignity. 'Thanks. Just . . . don't get your hopes up, eh? The other women looked scary.'

'Ah, but they're not you, are they, Em? You're amazing.'

His faith in me would be tested if he could see me now, skulking behind the phone box on the village green in Upper Findlebury. Unlike Heartsease's muddy excuse for a common, the green here is as lush as AstroTurf, and the freshly varnished benches gleam in the sunlight. Weird. The sun wasn't even shining when I left home, even though it's only six miles away.

Weirder still, in the centre of the green, half a dozen women are doing *synchronised pram-pushing*, swinging their buggies in wild movements with no thought for the babies inside. Their leader wears a turquoise all-in-one and barks commands.

'Wheelie to the right! And spin! And squat! Remember, buns of steel not butts of putty, gals!'

It's even more *Desperate Housewives* than I expected, but I also have to admit that it's, well, *nice*, if you like civic pride and hanging baskets. The cottages that horseshoe around the green are painted like a rainbow, blush pink giving way to pale orange and lemon, soft green, baby blue, and a parma violet purple. That kind of effect takes the kind of military organisation that I can't ever imagine in Heartsease.

Is that why I feel so unsettled at the moment? Is there an Upper Findlebury wannabe lurking under my Heartsease common-as-muck exterior?

I'm racking my brains to think where this place reminds me of, when I spot a mum crossing the green, pushing the very latest Pod-buggy. She gives me a curious look, and I realise I need to move on before they set the neighbourhood watch on me.

I should bugger right off, before I'm rumbled and yet . . . when was the last time I got to enjoy a full-fat cappuccino in peace? I spot a café called Pippin's on the corner, and my mind's made up for me.

'Cappuccino, please.'

'Fair-trade-Kenyan-Costa-Rican-Blue-Mountain-decaff-half-caff-or-treble-caff?' The teen behind the counter doesn't look at me as she recites the mantra for what sounds like the billionth time.

'Fair-trade's fine, thanks.'

'Soy-sweetened-soy-full-fat-skinny-half-fat-rice-milk-or-unpasteurised?'

I shrug. 'What's most popular?' Might as well start my research now. Perhaps we can sell these in our shop.

She looks up from the till and her milkmaid face twists contemptuously. 'Sorry?'

'What do you suggest?'

'Well, if you haven't worked out by now how you take your coffee, I'm hardly going to tell you, am I?'

I feel as though I've been slapped. 'Actually. I'll have it black.'

She sniffs. 'Suit yourself. That's two pounds. I'll bring it over.'

Out of instinct, I revert to secret shopper mode, taking a seat at the back of the room, so I can observe everything without being noticed. Normally, of course, my ordinariness is a gift because people look past me. But here I realise I stand out because I'm so average. In Upper Findlebury, beauty is the norm.

I hide behind the huge menu, which waxes lyrical about sourcing: the five varieties of apple juice come from orchards with a lineage longer than the royal family's. The soap in the loos is made in a Comic Relief-funded project in Liverpool – a place people here would probably find more exotic than Africa. The delicate green walls have been painted in a unique shade, containing pigments from local wild grasses.

So why does it all feel so artificial? It feels like . . .

Legoland! *That's* where the village reminds me of. I mean, I love Legoland almost as much as Freddie does, but I wouldn't want to live there. Would I?

I take out my notebook, and scribble. *Impossibly perfect. Completely free of chaos.* How would we transfer any of this to Heartsease? It'd take more than two hundred grand. We'd have to bulldoze the place, and start from scratch.

It's hopeless. I'm going to have to tell Will the truth – that I'm not up to it.

I jump as the café door opens. Four blonde women enter with buggies. I hold my breath as I check for bumps. Nothing there. Not even a muffin-top. I breathe a sigh of relief.

Because, if I'm honest, there was another reason I came to Findlebury, a reason that wears designer maternity wear and used to live with my boyfriend. Of course, now I'm in her territory, I am terrified that she'll spot me.

Luckily this is just the buggy workout brigade.

'Any treats, girls?' asks the turquoise one. Close up, her all-in-one is so seamless that it must have been sprayed on, along with her tan.

'Actually, I might indulge in something sweet. I'm feeling a little faint,' says the woman with the tiniest buggy. Her baby can't be more than a couple of weeks old. It blinks in shock every time the sulky waitress crashes plates together or rams the coffee drawer into the machine. 'A cranberry cookie, perhaps?'

The chorus line sighs as one. 'Dried cranberry is as loaded with sugar as Dairy Milk,' says turquoise woman. 'I'll get you some pumpkin seeds.'

I wouldn't last five minutes here, I'd tell that bitch where to stick her pumpkin seeds and be ostracised for ever. But I can see it's the perfect place for Abby.

Instead of obsessing about her, I should focus on the fact that Will chose me. But I keep wondering whether, if I could be slightly more like her – more elegant, less silly, say – then everything would be perfect, and I might even get Official Permission to Get Pregnant.

Finally the girl brings my coffee, which has gone cold. I leaf through the seven-page Green Goddess entry form and feel too exhausted to fill it in. Instead, I reach behind me and pull a magazine out of the rack.

The *Upper Findlebury Quarterly* is printed on the glossiest paper and looks as flash as *Vogue*. We used to have the *Heartsease Herald*, which the vicar wrote, and one of the lads from the village designed on the rectory computer. Well, until the hard drive collapsed under the weight of porn.

Maybe the *Quarterly* will give me ideas to steal. The front cover features an arty photo of a dog shaking itself after rain, droplets of water suspended in mid-air. You wouldn't know it was taken here except for the out-of-focus cottages behind him.

The left-hand page is an ad for a beauty salon offering

'mum and tot makeovers'. A letter from the editor urges locals to get spending for spring: 'After all, dear readers, it'll make you feel better, *and* give a much-needed lift to the economy. But do remember to spend locally, and help keep our wonderful village of Findlebury *Upper* where it belongs!'

The main feature is an interview with an alternative comedian who has swapped radical politics for an Aga and a second marriage with his former au pair. 'I love to get back from a hard day in the Big Smoke, take the kids and dogs out for a tramp round the woods, then head for the pub, where everyone treats me like every other harassed dad.'

The news round-up lists charity coffee mornings, cookery classes at the local pub, a meeting to discuss starting a literary festival. I flick through the pages, getting angrier and angrier with the photographs. And then suddenly I realise I'm the one in the wrong. This is the ideal place to live. The people in the magazine look a bit smug, yes, but then why shouldn't they? They've *arrived.*

Am I so much of a jealous, bitter person that I can't be pleased for them? I'm about to shut the magazine and go home, to remind myself of all the things I should be grateful for, when I spot her.

Shit.

The last page of the *Quarterly* features a section called *New Neighbours.* Abby beams at me from the centre of the page, with four photographs dedicated to her and her husband, and only one each to the two other recent arrivals. I guess 'parents-to-be Abby and Christopher Capper' have been granted pride of place because of their house: it's the great big whitewashed villa that you see as soon as you drive into the village. It's even *called* The White House.

'We fell in love the moment we saw it,' says Abby, who is expecting twins in the summer. 'We know we were in the right place at the right time, and we feel extremely lucky.'

Chris works in the City of London and readily admits that after work, 'the last thing I feel like doing is painting walls'. Luckily, as these pictures show, The White House is already a dream home.

'We are considering getting our garden done, though, ready for the summer,' explains Abby. 'I've seen so many gorgeous gardens in the village, so I'm planning to knock on a few doors to find out who can turn our little plot into paradise.'

From the photo, their 'little plot' is the size of three tennis courts, complete with a gazebo and a pond big enough to swim in. Their dining room table is as long as the one in my old school canteen, and their living room stretches behind them for ever. Are there really *three* fireplaces?

The house is stunning, but I keep coming back to her perfect face and her hair, so slinky it could be a wig. Her husband has the regular features of a Disney prince.

I slam the magazine shut and push my chair back so loudly that the little baby at the next table begins to cry.

'Well, really!' says the turquoise terror. I race towards the van, keeping my eyes fixed down on the litter-free pavements, because I'm now petrified I might bump into Abby.

I don't even feel safe in the Snowvan, because she's seen me get into it, and there's no other van so shabby in a fifty-mile radius. I put my foot down and *eventually* the clapped-out engine responds and I break the speed limit out of Upper Findlebury without looking at The White House.

My breathing doesn't return to normal until I'm a mile outside Heartsease. I pull into a lay-by. What the hell was all that about? I try to be rational: her husband being so clean-cut and gorgeous is a *good* thing, because it means she has no reason at all to come after Will (especially now he's banned razors for being wasteful and is growing a wholemeal beard like the one in my parents' 'secret' copy of *The Joy of Sex*).

So it's not about Will. It's about me. I am jealous, the same as I am about Sandie and her pregnancy and her lovely life. Shit. I always thought I was a *nice* person.

Well, it's time to get grateful, Emily. You got divorced, like a third of the rest of the population. Doesn't qualify you to write a misery memoir. And if Will gets exasperated with your air-headed moaning, then, frankly, who can blame him? Get on with your life and stop fixating on everyone else's.

I pull a 'get on with it' face in the mirror, like the one Anna Friel pulled in that movie about the land girls. From now on I will pull my weight and focus on the job in hand and I will enter that bloody competition because the single useful thing I've got out of my reconnaissance into enemy territory is the certainty that our side needs that euro jackpot a hell of a lot more than Upper Bloody Findlebury does.

I drive home like there's no time to waste, slam the van door so hard that a hill of flaky paint forms underneath, and I trample in dog poo as I cross the road which makes me even more determined to clean up our act. I march into the shop, full of pluck and ideas to transform all our lives.

'Will? Sweetheart, thanks so much for giving me the time off, it's completely focused my mind and we're going to blow them away with our—' I stop.

'Here she is! Last minute, as usual.'

I hear Will's voice, but I'm looking at his customer . . .

Abby walks towards me, twice as beautiful as in the photographs, and so serene in our chaotic store. She leans across to kiss me on both cheeks, though for a split second I imagine her as a vampire going in for the kill.

'So pleased I caught you, Emily. I don't know why, but this morning you popped into my head, so I thought I'd pop over and see how your application's coming along.' She pats her bump. 'Well, when I say pop, I struggle to pop anywhere these days, of course. Though I might be about to *go* pop.'

And Will laughs obligingly. He never laughs at *my* jokes any more.

Though maybe I've stopped cracking them.

'Anyway, it's been great catching up with Will, and I love what you two are doing here. Now, stop me if it feels like fraternising with the enemy, I'll understand – but I'd love it if you could join me and my husband for dinner one night? Fill us in on the best schools, the places to avoid, that sort of thing.'

I picture us in that huge dining room, like lucky peasants invited to the manor house at Christmas, but while I'm trying to formulate a polite way of saying I'd rather share dinner with a pride of ravenous lions, Will is nodding happily. 'That's a very kind invitation. We'd love to show you the ropes. The least we can do.'

He's probably just trying to make up for leaving her all those years ago, but I struggle to keep smiling as she kisses him goodbye and passes me her business card and mimes calling me with that delicate, manicured hand twisted into the shape of a phone.

CHAPTER 10

Sandie

I'm not in the mood for a dream wedding.

My ankles are puffy and my head is scrambled and the thought that I have another twelve weeks of this to go is beginning to get me down. And then there's the little matter of my big pitch to Garnett's.

But I never let down a client, and as Toby accepted this job on my behalf, I will keep my appointment with the Your Perfect Day Bridal Boutique in Kensington, to see if I can work out why women aren't flocking through their doors.

I've arranged to meet the owner, Lisabet, for a drink in a pub round the corner, so that the staff won't know what I'm up to.

'Over here!'

I look round to where Lisabet is waiting at the varnished wood bar. She's younger and pointier than the plump, pink fairy godmother figure I'd expected.

She shakes my hand. In her business suit she almost looks like a girl dressing up in her mother's clothes. I wonder what she thinks of *me*, with my incredible increasing bosom and my newly acquired maternity trousers.

'Sandie. It's good to meet you. Coffee?'

I'm tempted – these days I rarely feel fully awake – but as

I've just had a first encounter with the reflux Em warned me about, I decline. 'Mint tea would be good.'

We sit at a corner table. 'So, I understand you're concerned about a mismatch between your predicted customer base and your first year's turnover?'

Lisabet looks shifty. I guess it's always hard to admit failure to a stranger. 'I think we're getting everything right. So, yes, it's a shock that our figures could be better.'

'You have picked possibly the worst time in the last three decades to start a new business, if that's any consolation.'

She looks as though she's about to burst into tears. 'I need to make it work. I hear you're the best at what you do.'

Am I still? My failure to find an immediate solution for Garnett's is weighing me down. 'Thank you. I'll certainly do my best for you. I like to carry out a mystery shopping visit myself, first, and then research the market and the competition.'

'That's what's so weird. No one else is doing what we're doing.'

'If your business isn't meeting expectations, it could be that you're offering something no one actually wants.'

'Oh.' She looks hurt, and I feel like I've kicked sand in those Bambi eyes. 'I've put everything into this. It's the most important thing to me.'

'I understand.' I was like you, I want to say. I *know* how much it means, and I'll do what I can to keep you in business.

'Will it be . . .' she nods at my belly, 'I mean, will you get it done before the baby comes?'

'If I have to finish my report in the labour ward, I will, I promise, Lisabet. So let's see what you're offering . . .'

Your Perfect Day is in a small mews off Kensington Church Street, on the way up to Notting Hill. It could be the set of a Richard Curtis movie: the street is cobbled and the store takes up two adjacent houses.

I don't know where Lisabet got her money from – rich daddy or sugar daddy? – but it's been well spent. The stable door panels have been replaced with frosted glass, so you can catch a glimpse of white dresses beyond, and the signage above the windows is feminine but unfussy, dark leaf-green lettering on a creamy background. No tacky gold, no nasty flowers. I like it a lot.

To the side of the windows is a door painted the same green, and an old-fashioned bell pull in pewter, above a small engraved plaque reading *By Appointment Only*. I raise my hand, and the pretend engagement ring I've slipped on sparkles in the light. It looks all wrong. But the bell makes a satisfyingly musical sound, and already I feel like a member of a very exclusive club.

'Hello! You must be Sandie. I'm Beatrice, come in, come in.'

Beatrice is in her late thirties and could be Nigella Lawson's younger sister, with wonderful raven hair and a voluptuous figure in a beautifully cut velvety wrap dress. The room is elegant without being too country-house – the floor is sanded and polished, there are two small sofas by the fireplace, and a dining table overlooking the mews. The furniture is more Conran than chi-chi.

'Where would you be most comfortable?' she asks, and it occurs to me that the word *comfortable* has taken on a whole new importance since I've been pregnant.

'The table, perhaps?'

'Great. Now, what can I organise in the way of refreshments? We've got hot drinks, cold drinks, alcoholic drinks, and then, of course, there's sandwiches or cake. The scones are to die for, I must admit, and it's getting on for lunchtime, after all.'

'Some water would be nice. And . . .' I realise my mouth is watering. 'A scone does sound delicious, actually.'

She nods, as though my decision is a good omen, and disappears.

'On its way,' she says when she returns. 'Right, I usually start by explaining a little about what we offer here at Your Perfect Day. We like to think of ourselves as a combination of bridal shop and wedding planner, but taking the very best of both worlds. The women who choose us don't see planning a wedding as being so very different from anything else in their lives. It's incredibly important, of course, but there's something about the wedding "industry" that seems old-fashioned, even patronising. Perhaps you've found that yourself?'

I nod, though of course I have no experience of the wedding industry at all, beyond doing a single wedding-list secret shopping assignment with Emily, and hearing the gossip from Babs on the first floor at Garnett's.

'Some of the stories we've heard from our clients would make your hair curl. Literally in some cases. A hairdresser who gave a forty-seven-year-old bride a head full of golden ringlets even though she'd asked for a sophisticated bob. A dressmaker who produced a lace monstrosity, even though the bride was *allergic* to frills. Many wedding planners simply don't listen. Especially the male ones.'

'Right.'

'We don't have any preconceived ideas about your perfect day, though we are also aware that not every woman has been planning her wedding since she was in nappies.'

'It all sounds great.' And it does. If I *wanted* to get married, this is exactly the kind of place I'd pick. So far I'm struggling to see what's not to like about this place.

A girl appears with the water and scones, along with jam and clotted cream in small dishes. My stomach growls in anticipation.

'Dig in now. The next step is for me to take a little more information about you. Have you fixed a date for the wedding?' She is careful not to glance at my bump.

'Not this year,' I say. 'I'd like to be back in shape. So we're thinking of . . . spring.'

'When did he propose?' she asks.

'I've sort of lost count.' Which is true.

Beatrice giggles. 'Playing hard to get, then, eh? So when did you say yes?'

I try to remember the last time. Oh, yes. 'After we had a 4D scan. He said it was time he made an honest woman of me.'

'Ah. That's sweet. And have either of you been married before?'

'No.'

'Are you planning a religious ceremony?'

I stare at her. Why hadn't I prepared for this question? The fact that my gramma would have my guts for garters if I married anywhere other than in a Methodist church is yet another reason not to bother. 'We're open-minded.'

Beatrice writes this down. 'Any thoughts about venues other than churches?'

I shrug. 'Open-minded about that too.'

'Golly. Let's see if we can narrow it down a tiny bit. Are you leaning towards a big, traditional affair, or something more intimate or contemporary?'

'Hmmm . . .' I must be coming across as a total time-waster, so I decide the only thing to do is to be as honest as I can, with the obvious exception of telling her I'm not getting married at all. 'We probably want rather different things. I'd prefer low-key, but my . . . fiancé is quite a party animal.'

She smiles reassuringly. 'Now, forgive me for blowing our own trumpets, but we really are very good at finding perfect solutions in these kinds of situations. I think what might be an idea now is for me to give you our brochure, which also includes a section for the two of you to fill in individually, to see what's important.'

'Right.' I was waiting for a harder sell than scones and the glossy booklet she passes to me. I can't decide whether this soft approach is positive, or in danger of letting potential clients slip through their fingers . . .

'Oh, I can't believe I almost forgot the most important bit of all,' says Beatrice, standing up. 'Would you like a little look at our latest dresses?'

So *this* is when the hard sell kicks in.

We walk down the corridor and she opens the door marked *Gowns*. It's dimly lit, thanks to the frosted windows, so that the first thing that hits me is the smell, of gardenias and tea roses, with a hint of citrusy bergamot. Of course, I know it can't be the real thing, but I still can't help but picture a huge bouquet.

'One second,' says Beatrice, as though she can't find the light switch, which I think is unlikely given how polished her performance is otherwise. In fact, I'm now convinced that even the *Whoops, it slipped my mind to show you the dresses* line is part of her routine.

Soft ambient lights fade up, adding to the drama. If I were an excitable bride, then this would be getting my pulse racing. A cluster of spots highlights the central display, a polished wood mannequin dressed in the slinkiest long shift I have ever seen. The fabric drapes around her carved contours, flowing like water, even though she isn't moving. It's the purest of soft whites – like icing on a wedding cake – but it's also overtly sexy, for the woman who wants to make the male guests fantasise about her, and the female ones wish they were her.

I'm about to shake my head, when the light goes out, and another comes on, this time illuminating a shorter figure, in an embroidered, youthful dress that makes me smile. The tone of the lighting has changed, so it's like dappled sunlight, and I can imagine the wedding that bride will have chosen: a small country ceremony in a chapel with a lych gate. A bouquet of daisies and rosebuds, to match the lace that covers the tight bodice. Little bridesmaids in rustic dresses.

Not right for me, either.

What do I mean, not right for me? I'm not even getting married.

But my eyes continue to follow the changing tableaux, from a bouffant creation for the woman who always dreamed of being a princess, to an empire-line dress that makes me think of Jane Austen film adaptations, and finally the plainest of plain dresses, with a gently draping neckline, off the shoulder, nipped-in waist and full skirt. It's almost Grecian and I feel myself stepping forward to touch it, without knowing why.

'I thought of that one as soon as I saw you,' says Beatrice.

I leap back. Well, as far as a woman *can* leap when she's almost thirty weeks pregnant. 'It's early days to be thinking of that.'

'Maybe,' she says, 'although I always say that when you see the one for you, why waste time looking elsewhere?'

I smile. 'Waist's the issue, I think. I don't know if I'll ever have a waist again, do I? Not to mention the fact that my grandmother will never allow me to marry in white, under the circumstances.'

'One of *those*, eh? We have the solution for that, too,' she says, and she presses a button on the wall.

The fabric changes colour. Well, of course, it must be the lights that change colour, but it's surprisingly effective at taking 'my' dress through a rainbow of shades.

'Any of these appeal? We initially thought these would be best for picking bridesmaids' dresses, but we've had lots of brides playing around with the colours. You can change the intensity.'

And the dress goes from a rather sickly pink, through to cherry, and then scarlet, which would get Gramma even more aerated than white.

'Amazing,' I say, because it is such a clever, but simple, idea that I can't understand why no one else has done it.

I watch her turn the dress a hundred different shades. She ends with a light leafy green, and although I can't imagine a bride wearing green – wouldn't it be unlucky? – it strikes me that the shade would definitely suit my skin tone, and would show the guests that I wasn't trying too hard, that I was taking marriage with a teeny pinch of salt . . .

Hold on. This playing along has definitely got out of hand. I turn back towards the door. 'I'm afraid I'm out of time, but thanks so much for seeing me.'

'It was a pleasure, Miss Barrow. Once we've had your forms, I'll send my suggestions in writing within a week. I am sure we can help you find what you and your fiancé are looking for. Now, can I call you a taxi?'

I shake my head. 'Thanks, but I could do with at least attempting to walk off those delicious scones. I've already been warned by my grandmother that on no account should I be eating for two.'

Beatrice lets me out, and I walk along the mews. Before I step back onto the street, I look back at Your Perfect Day. It's making no sense to me. The right location, the right concept, the right staff . . . And the ability to make a seasoned sceptic like me begin to fantasise about frocks is the most impressive part of all.

It makes me want to extend this feeling to Garnett's, using the same combination of service, product range and a little bit of theatre.

So why isn't it working for them?

Usually I can identify the weak spots within seconds of stepping into a store. But here . . . it must be porridge brain, like Emily said, because I don't have a clue what to say to Lisabet. And if I can't help a tiny business like this, what hope do I have at poor old Garnett's?

CHAPTER 11

Grazia

How long is it now? Five days? A week? A fortnight?

My withdrawal symptoms are intense. My hands itch for him, and though embroidery keeps them occupied, floss and needle are no substitute for the warmth of his skin, the heat of his breath, the fire of his . . .

'Grazia? What do you think?'

I wrench myself back from the fire of Joel's . . . from my memories, and it is something of a shock to find myself back in Sandie's sombre little office on the top floor of Garnett's. 'I am sorry. Would you care to repeat yourself?'

Sandie sighs. She has recently developed an even more impatient streak than before. 'Grazia. You're worse than Emily. What's happened to you?'

Perhaps she expects me to answer *love*, or something similarly dramatic, but instead I shrug it off. 'I will pay attention now.'

The air conditioning vent emits a loud, farty puff followed by a long whine. 'Sorry about that,' she says, when it shudders to a halt again.

'Really, Sandie, you must stand up for yourself more. This is no place for a woman in your condition.'

'Ah, but it was personally selected as my headquarters by

Laetitia Garnett. I mean, as she said, it is a room with a view . . .'

'Of the delivery yard!'

'All modern conveniences.'

I look at the pre-war desk, and the drunken, bulbless anglepoise lamp, and the dark bookcase so crammed with dusty files that Sandie has to use her desk space as a shelf. There are four giant piles of paperwork, but the light is so faint that I cannot read the labels.

'And at least she gave me a chair.'

One chair. When I arrived, Sandie had to fetch another one from the boardroom so we could both sit down.

'Lucky you.'

'The truth is, Grazia, I had no choice. There's nowhere to work in our tiny rented house, and *definitely* nowhere for me to keep all my files. Plus, I get to hear the Garnett's gossip here, which wouldn't happen at home.'

'Even so, she could have found somewhere more comfortable for the mother of her grandchild.'

Sandie shrugs. 'There are only so many battles I can fight at once. And right now my priority is saving the store. So, tell me honestly what is wrong with Garnett's?'

'I—'

'Don't spare my feelings.'

I take a deep breath. 'All right. Well, this slogan. *The Greatest Store on Earth* is like a bad joke now. If this really is the greatest store, then heaven help the others. Sorry, but you wanted the truth.'

She pulls a face. 'No. That's good, that's good. Keep going.'

'It reminds me of somewhere ancient. Like the British Museum. And while that is also one of the best in the world, I have never wanted to fill my home with rocks or relics.'

'I'll write that down.'

I smile as she rests her little notebook on her increasingly large belly. Trust Sandie to find a practical use for the bump.

'But do not set too much store by what I say. Since Barcelona, I feel jaded by the grey days and formality of London.'

'Ah. Barcelona. Much more interesting than Garnett's. I do want to hear all about it, as soon as I've finished this. I'm a bit . . . well, *desperate*.'

'I have every confidence in you, my dear,' I insist, though in fact I am wondering whether she is out of her depth. 'But do remember that all things have a natural life cycle. And, well, perhaps even the most brilliant mind is no match for the biggest economic catastrophe in a century?'

I mean to soothe her, but to my horror her eyes close, and I fear she is about to cry. I have *never* seen Sandie cry. Should I pat her hand, ignore her pain, what?

She gulps. 'I might have bitten off more than I can chew, mightn't I?'

'No, no, that is not what I meant at all,' I say, reaching for one of her scribbled notes. '*Dreams for Everywoman?* That is absolutely what you should be offering!'

'No good if Everywoman is dreaming of George Clooney and all we can come up with is the same expensive coffee capsules as every other department store, is it?'

I put the note back, pick up another. '*Shopping as a mini break or spa experience?* Excellent. Yes. Free facials by candle-light.'

Sandie shakes her head. 'They already offer facials, like every other store in Oxford Street. But there's no way they can afford to employ any more staff, not with the state of the books at the moment. And lighting candles might save on the electricity bills, but we won't make any friends in the London Fire Brigade.'

I look at the rest of her notes. *Be selfish! Fresh start, fresh ideas!*

'I'd had lots of ideas,' she says, opening another file, 'but they're all *boom* ideas. Expensive ones. Even the idea of telling customers to be selfish right now feels wrong.'

Sandie is too smart to be fooled by false reassurance. My mind is blank.

She sighs, then slams the file shut. 'I'm bored with Garnett's, Grazia. Tell me something nice. Tell me about Spain and your mystery man.'

'The man is no mystery. His name is Joel, and already I cannot imagine a time when I did *not* know him. He is so inspiring and so bright and so sensual . . .' I hesitate a moment, because there is nothing so annoying as a woman in love. 'Oh, and then Barcelona. Wonderful. The two, for me, now are inseparable. The climate is good, of course, but what appeals is how the city blends the past, with . . . the now. You never know what is around the next corner, but you know it will be something amazing. *Surprising*.'

'Everyone I know who's been there has been surprised by a pickpocket at some point or other,' Sandie says.

I smile. 'No place is perfect. But I am a middle-aged woman, seen it all, done it all. And now I am reborn. The colours' – I decide not to mention that I have been stitching like a maniac since I returned, recreating the vibrancy of Gaudi's greens and turquoises and yellows on canvas – 'the girls, the boys, the bars. The cava. As you know, for me it has always been champagne, or a little prosecco. But the right cava is like cocaine.'

Sandie gives me a disapproving look, then touches her bump protectively. 'If you say so.'

I shrug. 'Falling in love with anything – a city, a person – is impossible to explain.'

'So have you fallen out of love with London now?'

'No . . . But I left behind a Europe of peasant ways and corruption and I have rediscovered a new continent. London is still wonderful but now the buildings seem . . . oppressive.' I wave at the horrible office which seems like a prison cell. 'I am a born-again European. The very worst sort. I apologise.'

Now Sandie smiles. 'No. I'm the misery guts, but I'm thrilled you're in love. It reminds me how I felt when I arrived here at the store. Oh, and when I met Toby, too, of course.'

Another silence. 'Perhaps I should leave you to the serious business of saving your first love. If anyone can do it, Sandie, you can. But do not lose sight of other important things.'

She sighs again, and touches her stomach. 'The important things? I feel even less equipped for them than I do for running a store.'

'You can succeed at either, Sandie. But perhaps not both at the same time.'

'Call yourself a feminist, Grazia?'

'No! Never. But a realist, yes. Of the three secret shoppers, Emily is the dreamer but you and I, *we* are the ones who know what it takes to make dreams happen.'

I take the lift – which smells damp – down four floors to haberdashery, and when I get there I feel as furtive as a shoplifter. But I am down to a single strand of black floss, and have almost run out of surfaces to embroider upon. Needs must.

I have to pass through the nursery section first, which is like travelling through a white-out. Poor Sandie must now navigate her way around this world of pastels and semi-surgical implements, and I can honestly say that I do not feel envious. With children, I could hardly have headed to Barcelona at a few hours' notice, or stayed there as long as I liked.

The transition from nursery to haberdashery is obvious. Suddenly, colour is everywhere. The malaise affecting the rest of the store has not spread here yet. A rose arbour marks the gateway to the section, but instead of flowers, the metal structure is covered in different shades and textures of yarn – an extravagantly fluffy aquamarine, a shimmering emerald green, a twining navy.

The department is packed, not with octogenarians, but with women younger than myself. All right, so the average

age at the Craftathon that Emily organised was low, too, but I imagined that was a fluke. Instead, I feel like the oldest embroiderer in London.

I walk up the narrow aisles, ignoring the yarn – knitting would definitely make me feel like a grey-haired *tricoteuse* at the guillotine – and the shelves of fancy contemporary books – because if you need to look to someone else for inspiration, why bother? Finally I reach the sewing section.

I let out a little sigh. Not just every single colour ever invented, but multicoloured flosses, not to mention a selection of textures – matt, silky, neon, glow-in-the-dark, metallic. Then there are the accessories: bamboo hoops, wooden hoops, a hundred kinds of pin-cushion, charming sewing boxes . . .

I may be some time.

I leave the store half an hour later, having spent over two hundred pounds. A lot perhaps, although nothing compared to what I could have spent in the same time on couture. I hail a taxi and as I settle into the back seat to admire my purchases – including a skein in the most perfect Gaudi turquoise – my phone rings. I see who it is. Ah! I allow myself a moment of delicious anticipation before I pick up.

'Hello, Joel. *Que tal?*'

'All the better for hearing your voice, Grazia. I'm back and I am dying to see you. I know it's cheeky, but if I sent a car for you this evening, would you come to mine?'

'I have a car of my own, thanks.'

'Ah, only I wanted to lead you on a bit of a . . . mystery tour.'

I consider turning him down, due to presumptuousness. But only for the briefest moment. I want to see him, he wants to see me. Simple.

'Eight thirty, then. But if you kidnap me, I shall be very cross.'

And he laughs and hangs up, and suddenly I crave his

company so much that I would jump in a cab and go right there now. If he had given me the address . . .

I am a little disappointed when the driver arrives. No limo. Not even a black cab.

The guy who greets me in the lobby of my apartment wears a rugby shirt, tracksuit bottoms, and trainers.

'I'm Maurice,' he says, reaching for my weekend bag, which I know is heavier than it looks. I was unsure what to pack so I have brought a little of everything: my finest lingerie, my highest shoes, my chicest dress, plus my make-up bag. Oh, and tucked into the side of the holdall, my latest embroidery project, a spidery abstract design inspired by the spiky Sagrada Familia cathedral. Not that I expect to spend much time sewing . . .

'Your carriage awaits,' says Maurice, pointing to the bland white car parked out front. I hope he doesn't want to make conversation.

'What *is* that, Maurice?' I say, pointing to the bright orange steering wheel.

'Oh. The wife is into crochet. She thought that it'd keep my hands warm on cold mornings.' He catches my eye in the mirror. 'Then, once she got going, well . . . she was unstoppable.'

I look past the wheel, and the contagion has spread: there is a shocking-pink cosy on the gearstick knob, and a vast collection of little crocheted dolls and animals lined up on the dashboard. I think of my own secret needlework habit, and I realise suddenly that Heartsease Handmade was a genius idea. Perhaps Emily is less of a dreamer than we all think.

As Maurice eases away, he says, 'There's something on the back seat there with you to keep you entertained.' I spot a willow basket and under the checked fabric covering there are treats, buried in straw. A half-bottle of champagne – no, of cava. There's a brown parcel label attached that says, *Drink Me*, and when I turn it over, I see:

I hope you don't need to be tipsy to spend time with me, but this is just in case . . .

I smile, and then delve deeper. There's a clear package of jewel-coloured macaroons from the little *pasteleria* we passed on the way back from the park. The label reads *Eat Me* on one side, and on the other: *if that doesn't sound too indecent . . .*

And I blush to my touched-up roots.

There is nougat, too – *because I am nuts about you, Grazia* – and a jar of manzanilla olives – *deep, savoury, memorable – who do these remind me of?* Then there is a tiny glass bottle of tawny coloured perfume – *Smell Me!* – that fills the car with the scent of lemons and basil and blossom as soon as I unscrew the cap. On the other side of the label he has written simply, *Remember?*

And I do, oh, I do. It smells of our last night together: a table set for two, a small improvised bouquet in the centre, of blossom and basil and lemon slices.

'What do you fancy in the way of tunes, Mrs Leon? Songs from the shows, rock 'n' roll, country?'

'Up to you, Maurice. After all, we will not be on the road long.'

He looks away, but not before I spot the flicker of doubt in his eyes. He puts on the easiest of easy listening, and I wince, but then I decide to open the cava and the olives and enjoy the ride.

Which goes on and on and on. After the cava and the olives, the red tail lights whizzing on the motorway make me nauseous. I'm about to take out my needlework, to tame my impatience, when I decide to take a final look in the basket for something else – mints, or water, perhaps. Instead I find a small red envelope at the bottom.

Dear G,

Hope you like the picnic. If you think I'm trying to soften you up, you might be right. In some ways, it's like we've always been together but, in others, we hardly know each other. Stay open-minded, eh? J x

Maurice turns off the motorway. What could Joel mean, *stay open-minded?* Is he luring me to his harem in the sticks, with no way home? Or does he live in a monastery, or a mental institution?

You are entering Mumford. Please Drive Carefully.

Mumford is a classic English market town: before Barcelona, I might have found it charming. Now it seems painfully restrained. This is not where I would have expected Joel to live, but he will have made the place his own. He will have interesting, creative neighbours. This is only a base for his travels.

Maurice slows down, then turns right towards a pair of high, reinforced metal gates. He winds down the window, types in a code, and is buzzed through. Beyond the gates, there is a wall of conifers, and a discreet carved sign reading *The Copse.* A mansion? The car turns to the left of the trees and I see not one, but *four* red brick houses, arranged around a spot-lit ornamental pond, at three, six, nine and twelve o'clock. They are large and angular and ugly. The fourth house, at twelve o'clock, is raised a little higher than the others, and a dirty people carrier sits in the driveway. Maurice's car circles around the pond, and stops outside.

'This cannot be the right place,' I say, but a security light has come on in the front porch, and I see the mock-Georgian door opening, and a silhouette that still makes me catch my breath, despite the strangeness of the setting.

Joel rushes towards me. 'You made it,' he says, and kisses me. When we break apart, Maurice carries my bag into the house, and then waves goodbye.

And then Joel and I are alone in this bland hallway, with its cream walls and fake plaster coving, and a clichéd blue-and-white photograph of a beach above a coat rack.

'So you *were* trying to soften me up, then?' I ask, watching his face. 'To prepare me for this?'

A nerve by his right eye is twitching. 'Hmm. Among other things.'

'It seems to me, Mr Ferguson, that you have some explaining to do.'

CHAPTER 12

Emily

I've had an entire week to come up with an excuse *not* to go to dinner at Abby and Chris's house.

But somehow I've run out of time to think anything up, and so here we bloody well are, parking our grotty van outside The White House. When we visit friends we usually take organic wine from the shop, even though it smells like compost, but we panicked at the last minute and Will made a mercy dash to the supermarket nine miles away to buy something fancier.

I have a hunch he's not looking forward to it any more than I am: the bright red circle marking our Saturday dinner date on the family calendar has looked about as tempting as a trip to the dentist. We've been snapping at each other over silly things – who forgot the van tax was due, whose turn it is to drop Freddie at playgroup, why people aren't buying our new and very expensive sheep's yogurt. And because we're tense, Freddie is too, arguing about whether to wear socks, whether to eat greens, why he should flush the loo after using it.

It was *almost* a relief when Duncan turned up this morning to collect him for what he's taken to calling Man Time.

'We're going to get *dirty* this weekend, son,' he said, and Freddie eyed him for ages, weighing up whether to disagree.

Then he caught sight of my face, and evidently decided that anything I disapprove of has to be fun.

'Yay!' he said.

'Please be careful.'

Duncan pulled a 'Mum's so boring' face at our son, and Freddie giggled.

'Emily, you have to be careful not to bring a boy up as though he's a girl.'

'What?'

'It's a big danger when single mums bring up boys. Women tend to mollycoddle them, when what they need is a bit of rough and tumble.'

'I'll give you rough and tumble, Duncan,' I whispered. Sadly it came out less menacing than I'd hoped, and he sniggered. 'I'm not a single mum, anyway. Freddie is lucky because he has two men in his life. Remember?'

Duncan smiled a nasty smile, and I noticed he'd had his teeth whitened again. He still hasn't found a job, and I think he's doing it on purpose, so he has less maintenance to pay. 'Oh, yes. The politically correct line we "agreed". Well, you can't lay the guilt thing on me from now on. I am a man and I don't care who knows it.'

And with that he marched Freddie down the stairs. I watched them from the window and it was only then that I noticed his horrible sheepskin coat – very *Starsky and Hutch* – and the fact that his sports car was covered in mud. God help us if he's been on some kind of male bonding course.

'You look lovely,' says Will, as we step out of the van.

'Hmm.' I look down at the rather baggy pink dress that I unearthed earlier. Somehow, in the midst of all this stress, I've lost weight. For the first time in my life I have *angles*. I wish I could say it suits me, but I feel as washed out as the frock.

'No, seriously. That colour really suits you. Brings out your eyes.'

'Is that a nice way of saying I've got conjunctivitis?'

'No, I . . .' And then he sighs. 'You know, we don't have to do this, Em. We could go home, watch a DVD. I've got the latest documentary by Al Gore.'

'It's too late to back out now.'

He shrugs, admitting defeat. 'We don't have to stay long.'

'And then maybe we can get an early night . . . and a very lazy Sunday morning . . .'

Will takes my hand. 'Sounds good. So we're going with Plan Migraine, then, are we?'

'I suppose you want me to develop the headache?'

'Well, trouble is, Abby already knows I don't have migraines.'

As we walk up the drive, I wonder what else she knows that I don't.

We are greeted by Abby like old friends – well, I guess that one of us fits that description. She's dressed in a shot silk purple kaftan thing, with leggings and Moroccan slippers, and I am ashamed to admit that her outsized bump and a slight puffiness around her elegant ankles makes me feel better about myself.

'Wow, you've grown!' I say, and she pulls a face.

'Horrid, aren't I? Like a water buffalo who has swallowed half the Nile.'

'Rubbish,' says Will, and as he leans over to kiss her, he adds, 'and anyway, it's not all bad,' before winking.

'Will, you naughty boy!' she shrieks. 'That was the one thing you always complained about – my lack of upholstering! No problems there now, eh?' She laughs, tugging her kaftan down a few centimetres, all the better to show off her boobs.

'Come through and meet the other half,' she says, and I only get the very briefest glimpse of their hallway – or should that be *entrance hall*? A six-metre mirror hangs from the wall, reflecting the kaleidoscope of colours from the leaded lights in the front door. The floor is honey-coloured parquet, and an antlered coat hook stands tall, holding only an 'ironic' black bowler hat.

'Chris. Meet Emily and Will.'

It's one of those moments when I don't know where to look first – at the kitchen or at the chef. My curiosity about Chris wins, even though I've already seen him in the magazine. If anything, the picture in the *Upper Findlebury Quarterly* didn't do him justice. There he looked a bit, well, computer-generated, with the smooth skin and the perfect crop of dark hair. But now he looks more likeable, with his striped butcher's apron and his broad smile. He's cutting large slices of country bread with a Japanese knife the size of a pickaxe. As he puts it down, I notice his hands are long and slender, almost feminine.

'All right, guys,' he says, sounding surprisingly barrow-boy. 'If I stop now, I'll never get the slices straight.' And he finishes off, one, two, three perfectly even pieces, before putting the knife down and turning to us.

'Emily? Delighted!' He kisses me on both cheeks then shakes Will's hand. 'You two are our first dinner guests here at The White House.'

'Really?' I can't help feeling surprised – I'd have assumed that Abby and Chris would be well into the social circuit by now.

'The house isn't quite ready to be unveiled,' says Abby, 'plus every time I think I have the guest list organised for our first dinner party, I realise I've left off the chairman of the school governors, or the bank manager, and it's back to square one.'

'So we're the dry run, are we?' says Will, and it's exactly what I was thinking: they want to see if they poison *us*, before letting loose on the village.

'No. You're our special guests,' insists Abby.

The kitchen is vast, at least as big as the entire shop floor, storeroom and backyard at the Emporium, but it's a bit eighties. The units are solid wood and the dusky pink marble worktops are a good ten centimetres thick.

'We were desperate to rip the kitchen out,' Abby says, noticing me looking, 'but time's pressing on.'

'Yes. I've got a good friend who's getting her new house completely rebuilt, even though she's got a baby due, and she's panicking it won't be ready in time.'

That's the same good friend who didn't call me back, even though I left her four agonised phone calls about this dinner over the last week . . .

'I know how she feels,' says Chris. 'I'm really panicking about my roast not being done in time, too.' And we laugh. 'Why don't you folks head into the dining room so that Abby can ply you with drink and you won't notice the food.'

She leads the way, and Will, who hasn't seen the photographs, is suitably wowed by the table and the three fireplaces.

'You've done well for yourselves here, Abby.'

She gives him a significant look. Is she trying to say *look at what you could have won*, like a cheesy game show host? Or, even worse, is she saying *you could still have this . . . me?* But all she says is, 'We were very lucky indeed. Now. Champagne?'

Maybe it is the champagne – or the expensive-looking reds that follow. Or maybe it's the incredible blue-cheese soufflés with port sauce that Chris served as starters, or the palate-cleansing lime and ginger sorbet, or the roast baby guinea fowl in sticky sauce, or the tiny bundles of buttered baby vegetables tied together with a chive leaf. But I am relaxing, despite myself.

I think Will is too. He didn't even start his standard 'have you ever thought about your food miles?' lecture when he came face to face with the mangetout.

'. . . we never went further than the Costas when I was a kid, but we love Bali. Went there for our honeymoon, even thought we might invest in a grass hut,' says Chris, though I don't see him as the grass hut type. 'But then things changed, eh?' He touches Abby's belly and my stomach lurches a little with envy.

We've learned a lot about our new friends. Chris is a medal-winning triathlete, and he also donates a portion of his bonus every year to a community project in the rough estate where he grew up. Abby and Chris met 'at a wedding', although the details were sketchy and I suspect online dating, as I can't see posh Abby and cockney Chris mixing in the same circles.

Classical music plays (and not the kind that's sold in a compilation CD of themes from TV adverts). We're sitting at the far end of their *seats sixteen* dining table, and they've put an enormous bouquet of exotic flowers and fruits at the other end, so it doesn't seem empty. Candlelight makes the food look even better, and all of us look golden. It's not quite real . . .

And that's when it occurs to me. It may not be real, but this is exactly what I used to imagine doing before I moved to London with Duncan: glamorous dinner parties with glamorous people. The reality turned out to be dinners for one as a single mum, of course, but maybe now this *is* it.

The wine has mellowed me and, actually, I don't think Abby's after Will at all. Why would she be? She has it all with Chris, who is rich, successful, funny, charming. There's no way Abby would swap life in The White House for the cramped style of our existence above the shop.

'. . . and are you almost there with your application, then, Emily?'

'Hmm?' I look up at her, trying to catch up.

'For the European grant.'

'Oh. That. Oh, yes, it's coming along. They like their paperwork, don't they?'

She smiles. 'That's a good thing, as far as I'm concerned. It'll weed out the no-hopers we met at the briefing day. Not one of them struck me as competition. Whereas your idea for expanding the craft centre into a whole sustainable village is just the kind of *knit your own yogurt* stuff they're looking for!'

Everyone laughs except Will, who scowls at the piss-take. But then I remember something. 'You weren't in my group at the training day, so how do you know about our plans?'

Abby frowns. 'Oh. Er. Well, Will told me, didn't he? When I came into the shop. That was when he wasn't trying to convince me to adopt a battery hen and install solar panels.'

Will shrugs. 'Your carbon footprint could certainly do with reducing, judging from the size of your house. But never mind me. I can't wait to hear how you're going to *regenerate* the slums of Upper Findlebury.' His voice is loaded with sarcasm, and his face looks different to me. Unfamiliar.

Abby takes a sip of elderflower cordial. 'We might not look impoverished, Will, but there's plenty of untapped potential in the village. Woman power, I'd call it. Or the Mummy Mafia. I'm majoring on the women's angle. A kind of training academy, and a network. I'm playing around with the names. The Findlebury Female Force. Or something like that.'

I smile politely, though it sounds even less thought through than my idea.

'That's rubbish compared to Emily's idea, Abby,' Chris says. 'I'm not surprised she thinks you're her main obstacle to world domination.' He smiles at me.

'Rubbish, Christopher.' Her face flashes with irritation but then she smiles. 'Well, yes, you were the most impressive person I met. Which is why I knew we could be friends.'

Friends? 'Either that or you're going to poison me,' I say, still feeling chuffed at Chris's compliment.

And she laughs more heartily. 'You're on dangerous ground there. My husband is good-humoured about most things, but he's ultra-sensitive when it comes to his food.'

Chris nods. 'Slag off my house. My wife. Tell me my future kids are ugly. But don't diss my puddings. Speaking of which . . .' He begins the clear the table. We get up to help, but he won't hear of it. 'You're here to relax.'

'Your husband is lovely,' I say, knowing I sound a little drunk.

'Well, so is yours,' she says, but with a big smile, and I suddenly do wonder if Abby and I could actually be friends, despite all that's gone before. 'Sorry. Your boyfriend. You always were the unconventional sort, eh, Will?'

'And you always landed on your feet,' he replies good-naturedly. 'I'm so pleased for you. You've got what you always wanted.'

A warning look passes between them.

And then Chris reappears, holding one jug of cream and another of custard. 'I do hope you've all still got room for afters. I will get very angry if you haven't and you won't like me when I'm angry.'

Later. Much later.

'Well, that was better than I expected,' I say. We're in bed, after the kind of lazy, tipsy, slightly noisy sex that only happens when Freddie's away. We daren't change position if he's here, because the mattress springs creak so loudly that he's raced in more than once, whooping and wanting to join in our game of 'Trampolines'. We've been planning to buy a new bed for years but, as usual, investing in the shop is more of a priority than upgrading our surroundings from squalid to acceptably shabby.

'Are you complaining about my usual technique?' he says.

'No! The dinner party, silly. I can't believe we were there till ten to one.'

'Only because you decided not to pull a migraine in the end. Though I was thinking of doing it myself when she started taking the piss out of my carbon footprint.'

'Ah, you need to lighten up. They're really nice people. OK, things were a bit awkward at first, but they were bound

129

to be. And then after a while, I really relaxed and I thought, you know, we might end up friends. *Proper* friends. And Chris is fabulous, isn't he? I never thought a city boy would be so genuine.'

I hear Will's breathing change, just a little. 'Mmm.'

'You're not jealous, are you?' I'm still trying to sound amused, but I feel chilly. What if he doesn't think Chris is good enough for Abby? What would that mean?

'Don't be daft. No. He's . . . charming. But didn't you think he was a bit, well, too perfect? The sports and the charity work and the money . . .'

I try to laugh. 'And the gourmet cooking.'

'Ah, well, I got to the bottom of that one, anyway.' He sits up, carefully, so he doesn't hit his head on the low eaves. Another thing that tends to curb the spontaneity of our love-making.

'Meaning?'

'When I went to the toilet, I took a wrong turning . . .' In the glow of the street lamp alongside our attic window, I see the shiftiness in his face.

'Will? You mean you had a nose around?'

'Easy to get lost in a house that size, isn't it? I managed to find myself in the utility room next to the loo. And guess what I found?'

'A Filipino maid chained to the washing machine?'

'Almost. I found the leaning tower of cardboard boxes, all marked "Findlebury Foodies, catering for all occasions". Complete with reheating instructions for the entire menu: the soufflés; the guinea fowl; the Sussex Pond Pudding. Even the veggies and the custard were made in advance. The most cooking he had to do was cut the bloody bread. Which, you know, he was doing when we turned up. Coincidentally.'

'Oh.' *Oh*. I pull the duvet up over my shoulders, feeling colder still. I suppose that apron of his did look suspiciously pristine. 'How weird. I suppose they're busy, though, aren't they?'

'Ye-es. But I reckon if you or I had the time and the money to get our dinners made for us, we'd make a joke of it. You'd never be able to keep it a secret. Besides, you'd want the real cooks to get the credit, wouldn't you?'

'I suppose . . . that's the difference between Heartsease and Findlebury. Here what you see is what you get . . .'

I don't finish the sentence out loud, but in my head, I do: *. . . and there, maybe nothing is quite as it seems.*

CHAPTER 13

Sandie

After a long week of doors slamming in my face – I've heard *No!* said a hundred different ways, by a hundred different suppliers – I return to the store just as it's closing for the night. From the outside, it looks almost as glorious as it ever did, though the paintwork doesn't shine, and neither do the dowdy window displays.

I push open the doors and, despite the problems, I feel safe and welcome. Trouble is, I think I'm the only one still feeling it. In the old days, we'd have to shepherd the last customers out onto the street, but the shop floor is already deserted this evening. And maybe it's my imagination, but the chatter of the assistants as they say goodbye to each other seems more subdued than it ever did before.

I take the grubby lift up to the management floor, hoping to have a word with Edgar about staff morale, but there's no one here. Great to know that everyone is so devoted to the cause that they skive off early on a Friday.

Rather than hole up in the horrible office Laetitia so kindly selected for me, I decide to walk the floor, as I used to back in the days when I dreamed of the dizzy heights of the management suite. Shame that now I've reached the summit, the view isn't nearly as good as I expected.

I start at the top, working my way around original art and limited edition photographs, through to electronics. The prints are staid landscapes and uninspired still lifes, but tonight I'm more distracted by the fingerprints all over the plasma screens and laptops. OK, so the cleaners don't arrive till later, but the geeky assistants up here used to love their products so much that they bought their own dusters to keep the kit tip-top.

Oh, Grand Dame Garnett, what's happened to you?

I turn the corner and I jump when I see the strangest-shaped woman reflected in a dozen gilded mirrors – and then jump again when I remember it's me. Of course I *know* I'm pregnant but the reality still takes me by surprise.

The next floor down is Home and Garden. Once upon a time, Arab princesses and home counties housewives alike came here to furnish their palaces. Now the floor looks as tempting as one of those massive out-of-town DIY sheds. Someone's decided to go big on flat-packs, even though there's no way we can ever compete with IKEA, or would want to. The only ready-made furniture we're offering is a range that might have suited a nineteen fifties vicarage, but the uncool chintz and dark-stained occasional tables are all wrong for now.

The gardens range is more up to date, but you could be forgiven for thinking there'd been a hurricane here. I stop to straighten a parasol that is listing dangerously, and try not to covet the hammock I'd imagined lying in with the baby through most of August. I pass through Kitchens, wondering if we're the only department store in London still trying to flog antique pine units. Do we deserve to survive, if we can't keep up with the trends?

At least the four-poster in Bedrooms looks tempting – I could lie down on it right now, if I didn't know how long it's had that same quilt and mountain of purple velour cushions out on display. I have a feeling that my weight on that bedding would cause a dust storm of its own.

I take out my notebook and write: *What is the most comfortable bed in the world? Source it and stock it.*

My best idea so far is to source an exclusive product for every department, something that will draw people to the store. And yet, is that any different from what we did before, or from what all our competitors are doing? Right now the only difference is that suppliers take our competitors seriously . . .

Down the stairs now to the Kids' floor, which fascinates me and scares me in equal measure. I've got my head round the baby clothes and the new mum paraphernalia, and I don't need to worry about buggies or monitors because Toby's in charge of the hardware, but it's the stuff for older children that disarms me . . . the Bratz dolls and the cricket sets and the fairy costumes and the pirate-ship bedroom furniture and storage chest.

'You'll have far too sophisticated tastes for this sort of tat, won't you, Bump?'

I make a note to myself to research what this Christmas's must-have toys are, and then descend to the fashion floor again, repeating the same mantra I use whenever I'm bracing myself for a visit to the construction site that used to be our house: *it has to get worse before it gets better.*

On this floor, we're busy shifting three years' worth of unsold stock to get ready for new stuff, and the disorder would put a *Blue Peter* Bring 'n' Buy Sale to shame. Even the bridal oasis isn't what it was, because I've co-opted Babs to work with me three days a week, so her domain is rather neglected. Amazing how little time it takes for a pristine wedding dress to take on a yellowy, Miss Havisham feel.

Another reason why being a bride has never been a dream for me: the whole thing seems heavy with a kind of nostalgic melancholy.

The one area I haven't dared investigate yet is the changing rooms – which were notorious, even back in my day.

'I'm going in,' I whisper to my belly.

Oh my lord . . . I thought I'd lowered my expectations to rock bottom, but it manages to be even worse. I've seen pictures of Soviet Bloc waiting rooms with more panache. And there's only so long you can hold your nose for before you have to breathe. Who *knew* that young girls could produce such a toxic combo of sour feet, overly fruity (and completely ineffective) deodorant and musky BO?

When I think of my Christmas-themed changing rooms the final year I was here – festive aromatherapy scents, red velvet curtains, comfy cushions – I want to weep.

I write fast, so I can escape as soon as possible:

Changing rooms (young style): complete redecoration and, if necessary, fumigation. To include usual painting, plus filling in of gouged holes in wall. New spec: replace carpet with industrial laminate; some kind of anti-stiletto coating for walls. If in budget, complete overhaul of lighting – so bad in here that would give Kate Moss cellulite.

'Hell-oooo? Who ees there?'

The voice makes me jump, but only for a moment, until I realise who it is.

'Don't shoot, Luis, it's only me,' I call out, as I step out onto the shop floor and fill my lungs with fresher air.

'Ah ha, my very most *favourite* girl and my very most favourite niño to be!' says Luis, trying to take me in his arms for a big bear hug.

'And my very most favourite security guard,' I reply, gently loosening his grip. 'Do I need to see you, Mr Cheerful! I could do with a dose of your optimism.'

He beams back, though I notice even he looks slightly less cheerful than usual. The right lapel on his uniform is frayed, and his slicked-back hair is now more salt than pepper. 'Of course, of course.'

'I'll join you on your floor walk, shall I, Luis?'

'Sure, sure, sure,' he says. 'I go to ground floor, now, huh, then back to my cubby 'ole.'

'So, how are things at the security nerve centre?'

He gives me a sideways look. 'Ah, pah. Different, but the same. Always. You know.'

'No, I don't know, actually. Tell me.'

We go down the stairs, then head towards handbags and hats. 'No, no, no. Nothing to worry yourself. Luis is always happy. Luis is especially happy to have a job right now.'

'Right.' He's hiding something. Maybe he's nervous about talking now he knows I'm expecting the boss's baby. Or nervous just because I'm no longer the ordinary shop girl he used to know, but the woman who could hold the future of the store in her hands. I bet he can't believe it: I can hardly believe it myself, sometimes. It's exciting, but so scary, too.

We keep walking, round the under-stocked cosmetic counters, and the early summer displays of bikinis and buckets and spades. I haven't bothered to get involved here, even though the mannequins are so patchy that they seem to have a skin disease, and the beach games look like they'd snap in seconds, but I have had to make myself focus on the relaunch, not the current state of the store. Otherwise I will never get anywhere.

Luis takes my hand as we step down the slightly too high steps on the switched-off escalator. Without music playing, the hum of the fridges and freezers in the Food Hall sounds sinister, and the pale light they cast around the darkened shop floor is even creepier.

'I'm worried, Luis,' I say.

He holds my hand tighter, even though we're now off the escalator. The lino is slippery with dirt and rain from thousands of shoppers' shoes. At least we still have customers for the Food Hall, but for how long?

'Do not worry, Sandie. Not good for Baby.'

'I don't want our store to go dark for good.'

'Go dark?'

'Close down.'

His eyes widen, as though it's the first time this possibility has occurred to him. 'But our jobs . . . the baby is coming, you need money.'

And he looks so worried for me and the baby that I feel guilty and responsible for everyone who works here and still cares. Even bloody Edgar.

I feel tears welling up and even though I turn away, I think Luis can see.

'Tea,' he says. 'For the English, tea always helps.'

In his 'cubby 'ole', Luis brews up and unwraps his wife's famous Dulce de Leche sandwiches from their foil packaging.

'Your favourite,' he says. 'I remember.'

I smile. They're tooth-rottingly sweet, but maybe sugar is what I need right now. The light is dim in here too, but comfortingly so, like candlelight.

'Pretty,' he says, pointing towards my necklace. I look down and see how the rich red colour of the garnet stone glows against my skin.

'Toby . . . Mr Garnett's first present to me, from before we were even dating. A garnet.'

'Precious?'

'Ah, it's not worth that much, garnets are much commoner now than they were in their glory days, when the Victorians loved them.'

'But like most valuable treasure for you, yes?'

'Yes, I treasure it more than anything . . .'

Something clicks in my head. *Treasure.* I think of the treasure chest on the children's floor, and then I think of explorers, of pirates, of gold and rubies and lost treasures.

And of *treasure hunts* . . .

That is the story I need to be telling our customers: that wherever they go in our store, whatever they're seeking in the new Garnett's, they will find treasures galore.

'. . . Sandie. You don't like more?' He's pointing at my sandwich, which is halfway between the table and my mouth, frozen in mid-air.

'Oh. Yes. Sorry. I *love* your sandwich,' I assure him, but then I lean over and I kiss him, Argentina-style, one on each cheek. 'But I love you more, Luis. You are a *genius*! Thank you. But now I must get back to work.'

And I leave him in his cubby hole, shaking his head, no doubt completely confused by what has happened to the shy, controlled Sandra Barrow he used to know.

CHAPTER 14

Grazia

'Just who are you, Joel? The bon viveur who whisked me off to Barcelona for three days of spontaneity, or a suburban dreamer who deliberately misleads women and has them abducted?'

'That's a bit harsh, isn't it, Grazia? Didn't you enjoy the journey?'

His jokiness infuriates me. 'A magical mystery tour is only magical if you end up somewhere you want to be. Either you tell me what is going on, or I am calling Maurice back here and putting the return on your account too.'

Joel sighs. 'OK. OK. I'm sorry. Will you come into my very suburban living room to hear me out?'

'If I must.'

The living room is boring, boring, *boring*, and dominated by a vast flat-screen television, and a living flame fireplace. There is deep pile carpet and a reproduction chandelier and more seaside prints. I feel an immediate sense of déjà vu, and it takes me a short while to work out why. 'Is it a coincidence that you have the same taste as the person who designs interiors for Travelodge?'

He flinches. 'I don't. But my wife did.'

I gulp. 'Where is your wife?'

'I suppose that depends on whether you believe in life after death.'

I stare at him, feel my cheeks colouring. 'When?'

'Three years ago.'

Leon died three years ago too. 'I am sorry for your loss. But you should have told me.' I stand up.

'You're right. I suppose . . . it didn't seem important. To us, I mean.'

His callousness shocks me. I walk away, towards the dining area. The bookshelves are full of pastel romances. There are no photos, but when I look more closely I see that the wood has a light covering of dust, except for frame-sized rectangles. 'You even moved her photographs before I came round, didn't you?'

'Grazia, sit down please. We were separated long before she died.'

'I will *not* sit down. If you split up, then why are you living here? What are her books doing on the shelf?'

He stands up and goes to the horrible fitted unit to the left of the fireplace, and pulls a photo frame out of a drawer. 'This is why.'

I take the picture. It shows this dining room, decorated for Christmas, with hundreds of cards on these same shelves. Four people. A younger version of Joel is on the left, though his body language is awkward – he sits apart from what is, obviously, a family.

His family?

A girl and a boy are in the centre. I am better at telling the age of antiques than of children, but I would guess that the girl is thirteen and the boy ten. And then next to them is a pale woman. She is pretty. Or, on closer inspection, she was. Her face is a little too thin, and her hair is blonde and stubbly. She wears an outsized red woolly jumper, perhaps to give herself some colour for the photo. And her smile is too wide, and I almost feel like I know this woman, I know that she feels that if she lets the smile drop, then it will all fall apart . . .

'That's Faith. Four Christmases ago. Her last one.'

'And those are your children.' It is not a question. Who else could they be?

'Daisy and Alf. Daisy's fifteen going on thirty now and counting down the days till her birthday in June, and Alf has just turned thirteen. He's quieter. But I don't know if that's a good thing.'

My stomach contracts. 'They are not . . . upstairs now, are they?'

'No. They're at school.'

'At this time of the evening?' I say, and then feel stupid. 'Ah. Boarding school.'

Joel shrugs. 'I'm not much of a dad. That was about the only thing Faith and I agreed on at the end. So when we knew she wasn't going to make it, we tried to work out where they'd be most stable. We found a school twenty miles up the road and, well, Faith wanted them to have a home, too, so' – he opens his arms – 'I moved into the place Faith bought after the divorce. Their home. Never been mine. Though I guess it is now.'

'It must have been difficult.'

'They've coped well. I'm proud of them.'

'Difficult for you, I meant.'

He sighs. 'I wasn't with Faith any more, was I? I wasn't the grieving widower.'

'It is never that simple. When my husband died, I was angry one day, paralysed the next, for years. And with you, it must have been much more complex.'

He stares at me. 'I don't want anyone's sympathy. I should have told you, Grazia, you're right. But, no one likes to dwell on their failures, and whenever I'm here, that's what I feel like. A failure.'

'I am sure your children do not see it that way.'

'No?' His laugh is bitter. 'Though if you can stick around, you'll see for yourself.'

'But they're not here.'

'They will be tomorrow. It's half-term. Look, you don't have to do this. Of all the girls I've met since I got divorced, you're the only one who hasn't brought up the whole subject of kids—'

'Because I am so old. And too self-centred.'

He holds up his hand. 'But you're also the only one I've ever wanted to introduce mine to.'

For the second time in ten minutes, I am silenced. I am certain I do not need two teenagers in my life. And although I understand the reason why he kept this from me in our first, seventy-two-hour 'date', it makes those amazing days seem less *shiny* somehow.

And yet this, too, is not simple. When I saw him that first night in the restaurant, when he came in soaking wet, what struck me was his vulnerability. Right now, he looks even more vulnerable. His face is carefully neutral but his hands are twisting around each other, like the roots of a tree.

'Why?'

'Why what?'

'Why would you want to introduce your children to me?'

He does not look up at me. 'Because I think they'd like you. Because I like you, more than I've liked anyone in a very long time.'

I pick up the photograph again. It is always British stoicism that is my undoing. There is something unbearable about the way each of those four individuals is pretending everything is normal: not simply the dead woman's smile, but also the fierceness of the son's glare, and the slight pout on the daughter's lips.

'Who took it?'

'Oh. I think it was Alf. He'd had a camera for Christmas –

he's a real techie – so he must have set the timer to get us all in there.'

And, of course, it makes up my mind. The English boy with his stiff upper lip, reading an instruction manual, even as his world is crumbling.

'All right. I *will* stay and I *will* meet them, on two conditions.'

'Go on.'

'First, that you tell them it is early days for us, treat them like adults.'

'Once you've met my daughter you'll realise that I wouldn't get away with anything else. And the second condition?'

'Promise me there is nothing else to come out? No more secrets?'

He takes the photo from me, puts it down carefully on the table, then takes my hand. 'I promise. No more skeletons.'

'No more children?'

'Definitely no more children. And no more houses full of awful soft furnishings. What you see is what you get.' He smiles. 'Whether that is a selling point, well, I guess that's up to you.'

I cannot bear to see him so humble, so I decide it is time to change the subject.

'Perhaps,' I say, 'it may be time for you to prove again what you are offering. To remind me it is a worthwhile deal . . .'

We make love once, with extreme tenderness, in the guest bedroom of his dead wife's house.

Sleep does not come easily to either of us.

Teenagers!

The only contact I have had with teenagers in recent years is while secret shopping, and I was unimpressed. Surly girls and shy boys, unable to spell or speak in most cases.

But will they judge me any less harshly than I judge them? This is all too soon.

143

When Joel's alarm goes off, we both pretend it has woken us. I wait for his first touch, anticipating the kind of mornings we had in his apartment.

'Morning, Grazia,' he says, kissing me, but then leaping out of bed before I have a chance to respond. Because he sleeps naked, I can see this is not down to lack of desire . . .

'No lie-in?'

'I wish. I need to pick up the kids. But stay in bed, please.'

I lie rigid while he gets ready, and when he is dressed, I sit up. 'You look like a father.'

He laughs. 'In what way?'

'It is . . .' I gesture at his clothes. 'I cannot put my finger on it.'

Actually, I can. His clothes look dowdier, more practical. He has combed his hair, which makes it look thin but, I suppose, more respectable. And his expression is sombre. He looks like every other man with a mortgage.

'They take the piss if I turn up in my normal gear. They reckon the other kids take the piss out of them if I look like I'm trying too hard.'

Suddenly it occurs to me. 'What am I going to wear, Joel?' I jump out of bed and rifle through my overnight bag, even though I know that neither the dress, nor the lingerie, is at all suitable. 'Do you have time to drop me at the shops?'

'No. I daren't be late, that'll give them another thing to beat me up with.' He pulls a face. 'Look, I know this sounds ghoulish, but Faith was always buying clothes she never wore. You aren't far off her size, either. Her wardrobe's full of stuff with the labels still on. I mean . . . you could take a look?'

I consider this, and even though I do not like the idea of wearing a dead woman's clothes, I will admit I am curious about her. In addition to being almost naked. 'It does make sense, I suppose. But only if you are sure.'

'Of course. You've got about an hour, make yourself at home.' He kisses me again, a marital peck on the cheek.

I wait until the people carrier has accelerated away, and then I do what he instructed. It is ghoulish, yes, but I can hardly greet the children in my Janet Reger underwear.

The first floor has the two guest bedrooms – one of which Joel uses – plus a large office, and Alf's room, which has a lock on the door, as well as the compulsory KEEP OUT notice. The shower in the 'family bathroom' is powerful, but there is a lack of feminine soaps and gels and moisturisers. Only spot cream and deodorant and toothpaste. Daisy has her own bathroom and bedroom on the top floor.

Next door to her room is the entrance to a vast, ghostly master suite. I know it is only superstition but it does feel cold and sad, even though the heating is on and the colours here are relentlessly cheery. The ornate four-poster bed is made up in lacy fabric, there are towels in the bathroom, along with full bottles of hand wash and body lotion. The bath has spa jets, and a bottle full of lavender 'relax and recharge' oil next to the taps. Any evidence of medical treatment – pills and appliances – must have been cleared out after she died.

There is a large dressing room linking the bedroom and bathroom. I open the wardrobes tentatively. Am I expecting her ghost to leap out at me? Instead, I find rows and rows of differently sized clothes arranged in colour order, again with a bias towards bright primaries and Boden-style relaxed casual. Her shoes, in plastic stack boxes, reveal her feet to have been larger than I would have expected from that photo, but otherwise everything that fitted her would also fit me.

I reach in and, as Joel said, at least a quarter of the items still have their labels, thankfully. I can hardly greet them in their mother's favourite jumper. The items range in size from eight to twelve, perhaps because she lost weight faster than she could wear her purchases. The thought makes me shiver. I rifle through quickly and pick a black linen blouse with matching capri pants. My own jewellery will transform them into something more . . . *Grazia*.

The end wardrobe door is slightly open and I wonder whether Daisy might sneak in here occasionally, perhaps even try to talk to her mother.

I slide the door a little further, and I gasp.

It is a tiny space, and must have been built specifically for what it houses: a wedding dress, and a morning suit. His and hers. I do not touch the dress but I can see enough of it to work out how it must have looked: tight and lacy, moulded to her more generous pre-sickness frame. The lace is like a field full of Michaelmas daisies. Next to the dress, the black suit looks unfussy, but as I move, I see there is a hint of purple that catches the light, like the sheen on a blackbird's feathers.

She still loved him, to have kept this.

Now I feel dirty. I slide the door back to its just-open position, and head back to the guest room to change into the wicked stepmother.

The people carrier returns ninety minutes later. I have a moment of panic wondering whether I should come to the door, but then I realise that might seem too freaky, so instead I wait in the kitchen, stirring the same mug of coffee over and over again.

I hear the key in the lock, and footsteps in the hall, but none of the wild noise I would expect from children. For some reason, this makes me more nervous.

The door from the hall to the kitchen has frosted glass, and so the first thing I notice is the size of the kids: the girl almost as tall as her father, and the boy stouter and shorter.

'Shoes off!' Joel's voice sounds so different: weary is the best way to describe it.

The door opens and I clutch my mug, trying to look relaxed. The girl stomps in, wearing high-heeled boots. *Daisy*. Pretty, of course, in the way they are at that age, though they do not realise it. But maybe more than pretty: intense eyes that would be knockout even without the turquoise kohl.

Pale skin that will surely soon turn to irresistible alabaster. Shoulder-length blonde hair with a fringe to hide behind or flick (and I suspect she does the latter more often than the former). Her body is a little out of balance, with legs that look too long, although better that than too short. And her teeth are kookily crooked, either cute or in need of a brace, depending on her dentist.

She looks at me with astonishment. 'Bloody hell. I thought you'd be way younger.'

Before I can respond to that, her brother joins her. He is wearing filthy trainers that have left marks all over the hall carpet. Alf has the same bright eyes as his sister and his father, but he looks everywhere except at me. He has a plump face that makes him seem much younger than thirteen.

The girl, I understand. The boy has an aura of trouble.

And behind them, their father, wearing an expression of defeat. 'OK, you two, Grazia is my friend. I really like her and, amazingly, so far I haven't done anything to put her off. So I would be very grateful if you'd help keep up the illusion that I'm a catch, OK? Remember who pays your pocket money.'

'Hello,' I say. 'I have just made coffee. Would you like one?'

'Er. No, *thanks*,' says Alf, as though I had offered him crack cocaine, and turns on his heel and stomps up the stairs.

'Alf. *Alf! At least take your shoes off in the house*,' Joel says, but even I can tell his heart is not really in it.

'I will,' says Daisy. 'Black, like yours.'

'Coming up.'

Joel looks ridiculously hopeful at this tiny concession, and sits down at the breakfast bar. 'I'll have one too.'

'You don't even like black coffee, Dad.'

'And you don't know everything about me, young lady.'

'So you're Italian, then?' says Daisy, ignoring her father. 'I love Italy. It's so romantic. The men are beautiful.'

'When did you go?'

'Last month. We did Florence, Rome and Venice, all with school. It was *super gorgeous*! I totally want to live there as soon as I'm sixteen.'

I smile. I wonder which boy turned her head.

'Grazia thinks all Italian men are mummy's boys who care more about their own reflection than giving their girlfriends a good time,' Joel says.

Daisy looks dubious. 'Maybe that's what the older men are like, but the young guys are charming. And so what if they look after themselves? Better than going to seed, eh, Dad?'

'So what else do you like, Daisy, apart from Italian boys?'

She frowns at the question. 'Music. Mates. The usual. What about you? What do you like, apart from my dad?' She says this with a slight sneer, as though she cannot imagine why anyone would like her father.

'I adore England. And also Barcelona, now that Joel has introduced me to it. In addition, I prefer champagne to cocaine, and embroidery to knitting. Now, do you take sugar?'

She gawps at me, and then manages to shake her head. She almost snatches the cup away from me, and turns on her heel without looking at either of us, before stomping up the stairs.

'Impressive,' Joel says.

I shake my head. 'No. I should not have mentioned the drugs, should I? It was very infantile.'

'Don't worry about it. She has a unique gift of bringing out the worst in people. Especially me.'

Perhaps it is too soon to suggest that he is a pushover. What do I know about parenting, after all? 'Anyone would find it tough bringing children up alone.'

'You mean, alone except for the staff of the boarding school, two sets of grandparents, and a cleaner.'

'Stop being so hard on yourself, please, Joel, if only because it is beginning to sound tiresome.'

He shrugs. 'Look, I know, you didn't sign up for the

stepmother business. You didn't sign up for anything except a fling. I've been stupid even suggesting you should get involved in all this carnage. I'll call Maurice. Or I'll drive you back myself. It's the least I can do for leading you up the bloody garden path.'

It would be easy to duck out now, of course. I am completely ill-equipped for this role. And yet are any men of my age without complications?

'No. I will stay. After all, perhaps it is time for me to embrace something a little more meaningful in my life than champagne and cross-stitch. But I have a new condition.'

'Go on.'

'That you stop putting yourself down. I myself know nothing of children, but I think they do want to know you are interested in them. So stop looking inwards and start listening, yes?'

He nods.

'Right. So what does a Saturday with the Ferguson family consist of?'

'Supermarket, bowling, junk food for them, hard liquor for me, plus a row with Alf over his bedtime, and some arguments with Daisy over everything else.'

'Marvellous. Sounds like the best weekend in months.'

I am still wondering why I did not call for Maurice to pick me up and take me home . . .

CHAPTER 15

Sandie

Just now, in the shower, I saw . . . a foot.

At least, I *think* it was a foot. I suppose it might have been an elbow or a heel or even a buttock, but it seemed to be kicking out, like someone in a serious hurry.

Someone . . .

I call down to Toby, but by the time he gets upstairs, my stomach is back to its drum-tight smoothness.

'Come on, kiddo. Wave at Daddy, will you?' He strokes my belly. 'Shall I rub some lotion on it? Or put on some Motörhead?'

We've noticed lately that the bump is a fan of heavy metal, but classical produces no reaction whatsoever. The idea that the *someone* is already developing musical tastes, and bad ones at that, is so strange.

'Much as I'd love to sit here all day with you watching my belly, I do have meetings.'

'I love it when you get school-marmish, Brains.' He leans forward to kiss me. The bigger I get, the sexier he seems to find me. Whereas I feel like a minibus.

'Sorry. Have you seen my schedule?'

The only thing more terrifying than the hard rock fan in my belly is the number of appointments in my diary.

Yesterday I had three profoundly depressing meetings, and I only hope this morning's is going to be an improvement.

'Miss Barrow? Golly, aren't you enormous?'

Why do people keep *saying* that? Do they think I haven't noticed? I take the hand of the perfectly petite woman in front of me. 'Yes, I am rather.'

'Come on through.'

The offices are beginning to merge into one. They're all glass walls and Nespresso machines and legions of gorgeous staff racing about looking purposeful. She leads me into a small conference room, where a frowning man with a pair of horn-rimmed John Lennon glasses glances up briefly from his iPad, and then looks down again without a word.

I knew I should have done the full multimedia presentation, but of course I haven't had the time or the money to commission a graphic designer. I try not to fumble as I unpack the mood boards from my portfolio case.

'So, what can we do for you, and for Garnett's?' says Ms Petite, nudging her frowning colleague.

As if she doesn't know already. It's taken weeks to get this meeting. She's concession manager for a hot gold jewellery firm with an A-list clientele. And I *need* their brand in my store.

I take a deep breath – something that's getting much harder as the Bump keeps expanding. 'We believe your brand is the perfect match for Garnett's. I think we can benefit each other. Let me talk you through our plans for the next season. Our store is one with a grand and illustrious past and, we believe, a vibrant and profitable future—'

The girl holds up her impossibly delicate hand. 'Can I stop you there? Because I'm sure neither of us has time to waste. We are not convinced we are a match for Garnett's with your current figures and clientele. To be blunt, at present your store does not have the right image. Today you need to convince us otherwise.'

Finally the frowner makes eye contact, and a rather sneery smile spreads across his face as he crosses his arms.

I gulp. It's not as though it's the first time I've heard a version of that this week. But I'm not giving up. I pass them the mood boards.

'I am sure you'll agree that this image is more of a match.'

The boards feature a wonderful ink and watercolour promotional image I found in the archives, from when the store first opened in 1909. I've magnified it, and then added my wish list of top names and dream products, floor by floor. The only thing I have splashed out on so far is a tweak of the Garnett's logo and livery: keeping the same ruby and cream colours, but adding a little drop shadow and a subtly enhanced font.

Too subtle for iPad man, judging from his expression. He's switched off already, going right back to the iPad. I hear pinging – I think he's actually playing a game.

'How many of these brands do you have on board at present, Miss Barrow?' the woman asks.

'We are in advanced talks with all of them,' I say. Well. Except for the ones who told me a straight no yesterday. I did try to pull the photos off, for the sake of honesty, but they tore the black blacking, so I had to glue them back on again.

Frowner sighs.

'If I could ask you to read our projected figures and our anticipated client profile? We are aware that there's no time to waste with this one, and so we'll be aiming for the fastest store makeover in UK retail history, which should generate lots of publicity in itself.'

The documents lie on the table, untouched. Frowner smiles as a small victory fanfare sounds: he's evidently just got himself a high score.

Mini-girl shakes her head. 'The fact is, we are on the ascendant. Garnett's isn't.'

'What makes you say that?'

'It's about confidence. Chances are, your store won't be here this time next year. So why would we go to the trouble of putting in a concession that will need to be ripped out before the receivers try to asset-strip?'

I gulp again. 'Is that really what people are saying?'

Her face softens a little. 'Yes. I'm afraid it is. Are you OK? You've gone a bit . . .'

She wants to say *pale*. But I guess she's worried about seeming racist. I decide to play it to my advantage. 'Perhaps you have some water?'

'Of course.'

She races out and Frowner looks up, thinks the meeting's over and leaves without a word.

'Here we are,' the woman says, proffering two bottles of Fuji water. 'One room temperature, one chilled. We've got this fab new fridge with different zones. It's the *in* thing in Hollywood.'

'Golly.' I take both, and make a mental note to check it out as a potential 'treasure' product for our domestic appliances department. 'You were saying. About the word on the high street.'

She looks at her watch. The last thing she wants cluttering up her pristine meeting room is a weeping heffalump, but until I feel better, I'm as good as a sitting tenant. 'Look, Miss Barrow. *Sandra*. I'm genuinely impressed by your vision, but Garnett's isn't looking promising. We have our spies and frankly we'd need more than fancy pitches to back you over the others. The rumour is that you're being run down for a takeover.'

'Where does that come from?'

'Sources. But reliable ones, from the top of the food chain. Still, maybe a nice Russian oligarch has his sights on you. Or the Chinese. Now, if that happens, come back to us. We're *gigantic* in Shanghai right now.'

'I assure you, we have no plans to sell.'

She smiles at me sympathetically. 'What was it Shakespeare said? Life is what happens to you when you're busy making other plans?'

'I think that was John Lennon actually.'

Tiny girl nods as though it was what she'd meant in the first place. 'Precisely. Look what happened to *him,* poor guy.' She looks up at the clock. 'Are you feeling better now?'

'Yes, thanks. I take it that's a no?'

'I hate to close the door completely, but . . . well, it's a not right now.'

When I stand up, I do feel a bit faint. The power of suggestion. Plus the realisation that I have precisely *nothing* to pitch at tomorrow's board meeting.

The only thing I can hope for is that the codgers realise that at least I give a shit (sorry, Gramma, but it's the only way to say it right now). Unlike, it seems, our current general manager. *The top of the food chain.* Does that mean the rumours are coming from him?

Why the hell would he want to do himself out of a job?

After a hellish day, the baby – yes, I have admitted it's a baby now – grants me a mercifully kick-free night, and this morning I feel that we're on the same side.

Which is more than can be said for Toby.

'Are you sure you're up to this, Brains? Only you don't look well at all.'

Neither of us has slept well. Our bedroom here in the rental house is piled high with stuff Toby keeps buying for the new home: I thought it was meant to be women who got the nesting instinct? But every time he brings something back, he's trying to reassure me that we will be there in time for the baby.

I give him what is meant to be a silencing look. 'I'm fine.'

'OK. Enough with the crazy eyes. I am scared of you, you know that. But I'm more scared of what you're going to do to yourself if you overdo it.'

I look up from trying to fasten the zip on my very loosest pre-pregnancy skirt. 'Doesn't saving Garnett's matter to you?'

He walks across the bedroom: it only takes two steps and the static electricity from the acrylic carpet crackles and pops. In our master suite in the House of Our Dreams, he could stride masterfully across the reclaimed oak floor. 'Don't be silly. Of course it does. But not nearly as much as you matter to me.'

It's so tempting to lean on his very broad and supportive shoulder and forget it all. I haven't mentioned what the tiny woman said yesterday about Garnett's being on the rack, because it feels like popping a child's balloon. But I'm going to have to do a lot of popping this morning, and I cannot be weak.

'It doesn't have to be a case of choosing one over the other, though, does it, Toby? This isn't the fifties. Pregnant women are allowed to work.' *Even if they have to do it in tracksuit bottoms*, I think, finally abandoning the battle against my skirt. It's the watershed moment.

'Oh, Sandie, when will you stop being so stubborn? This isn't about me trying to cramp your style or stop you having a career. God knows, I don't have much of one myself so it'd be nice if Junior had someone to look up to.' He puts his arms round me. I breathe in his old school cologne: fresh yet reassuring, like its solidly manly wearer. 'But I *know* you. I know you're brilliant, but you can also lose perspective.'

I shrug him off, with some difficulty as part of me longs to be taken care of. 'Once this is out of the way, I promise I'll relax. This afternoon, we'll know for sure, won't we? My consultancy work will be out of the way, and then it'll be easier.'

He sighs. We both know that's not true. It'll only be easier if they reject my plans, and even then, I don't think I can give up on Garnett's.

'Remember, Sandie. This isn't just about you any more.'

I choose Stella as my perfumed weapon today. Girlier than I usually wear, because I suspect a touch of vulnerability might soften up the Muppets.

Laetitia is standing with her back to us as we walk up the panelled corridor towards the boardroom. Even from behind she looks fierce – there'll be no softening *her* up. She turns when she hears our footsteps, and I realise she's smoking, which makes her look even more of a dragon.

'Mother,' says Toby, leaning in for the most formal of kisses. They are barely speaking these days, not since he took my side at the last board meeting.

I ignore her, but as I walk towards the boardroom door, a puff of noxious smoke is propelled towards me. She shouldn't be smoking, of course, but the unpleasantness is more than simply nicotine – there's an unmistakably stale, bitter smell.

'I can't *wait* to hear what you have to tell us,' she says, and I wonder how it feels to be so evil inside that you reek.

I feel Toby's hand on the small of my back and, momentarily, I feel sorry for the woman because she's almost lost him, and when the baby's born it really will be game over for her.

Will I ever fall out that badly with the Bump? Maybe I'll end up being as awful a mother as Laetitia?

Edgar looks at me warily when I enter the boardroom. He acts like a man with something to hide, but what? I've thought it over, and I don't see how he could gain from running us down. So it must be simple incompetence.

'Good morning, Miss Barrow. Planning another character assassination, or are you actually going to focus on helping us to make things better this time?'

'I don't remember anything personal being said last time.'

'Oh, come on. I mean, I'm not naive enough to expect loyalty, but the first stage of your . . . *takeover* bid was obviously to undermine my authority and credibility, so I am intrigued to know what's for seconds.'

'Don't talk to her like that.' Toby is behind me, his open face creased with indignation.

Edgar still looks defiant. 'So you can dish it out, but you can't take it, is that right? We don't all sleep our way into the boardroom.'

I put my arm on Toby's hand to stop him lashing out to defend my honour. 'Thank God he's never tried,' Toby whispers. 'I'd rather sleep with old Stoddart than roger Edgar.'

'Could we possibly make a start on things,' Edgar barks, 'as some of us actually prefer running a store to having meetings about it?'

Which is a bit rich considering that in the old days whenever we wanted our manager urgently, he was permanently *in a meeting*.

The door closes and as it creaks, I feel the Bump shifting slowly around the confines of my abdomen, settling right in the most uncomfortable position, with a knee poking into my bladder.

But I can't excuse myself now, not when all eyes are on me. OK, there's less hostility than last time, but I do feel a bit like the bull at a Spanish fiesta.

Laetitia bares her teeth.

I think I've spotted the matador . . .

'Miss Barrow, are you ready to present your proposal to the board?' says Edgar. I nod and take as much breath as I can into my lungs. As I stand up, Stoddart checks his pocket watch, and then winks at me.

The old dog.

'Thank you, Mr Murray. I appreciate the opportunity to talk you through my findings. I have prepared a very brief report which I will distribute shortly. One thing I do promise you, and that is that I won't waste your precious time. Not only because you are all busy people. But also because Garnett's definitely does *not* have time on her side.'

I pause, to let this sink in. *Kick.* The Bump is making its presence felt.

'I call the store *she* because to me Garnett's is more than another assignment. This shop was my world for seven years, and I saw her as a friend, one I admired, but also felt in awe of. For as long as I remember, Oxford Street was unthinkable without her.

'But, times have changed. The British high street without Woolworth's was unthinkable not too long ago, and yet we all know what happened *there*.'

I hate using the W word. It's the retail equivalent of saying *Macbeth* in the theatre dressing room, and I feel for the ex-employees. But shock is all I have.

'By my calculations, the unthinkable could happen here. I estimate that as soon as Halloween this year, our beloved store could be a ghost building. Everything from the shopfittings to the hand-dryers sold off to the highest bidder. It'll be the busiest October we've ever had, but the customers will be scavengers picking over the remains.'

The board look horrified to a man. Even Toby seems to be saying *steady on, Brains*, with his eyes. Edgar has his head in his hands . . . though Laetitia is busy fluffing up her cashmere cardigan. I'll give her one thing: she's ice cool.

'It's bad enough that customers are staying away. But what will kill the grande dame off for good is industry gossip. The rumours aren't good. In fact, the brands I've been talking to are united in their opinion that Garnett's is already on her deathbed and that it's only a matter of time before her obituary is published in *Retail Week*, and the asset-stripper is at the door—'

'Hang on!' Edgar is on his feet, and quite red in the face. It's the first sign that he still cares, which is something. 'You've got some cheek, Sandra Barrow. Coming in here with your anonymous scandalmongering and your nasty sniping, well, I won't have it. If the board choose to believe some girl over me – that's me, remember, Edgar Murray, shepherd and . . . guardian angel to this store and its flock for the past fifteen years – then fine. I resign. And good luck to you all!'

I don't know what's more astonishing – his resignation threat, his fury, or the fact that he thinks he's the Angel Gabriel.

'Mr Murray, please, you misunderstand me.'

'I don't think I do,' he hisses. 'You've always wanted my job. Well, you're welcome to it.'

He begins to gather together his papers, but he's so apoplectic that he keeps dropping them and swearing under his breath, and I worry he's going to have a heart attack.

'Do something, Toby,' I whisper, and Toby places a calming hand on Edgar's arm, but it's slapped away. Now Stoddart is next to them, and the 'guardian angel' is lashing out and might do someone an injury if he's allowed to carry on. Stoddart wraps his plump arms around Edgar's skinny frame, putting him in some kind of straightjacket hold. For a while, Edgar's mouth moves up and down, but there's no breath in his lungs to get the words out, and after a few agonising seconds, Stoddart loosens his grip a little.

'That's it, my boy. Nice and calm. It really doesn't do to let yourself lose control like that. Five-minute adjournment, ladies and gentlemen. Hilary, would you mind seeing if we can have an early tea?'

And although I'm shocked by the outburst, there's a bit of me that's thanking my lucky stars for the diversion because at least now I can nip to the Ladies.

Edgar is sent home, with a copy of my proposal, a bottle of Valerian from the health and beauty section, and a suggestion that he might like to take the day off to consider his next step.

'I'll be at the helm for the rest of the meeting following our little interruption,' says Stoddart. 'Now, then, Miss Barrow. Please do continue.'

He gives me an encouraging smile. At least I have one fan here, and he's formidable. During the break, he confided in Toby that he'd only ever seen the Korean Coma Grip during National Service, so trying it on Edgar took guts.

'So, as I was saying—'

Stoddart holds up his Coma Grip hand. 'Sorry. One thing. You did promise you wouldn't waste our time. Yet you've spent a long while telling us what's wrong, instead of how you propose to put it right. I trust you're about to remedy that, my dear.'

Maybe he's not quite such a fan. 'Of course. You may have noticed that I too am somewhat short of time.' I nod towards my belly, and wait for them to respond. If they smile, I'm OK, if they don't, I'm sunk. They smile. Nervously, but I do catch a glimpse of their teeth. Though Laetitia's are always bared.

'We need to work on four fronts. We need to convince the trade that we are not going to fold. We need to source killer *exclusive* products for every department of the store. We need the biggest revamp in the store's history, to make the place feel fresh and appealing again. And finally, we need an autumn relaunch with events that will bring the punters back to see what they've been missing.'

I look at Toby. He nods vigorously. But then he's not exactly unbiased.

'My theme for the relaunch is "Garnett's: All the world's treasures under one roof". I want customers to feel they will uncover a treasure trove of beautiful, practical, covetable things, so much so that they need go nowhere else. To complement this, the launch will include a first-week Treasure Hunt, with hundreds of prizes, including specially commissioned jewellery of gold and garnets.'

'Sounds pricey,' murmurs one of the Muppets.

'Cheaper than bankruptcy.' I pull my reports from my briefcase, and pass them across the boardroom table. 'Proposal on the front, with costings on the back. Only a sheet of A4. The figures may shock you, but we need money to make this happen. Usually a relaunch like this would be planned for at least two years. We are talking three *months*.'

'But what's the money for?' asks Stoddart.

'New fittings. Marketing. Ads. New stock. Plus, as a matter of urgency, we need to contract decorators for the outside and inside. They'll want payment up front, given our current state of affairs.'

One of the Muppets is shaking his head. 'Waste of money. Not like the paint is flaking off the windows, is it?'

'No, but it is a nasty polluted grey. A lick of paint isn't simply a facelift. The smell also suggests energy. Faith, even. Would you paint if you didn't expect to be here past the summer?'

I don't add that the paint job was Toby's idea, and that I took some convincing myself because right now the smell of paint gives *me* sleepless nights: it reminds me we don't have a cat in hell's chance of our house being ready in time for the baby.

They each take a copy of my report and I sit down while they read.

'You are brilliant, Sandie. If anyone can save the old lady, it's you,' Toby whispers. I notice Laetitia staring at him, and I have to look away, because there's a kind of raw distress on her face that makes her look at least a hundred years old.

'I'll need your help too, Toby,' I whisper back. 'Your connections. Your networking. You're my secret weapon.'

He shrugs. 'You're only saying that.'

But I'm not. Together we're a winning team. Though whether the board will agree is far from certain.

The men have finished reading. I stand up again. 'You're bound to have questions, and ideas. I'm happy to talk about any aspect of the report, but I can't overstate the importance of doing whatever it is you decide to do *as soon as possible.*'

Silence. Then Laetitia stands up too. 'Thanks for coming. A little . . . thin, I suppose,' she says, letting my report slip out of her fingers and onto the table, 'but then again, those who shout loudest often do have the least to say, I find.'

'Mother, I've warned you.'

'Oh, please, Toby, I'm sure we've already had one scene too many today. We're very grateful to Miss Barrow for her efforts, such as they are, and, of course, we'll pay her fee in full, but now it's time to let the grown-ups talk among themselves. Easier for us to be honest while you're not there. This is serious business, not a college project.'

I wait for Stoddart to say something in my defence. I *know* this is the only thing that can possibly save this store. Surely even that cow could put petty rivalries aside for the sake of her late husband's business – not to mention her son's inheritance . . .

Stoddart looks from Laetitia to me and then back again. 'All right. If you would allow us some time, Miss Barrow, it might permit freedom of discussion. Perhaps you'd like to wait in your office—'

'Oh, there's no need for her to wait. I think we can run to a black cab for Miss Barrow,' says Laetitia. 'In her condition, we really don't want her to be hanging about any longer than necessary.'

I'm getting the message, if no one else is: Laetitia will block me, even if it means Garnett's goes down the tubes. There's no room here for the common girl from the sticks and there never will be.

And that's where I decide I've had enough. 'Well, thank you all for listening,' I say, and then I walk out. I'm almost beginning to sympathise with bloody Edgar Murray.

Toby follows me outside. 'Don't go. I'll insist you stay. You can't let her win,' he whispers.

'I'm not *letting* her win. It's just . . . well, I tried. If they don't want to save the store, what can I do? You were right. I've let it take over. Let's go home.'

I start walking and he calls out. 'Go to the café. Wait. I won't be long. I promise.'

I shrug. 'Half an hour, then I'm getting a cab.'

Half an hour is too long to spend in the Jewel Café. I can't believe I've missed the woeful state of this place, but I've been too busy on the shop floor to hang around drinking tea until now.

This is awful. I don't think the cooker filters have been replaced since 1978 and I'm going to need a shower when I get in, to get the stink of deep fat fryer out of my hair. My scone is nice enough, but the cutlery's tarnished and the rap music they're playing must be the choice of the tough-looking teenage trainee.

I formulate a plan for the café in my mind – open up the windows to turn the flat roof into a terrace, ditch the fish-fryers for a salad bar, maybe find a new name, or at least revamp the signage, make it more bling than beef dripping. But then I stop. I've given enough to this place already.

Now I have to focus on project-managing our house, not to mention project-managing our baby. At least I can make some kind of difference there . . .

It's been forty minutes now. Time to leave. I take the lift down and step onto Oxford Street. I peer up: the lights are still on in the boardroom. Laetitia will be holding forth on my faults, Toby defending me, the Muppets watching like Wimbledon spectators. A cab pulls up and I climb into the back. I close my eyes. I *never* have to go back there, and if I concentrate really hard, I can make myself believe that's a good thing.

I must have fallen asleep, because by the time I realise my phone's ringing and manage to find it in my bag, I've missed the call. The taxi's in our street anyway, and I pay without getting a receipt because I don't want to demean myself by begging Laetitia for petty cash.

The sofa beckons, the best sight I've seen all day, and I lie down and the Bump is tired out too, and as soon as my head is down I feel sleep, lovely sleep, taking me over . . .

'Sandie? *Sandie?* Wake up.'

'Eh?'

Toby is leaning over me, beaming. 'You've done it, Brains. You've got all the money you wanted. And they want to offer you a contract, plus a heck of a title. Hang on, let me remember . . . Relaunch Executive Director.' And he produces an enormous bunch of red roses.

I'm not sure whether this is a dream, or a nightmare. '*Director?*'

He's nodding. 'Unanimous. Well, obviously, my mother didn't vote for you. But you blew the rest away, Sandie.'

'I'm on the board?' Despite my grogginess, I begin to feel excited.

Toby shakes his head. 'No, not quite yet. That might have been a step too far for the old codgers, but I know it's only a matter of time. The title's honorary, to show how important you are. But you're going to be in charge of the entire thing.'

I sit up and my head spins. This is as close to my ultimate ambition as I've ever got, and yet the way they can't bring themselves to make me a director, even temporarily, niggles at me. 'I'm not sure I wanted to be in charge of the entire thing. Toby, only this morning you were warning me against taking more on.'

'No, I know, but this way you totally call the shots. You can hire, fire, work from this sofa, work from the management suite, whatever you want. And, of course, I'll be your right-hand man.'

'But I've only got ten weeks before the baby's here.'

'Even if they only get you for five weeks – and I'll

be keeping a close eye on you – then Garnett's is in with a chance.'

'And Edgar?'

'Um. Stoddart called him up and told him we wanted you in charge. Edgar's reaction wasn't positive. He abandoned ship. They're putting his deputy in charge of operational management until they can advertise. But that's just about keeping things ticking over. The focus now is on the re-launch.'

'Poor Edgar. He gave the best years of his life to Garnett's.' I can't imagine where he'd find another job. How weird that he's resigned after so long. 'So now your mother's my greatest obstacle.'

He smiles. 'That's the weirdest thing of all. *Right* at the end of the meeting, after she'd realised that I wasn't giving in and that Stoddart had decided to back you, she took me aside and asked me if we really were making a go of it.'

'You and me?'

'Yup. So I told her, well, yes, obviously. And she pursed her lips in that way she does, and I waited for another lecture, but then she dug down into her handbag and passed me a piece of paper with a number on it.' He takes the paper out of his pocket. 'For the family gynaecologist.'

'I don't get it.'

'She said, and I quote, "If this is really going to be my first grandchild, then I suppose we'd better make sure it arrives in one piece. I'll pay." It's up to you, of course, Sandie. We don't have to use him. But he's good. The celebs use him, minor royals. That sort of thing.'

I take the paper from him. 'I can't get my head round any of this. The job's overwhelming enough, without trying to work out what your mother's plotting.'

'Maybe she's not plotting anything. Maybe she's finally admitting defeat?'

'Oh, Toby, I wish I had your faith in human nature. It's all been too much for one day.'

'You hungry?'

I consider this and realise, to my surprise, that I am.

'OK. Don't move. I will fetch pizza, run you a bath, iron your blouse and tuck you up in bed afterwards, all ready for tomorrow.'

'Tomorrow?'

'Yes. Didn't I say? Stoddart would like to meet you in the boardroom at nine to go through the budget . . .'

CHAPTER 16

Emily

'Are we nearly there yet?'

I shut my eyes. Is that one of those phrases that's hardwired into kids' brains when they're born?

'Have we moved at all since you last asked, Freddie?' Will asks, with dangerous-sounding patience.

'Um. Not sure. Maybe a little bit? Maybe as far as a little, little ant?'

Then again, maybe we bloody well haven't. We've been building up to this outing for weeks, but judging from the queues on the motorway, so has every other family in the south-east of England. Even though it's bloody freezing out there.

'You'd think we were in a disaster movie, fleeing from certain eco-death,' I say, offering Will a Malteser.

'Might happen before long,' he replies, with a certain relish that suggests he'd almost like it to, so he could tell the world *I told you so*. 'And if we are trapped here for ever, then I think we need to go easy on supplies.'

The footwell of the Snowvan tells its own story. An empty pack of Oreo cookies, another of organic crisps, and a large water bottle with less than a quarter left. Let's hope this *isn't* the apocalypse.

We should have known it might be like this on the May Bank Holiday, but we get so few family outings because someone always needs to mind the shop. So Freddie's excitement about today's trip – all paid for, as one of Sandie's secret shopping assignments – has been running at record levels.

I want it to be right, because despite our new friends Abby and Chris, our slowly rising profits, and our declining carbon footprints, things still don't feel quite . . . right in my life.

'Are we nearly—'

'No, we are not!' Will shouts.

'Let's play I Spy,' I suggest, though I wonder if that'll entertain a child who is getting scarily accomplished at the Thai Masters Kick-Boxing game on his best friend's Wii.

'So long as I am *it* the entire time.'

'Fine, Freddie. Remember how it goes?'

'*Obviously* I do.' Obviously is his new favourite word. He came back from his weekend with Duncan with heaps more macho attitude and an extensive repertoire of fart noises.

'I spy with my little eye something beginning with . . . a Wuh.'

'Wuh,' I say. *Wuh.* I look outside. The first thing I see is an enormous dark green four-by-four. The driver gives us a superior look as he crawls past, so much higher up than us that I feel like an earthworm.

'W is for . . .' I want to say wanker, but instead I say, 'wheel'.

Freddie growls. 'Yes! Wheel! You cheated. But it's my turn again! I spy with my little eye something beginning with . . . c.'

Oh, don't tempt me, Freddie. The road is full of them.

'Is it cars?' I ask.

'No,' says Freddie.

'Is it . . .' I see the sign for the next junction, a mile ahead. 'Will, we could always turn off. Go home. Play board games. Sandie would understand.'

'We're not giving up now,' he says, in a way that sounds spookily like my dad always did when I was a kid. 'Anyway, it's important for us to do stuff together, we so rarely get the chance. It's important *to me*.'

Something about the way he says it makes me feel unsettled. He was the same this morning, refusing to contemplate cancelling, even though the forecast gave us a fifty-fifty chance of *snow*, which could make our journey back even more painful.

'Guess again! Guess again!' Freddie insists.

'Cat? Catapult? Crow? Carrot?' I try my hardest to think of more things. 'No, Freddie. I give up. You win!'

'Ha ha!' he says, then points up towards the bridge across the motorway. 'Camera!'

And I look up at the camera and I wonder whether the policemen in the control room are having more fun than us little, little ants down here . . .

By the time we arrive at the Super-Science Playground, it's past two o'clock. Three hours to go forty miles. The car park is packed, and after circling for twenty minutes Will finally eases the Snowvan into a space, and we tumble out, desperate for food.

The building itself is shaped like a giant squid, covered in a space-age silvery coating. It's quite impressive if you like that sort of thing.

'Look at the amazing tentacles, Freddie.' Will points.

'Cool,' says Freddie unenthusiastically. 'Where's the café?'

It turns out to be in the centre of the octopus's body. There's a queue at the entrance to pay forty quid for a family ticket, then another at the door to the café, which is as busy as a West End brasserie, with prices to match. Thank God we're doing this for Sandie, otherwise spending eighty quid before we've seen a single exhibit would leave a very nasty taste in my mouth.

Silence reigns once we sit down to tuck into the scientifically themed menu. There's a black bean 'Night Sky' dip with rocket-shaped corn chips; hot Submariners' Rolls with Rainforest Salad; a livid-green Swamp Smoothie, and then Meteorite Pudding, with a topping of old-fashioned space candy that explodes in your mouth. I write it all down in my notebook, along with the numbers: time in queue, number of people in queue, number of dirty plates and cups on uncleared tables.

'Eeek!' Freddie shrieks delightedly as he feels the popping of the candy against his tongue. 'It's a-LIVE!'

Will and I exchange smiles – however good the exhibits, the only thing my boy will remember about today will be that pudding.

'Right, let's do the educational bit, now,' I say, 'before the post-lunch slump.'

Will puts his hand on mine. 'No. Hang on a minute. I've got something to talk about.'

Wtf? I don't want to hear anything serious. It's been a serious few weeks, what with organising a whole 'Dads' Day' craft session for June, plus working till midnight on Friday to get my application for the bloody Green Goddess in the post. 'Can't it wait? You know we have to go round this entire exhibition to earn our fee back.'

He hesitates. 'OK. Later. But I do want to say how pleased I am to be here with my two favourite people.' He squeezes my hand.

We start in the first tentacle, Under the Sea, walking through a digital coral reef and befriending the fishes. I'm trying not to read too much into Will's comment, but I can't help myself . . . I watch him as he watches Freddie's reaction, and I wonder whether seeing Abby pregnant has changed him. Made him realise that if three is fun, then four of us might be perfect.

But I've had my hopes raised and dashed before.

The second tentacle, the Chemistry of Life, is mind-numbingly worthy and apart from the pretty coloured test tubes, we're underwhelmed, so we take a quick detour to number three, Weather World. This is more like it – we follow the crowd through a climate maze, starting in the freezing Arctic, through a simulated hail- and snowstorm, followed by a tornado, thunder and lightning, and a deliciously hot Saharan wind, which helps to warm us back up . . .

'Again! Again,' Freddie says.

'Not until we've had a little talk.' Will leads Freddie up to a gallery overlooking the whole centre. 'Now. What did you think of the weather maze?'

'Brilliant! I want to go again!'

Will's forehead creases momentarily. 'Yes, it's a lot of fun, Freddie, but it also has a serious message. Do you know what that is?'

Freddie pulls an obligingly serious face. 'Is it about always remembering your umber-ellas?'

'No. Well, sort of. Er. Imagine that it started to snow but then never stopped.'

'Cool!'

'Well, it would be cool. Cold, in fact. But imagine somewhere else on the planet, it's so hot you can't walk down the street without your shoes melting.'

'Ha, ha, except what if you walk very, very quick, then you're OK!'

Will sighs. 'OK, let's start again. You're a penguin, Freddie.'

'Yes.' Freddie pulls a penguin face, puts both arms down by his sides, and does a little penguin waddle.

'You live on a cosy bit of ice but one morning you wake up and your ice island is melting. You're clinging on and clinging on, but you can't see your friends, and the island's getting smaller and smaller and before you know it you're in the water.'

'Tee hee, I'm a penguin and I love swimming.'

'If you have to keep swimming for ever, your wings will get tired, won't they?'

'Suppose,' says Freddie uncertainly. 'Not for ages, though.'

Will looks pained. 'The point is, Freddie . . . it's not nice if the ice caps melt and Pingu has nowhere to live. And that's what's happening. Right now.'

'Mummy?'

'Yes, darling.'

'Could we have a penguin come to live with us?'

I shake my head at Will: *Look what you've started.* 'Where would the penguin live, sweetheart?'

'Um. Um. In the bath! I could get ice from the freezer for him. Or her. Could be a girl penguin.' He nods, pleased that he's being thoughtful. 'That would be all right, like when Daddy asks whether I'd prefer a little brother or a little sister.'

I stare at him. 'Daddy asked what?'

'Obviously I fibbed a little bit because everyone knows sisters are rubbish.'

I don't want to ask the next question, so Will helpfully asks it for me.

'Did Daddy say that a new brother or sister might be arriving . . . soon?'

Freddie bites his lip as he considers this very carefully. 'He said not to tell you, or Mummy. Especially Mummy.'

'Oh, God, Will, she's pregnant. Bloody Suki is pregnant.'

Freddie shakes his head. 'Daddy's not going out with Suki now. Daddy's going out with Marianne. She has a little dog. Can we have a dog instead of a penguin?'

Marianne is news to me. I didn't like Suki one bit, but if Duncan is introducing his girlfriends to our son, surely the least he can do is tell me their names?

'But is she . . . expecting a baby?'

'Don't know.'

'Did she have a big round tummy? You know, like Mummy's friend Sandie?'

Freddie is bored now. 'No. She has a very flat tummy. Much flatter than yours, Mummy.'

Ouch. 'So no one's mentioned a baby in her tummy?'

Freddie tuts impatiently. 'No-o. Tummies are boring. Babies are boring. I want a dog, like Marianne's. He's called Patch.'

'We're not getting a dog, Freddie,' I say.

'A cat?'

'We're not getting a cat either.' Maybe Freddie started this whole conversation with the aim of talking me into getting a goldfish.

I look at Will, pleading with my eyes for rescue.

'Come on, Fredster. Let's get a move on round the rest of the museum and then if you're lucky, we might treat you to a plastic dinosaur in the shop.'

After three hours at the centre, we're knackered and crabby and ready for bed.

There's a light dusting of snow on the road, which means everyone's driving as if they're on tiptoes, and we're in for a long return journey.

'Guys, I need some help with my secret shopping report. What did we think of the museum?'

'Good and boring,' says Freddie.

'You liked the weather tunnel, didn't you?'

'Shop was the best bit,' he says, stroking the pea-green stegosaurus in his lap.

'What did you think?' I ask Will.

'It was fun, but disappointing on climate change. To have that entire weather exhibit and not follow it up with educational messages is a missed opportunity.'

I sigh, and he gives me a dirty look. Right up to the eighth tentacle – The Human Body – I kept hoping he was going to suggest making a brother or sister for Freddie, but when we got to the reproduction section with cartoon sperm and eggs, he began to mumble about *over-population* and *thinking globally, acting locally*. I realised that whatever thrilling announcement he had in store didn't involve a stork.

I doze until we're back in Heartsease, and I even allow Freddie to go to bed without his bath, because neither he nor I have the energy. As I slump down on the sofa with a glass of white wine, I feel Will stiffen. And not in a good way.

I take a mouthful of wine, swallow, then close my eyes. 'OK. What's up?'

'What makes you think something's up?'

'The weird speech in the museum café, the pained silences in the car . . .' I tick them off on my fingers. 'Oh, and the way you look like you've got piles. Now that I'm reading the monthly accounts, I know it's not bad news about the shop, so what is it?'

Will frowns, then gets up and pulls something from the stack of papers on the sideboard. 'Here.'

It's a brochure for something called the *Green University*, thick as a blockbuster paperback. 'You think I need to get some more education?'

He sits back down. 'Not you. Me.'

'But you've already been to college.'

He opens it at a page bookmarked with an old envelope and I read aloud. 'Masters Degree in Sustainability. You want another degree? But why? And, more to the point, when? We hardly have time to blow our noses, you know that.'

'It's not full-time,' he says.

'Even so . . . we're only just starting to make any money, aren't we? We can't take our eye off the ball.'

'Says the woman who wants a baby. Like *that* wouldn't take our eyes off the ball.'

'That's below the belt, Will.'

'Sorry. But Freddie starts school in September, so we'll both have more time. I want to make a difference, Em. Because it's not us who are going to suffer the consequences if we don't. It's Freddie. And *his* kids, if the earth is around long enough for him to have them.'

I manage a smile. Part of me loves to see his passion for the cause, but I do wish his sense of humour hadn't been eclipsed by the eco-doom. 'So how would it work? The degree?'

'Like I say, it's part-time. Mainly distance learning, like the Open University. Although . . . well, like the Open University there's some residential time. Like a summer school.'

'A week?' I try to ignore the feelings of panic at the idea of managing here alone for a whole week.

'Um. Well, three, actually. But not all in one go.'

I gulp. 'In London? You could commute.'

Now he looks as sheepish as Freddie does. 'No. North Wales. It's the greenest campus in the UK.'

'When?'

'A fortnight in July, then another week in August.'

I stare at him. 'So you're asking me to hold the fort here, in the summer holidays, while you . . . I don't know, get drunk on organic rhubarb wine, and have group sex with eco-warrior chicks who don't shave their armpits?'

Will shakes his head. 'It won't be like that. It's serious academic study.'

I have to stay calm. He's always been the calm one, which means he wins all the arguments.

'I know the timing isn't ideal, Em, but a relationship doesn't mean we can't explore new things, does it? I want us both to grow. To be happy.'

'How long have you been planning this?'

He looks *properly* shifty now. 'Not long. I just . . . wanted to see if it was possible. I hoped you might support me. Like I'm supporting you with the Green Goddess thing.'

I grip the sofa cushion, knowing I mustn't storm out because then he's the one left looking like the grown-up. 'That was *your* idea.'

'At first, maybe. But don't tell me you're not excited about proving yourself. About being an entrepreneur. A winner.'

'I don't want to be a fucking entrepreneur. I want to be happy. To be like . . . Abby. You know. Normal. Married. Babies. The works.'

He's not looking at me.

'Unless that's why you've applied for the course in the first place. Because you're running away, like you did from Abby when she started to get serious.'

'That's not true, Emily. I love you.'

I'm channelling my inner Jeremy Paxman now, trying to get to the truth. 'No, you didn't run away from her, or no, you're not running away from me?'

'We went through this at Christmas, Em.'

'Yes, and I kept my side of the deal. I read the accounts and I ask questions and I don't bury my head in the sand. And it turns out *you're* the one with the secret.'

'You want me to give up on what I believe in?'

'Don't get on your high horse. Of course I don't want to stop you being green. But aren't we doing enough for the world already in Heartsease? You could do the course when we're more settled. Isn't what we've got enough?'

Will looks up at me for too long. 'I don't know,' he says, finally. 'I honestly don't know if it is enough.'

'Or if I'm enough? If the two of us are enough for each other?'

He sighs. 'You're not the problem. Maybe I am. I love you. I love Freddie. I really like Heartsease and the people here, and what we've been doing but . . .'

'Always a but, eh, Will?'

'There's a whole world out there, Em, and I want to find out if I'm here to do more than run a little shop and be a good stepdad.'

I want to rant and rave. But if this is Will's early mid-life crisis, I must prove I'm the grown-up. It takes everything I've got, but somehow I manage not to throw my white wine in his face, or throw insults either.

'Sounds like you've made your mind up already. I'm going to bed.'

As I leave the room, I keep my back straight and my chin up, like a kid trying to learn good posture by balancing a book on her head. I even manage to brush and floss my teeth. I shut the bedroom door, guessing that Will is bound to wait until he's sure I'm asleep before coming to bed himself.

It's then that I feel the most alone I've ever felt. I know it's irrational. He's only talking about three weeks. Well, to begin with, anyway. So why do I feel almost as devastated as I did when Duncan abandoned me when Freddie was a tiny baby?

But, to my surprise, I don't cry. Maybe I won't crumble. Maybe this time, I will cope on my own.

June

CHAPTER 17

Grazia

I appear to be living a triple life.

The first is my old life, with a little embroidery on the side, when I have the time. The second is that of a courtesan: all caviar and champagne truffles and caresses from my lover.

And the third . . .

'So, does your generation think that snogging counts as infidelity, Grazia?'

Daisy, fifteen and eleven-twelfths, is my new best friend, though she is testing the limits of our friendship quite forcefully.

'Snogging is such an ugly word, I think.'

We are viewing a rather sweet photography exhibition at the town's art gallery, featuring pictures taken by children to represent their own lives.

'Yeah, but that girl looks like she's trying to swallow that boy's entire face.'

She is right – the photo features very young teenagers engaged in a kind of kissing that could almost qualify as an Olympic sport. I walk towards the next picture, of a child's pet kitten.

'What about blow jobs?'

I turn back to Daisy. Her voice was deliberately loud, so

now the other visitors are looking on curiously. 'What about them?'

'Well, you wouldn't answer my snogging question.'

I lack the experience to know how one responds to such questions. When I was her age, I was already out of control, and too jaded and smart to listen to any adult. But even though today's teens are supposed to be so knowing, there is still a freshness about Daisy, underneath the pretend world-weariness.

I check my watch. Another half-hour before we have arranged to meet Joel and Alf, who are having quality time in Mumford's premier sports shop. Joel hopes that by suddenly developing an interest in football he can bond with his son, not to mention help the boy shift the extra pounds he is carrying.

'Teatime, I think.' I need to buy myself time to decide how far to go.

I manage to kill ten minutes selecting which homemade cake to buy, and Daisy is equally torn between the toffee fudge slice and the raspberry Danish, so at least she has not succumbed to a fashionable adolescent eating disorder. She's very excited that this is our first joint secret shopping assignment – one of the contracts that Sandie keeps on as a little perk for her ex-colleagues, so we can grab a free coffee and cake whenever we fancy one. Daisy is keeping a mental note of the freshness of the sandwiches and the freshness of the cashier's smile.

'I'd give her four out of ten,' says Daisy, 'and it would have been higher, except that I don't think her nose ring looks very hygienic.'

I will have to remember to tell Joel what she said: he is terrified that his baby girl will come home one weekend with a tattoo and a full complement of piercings (even though he admits to an interesting night a few years ago with a woman whose tongue bar was the least shocking of her adornments).

By the time we sit down, I have decided that honesty is the best policy.

'Daisy, you appear to want to provoke me with your questions.'

She dips her little finger into the frothy top of her mocha, then licks it clean. 'No. I'm interested in how you think. You're different. You're the oldest person I've ever met that I can actually talk to.'

'Why, thank you, Daisy. What a compliment.'

She picks up on the edge in my voice. 'Sorry. I don't mean that you're old, but you are older than me, obviously, so I know you must be all sort of wise and knowing, and I'm not. And I want to be. I want to learn from you.'

I smile. 'Avoid making mistakes by hearing about mine?'

'Exactly!'

'That never works, Daisy. But if you are serious about wanting to listen, then I will talk. So. Remind me what you wanted to know.'

She blushes. Sitting face to face over coffee and cakes is much more intimate than walking through an exhibition. 'You know. Kissing. Cheating.'

I nod. 'I think every relationship is different when it comes to what counts as infidelity, Daisy. My husband was unfaithful to me many times, although I only found this out after his death. It hurt, yes. But whether it was kissing or a Roman orgy, the act itself is of little consequence. The exclusivity I wanted – and I thought we had – was exclusivity of thought, of trust. That is only the view of a middle-aged woman. Young people are different. More passionate.'

'Mum cheated on Dad.'

I look at her. 'I did not know that.'

'I mean, they weren't getting on for ages before that, but that was why he left. They never told us, but I'm not deaf, am I? I heard the rows.'

'That must have been difficult for you.'

She picks the dried raspberries off the pastry, and licks her fingers again. 'Almost everyone at school has divorced parents. The horrible bit was I thought they'd get back together, because Mum always said they would. And then she got sick and so bang goes the happy ending.' She tries to laugh, but it sounds wrong.

'I think that now must be the worst time in a girl's life to lose a mother.'

Daisy shrugs. 'Shit happens.'

'True.'

Now she looks close to tears. What I remember most about being her age is the anger I felt against everything, and everyone. In Daisy's case, perhaps her rage is directed at her mother, because she died, and her father, because he is still here.

'Daisy, my years do not grant me any particular wisdom. But I am a foreigner, and an observer of people. I also happen to be very fond of men, which is not something that can be said for all women of my age. So I am happy for you to ask me anything that you would want to ask your mother. I cannot promise to be as wise as she would have been. But I give you my word I will be honest.'

She looks at me, and nods. 'About everything?'

'Well, perhaps questions about your father and I should stay out of bounds. But otherwise, yes. See me as the Encyclopaedia Grazia. Though I warn you, I know nothing whatsoever that might help you with your homework.'

'Homework I can do. It's life that gives me the shits.'

So, Daisy is a doddle.

Alf is a conundrum. He refuses to look at me when I speak to him, yet if I turn suddenly, I often catch him studying me. He makes me feel like his prey.

'How did you two get on at the sports shop?' I ask, and then notice that neither of them is holding any shopping bags. Alf has his hands full all right, clutching a large portion of chips wrapped in paper in his left, and shovelling them steadily into his mouth with his right.

Joel gives me a pained look. 'Alf wasn't keen to get fitted for soccer boots today.'

Alf's mouth twitches upwards between bites. I want to tell him exactly why I think he should be prioritising football over food but that may not help our 'bonding'.

'No girl's ever going to fancy you if you keep guzzling like that, bruv,' says Daisy. 'They're already calling you Fatty Ferguson.'

'Don't care.'

'You might not, but it's doing my reputation no good having an obese brother.'

'Daisy . . .' Joel tries to sound mildly threatening, but I have spent enough time now with this family to know that it has no effect at all on either child.

'It's true, Dad. You don't know what kids are like. If he doesn't shift a few kilos, his life won't be worth living.'

Maybe I was wrong about her being safe from eating disorders.

'At least I wasn't born ugly,' says Alf.

'OK, leave it, you two, please. I know you don't care what I think, but the least you can do is behave yourselves in front of Grazia. We talked about this.'

And something amazing happens. Alf looks up from his chips – I think he has finished them anyway – and gives me something resembling a smile. 'Sorry, Dad,' he mumbles.

'That's OK, son. It's not always easy, this family business. But the trick is to remember that we're all on the same side. Now. Shall we go head down to the Super Bowl? See if they've got a lane free for the four of us?'

'I don't think so,' says Daisy.

'Or the dry ski slope is great fun.'

Daisy tuts. 'Da-ad. There are *limits*, you know. We're not

on some *sit*com. Can we go so I can get on Messenger and Alf can get back onto Fatbook, sorry, *Face*book, and then you and Grazia can spend the rest of the afternoon . . . well, pretending we don't exist.'

'You *paid* them?'

'I am a great believer in the market economy,' says Joel, though he looks shifty. 'Besides, most of the kids at school with them get far more pocket money. Call it a performance-related bonus.'

Finally we are alone again. Alf has been dropped at a boys' sleepover where video games and takeaway pizza are on the menu, while Daisy is at a friend's getting ready for a big night at an alcohol-free nightclub. Or, at least, that is what she has told her father.

But though we are in bed, I am not in mistress mode. Joel and I are in the spare room, with its ocean-blue decor and its print of beach huts, and sex is definitely not on the agenda. We sit up against a stack of pillows, drinking tea instead of champagne, and analysing the children's behaviour.

'So there is no way of knowing whether they like me, or like the money.'

Joel takes my hand. 'It's not like that. Daisy definitely likes you. She wants to be your new best friend. Haven't you noticed that she's already started wearing the same colour lipstick as you?'

Actually I had. 'But Alf?'

'Alf doesn't like anyone. He doesn't much like himself.'

'I suppose it must be difficult telling what is normal teenage behaviour, and what is related to their mother's death.'

'Or to having a useless dad.'

'What did we agree? No more self-criticism. Anyway, apart from the bribery, you are trying your best. What else can you do?'

'I could have stayed with their mother.'

'We would all love to change the past. But what is it they say? The past is a foreign country: they do things differently there.'

'*The Go-Between.*'

'Pardon?'

'The opening line of *The Go-Between.*'

'Oh. I thought it was a proverb.' But suddenly the other things matter less. I adore a man who can quote at will and for the first time since I came back to this house, I see a glimpse of the man I knew in Barcelona, behind the stressed parent. 'It is true, though, is it not? We cannot judge ourselves by what we did in the past.'

He sighs. 'You can tell you don't have kids. Even if we don't judge ourselves, they'll do it for us.'

For a moment, I wonder whether to take offence – so many people treat you as somehow subhuman because you have not procreated, but I had not expected it from Joel. And yet . . .

'How many hours till you have to pick up Daisy?'

Joel looks at his watch. 'Four. Maybe five.'

'So, we have two choices. We can easily occupy five hours – five months maybe – detailing your inadequacies as a parent. Or . . .' I smile at him.

He smiles back. 'Tough decision. But I think I'll take the or . . .'

Back to London, and another of my triple lives.

Somehow, returning to my apartment in Kensington does not, quite, make my heart sing as it always did before. I know my *intoxication* with Joel is the reason, but I must stay cautious. Grazia Leon does not place all her (ancient) eggs in one basket. Never again.

I have invited Pierre, my New Best Gay Friend from the V&A party, to tea at my apartment. I must stay the Grazia I was, the one Joel fell in love with – for his sake, and for my own. Time to extend my social circle, make new friends who share my love of beautiful things and beautiful people.

And, OK, if he happens to be able to give me a little more insight into Joel, then that is merely a lucky coincidence – after all, I knew Pierre before I knew Joel, even if it was only by an hour or two.

Pierre ambushes me with compliments. My décor is divine, but my Russian concierge, Boris, is *diviner*. He makes himself at home on the raspberry sofa – 'it matches my eyes, Grazia, after the night I had last night!' He helps himself to a plateful of pastries I bought from Patisserie Valerie, takes a glass of champagne, and leans back.

'So. Cut to the chase, then, madam. Joel and you. The real deal?'

I smile, trying not to notice the flakes of puff pastry exploding from his open mouth and floating down onto the unblemished nap of the velvet. Leon always used to say that sculptors had the worst manners on the art scene, 'stuck at the toddler stage of fiddling around with Play-Doh and sticking their fingers up their noses and arses'.

'We are having fun,' I say.

'Aren't you *coy*, Grazia! Still, fun is what he deserves, he hasn't had much of that in a while.'

'How long have you known him?'

'Oh, donkey's. We met at art school, did he tell you?'

I shake my head. 'He appears to have led a thousand lives.'

'Hmm. Well, he wasn't studying – I'm a fossil compared to him, though of course I look young for my age.'

'Of course.'

'No, he was modelling. Well, I understand why he wanted to show off. I mean, his physique itself was nothing special, but young Joel is not one who needs to be shy in the shower, we *both* know that. I took rather a shine to him for . . . obvious reasons.' He winks. 'But despite my best efforts, I couldn't convert him permanently.'

188

I blush. I know Joel was wild, but I did not know he'd experimented. Still, Pierre is almost feminine, so a man might be able to dally without feeling too much need to question his sexuality. 'Was this in Paris?'

He laughs. 'Oh, no. Chelsea. I'm as English as they come, Grazia. Pierre is my little affectation. I'm old school. I was making my name before the likes of your husband made it cool to be British, so I'd never have cut it as plain old Peter.'

'Actually, even my husband changed his name to make himself seem more sophisticated.'

'Yes, that's right, I'd forgotten.' Pierre looks around. 'Nothing of his on the walls, then? I heard you sold a stack of his work off. Which painting paid for this glorious sofa, then?'

I flinch. And then wonder momentarily whether our first meeting at the party really was a coincidence. Surely he did not *target* me to become his friend, like some sort of art-world ambulance chaser?

'It is a little . . . vulgar to think of things in those terms, Pierre. I prefer to think that Leon would have wanted me to enjoy life as much as he did.'

Pierre looks unabashed. 'Just curious. It's my downfall. And I've always had something of a low tolerance for muses. Artistic gold-diggers, most of them. Not you, of course. Now. Tell me, have you met the kids yet?'

I nod.

'Joel *is* serious, then. Be gentle with his heart, please, my Italian temptress. He might seem like a man of the world but he has more tender spots than a newborn baby.'

'He told me about his wife.' Although he did not mention her adultery – only his own weaknesses.

'She was awful. Oh, I know it's bad to speak ill of the dead, but really, in her case, it's justified. A serious lapse of judgement on his behalf. You know all those girls who want to be WAGs? Well, she was like that, except she wasn't pretty enough to compete in the Premier League, so she went for businessmen instead. As soon as she spotted Joel, she was on a mission to score kids with his cute genes, and then a whopping divorce settlement. Job for life, in her eyes, being his ex.'

It feels terrible to hear the woman bad-mouthed, when she cannot defend herself. 'The children seem nice.'

Pierre gives me a quizzical look. 'You reckon? Daisy is a trollop and a half, and Alf has that serial-killer look about him, don't you think?'

'No. Actually, I think he is a confused boy who is still mourning the loss of his mother.' Well, maybe that is not entirely truthful, but, yet again, I feel a strange loyalty to the child.

'Sorry. I can be an awful bitch at times. It's that bloody gay gene. Nothing I can do.'

An awkward silence follows. Pierre's eyes focus on something behind me, and he stands up, sending more crumbs raining down onto my Versace rug.

'Ooh. I like this,' he says. 'Where did you find it?'

I turn to see a large embroidery hoop. I really did not mean to leave *that* one out. I made it when I first returned from Barcelona. It is sewn in two colours – turquoise and *azul* blue – in an attempt at subtlety, but actually it is immediately obvious that each colour represents a naked body. Even now, I blush as I remember the moments it portrays . . .

'I've heard about the movement in embroidered erotica, but I haven't seen any in the flesh before,' Pierre continues.

'There is a movement?'

'Hmm. Yes, of course. Big bucks, too. Probably a fad, it'll be crocheted phalluses next, though imagine the chafing! But I thought you might be a collector. You have a good eye for the quality stuff.'

'I made it.'

I do not know why I say this now. Perhaps to prove that I am more than an 'artistic gold-digger'. But he looks at me, and then my work, with such intense interest that I feel my cheeks blaze hotter. It feels as though he was in the bedroom with us when Joel and I first made love.

'Do you have more?'

'No,' I lie. I have half a dozen in what I suppose is my Barcelona Bedroom Collection. Each in different shades: bronzes and oranges for *that* afternoon, a tiny square of the two of us in the closest I could find to our two skin tones. Oh, and a white-silk-floss-on-black linen, where you can no longer tell where his body ends and mine begins.

'Come on, Grazia. No way is this a one-off. Don't believe a word of it. You *are* a tease.'

'There are others that are not erotic,' I say, realising Pierre is not the type to give up easily. I walk to the inlaid trunk I bought recently, to house my growing stash of fabrics and silks and frames. But as I lean into the trunk, it occurs to me that even if they are not sexual, they are no less intimate. They speak of loss, of loneliness, of bliss, of anticipation . . .

But before I can close the lid he is there, grabbing greedily at the pieces of fabric. He holds up the one that kicked off my habit again, the grey broken hearts from Emily's Craftathon. 'Oooh. OK, the rude one's good, but this is darker. Angry. Bloody hell, Grazia. All that time with Leon must have rubbed off on you.'

Angry? I will give him angry. 'Are you saying I am some kind of copycat? Is it so impossible to imagine that I might have some tiny talent of my own?'

He smiles. 'Ah. Now I see where this anger is coming from,' and he waves the embroidery. 'But, you know, people are bound to think that about muses. Pretty girls with such empty heads that the artist can project what he likes onto them.'

'Is that really what people think?' I say, even though I know it *is* true.

'Well, there's one way of proving you're different.'

'Which is?'

191

'Exhibit, of course.'

I slam shut the lid. 'Please, do not mock me.'

'What makes you think I'm mocking you? I'm serious.'

I try to grab back the pieces he's holding, but he ducks away and heads back towards the sofa. He lays them out on the velvet. 'Freehand, are they?'

'Yes.'

'I can tell. There's a flow about them. A lot of the stuff I've seen in the magazines is more regimented. Twisted tapestries with a few additions. Or those stupid cross-stitched swear words. Novelty items, really. I mean, it's no harder to cross stitch "quim" or "queer" than it is to spell out the alphabet, is it?'

'I really was not aware that anyone else was experimenting.'

'How many have you done? Including the top secret smutty ones.'

I shrug. I am torn between wanting to keep this private, and wanting to prove myself. 'A couple of dozen? Perhaps another ten I am working on. I get bored easily.'

Pierre nods. 'That's definitely enough for the place I have in mind. Friend of mine has a little gallery in Hoxton. Not your usual twattish stuff, but not a stuffy fine-art place, either. He likes textiles, sculpture, anything really, so long as it's good.'

'I am not interested in selling. This is for myself. A little hobby.'

He stares at me. 'I'd like to believe you, Grazia, but I think that's only half-true. You might have started out thinking they weren't for show, but I can see the interest in your eyes now. The idea of being valued for something more than being the merry widow must surely have some appeal?'

I look away.

'And the idea that someone might pay to have your work in their home. I mean, it's evident you don't need the bunce, but, for me, part of the thrill is the approval. Money means people like me. And the more money they offer, the more loved I feel . . .'

'Your tea is going cold.'

Pierre smiles slyly. 'Playing hard to get, eh, Grazia? Well, it's a woman's prerogative. But when you're ready, I can set up a meeting, just like that. And, you know, there's nothing Joel loves more than a woman with a talent.'

'What was Faith's?'

He laughs, then refills his cup with tea. 'I can't be sure, but the word on the street at the wedding was that she learned it while backpacking in the red light district of Bangkok.'

CHAPTER 18

Sandie

OK. Don't panic. If anyone can fit four months' worth of work into four weeks, it's me.

I have over two hundred meetings to organise and chair. Dozens of exclusive products to source and sign up from all over the world. Paint colours and finishes to choose (how can there be so many shades of off-white?). Impossibly high decorators' quotes to knock down. An ad campaign to commission. Staff to sack and hire and brief and retrain. Rumours to quash. Contracts to broker. Prizes to find.

'All looking good for the big day, whenever it turns out to be.' The snap of rubber gloves brings me back to right now. 'You can pop down whenever you like.'

Mr James Waverley, who delivered Toby and countless members of the landed gentry, is nicer than I'd expected, even though I wasn't sure how to take it when he told me I was 'built for babies'. He has an old school gentlemanly quality about him that I find reassuring. He won't shy away from telling me the right way to push. The more I hear about the business of childbirth (and I am trying to avoid hearing too much about it), the more I know that I don't want it to be empowering, any more than I want a trip to the dentist to be empowering.

I just want it to be over with as soon as possible.

'Right, so, from now on I'd like you to pop in weekly, so we can make sure everything's still tickety-boo. You're working in the area, anyway, aren't you, Miss Barrow?'

I nod. 'And that's still all OK with you? My continuing to work.' I don't mention that I feel tired all the time. I'd feel that way even if I weren't pregnant, with this workload.

'Not like you're digging coal, now, is it? So long as you're feeling well, it's fine. But the moment you don't feel like it, then tell that young man of yours to order you a taxi and then enjoy doing nothing for as long as you can. Don't lift a finger!'

The idea of a get-out clause sounds appealing, but laziness isn't my style. 'He's being very attentive.'

'And Mrs Garnett?'

I hesitate.

Mr Waverley smiles. 'Two strong women in one family can be tricky to manage. Toby will have to be quite the juggler to keep everyone happy. Good job I have a habit of delivering fearless infants, isn't it?'

One benefit of my bump is that it's a cab magnet. I get one immediately, and use the 'free time' to switch from Garnett's business, to my own life. First I harangue our builders about delays, which they blame on the suppliers, so then I call the suppliers to harangue them instead. Then I decide to ring the architect and harangue him too, to get the hat trick.

Maybe it's the earth-mother hormones kicking in, but I'll do whatever it takes to make sure we have somewhere our baby can call home. My inner bear is rumbling, and the cabbie looks distinctly intimidated when I pay him and lumber out at Olympia.

I see Emily before she sees me. She's standing on the steps, staring into space, and there's something flimsy about her, somehow. Of course, a hairy mammoth would look flimsy compared to me right now, but it's more than that.

Maybe the theme of the exhibition isn't helping her mood . . .

She spots me at last, and gawps at my belly. 'Bloody hell, I hope they've got your dates wrong, because if you've got another four weeks to go, you'll burst.'

I wince. 'Thanks for that.'

She blushes. 'You look gorgeous, though. Really. You look like a huge, ripe . . . um . . . *bouncy castle.*' She stops. 'Sorry. I am useless at compliments, aren't I?'

'No one's ever called me a bouncy castle before. Fortunately I'm too busy for body image issues at the moment.' I push open the doors, and the security guard checks our tickets and waves us through.

'I hope you're feeling brave, Sandie. The place is absolutely *crawling* with Bridezillas.'

'What on earth is a bride—'

And then I see them. Women in their twenties and thirties, with the same crazed expressions I recognise from the days when the Garnett's sale was The Sale that mattered. These women are clutching honeymoon brochures rather than shopping bags, but they're every bit as dangerous.

'It's a whole other world through here, I warn you.'

Emily and I have come to the Beautiful Brides Fayre as part of my research into why the Lisabet's wedding store is failing and within a few short, scary seconds I am beginning to understand . . .

If Your Perfect Day is Harrods, then the 'fayre' is Primark. I see stall after garish stall, filling the exhibition space to bursting. Already people are approaching us with money-off leaflets and competition flyers. No one looks twice at my belly – maybe it's not unusual to be planning your wedding in advanced pregnancy.

'Were you a Bridezilla, then? When you married Duncan?'

She pulls a face, as though she's smelled something nasty. 'I was so grateful to him that I went along with everything he wanted. If I did it again, then . . .'

And then she bursts into tears.

'Oh, Em, I'm sorry. I didn't mean to upset you.' Even as I try to comfort her, I feel slightly impatient. This is why I've been a rubbish friend lately – I do love Emily to bits, but being with her is like riding an emotional rollercoaster and right now my own stresses are quite enough for me. But I must try harder.

I grab the arm of a passing model, who is wearing a hat that resembles a bird's nest. 'Excuse me, is there anywhere to get a coffee around here?'

She shrugs. 'There's a champagne-tasting tent over in the corner. Or the Cake Walk, maybe? It's by the loos.' And she points to the right.

The toilets, traditional port in a storm for girls in tears, are too packed with hyperventilating brides-to-be. In fact, by the time we get to the Cake Walk, Emily's managed to stop the waterworks, but keeps trying to apologise.

'Don't worry about it,' I say, aware that I sound a bit short. 'You'll be better once you've had a muffin.'

Her pink-rimmed eyes brighten, and we enter the café. Except it's *not* a café.

'Have you ever considered a cheesecake for your special day?' a man asks the two of us as we realise we're still in wedding fair hell.

Emily's bottom lip wobbles again. I wish Will would take the hint and marry her. It would make life so much easier for all of us.

An old sock smell hits me.

'Yes,' he says, noticing my surprise. 'Our cake is made of the finest English cheeses, arranged one on top of the other, for a top-table display your guests will never forget. We can *even* carve miniatures of the bride and groom in Stilton or Parmesan.'

The 'cake' looks handsome enough, with tiers of veiny blue, dairy yellow and pure goaty white, but it'd be about as welcome as a stinky old tramp by the time you got to the first dance . . .

'Thanks,' I say, as I bustle Emily along to the next stalls. 'So, what's up, then, Em? I thought everything was going better at the store.'

'It is,' she agrees. 'But Will is leaving me.'

'Leaving you? When the hell did this happen? Why didn't you ring me?'

'I *did* ring you. Eight times. Anyway, I don't mean leaving me for good, but he's definitely leaving me in the lurch. He's going to study for a green degree which means going on not one but two summer schools, and guess who is meant to run everything while he's hanging out in the student bar?'

'Ah. But being a green expert might be good for the business in the long run, mightn't it?'

'Might be a good excuse to get away from me, more like.'

'Ladies? There's only one thing sweeter than a happy marriage, isn't there?'

An appetising scent of a cocoa wafts our way from a rather wonderful flower-shaped creation in deepest, darkest mocha. The chocolatier sees Emily's tear-stained face, and gives us two free truffles, 'perfect for your wedding favours. We can make any flavour you like. Salted caramel is the big sensation this summer.'

'It'd be salty tear flavour, in my case,' whispers Emily, and she gives me a smile. 'He'd more or less decided without asking me. We're meant to be a team. Or we were.'

Next, there's a self-styled 'wobble artist' trying sell his 'jelly' cakes, which feature happy couples buried under aquamarine gelatine, like deep-sea divers. And a vanilla-scented baker who offers 'make it, ice it, love it' courses so the bride and her hens can prepare the cake from scratch. I take cards, because I wouldn't mind stocking some of this stuff in Garnett's, but I still don't know where Your Perfect Day is going wrong. Sometimes I wonder if I am being pulled in one too many directions.

'Are you listening to me, Sandie?'

I look up at Emily. 'Sorry, yes. Um. Is it possible that you're overreacting a bit?'

She glares at me. 'Eh?'

'How many weeks are we talking? That he'll be away.'

'Three.' She doesn't look at me now.

'It'll go like that,' I say, clicking my fingers. 'Maybe it's just something he's got to get out of his system.'

'While I hold the fort?'

'Are you sure that's not the part that's really worrying you? That you might not cope?'

She gives me the hardest stare yet. 'Ha! That's where you're wrong. I've decided to act as though I'm on my own *all* the time. If I'm going to survive and make a future for me and for Freddie, then maybe that's got to be without any bloke on the scene.'

Her answer shocks me, 'Right. Good. But . . . I mean, it's great to be independent but be careful, eh, Em? You might end up alienating him if you overdo it. Squeezing him out. I've been reading all about that in the one baby magazine I bought, that unless men feel involved in a pregnancy, or anything really, they end up withdrawing from the relationship.'

Emily's eyes narrow and I think she's about to cry again. But then she turns on me. 'Oh, well, thanks for your bloody wisdom, Sandie. So according to you, it was *my* fault that Duncan decided to bonk Heidi the Swiss roll when I was pregnant?'

My jaw drops. I'd forgotten that Duncan had started an affair before Freddie was born. Though maybe he *did* feel left out – I know how wrapped up Em gets in her dreams. 'Sorry. Of course, it's completely different. Duncan was a git. There's no excuse for what he did.'

'But I'm making the same mistake again, am I?'

The baking lady is listening in, so I try to usher Emily out of the Cake Walk. The grand finale is the Bake-off Battle, with two breathtaking cake extravaganzas on matching pedestals. On the left is a traditional white edifice that makes me think of Garnett's: a dozen tiers and a hundred hand-iced pillars. And on the right, the young pretender, a *cascade* of cupcakes, top-loaded with buttercream in every shade imaginable: not just every colour of the rainbow, but also bronze, silver and gold.

'Bloody hell, Sandie, stop gawping at the cakes and at least pretend you give a shit about our friendship, will you?'

'I . . . Sorry, Em. Of course I care. I'm so tired.'

'Of me?' She waits for an answer but before I can think of one, she storms off.

'Wait, Em, wait.'

She tries to push through the crowd, but the place is too packed for a quick getaway. I catch up with her by the Spa and Surgery Bridal Boot Camp stand.

'What?' she says, and her face is full of righteous indignation.

'I know I should have been there for you more than I have, but it's tough going at the moment for me. The house, the store, Toby's mum. I've not had much time for anything else.'

'Poor you, Sandie,' she says flatly. 'Poor you, with your little store project that won't make any difference either way because Toby is so loaded. Poor you with him proposing to you every five minutes, and with the lovely house that you're making even lovelier. Oh, and poor, *poor* you, having friends who have the nerve to want you to return their calls. Well, don't worry. I won't be bothering you any more!'

And she elbows her way back into the crowd before I can respond. Which is a good thing, as I don't know what the hell I'd say. Is she right? Am I too selfish? Or is she too needy?

I know one thing for sure. I'm not about to try to force

myself through thousands of brides-to-be to take even more abuse.

I head for a quieter corner, the tiny Top Gear for Grooms section. Apart from two bored-looking young lads manning the waistcoat and the kilt stand, I am the only person here. Men and weddings are not a match made in heaven.

Though Toby is the exception. He can't wait to don a morning suit and make an honest woman of me.

Maybe Emily is right, and I'm the problem. Anyone else would jump at the chance to become Mrs Garnett. I should be listening to Emily's woes without running out of patience, and I should be knitting bootees and eating cupcakes instead of trying to save a department store single-handed.

Perhaps I'm not cut out for being a mum, either, despite Mr Waverley saying I'm built for childbirth. Emily might be needy, but she's the best friend I've ever had, and I've hurt her. It doesn't bode well for me being able to care for a helpless baby, does it?

I touch my stomach. 'Sorry, Bump,' I say, in my head. 'I'm going to try my best but you have to accept that my best might not be up to much.'

And then I feel the strangest thing. Dampness. I look down at my body and see two small circles of liquid leaking through my blouse.

Breast milk? Before the baby's even born? That's . . . freaky. I put my jacket back on, to hide it. Is this my body trying to tell me it's a bit late to be worrying? That I've already lost control. All I can do now is hope that Mother Nature comes up trumps and miraculously gives me the tools I need, as well as the anatomy.

Father's Day

♥

CHAPTER 19

Emily

Dads have it *so* easy.

All it takes is a kick-around with sons or, even better, a jig-around with daughters, for women to adore you for ever.

'Will dads intending to take part in the tug-of-war, please line up by the goalposts. And a reminder that the Emergency Carpentry for New Men class is about to begin in the pub.'

OK, it's possible that I'm a bit jaded right now, what with Will about to do a bunk to wildest Wales, and Duncan getting chippy on the phone with me this morning because his Father's Day card from Freddie hadn't arrived yet.

Which, of course, has nothing to do with the fact that I only posted it yesterday. Which, in turn, has nothing to do with the fact that my ex returned my son to me last weekend *minus* the gorgeous floppy waves of blondish hair he's had since babyhood.

'He'll be four this month, it's about time he looked tougher,' said the oh-so-tough Duncan, who refused to get out of the car because he was frightened of what I might do to him.

I ran my hand over Freddie's buzz-cut hair do. It felt like a clothes brush. 'Tougher? We're not living in the Bronx.'

'You'll see. He needs to be ready for school. We can't have

him looking like a baby in the playground. Unless you *want* him to get bullied?'

Playground? The word fills me with raw terror, even though I loved school. Well, not lessons, but gossiping and hopscotch and kiss-chase.

But Freddie's too young, surely. The idea of sending him into a playground is like sending a duckling into a boxing ring . . .

'I'm told that you're Emily?'

I feel a tap on the shoulder, and turn round to see a giant. 'Oh. Yes. And you must be . . .'

'Mickey. Mickey Burke. Sorry about the hour. Help didn't show this morning so I had to load all the bales myself. They're heavier than they look.' He waves towards his truck, but I can't get any further than looking at his hands.

Men's hands. Easily twice as big as mine, brown from working outdoors, but with clean, strong nails. No wonder he's known as Giant Haystacks in green building circles.

'Yes. I bet they are.'

My eyes travel up his arms – thick as my thighs, and that's saying something – and covered in fine, straw-coloured hairs. Then a checked shirt that looks suspiciously ironed, so he must be married.

Why did I even think that?

And back to his face, which I'd originally looked away from because I couldn't quite believe it. Mickey is the most organic-looking man I've ever seen, and that's a compliment. Apart from his clothes, he seems to be the same light gold colour all over, from his fringe to the gloriously muscular calves that emerge beneath his cotton shorts. He looks like he's been sculpted from sandstone over thousands of years.

Though, actually, he's probably only thirty-five.

Mickey smiles. 'I'll get started, then, shall I?'

And as he strides off towards the space we've allocated for his demo of straw-bale house-building, he looks back, for a millisecond, and smiles again. A lazy, confident, summertime smile that makes me think of cider-fuelled parties as a teenager back home.

Will's crossing the common, looking vaguely harassed. 'He made it, then?' he says, nodding towards Mickey. 'I'd been warned he wasn't the most reliable.'

I tear my eyes away from Mickey and back towards Will. When did he get so pale? All that time in the shop isn't good for him, and his forehead is creased in a permanent frown.

'Perhaps he makes up for it in other ways,' I say. 'Golly, summer's arrived at last, hasn't it? I think I need to go and get myself a fresh lemonade to cool down.'

The Upper Findlebury fathers are out in force, in their French linen shirts and Masai barefoot trainers. I suppose it must be a sign that the word is spreading about our crafts workshops. As well as the straw-bale building, we have a Whittling Workshop, the mystifyingly under-subscribed Men-broidery, Bush Craft Basics and – most popular of all – a King of the Barbecue Course.

Will was quite sceptical about anyone signing up for the barbecue one, on the grounds that most blokes already think they've mastered the grill. He forgot that it's the women who've been signing up their menfolk for the workshops as they're also the ones who've suffered endless weekends trying to chew through their husbands' scorched sausages without breaking a tooth.

And there's no hardship in watching your husband being tutored by Jeff, the handsome Aussie chef who is taking the boys to new heights of barbie magic, from lime-marinated salmon, to chocolate brownie bananas . . .

Another triumph for Heartsease Handmade.

'Who's the hunk?' asks Wendy, who is in charge of the fresh lemonade stall.

'Oh, that's Jeff from Melbourne.'

'Not *him*,' she says, and then points towards the straw-bale demo. '*Him.*'

Seems I'm not the only one who has talent-spotted Mickey. 'His name's Michael. He's the sustainable-building specialist from Oxfordshire. Must admit, I was expecting more of a hippie type, because he said he'd have to leave on time so he could get organised for the Solstice.'

'He could get me naked at Stonehenge any day,' she says, licking her lips, and putting an image into my head I know I'm going to struggle to wipe out for days on end.

I take my lemonade – fabulously sweet and sour, like my mum always made for Wimbledon – and wander away. Despite the success of today, something's missing. Well, some people: Sandie's at work, as usual, and even Grazia is hanging out with her new family. Who'd have thought it – Grazia doing a Maria von Trapp to two motherless children? Though I suspect she'll be teaching them more useful skills than doh, re, mi and how to make clothes from floral curtains . . .

I decide to cheer myself up by going to look for Freddie, who has been transfixed by the Small-Holdings for a Big Difference enclosure, complete with ducklings, bantam hens and a very smelly nanny goat. But on the way over, I pause by Mickey's demo. There's quite a crowd building up there now, and it doesn't only consist of moony mums. The dads are out in force, too, watching closely as Mickey builds a surprisingly solid-looking wall from his straw bales.

Aside from his very obvious physical appeal, there's something satisfying about the process itself. Something . . . earthy.

Mickey is sweating as he hauls the last bale into place. I've never found that horny-handed man-of-toil look attractive before – I mean, really, deodorant was invented for a reason. Yet I can't help thinking that Mickey would smell rather good close up. Of sunny afternoons making hay.

He looks up and winks at the woman behind me: a slow, lazy wink. But when I look behind me, no one's there . . .

When I finally find Freddie – oh, that short hair still gives me such a horrible shock – he's posing for a picture for Will, and I join my son next to the goat, who looks like she's about to make a break for freedom.

'We should make a few of these courses a regular thing,' Will says. 'The carpentry is massive, and so is the bloke with the bales. Weekend workshops, for the commuter who wants to get macho on his days off. The wives would love it too.'

I'm about to remind him about Mickey's reputation as the least reliable man in the conservation business, but then I decide against it. If I'm going to be holding the fort over the summer, surely the very least I deserve is to enjoy the scenery . . .

CHAPTER 20

Grazia

After my secret shopper bonding success with Daisy, Alf is next on my radar. I plan to win him over by trusting him with an assignment of his own.

'Kit's not bad,' he says grudgingly as I show him the controls on the secret camera that is stitched into the straps of his rucksack. 'Could do with a few more megapixels.'

'It is capturing the conversation that matters the most,' I say. 'Now, I know it will be difficult for you to play dumb in the store, as you probably know more about the games than the assistants, but you must see it as acting a role.'

He accepts the compliment with a shrug. 'No worries.'

We drive with him into the town centre, and drop him off outside a branch of a national chain of gaming stores, then park up and go to the supermarket. In London, I have my groceries delivered on a weekly basis by Harrods, though I eat out so much that the order has been scaled down to fit into a shoe box.

With teenagers, I learn, it is a little different.

The store is quiet because it is Father's Day. Joel pretended not to expect anything from the children, but I still saw a resigned disappointment when he came down for breakfast and saw no freshly made coffee, no cooked breakfast, no card.

In fact, neither Alf nor Daisy emerged from their rooms before midday, and neither seemed to have remembered there was anything different about the day.

'It's just a commercial thing, anyway,' says Joel, as we push our trolley past the end-of-aisle offers for gift sets of 'Dad's Favourite Beer' and Pub Game Compendiums. 'What did dads do to deserve a day of their own, anyway?'

'What was your father like?'

Joel shrugs, and the gesture is so much like Alf's that I would laugh if I did not sense that I may have touched a nerve. 'Below average. Like father, like son.' And he turns the trolley sharply into the snack aisle, to throw in the half-dozen multipacks that make up Alf's weekend diet.

'Has he knowingly eaten a vegetable in the last two years?' I ask.

'I tried buying beetroot and parsnip crisps once, to see if I could sneak in at least one of his five a day that way,' Joel says. 'I thought it's so dark in his bedroom that he wouldn't notice the difference. I found them a few weeks later, soggy and untouched. Anyway, they feed him properly at school so I'm not too worried about malnutrition yet.'

'But would it not be better to try to be stricter? Friends tell me that children may pretend to hate strictness and discipline, but deep down they see it as evidence that you care.' I am lying about the friends: in fact, I read this in a women's magazine I had picked up specifically for the headline: Tame Your Terrible Teen. I cut the article out, though it did occur to me as I scanned it that none of the taming techniques would have diminished my own terribleness at that age.

Joel simply gives me the look, and doubles back to the produce section, to stock up on Daisy's ever-changing food demands. Today she wants sweet potatoes, on the grounds that yams might possibly contain a hormone to increase breast growth, and celery juice, which is supposed to detox away the cellulite she does not even have before her party next month.

It would all be worrying, if it were not for the fact that I know she intends to consume the yams and celery in addition to, rather than in place of, her usual favourites.

So in go a huge ready-made pizza, a pack of pasta, crumpets, bread rolls, oven chips, fizzy drinks (diet for Daisy, full-fat for Alf), and a good Rioja to see Joel and me through the rest of Sunday. The bill for just one day and one night's family life is over forty pounds.

Even though I know none of it will be eaten tonight . . .

Alf texts to say he is having so much fun on assignment that we have no need to hurry back. Good boy.

We load the car up, then amble through the pedestrian precinct towards the games store. Joel insists on taking my hand, something he is not permitted to do when the kids can see us.

'You know all about my parents, Joel, so is it not time to spill the beans on your own?'

'Actually, I didn't know them very well.'

'No?' I wait for a drama to match the rest of Joel's high-octane life: a prison sentence, a vendetta against his family, an appalling accident.

'Oh, don't look all sympathetic. It's nothing remotely tragic, unless you count a typical sixties middle-class upbringing as tragic. My dad worked too hard as an accountant and keeled over a year after retirement, leaving me none the wiser about what made him tick. And my mother seemed to feel that having children was something she'd been conned into and so she wanted nothing more to do with us once we got to school. A very average childhood.'

Behind his defensiveness, I see a lost boy. No wonder he has no clue about how to treat Daisy and Alf.

'Just because it was average, it does not mean you cannot be sad, Joel.'

He looks at me sharply, then kisses me, full on the lips.

'And just because I adore you does not mean you can turn me into a project.'

That is what *you* think, Joel Ferguson.

After my impertinent questions, Joel is stressed and irritable. Exactly as I intended. It is easy enough to persuade him into the pub for an 'impromptu' drink before we collect Alf.

The look on Joel's face as he realises his kids are waiting at the corner table is far more valuable than the bottle of champagne that Alf and Daisy clubbed together to buy: I insisted they put in their own pocket money, but they've gone further, and bought a card and a naked blow-up doll for him too. I suppose it is the thought that counts.

'All right, Daddy? Did you think we'd forgotten?' says Daisy, and I think she's already been at the fizz. Or maybe the flush in her cheeks is because she really is enjoying springing a surprise on her father.

'Bloody hell,' Joel says.

'Need to sit down, Dad? At your age it doesn't do to be on your feet too long, no good for the knees.' And Alf pulls up a chair for his old man and the insults continue for a good ten minutes, but every time I look at Joel his smile gets broader.

CHAPTER 21

Sandie

Babs is speechless when she sees the necklace design that the jeweller has emailed through. Garnets, seed pearls, and two grand's worth of gold. To my surprise, when I met Stoddart to go through the budget, he actually upped what I'd allocated for the prizes.

'Got to make it worth their while, eh?'

Babs's silence doesn't last long.

'Oh, wow, wow, wow! It's going to be so brilliant, Sandie. Like that eighties thing with the bloke and the picture book and the hare thing he buried in a field.'

I don't know what she's talking about, but if the top prize in the Garnett's Treasure Hunt looks even half as wonderful in reality as it does on paper, then we are going to make one of our customers very, *very* happy.

Almost as happy as Babs. My decision to promote her to right-hand woman is one of the best I've made. She's putting in longer hours than I am but despite all the work, she looks ten years younger and has found time to cover the grey in her hair with a perky shade of chestnut. She was really pleased when I asked her to work with me this Sunday, even though it means her almost sitting nose to nose with me in my awful office. On the plus side the extractor fans are off on

Sunday – on the minus, it happens to be the hottest day of the year so far.

Babs, and Luis, and all the other employees who still care are the best reasons I know for trying to save this place.

'Right, so where are we at with the rest of the exclusive products?'

She opens her file. 'From the basement up, OK? Right, in the Food Hall, we have seven chutneys, seven dressings and a range of farmyard cheeses confirmed as London exclusives from your friend's store at Heartsease Common.'

My friend. I wonder how it's going today with Emily's Dad's Day event? I wasn't sure if I should turn up, but since that row at the wedding fayre, I don't even know if we are still friends. 'Good.'

'And I'm getting *very* positive noises from the Superstar Who May Not Be Named about her gluten-free cupcake launch. It seems pretty likely that it'll be in September and we could be the only outlet outside Beverly Hills.'

Let's hope they don't make the trip from Beverly Hills to visit the store and discover the truth behind our glossy pitch, I think, or the range will end up in Selfridges.

'That could be terrific. Make that a priority.'

Babs grins. 'Along with the other forty-five priorities?'

'Touché. But you can do it.'

She glows. All that time hidden away in bridal like Miss Havisham, and she just needed the odd word of thanks to fire her up. Bloody Edgar has a lot to answer for.

'Good. Right, well, the French kitchenware in the exclusive Garnett's red enamel has been confirmed and the foodie press are definitely running a few spots. Moving up, we've got Aguasalisnectarin from New York, it's already massive out there. First results say it makes the nearest competitor look like Vaseline when it comes to wrinkle reduction. Then we've got those Tuc-Tin bodyshapers from Japan, the ones with the green tea for inch loss. I've tried a sample and it's like wearing a lightly fragranced sausage skin, but I did lose a dress size while I had it on.'

'Do you think it'd work for me?'

She gives me a nervous look. 'Is it really awful? Being preg-gers?'

'Um . . .' I don't know how to answer her. I'm still not sure whether Babs sees me as a traitor for finding a man, or whether it gives her hope that it could happen to her too. 'Not awful, no. Just . . . strange, I guess. Have you ever wanted kids, Babs?'

'That's like asking me whether I've wanted to represent England at basketball.' Babs is five foot nothing. 'I don't think I've got what it takes to qualify.'

'Ah.' I can't tell whether she wants me to pry further.

'Then for the fashion floor we have the capsule and cruise-wear collections from . . .'

Evidently not. As she runs through her plans to source the animatronic polar bear – bound to be the Christmas must-have toy, apparently – it occurs to me how close I came to *being* Babs. Not that it would have made me sad. It's just another route, isn't it? There are a million different ways to be content, and Garnett's can be more stimulating company than an awful lot of men.

'. . . and then the Window Box Oasis is a firm yes, they're already planting the seedlings for us. I might even buy one myself.'

'Phew. Babs, you're amazing. No one else could have done what you've done there.' I suddenly realise we've been sitting in my office for over three hours. 'But I am losing all feeling in my left side, so I think we've earned ourselves a stroll.'

All the action today is on the second floor, where Captain Toby is surrounded by the inaugural members of the Garnett's Gang, our new initiative for kids.

It was Toby's idea. After his triumph as a Santa stand-in at

Christmas, he knew that where the kids lead, the parents follow. So we're trying it out, offering beer and sandwiches for the fathers in the Jewel Café (which already has a new extractor fan and no longer leaves customers smelling like a chip pan), while the pirates conduct a treasure hunt.

Seeing him now, being tied up by half a dozen children armed with plastic cutlasses, makes me realise how mad I was ever to doubt Toby's potential as a dad. He's shrieking with faked fear – at least I think it's faked – and the pirates are loving it.

He sees us and winks. 'OK, kids, I *will* walk the plank. In twenty minutes. Meanwhile let's all head for the galley where you can spend your pieces of eight on whatever you like.'

There's a general whoop, as he fights his way out of his shackles, and we follow the pirates up to the café. Luckily the only people in there seem to be their parents, who barely register it when the children race in and begin an ear-splitting game of pirate rounders.

Note for the relaunch: designate a *separate* area of the kids' floor for refreshments . . .

Babs and I get our food, while Toby slips unnoticed onto the terrace, which is a work-in-progress: a great view of the West End, but no barriers yet to stop us falling down on to Oxford Street below.

'You're very charming. With the little ones, I mean,' says Babs, who never quite knows what to say to Toby.

'I need the practice.'

We sit on concrete slabs and eat our old-school sandwiches – cheese and pickle or ham on white bread. Eventually, Babs wipes her mouth, coughs and stands up. 'Better get back to work.'

'No!' I say. 'You've done enough today. Please go home. Relax.'

She smiles. 'This feels like home to me.' She waves

awkwardly at Toby, and then picks her way carefully through the building works towards the door.

'Funny old stick, isn't she?' says Toby once she's gone.

'Don't! You only say that because she doesn't flirt with you. And I couldn't do all this without her.'

He nods. 'Whereas . . . I've been thinking, Brains. About the future. You could easily do all this without *me*.'

I stare at him. 'Don't be silly.'

'No. Listen. I know I'm decorative and I'm quite good at getting people to parties, and I'll be some use on launch day, but aside from that, well . . . what I'm trying to say is, how would you feel about *me* holding the baby while you stay at Garnett's after the relaunch?'

'You . . . you'd do that for me?'

'Not only for you, Sandie. For me, too. And for the baby. I rather like little people, I'm discovering. I've always been called a playboy, but I think perhaps I'm just a boy who likes playing.'

'What would your posh mates say?'

'Oh, they'll rip the piss out of me for a while. But I'll give as good as I get. After all, what are they doing with their lives? Playing tennis and playing at business. Whereas I could be raising the next generation of Garnetts. Speaking of which, what about a nice autumn wedding . . .'

'One thing at a time, Toby. We were talking about the baby, weren't we? You know that it's bloody hard work when they're tiny. Nappies and feeding and the rest.'

'Give me *some* credit, Brains. Yes. Obviously for the first few months there won't be much intellectual conversation. But after ten years at a boys' boarding school, I can assure you there isn't a noxious smell I haven't encountered and survived.'

'I guess not.'

'Absolutely. And we won't need a nanny, either, because I will do it all!'

'You're serious, aren't you?'

He says nothing, but puts one arm around my shoulders, and rests the other on my belly.

'Happy Father's Day, Toby,' I say, kissing him on the cheek.

July

CHAPTER 22

Emily

God knows, dignity doesn't come easy to me, but I am trying my best.

'I'll call you every night,' Will promises. 'You'll hear so much from me that you'll be sick of the sound of my voice.'

'If you have time between lectures.'

'I'll make time.'

Upper Findlebury station is deserted. Even the laziest commuters headed for London hours ago. I can't help but remember the last time we stood on a train platform: the morning after our first night together, when it took my angry husband to prise us apart.

Right now you'd never guess we were a couple. We stand at arm's length, while Freddie tears up and down the platform, because even he senses the awkwardness between us and wants to stay as far away as possible.

'I hope it's on time, or I'll miss every one of my four connections.'

I want to beg him not to go, but I keep myself together. Just. 'That would be a nightmare. You'd probably end up getting to Wales just in time to start the journey back,' I say, and we both pretend to laugh, even though it really isn't funny.

By the time we see the train in the distance, I'm exhausted from the effort. We do, finally, exchange a kiss before he gets on board, but Will looks almost relieved as the train leaves the station.

'Mummy, is it blue whales they have in Wales? Or grey ones?'

I can't summon up the energy to explain. 'Both, I think. Shall we drive past your new school on the way back?'

'Um. Hokay,' he says, sounding uncertain. The concept of school is something that Freddie changes his mind about roughly ten times a day. Sometimes it is, *obviously the world's most excellent thing ever*. And sometimes it is *quite proper scary*.

As for me, I am *terrified*. A whole village full of school-gate mums, ready to judge my imperfections even more harshly than I judge them myself. It doesn't seem more than a few months since Freddie was a tiny baby and all that mattered was keeping him fed, and out of danger, and remembering to put socks on my own feet before I left the house.

And now I've got this whole beauty parade to deal with. The Findlebury mummies are the same types who come to my craft workshops. It's not simply about being immaculately groomed: it's also about being impeccably green, and fiercely ambitious for your kids. Apparently there's a waiting list for Mother and Baby Cantonese.

I'm not about to meet new friends, either. Not that I want to. The row with Sandie has made me wary of getting close to anyone again.

'Look, Mummy, it's playtime. Can we look?'

I park the Snowvan out of sight. Maybe we'll have to *walk* the three miles every day to keep *that* particular guilty eco-secret. But how will I do that *and* open up the store and the craft centre in the mornings without help?

Shit. I'm already planning for a future as a single mother. And even though I survived before, when Freddie was tiny, it was different then. I was in that post-birth fog, too preoccupied with survival to expect anything much from life. Whereas now I am used to our little team of three against the world . . .

'Come on, Mummy, don't dilly dally!'

The two of us tiptoe towards Upper Findlebury Primary School, with its architect-designed 'poppy' railings, and its pioneering 'bully off' friendship zone in the playground. Even Freddie seems to sense that we might be imposters.

We find a vantage point at the edge of the railings: the poppy seed-pods are cast in chrome, and stretch three metres into the air. I know it's for security, but they remind me of prison bars.

'They're big, aren't they, Mummy?'

'The railings?'

He shakes his head at my stupidity. 'The children. They're all at least *eight.*'

Since his fourth birthday last week, Freddie is no longer in awe of five-year-olds, and eight is his current definition of *properly grown up.* Obviously adults are grown up, too, but in a crusty, past-it way, whereas he is completely convinced that eight-year-olds have the world at their feet. But that doesn't mean he wants to share the playground with such super-human creatures.

I look for smaller children, but all I can see are organically fed, unnaturally tall and leggy kids, their shiny hair glowing in the sunshine, the girls dancing and skipping, the boys kicking around footballs in the spirit of healthy, but not aggressive, competition.

'The infants must have a separate break time,' I say, dismissing a sudden vision of a factory on the outskirts of Upper Findlebury, churning out high-achievers.

Freddie looks at me. 'Can we go home now, Mummy?'

I don't think he's relishing the prospect of school any more than I am.

*

Staying busy helps a bit over the next couple of days.

The rest of Friday is the usual juggling act of selling weekend supplies to the right-on brigade, getting the workshop area ready for Saturday's workshops, and trying to control my temper. It must be a full moon, because the mad questions I'm asked make me wonder whether going green means people end up with a severe Common Sense Deficiency. If organic food makes you that thick, then maybe pesticides are good for the brain.

The only high point in the whole day comes when I get a call from old brown eyes, aka Mickey the Straw Bale hunk. 'I promise I haven't been ignoring your messages. It's proving to be a very busy summer so far.' Now that I can't see him, I notice his accent: a soft burr that reminds me of home, but somehow sounds so much sexier than any of the yokels I grew up with. I think it must be because he *knows* he's in demand.

And not just for his straw-bale buildings . . .

'Anyway, Emily, the good news is I've had a cancellation and I can sneak you in a workshop in a fortnight, if you're interested. I know it's short notice, but otherwise I can't see it happening before next year.'

I check the date against the calendar, but I already know it's while Will's still away, and I feel the briefest of frissons. I would *never* act on them, of course, not after what Duncan did to me, but there are worse things to look forward to than an afternoon of watching Mickey with his shirt off.

'It's a date.'

With Will away, Freddie is super-needy, refusing to leave my side, even as I tear from the store to Handmade and back again four million times. By bedtime, I'm feeling pretty needy myself. Usually I'd call Sandie, or Grazia, but under the circumstances, neither would want to hear from me. Instead I let Freddie sleep in my bed, which means I'm woken every ten minutes or so by a foot or elbow. For a small boy, he needs an awful lot of space.

Oh, and I ignore my mobile when Will calls, and then spend the wee small hours regretting how childish I am. I guess I'm testing myself, to see if I can cope alone.

Can I?

Saturday is even busier. Three hen night parties, back to back, with full-on hysteria. At least they keep an eye on Freddie, in between necking cava and fiddling with feathers for their wedding day fascinators. As I top up their glasses and hand out cupcakes, I long to sit down, join in the gossip. But there's no time.

Finally, when I am about to drop, I call Will at ten to eleven, resolving to be nice as pie to make up for last night. And within seconds I am sniping like a fishwife.

'You woke me up,' he says.

'I didn't realise Wales had a different time zone. Some of us haven't even finished work yet.'

'I'm not on holiday, Em. I haven't stopped all day.'

He might as well be in Timbuktu, I feel so lonely.

And now it's Sunday and Freddie is working on his own fascinator, having charmed wedding invitations out of two of yesterday's brides. I should be balancing the books, but as 'balancing the books' is possibly the least enticing thing ever to appear on my to-do list, I am getting nowhere. I've been trying to read the same column of figures for the last half-hour now, and never got more than a third of the way down the page.

Sandie would be able to do it in seconds. But then I'm not exactly in a position to ask her right now.

'Did you have a fascinator at *your* wedding, Mummy?'

I put down the paperwork. 'Well, brides don't usually have head-dresses. I did have a pretty tiara, though, with crystals all over it.'

'Can I see?'

'Sorry, Fredster, you'll have to ask Granny to get it from the loft next time you stay there.'

'When?'

'Um . . .' I've been avoiding my folks, like I always do when things are going tits up. They're the best parents in the world, but I hate to disappoint them, especially when my big sister Jane is so damned *perfect*, with her kinkless life and kinkless hair.

'Soon.'

'OK,' he says, then after a bit, 'Mummy, what's your favourite colour?'

'Um. Pink?'

'Good. I will make you a pink fascinatingator for when you and Will have your wedding, OK? And I will make a blue one for him, and a purple little one for me.'

'Er . . .' I don't know where to begin. 'What makes you think we'll get married, Freddie?'

'Well, Tyra's mummy has had three weddings, and Abigail went to one of them and said it was completely wicked, because everyone is your friend and you get to wear the best clothes and people give you presents as well. Like sandwich toasters. Abigail has a sandwich toaster and it is the best thing ever.'

'We could buy a sandwich toaster, it's cheaper than a wedding.'

'Mummy!' He holds up a finger. 'Obviously a wedding is not only about the presents. It is about love as well. That you are together as soul makes for ever and ever.'

'Like Tyra's mum?'

He looks puzzled. 'I don't know. What is a soul make, Mummy? Veronique said it yesterday.'

Veronique was one of the crafting brides to be. I shouldn't have left him with her, putting dangerous ideas in his head. 'A soul*mate* . . . is when you think that there's only one person in the whole wide world that you can love.'

'Oh. Is that true?'

'Come here.' He climbs onto my lap, not *quite* too grown up to do that. Will he stop once he starts school? 'The good thing about love, sweetheart, is that it's something that grows and grows so you can love lots and lots of people.'

'Grows like a tree?'

'More like . . .' I remember a song my mum used to sing to me. 'Granny says that love is something if you give it away, you end up having more.' I hum the tune, from way back when I still thought I'd marry a frog prince and live in a castle.

Way back when? Who am I kidding? I believed in fairy tales right up until I moved to London. Well, I still do. No wonder I irritate the hell out of Will and Sandie and everyone else . . .

'You're *my* soulmate, Mummy.'

I kiss him on the forehead, his skin so sweet and soft that it almost feels that it would be enough to be me and Freddie against the world. But that's too much of a burden to lay onto any kid, to make them responsible for your own happiness.

'Oh, you're going to break more hearts than mine in your time, my little Londoner.'

'*Mummy!*' he says, shaking his head at my silliness. So I tickle him and he giggles and it sounds like little bells and I know I'll sleep better tonight.

Mondays are quieter, so I'm surprised when Jean turns up to help me out.

'Thought I'd keep you company, while William's away!' she announces, putting her bag of knitting down on the counter with a woolly thud. Ever since she's started running her own Knitting Wisdom Workshops (with the emphasis on wisdom, aka poking her nose in where it's not wanted), she's become more and more full of herself. Well, today, I'm not in the mood for her advice.

'Good. It'll give me a chance to do a clean-up next door. Help yourself to tea.'

It stinks of Pringles and stale wine in Handmade, so I open up all the windows. The industrial Hoover roars into life, and I wave the nozzle about in the air, hoping it might guzzle the feathers and dust that are dancing in the sunlight, and then I spot an enormous tangled ball of wool and thread and paper cuttings and aim at it. Sure enough, it sucks in the ball with a satisfying gulp.

And then it gives a phlegmy, forty-fags-a-day cough, and stops sucking. The wheezing is horrible.

'Shit.'

I pull the plug and crouch down, trying to unscrew the hose so that I can remove the offending ball. But I can't unjam it because it's so tightly wedged, so I grab the nearest pair of craft scissors, the ones with the tiny tips as sharp as sharks' teeth, and try to force them into the gap.

One more push, almost there . . .

The Hoover gives a big sigh, as though it has cleared the blockage. And then coughs up three days' worth of dust and dirt and cupcake crumbs all over me.

'Shit, shit, shit.'

I sit there, eyes and mouth closed, trying not to breathe in the muck. I wipe the dust away from my eyes with my sleeve, and when I open them, my eyelashes are clogged. I glance down, and my clothes are white, like an earthquake victim's. The smell is pure old lady's wardrobe.

'Need some help?'

I don't turn around. Just when I thought my day couldn't get any worse. The voice is Abby's.

'Er . . . give me a minute will you?'

I go to brush away the dust, but make more mess.

'Here, let me.' She brandishes a pocket-sized clothes brush. I mean. What kind of woman carries a *clothes brush* around with her? I don't even own a normal-sized clothes brush. I don't think anyone in my whole extended family owns one.

She begins to attack my clothes, staying at bump's length

from me. I accept as gracefully as I can, and when she's finished, there's a black fairy ring of dirt around me on the floor. I step out of it.

'Thanks,' I say, trying to sound grateful. 'I don't know what I'd have done without you.' I do, of course. I'd have kicked the bloody Hoover into next year and then got under the shower without taking my clothes off.

'No trouble. What happened?'

'Cleaning malfunction. Otherwise known as everything I touch turning to shi— I mean, going wrong today. But if you're prepared to take the risk of being near me, then pop next door with me for a cup of tea.'

I go back through the connecting door and Jean's jaw drops when she sees my ghostly appearance.

'You don't mind minding the shop for a bit longer, while I get cleaned up?'

Jean nods. It's only as Abby follows me up the stairs to the flat that I remember the state it's in.

'You'll have to take me as you find me,' I say, 'it was quite a busy weekend and I haven't had the time to clear up.' Or the inclination.

'Oh, no problem, I remember that the living space here was . . . petite even when it was Will on his own, and I bet with a young boy too, it's—' She stops speaking as she steps into the kitchen. Her face drains of colour and she struggles to control her eyes as they take in the mess.

'He's a bit of a whirlwind,' I mumble.

'Golly. It's good to know what to expect.'

'You'll be having help, I guess?'

'Only because it's twins,' she says, defensively. 'I only have two hands.'

'Two hands aren't enough for *one* baby. Sit down, if you can find somewhere to perch.'

Abby eventually settles on the sofa arm. 'If I sit all the way down, I'll need scaffolding to get me back up again.'

I smile. I'd planned to get in touch with her again after the dinner, but the business with the 'home cooked' convenience food made me think again. But maybe she could still become a friend? God knows, I need *someone* to talk to. 'I remember that feeling. Still, not long to go now, eh?'

She shrugs. 'What about you? How are you getting on without Will?'

I frown. 'In what way?' Jean must have been gossiping with Abby in the shop before she came next door. 'Oh, the course. Well, it's harder work while he's off, but that's the thing about being a couple. You have to support each other's dreams.'

'Yes, that's what Will said, that it was amazing how good you've been about it.'

'Well, I don't know about that . . .' And then the penny drops. 'He spoke to you about it? When?'

'When he popped over to lend me the eco manuals,' she says, and seeing my clueless expression, she adds, 'Don't worry, he wasn't trying to help the competition! They were really boring, actually. Great for insomnia, but they've done nothing for my proposal. *Anyway*, it's a bit academic now, isn't it?'

'In what way?'

'Because . . .' she reaches into her magic bag, and I wonder what she's going to bring out now, 'ta-da! I'm through to the pitching sessions!'

She passes over an envelope, ripped open with neat precision. I pull out the letter and scan it: *following the primary judging process . . .* blah, blah, *pleased to inform you that your proposal, Upper Findlebury Females Save the World, is through to the final stage of pitching in person to the EU funding committee in August.*

'When did this arrive?'

'This morning!'

'Oh. Congratulations,' I say, surprised at my own

disappointment. It's not as though I thought my proposal was that good, but I feel upset for poor old Heartsease. Last place, as usual. And with even bloody Will helping the next village along, what hope did we have?

'Surprise!' she says, holding out another envelope. An unopened envelope. When I take it, it's addressed to me . . .

I rip into it and pull out the paper so fast that it tears the page in half.

'I got through?' I have to read the letter a couple of times before I can believe it. 'But how come you've got *my* letter?'

'Relax, Emily. I'm not intercepting your post.' She giggles. 'No, I talked the old lady downstairs into letting me rifle through your mail once she'd wormed out of me why I was here. Did she work for the secret service in World War Two?'

'Wouldn't surprise me.' I look at the letter again. 'Blimey. I only entered because Will made me.' Though is that true, really? I wanted it for myself, as well, and the way I felt disappointed just now must mean some part of me believed I could do it too.

'Ah, the miraculous persuasive powers of Will Powell,' says Abby, with more than a trace of sarcasm in her voice.

'Was he like that with you too, then?' I feel odd, asking, but I want to know what she means.

She gives me an appraising look. 'I was ambitious enough on my own. Plus, of course, I was the *older woman.* I was the one trying to push him. But he won't be pushed, you know, Emily. He's all smiles but he's stubborn as a bloody mule when it comes to what he wants.'

I nod. 'If he knows what that is . . .'

Abby smiles. 'Ah,' she says, and I suddenly feel disloyal. I take the mugs out of the cupboard and pick the least stained one for my guest. 'Anyway, if you're the competition, doesn't that mean I should be putting arsenic in your tea?'

And I wonder whether we're still just talking about the Green Goddess money.

'Well, you could,' she says, 'but I have a feeling we might be better as a team than as enemies.'

CHAPTER 23

Grazia

Daisy is sixteen today.

Sixteen!

The idea of being so young makes me feel dizzy and more than a little nauseous. Like standing on the roof of a skyscraper after one too many cognacs.

'You're definitely not coming back until two?' Daisy asks, as we prepare to leave the house. She is utterly beautiful tonight, despite her best friend Chloe's efforts to make her look like a circus clown. Chloe never eats, and looks less like a supermodel and more like a homeless woman in her fifties. Perhaps that is why she has used hideous shiny foundation that highlights Daisy's slightly oily skin.

Her sabotage is in vain, however. Daisy is . . . luminous.

'Two o'clock, *or* when the neighbours or police call, whichever comes sooner,' Joel says. He is convinced that the place will be trashed by Facebook gatecrashers, and has asked the twenty-year-old black-belt son of one of the neighbours to act as a bouncer in return for fifty pounds. Though given Joel's feelings about the general awfulness of the house, I wonder whether he's secretly hoping to come back to find the place in flames.

He would *never* have allowed Daisy to have a party in the Barcelona apartment.

'I'll make sure nothing bad happens,' Alf pipes up.

I smile, though the boy's new helpfulness alarms me somewhat. It started the weekend before last and at first I thought I had won him over with gifts. I had bought him a tiny wireless video camera, which Sandie tells me is *absolutely* the latest gadget. For Daisy, I'd chosen an exquisite French skincare set that helped the entire teenaged cast of Harry Potter stay spot-free and high-definition-camera ready. She was delighted, but Alf was characteristically surly, as though he was doing *me* a favour by accepting the camera.

However, the next day he actually smiled at me over breakfast, and even offered to make me toast. So dramatic was the change that I asked Joel if he had given the kids more bribes to improve their behaviour, but he denied it outright.

'Planning to grass me up, are you, Fat Alf?' asks Daisy.

'Why? You planning to do something bad?' he snaps right back.

'I'll let you know in advance so you can catch it on your new camera!'

'Your mates would crack the lens,' he says, and stomps off to the kitchen, where the town's most sought-after caterer has prepared an American teen feast of organic burgers, brownies and milkshakes, to mark Daisy's own Independence Day. Personally I suspect the shakes will be spiked within ten minutes of us leaving, and the best we can hope for is that guests make the most of the balmy evening and throw up in the flower beds.

Joel is driving tonight, ready to head back and play Strict Dad at a moment's notice. We're eating at a Japanese restaurant that is absolutely the hottest ticket in a ten-mile radius.

We sip indifferent sake, and try to pretend that this is a normal night out.

'It'll be fine, won't it?' Joel asks.

'Daisy is a sensible girl. I do not doubt there will be tears and a few other bodily fluids featuring tonight, but they will not be hers.'

He winces at the mention of bodily fluids. 'Times like these, I always wonder what Faith would have done.'

'And?'

'I don't know. It seems like such a long time since . . .' He picks up an edamame pod. 'There should be a course for dads. Women are naturals with children, but men. No.'

'I have no maternal instincts.'

'Rubbish. It's only taken you a couple of months to manage what I still haven't managed after sixteen years. Daisy wants to be you, and Alf wants to . . .' He trails off, shrugging. 'Well, let's not go there.'

'Ooh? No. You do not really think he . . . I mean, he is only thirteen.'

'I was a randy bastard by thirteen. Maybe he doesn't *quite* know in detail what he wants to do with you yet, but the urge will be there. Like father, like son.'

'Heavens.'

Somehow, after that revelation, I find it more difficult to concentrate on my sushi.

Later, to kill time, we walk around Mumford's grim town centre, looking for somewhere quiet to drink.

'So much for the new British café culture,' Joel says.

We have three options: Lollipops, a club populated by girls who look younger than Daisy; the Golden Fleece, a pub where the live entertainment involves waiting to see who will thump who first; or Platinum's Nite Spot which, Joel informs me, is popular with 'the older crowd'.

'And that is supposed to make me feel better?'

'Well, it's that, or a two-litre bottle of strong cider in the graveyard. But by now,' he looks at his watch, 'it'll be standing room only. All the tombs will have been taken.'

'Platinum's it is, then.'

The thing I like most about Joel is that anywhere is transformed by his presence, and so it is with this small underground space that reeks of nicotine, years after the smoking ban. The 'older crowd' pays a fat entry fee for nineties dance music and pretty barmen. Joel knows more people than I would expect, given his loathing of the town: the vaguely satanic chairman of the council, and his much-operated-on wife; the local-boy-made-good who plays a detective in a long-running police show; the headmistress of Alf's primary school.

'Poor woman, she was desperate enough to try it on with me at Alf's leaving ceremony. She'd had some Dutch courage beforehand, so her breath smelled of Bailey's and extra strong mints.'

'A winning combination, surely?'

'Oh, she's a sweet, sweet woman. She used to send sandwiches *home* with Alf, in case I wasn't feeding him properly. But she'd been single for so long that the thought of living up to her expectations was so exhausting.'

'Whereas a woman of my age is glad for what she can get?'

He laughs. 'Not at all. But she wanted a father for her children. I didn't fancy messing that up all over again. Whereas I had a feeling that our expectations might be more . . . um, complementary.'

I move closer to him. 'I cannot wait to return to Spain. Joel the father is not nearly as awful as he thinks he is, but I still prefer Joel the lover.'

'Hearing that makes an old dad very happy.'

And he pulls me up from my chair, and then out of the club, and towards the graveyard which, surprisingly, is empty except for us, though the empties suggest it was busy earlier. And he proceeds to kiss me like a lover, not an old dad.

I half-expect bright, alcohol-fuelled flames to light up our journey home, but we drive past the security gates and into the close and there are no outward signs of Party Gone Badly Wrong.

Even when we park the car, the music is barely audible from outside, and though there is a slight aroma of cannabis when we enter the house, nothing seems to be on fire. A few teens are groping in dark corners, but after our tomb-side tryst, we do not feel in any position to judge. Instead, Joel gradually fades up the living room lights, and the kids blink like baby animals, before slinking away.

Daisy is in the garden, talking intensely to the Black Belt Bouncer from next door, while Chloe attempts to get herself noticed by flicking her hair aggressively and blowing cigarette smoke into the boy's eyes. But it makes no difference. Black Belt and Daisy are falling for each other, I can see it, and it makes me warm inside. *Young love.*

Where did the cynical Grazia go?

'Hey, Daisy, what's going on here?' says Joel, and even in the half-light, I see the two of them blush. 'Well done, kiddo. No sign of any lasting damage. Where's your brother? You haven't sacrificed him in some coming-of-age ritual, have you?'

'Upstairs, I think, with his cronies.'

'OK. Well, we're off to bed now, so can you send your guests on their merry way, please?'

We leave the lovers – and Chloe – to it, and head upstairs. The door to Alf's room is ajar, and a loud cackling emerges as we cross the galleried landing.

'I'll go,' says Joel.

'Yes, I think you had better, after what you said about him in the restaurant.'

But I think they have heard us, as Alf appears, followed by two other boys.

'Hey, Dad. Hey, Grazia. Meet Rob and Lucas.'

Rob and Lucas stare at me. Rob blushes to his blond tufty

roots, and Lucas simply keeps gawping, as though he has never seen a woman before.

Oh, Lord, Alf must have *told* them about his sordid little fantasies.

I wave, vaguely, and turn tail. When Joel comes giggling into the bedroom, telling me he's pretty sure the boys were watching porn on the Internet, I decide I rather preferred it when Alf was the surly brat and I was the wicked stepmother.

'Barcelona! Barcelona!'

I waltz around my own apartment, singing like Montserrat Caballé in the shower, even though, actually, we are not going to Barcelona at first, but to Sitges, which Joel tells me is a beach-side idyll, full of the world's most stylish homosexuals. Pierre has rented a place there, and apparently has 'news' on my forthcoming embroidery exhibition. An exhibition I am pretty certain I never actually agreed to.

But before we go to Spain, there is an ordeal to be endured.

'I don't think she's going to be very pleased to see me, Grazia.'

Emily sits on my sofa, picking at her nails. Back in May, when I thought of hosting a baby shower for Sandie, it seemed an inspired idea. And an excuse for oodles of embroidery, of course. I embarked on a project to stitch the most beautiful quilt featuring all the things I hoped her new baby would experience in life: love, beauty, fun, happiness, friendship . . .

Ah, yes. Friendship. Not nearly as simple as it seemed. Because since I organised the shower – ordered the cupcakes and booked a holistic therapist who is, at this very moment, preparing to give us the most blissful massages in London – Sandie and Emily have fallen out spectacularly. I suppose I should be pleased that they both value my friendship enough not to let me down, but I do not think today will be the celebration I had hoped for.

I want to knock their stubborn heads together.

'She might be touched that you have made the effort to come.'

'She thinks I'm silly and pathetic.'

I sigh. I have, at times, felt exactly that about Emily, just as I have thought that Sandie can be dogmatic and humourless, and just as they must have thought I am hard-nosed and spiky.

But surely the key to friendship is accepting your friends' faults as they accept yours. Forgiving, if not forgetting. And realising that we all change over time. I am certainly under-going a metamorphosis myself.

Funny how such wisdom has crept up on me.

'What would you say to Freddie if he fell out with his best friend over a tiny thing?'

'His best friend is a junior thug, so I'd be relieved!' She grins at herself. 'I know I'm being childish. If only she'd even be the tiniest bit, I don't know, *humble* about all the good things in her life, then I'd find it that bit more bearable.'

I know she wants to talk about what is wrong with *her* life, but I cannot summon up the energy. Instead, I go to the kitchen to fetch a bottle of chilled cava, reasoning that a tipsy Emily might be less trouble than a sober, maudlin one. As I pour the first glass, the intercom sounds, and I buzz Sandie in.

'Before you say anything, please don't mention the bump or try to pretend I am blooming in any way,' she says, as I open the door. 'The next person who assures me I am glowing will get a punch in the nose.'

I kiss her on both cheeks. 'I rather like my nose, so I will say nothing. But do try to embrace the party spirit a little more, Sandie.'

At least she has the grace to look embarrassed. 'Sorry, Grazia. I'm a bit stressed.' She steps into the living room and cannot stop herself scowling when she sees Emily. 'Hi,' she says, waving, but then pointedly sitting down on the opposite sofa without the customary hug. 'How's Freddie?'

'Good,' says Emily, equally cool. 'He had a nice birthday, thanks for the card.'

'He's still into penguins, is he?'

'Not sure,' she snaps, then adds, 'to tell you the truth, even I struggle to keep up with his fads.'

I lift up the bottle of cava and am about to uncork it, when I put it down again. 'Is there any point in opening this, if the two of you are going to behave so childishly?'

They look anywhere except at me or at each other, exactly as Joel's two do when he tells them off.

'Any minute now, one of you will stick out your bottom lip and say, *she started it*, am I right?'

Sandie stands up. 'Maybe this was a bad idea.'

'Are you really so stubborn that you're prepared to lose a good friendship over a schoolgirl quarrel? Shall I send the masseur home?'

Sandie sits down again. 'I'm sorry, Grazia. I know you've gone to a lot of trouble and I'm being ignorant.'

'Sorry,' says Emily, though she still refuses to look at Sandie.

I ease the cork out of the bottle, and fill three flutes. 'Fizz first, then presents, then massage. Then, with luck, happier faces all round.' I hand out the glasses. 'To a safe delivery and to the best future for baby Barrow stroke Garnett.'

'To the baby,' says Emily.

We clink, and sip, but the cava does not taste anything like as good as it did in Barcelona. The bubbles are too harsh and the bouquet too musty. I remember the times we secret shoppers have toasted our good fortunes previously – Emily's divorce, Sandie clearing her name, me clearing my debts – and I realise how fake this 'celebration' feels.

'So, when are you planning to give up work?' I ask.

Sandie looks shifty. 'Not sure. My consultant says I can work as long as I am feeling up to it, and there's too much still to do at the store for me to feel right about putting my feet up and watching *Loose Women*.'

'But is that safe for the baby?' says Emily.

'Women in Africa or Asia give birth in the fields while they're working,' Sandie snaps back.

'Not through choice, I'd say. I mean, I know you're not doing anything physical, but it is stressful. Be careful, please. Babies are hardy but . . .' Em shakes her head. 'I don't know. It seems like asking for trouble to me.'

'Thanks for the advice, Emily, but I think my obstetrician, with forty years' experience, knows what's best for me and the baby.'

'Presents!' I say, attempting to sound jolly.

Emily looks uneasy as she reaches into her handbag. 'It's not much . . . I mean, I didn't quite know what . . .' She pulls out a slightly battered gift bag and hands it over. 'I know you're bound to have strong opinions about what the baby has, and how the nursery is decorated, so I thought you could come to the shop after the delivery, and choose something yourself.'

It sounds plausible, but something about the way she says it makes me think that Emily had not even decided she was coming to the shower until the last minute.

'Actually, I don't care how the nursery is decorated so long as it has walls and a ceiling, neither of which is a given right now,' Sandie says.

She tips the gift out onto the curved ledge at the top of her belly – really, she is very big now, not fat, but as solid as a cruise ship – and the paper is already falling off. Usually Emily's gifts are too pretty to unwrap, with bows and flowers and glitter. Perhaps it is simply that Will has cracked down on her unecological habits. Perhaps . . .

'Oh!' says Sandie. She holds up a box of chocolate truffles, and a pot of cheaply packaged face mask. 'Thanks.'

'I thought you could make the most of your remaining child-free life by eating truffles on the sofa . . .'

'. . . with a face mask on?' Sandie finishes for her. 'Right. Thanks.'

More likely, Emily grabbed the first thing that came to hand on her way out of the door. I see that Sandie is trying not to let her hurt feelings show.

'Right, well, some of my gifts are rather more homespun,' I say quickly. I retrieve the packages from underneath the coffee table. 'Though the ones at the top show I was thinking along the same lines as Emily.'

Sandie unties the ribbons at the top of the first box and the silk wrapping falls away. 'Oooh.'

'It is from Paris. The only product *Elle* magazine says actually works on stretch marks. And even if it doesn't, it smells *divine*.' And costs the earth, of course.

Emily drains her cava noisily.

The next parcel is an exquisite collection of limited edition Beatrix Potter children's books, in a hand-carved book box. 'I loved these stories, and so did Toby, despite our different backgrounds,' says Sandie, pulling them out and looking at the illustrations. '*Peter Rabbit. Mrs Tiggywinkle*. I think the baby will have to fight his parents for them. Thank you *so* much, Grazia, they're gorgeous.'

'Better read them before the baby comes, because that's going to be the last thing you have time to read for about ten years,' Emily mutters. Never has my desire to slap her been so strong.

Finally, Sandie rips into the last package. 'This must be the homespun part, as the other gifts are anything but . . . oh, wow!' Sandie holds up the little bedspread.

'I wanted to embroider the life I would want for your baby, Sandie.'

Emily leans over to look. 'You want him or her to have a Louis Vuitton trolley case?'

'That represents travel,' I say. 'And the book is knowledge, and the sun represents happiness, and the moon is about sweet dreams—'

'And the dumb-bells?' asks Emily, her voice sour.

'Just body confidence.' I laugh. 'It is quite difficult to find images that apply equally to boys and girls. I would like to take it back when the baby is here and sew some more. Perhaps you have some other ideas, Emily? What would you give, if you were the fairy godmother?'

'What about a rich daddy?' she says, and then fakes a giggle. 'Oh, no, I forgot. Baby Barrow already has one of those. So that means he or she's not going to need anything else, eh?'

I am about to say enough is enough, but Sandie gets in first.

'That's *it*, Emily. I've tried to be patient and to be nice and to let you off the hook because I know it's hard for you at the moment, but you've overstepped the mark. What's happened to you? When I first met you, you weren't a jealous cow.'

'When I met you two, we were all on the same level. Broke, fed up. There was a bond there. Do you know what I got for *my* baby shower? Nothing. Because I was in London, on my sodding own. Then I found you lot. But now,' she sighs, 'now it's different. It's clear who's been left behind.'

'It's not like that, Emily,' Sandie says.

'Easy for you to say, over on your side of the picket fence, where the grass is so much greener.'

'Yeah, because Grazia and I have always had it so easy, haven't we? Grazia's man moving halfway round the world, me treated like the scullery maid who got herself pregnant on purpose. You need to look at yourself, because if you're not careful you won't only lose us, you'll lose Will too.'

'If you were my real friends, then you'd know that I think I already have!' She stands up. 'I'm off. Leave you to it.' She grabs her coat and stomps to the door. I am about to get up and stop her, but she turns at the last moment. 'I'll be thinking of you on the fourteenth, Sandie. And after that.

But for my sake, eh, leave me alone? All you two do is remind me of what I don't have, and what I never will!'

When she slams the door behind her, I feel no inclination to follow. Sandie and I sit staring at each other, Emily's absence sudden and, I will admit it, painful too. This is not how it should be and, as the person who organised today, I feel I have failed, I have made everything worse.

'Well—' I start.

Sandie leans over, and takes my hand. 'Thank you for this, I cannot imagine a present I'd have loved more.'

'But—'

'But nothing. Don't we have a masseur waiting for us next door?'

'I hate to see you girls like this.'

'Perhaps she's right, Grazia. Perhaps we have all changed. Not in material ways – I don't really care where we live, so long as it's safe – but fundamentally.' She touches her bump. 'Sometimes we can't help it.'

I think of the teens and of Joel, and of how hard I have been fighting *not* to let them change me. Not to allow myself to be vulnerable. Ha! What a vain hope, from a vain woman. Everything changes. 'You seem . . . tougher?'

'Do I?'

'Would you still give free pyjamas to a distressed woman because you thought she needed them?'

She thinks it through. 'I *hope* I would.'

But she does not sound entirely sure.

CHAPTER 24

Sandie

'You lied to me.'

The site manager shakes his head. 'No, we didn't. It's not our fault that the last lot were cowboys.'

We are standing in my 'glorious' living room. There should be dove-grey walls, ornate plaster cornicing, a huge marble fireplace and a six-windowed bay flooding the space with soft autumn light.

Instead, the walls are bare and held up with scaffolding. The ceiling is cracked. There's a London-cab-sized gash where the fireplace should be, and the sash window frames have been removed, with burglar-proof metal panels in their place.

'The last lot were the Victorians who built the place,' I snap back. 'Their work has held up pretty well for the last century, yet when I opened the door to the bedroom just now, the handle that was only fitted *yesterday* fell onto the floor.'

I gesture with my hand, resisting the urge to turn it into a punch. Those calming pregnancy hormones really are long gone and my angry inner bear is straining to get free. I always knew there was a risk that we'd have to make do with a few of the rooms unfinished. I imagined the baby with a tiny yellow hard hat and a fluorescent bib as the odd decorator finished hanging our lovely wallpapers.

I *didn't* imagine I'd be bringing a baby home to a space that's only open plan because half the walls still aren't up. I didn't expect that the baby would need a dust mask to protect its tiny lungs, or have to sleep with the sound of cement mixers as the lullaby. I didn't expect to have to wrap the baby up in swaddling clothes because most of the glass in the windows is missing, which makes the house look dead.

I turn my back on the living room, too depressed to stay there. But the entrance hall is no better. The staircase has no banister, and the black-and-white herringbone tiles have been shipped off for 'restoration', leaving a kind of dirt track behind.

He follows me, bleating away. 'And then there are the supply issues. The delay with the heritage paints put us back at least a month.'

'Excuses! Excuses! Everywhere I go I hear so many bloody excuses! This baby isn't going to accept any excuses.'

He looks sullen. 'I can only do what I can do. I'm not a miracle worker.'

'But you *promised*!'

I should know by now that promises mean nothing. All round me, people break them. At work, it's worse. I spend my life with my BlackBerry permanently attached to my ear, as I cajole and beg and rant and rave to the suppliers of the world's most comfortable bed, who are claiming catastrophic spring shortages, or the New York-based Retoxygene super-powered coffee bar franchise who pulled out of a prime space on the ground floor for 'operational reasons', and next day announced their first UK store will be in bloody Selfridges.

I don't often swear out loud, but really, the foul thoughts whizzing through my brain these days would be a great disappointment to my gramma. I am impatient, unreasonable, the exact opposite of what a woman is supposed to be like in her last few days of pregnancy. I have no desire to nest whatsoever. Good job, really, given the state of this house.

'It's exceptional circumstances,' says the man. 'Worst winter for decades, weren't it?'

'Stop taking me for an idiot! We didn't complete on this house until the end of February and most of the snow fell before that. I might be pregnant, but I do still have a brain, so don't you dare—'

And then I feel it. A deep, dark, evil pain inside me, as though all the people I've shouted at in the last week are getting their own back. I lean against the banister-less staircase, hoping it won't give way.

'Ugh.'

The site manager scowls at me. 'You're not going into labour on my site, are you?'

'I . . . I'm not sure.' My voice is embarrassingly feeble, as there's hardly any breath to power it.

'Is this the first contraction you've had?' he asks.

Contraction? Shit, this can't happen now. My due date isn't till the day after tomorrow, and first babies are always late. For a few moments I can't manage a reply, but then, as suddenly as it came on, the pain is gone and I feel normal – and stroppy – all over again. 'I'm fine.'

'Chances are, it's a Braxton Hicks,' he says, smiling for the first time. 'You know, the warm-up contractions? Getting you ready for the big day? My wife—'

'Thanks for the antenatal class, but I know what a Braxton Hicks is, and right now I'd prefer you to focus on the only "big day" I'm interested in, the big day when we will be able to move in.'

As soon as the words are out of my mouth, I regret how harsh they sound. His mouth goes tight again and I have lost him, all because I wanted to prove that I'm not some feeble woman. When will I ever learn that being vulnerable can work as well as being feisty? Emily is the expert at that . . .

That's the same Emily who more or less told me I was endangering my baby by working till the end.

I feel a lump in my throat, because it was meant to be so different to this. Even with my limited imagination, I had a very clear picture of the summer ahead: of organic picnics and intimate shared secrets on Heartsease Common, of Freddie playing with the baby, of learning to do motherhood the way Emily does it: less chaotically than my mother, more laid-back than my gramma, and with the kind of intense love that I am so scared I won't be able to give to my baby.

'. . . might be better if Mr Garnett attends the site from now on, because we wouldn't want to risk any accidents.'

'Sorry?' I realise the man is talking to me. 'You don't want me here?'

'For safety reasons,' he says.

I am about to argue, to tell him that I know it's nothing to do with safety, and all about keeping the awkward bitch away . . . but then I wonder whether it *might* be a better use of my energy to focus what limited time I have left on the store. 'All right. But don't think he won't be every bit as tough on you as I am. It's his baby too.'

The hours drag by now. This July is getting hotter and hotter, and getting anything done feels like wading through a sweaty swamp, with a hundredweight strapped to my belly. I don't sleep, and neither does Toby, who leaps up every time I move or take a breath, asking *is it time*?

Between them, Gramma and Marnie call and text five times a day at least. My mother is making the most of the time before she becomes a granny to go out on the town, while Gramma is waiting for her summons to save the day with terry nappies and West Indian wisdom. Not that we have room for her or anyone in the rented house which I'm pretty sure is going to be our home for the foreseeable future . . .

It's five o'clock on the sixteenth of July, two days past my due date, and Toby thinks I am having a long, luxurious afternoon tea with Grazia. He's playing golf – a rare escape from the full-time schmoozing of journalists he's been doing on my behalf – so I knew I was safe coming in. I've sworn the entire management floor to secrecy, but I *had* to get back here. After spending the last couple of days on my backside, building up worse and worse pictures of what lies ahead in the labour ward, I needed the distraction.

'On my way down.' I put the phone down on Babs, who is more or less living here now, and who sends me on-the-spot reports from the shop floor. I'm so huge that I try to restrict myself to no more than two trips outside my office a day, because even one flight of stairs tires me out. Hilary keeps me supplied with tea and sandwiches. But sometimes I need to see what's happening for myself, and this time I'm off to the new espresso bar, to see whether the lighting really *is* making the salads look radioactive, or whether Babs is exaggerating.

The doors close and the signal on my phone peters out.

'Third floor for . . . the little ones. A children's paradise for new arrivals onwards.' The voice in the lift – a Hollywood starlet – is one of the new touches designed to give the place a more contemporary feel.

'Owww.'

That hurt. I mean, it really hurt.

Still hurts . . .

'Second floor for the man in your life and the life in your man . . . First floor for glamour, for romance, for relaxation and rocket fuel coffee . . .' Right now, it feels like the starlet is mocking me. *This* is a pain that means business. I've always had quite a high tolerance for discomfort, but right now I wonder whether I will cope.

I don't suppose I have a choice.

The doors open, but I can't risk my waters breaking on our brand new store carpet, so I try to get my breath back, and put my foot between the sliding doors. The elderly man waiting to go up gives me a horrified look, and heads for the stairs.

The pain goes as quickly as it arrived. I dial Babs again, my hands shaking as I lean out to get a signal. In the one antenatal class I did manage to attend, the teacher said we should see contractions like beautiful, powerful tidal waves. This must be the bit as the sea leaves the shore, before returning as a tsunami.

'Sandie. Where are you?'

'Um. I think I might be . . . in labour.' Those words sound unreal.

'Oh *shit*. Where are you?'

'By the lifts. I don't suppose . . .'

And I hear her running, and then she's there, and then we're back on the top floor, and she's ringing Toby, and somewhere very, very deep down, below 90 per cent of pure terror, there's 10 per cent of excitement that, God willing, this is the start of the journey to the place where I will meet my baby.

'Perfect timing, Toby,' says Mr Waverley, after he has finished his inspection between my legs. 'I can't tell you how often I get called in from the opera or concert hall, even though the lady in question has *hours*, if not days ahead. Whereas today I'm running my career girls' Saturday clinic, so I can pop in to see how you're getting on.'

The last fourteen hours have been the longest in my life. Last night, when Toby raced from the thirteenth hole to my side, we went to the hospital where they told us firmly that there was no hurry whatsoever, 'so cuddle up at home, watch some DVDs, take warm baths, sip raspberry leaf tea if you want, and then come back in the morning when there's something for us all to do'.

But when Toby fell asleep next to me on the sofa, I gave up on the allegedly relaxing stuff and went back to Garnett's paperwork, which passed the time until six this morning. That was the moment when I suddenly realised that what I'd been having before hadn't been real contractions at all, but these totally bloody well were . . .

I open my mouth to tell Mr Waverley that he should be congratulating *me* on not calling him out of the opera, but I can't speak. The pain has transformed me into half baby machine, half wild animal. So far, I am managing not to swear, but I don't know how much longer I will be able to stay true to Gramma's rules. When the pain is there, all I can think about is whether I can stand it for another second. And when the pain goes, I try not to do anything else – not move, not breathe, not think – to save every ounce of energy so I can face the next time.

Toby is timing my contractions with an iPhone app that even gives him an estimated time of delivery. Like Parcelforce.

'When *will* this be over?' I ask, when the midwife and Mr Waverley have left us and, seemingly, taken the pain with them. 'It must be soon, surely? An hour?'

'I don't want to put you off.'

'More than an hour? Am I going to be in labour for weeks?'

'No-o.' He looks at me nervously. 'Not *that* long.'

We both look up at the clock on the wall. It's an official-looking clock, one that screams, '*I will record the time of birth with Swiss Quartz accuracy.*' I'd imagined that paying the horrifying rate to go private would buy the odd soft furnishing, but it's all shiny surgical steel and eau-de-antibacterial hand-wash.

'Define *not that long*, please, Toby. But before you do, consider what *not that long* would be, if you were being tortured.'

'Oh, Sandie. I'm sorry about all this.' He takes my hand and I let him, even though any kind of physical contact at this point feels too much for me. 'I am feeling extremely guilty, even though, God knows, I didn't get you into this condition on purpose.'

I say nothing. Maybe an NHS hospital would have been

better. I might almost have welcomed the moans and cries from neighbouring delivery rooms, as a sign that I wasn't the only one going through this.

Toby picks up the menu. 'How about afternoon tea? Would that help?'

I give him *that* look. The one that says, *how can you pretend everything's normal when this terrifying thing is happening to me?*

He frowns. 'You might need some sustenance to keep you going.'

'You're going to have to tell me how long now, aren't you?'

Toby sighs, fiddles around with his iPhone. It's all the more galling that he's still online, after he confiscated my Black-Berry because I took a call from China about the iPolar Bear. He sighs again. 'Well, according to the app, we should see the arrival of Junior Barrow-Garnett in time for elevenses.'

'Two and a half hours more?' I stare at the clock again, trying to make sense of the numbers as a grumble inside me tells me it's about to start again.

'Give or take.' When he sees my face, he adds, 'Sorry, that's not helpful, is it?'

I manage to whisper the words *midwife* and *epidural* and he pushes the help button about twenty times in succession and I can hear the cavalry pounding up the corridor towards us.

Things speed up, suddenly. The clock no longer seems to be going backwards. I am beside myself with fear.

Turns out I'm too late for an epidural, so I'm on the gas and air which makes me feel hideously sick, but puts some weird distance between me and the pain.

'I can have the peth . . . the ped . . . the stronger stuff . . . later . . . can't I?'

''Fraid not, sweetheart. You've left it a bit late for that too. But you won't need it. You're doing so well! Remember, every contraction gets you closer to the big push.'

The big push?

254

Oh, shit, Gramma, this is really happening. There's nothing I can do.

But being a mum isn't simply biology and breathing, is it? There's heart and passion and patience.

I can push, yeah. But the rest of it . . . what if I can't do that?

A tear slips from my right eye, and down my cheek, followed rapidly by one from the left. I try to wipe it away before Toby notices, but all morning he's been staring at me, watching for the moment when he might be able to administer chocolate truffles or the clary sage aromatherapy oil he's packed.

'Oh, my darling Brains, what's the matter?'

'I'm going to be an awful mother,' I say, and then great floods of self-pitying tears cascade down my face. 'I'm too selfish. Too cold.'

'No way.' He pulls me towards him, as far as he can without touching my sensitive belly. 'You're clever, but you're also one of the kindest people I've ever met. Between us, we'll be *brilliant*.'

The monitor is beeping rhythmically and I try to zone into it, to focus on the new life that's coming. Oh, the pain's back. Sharper. Nastier.

'Can't do this,' I whimper.

'Oh, dear, sweetheart. You've been so brave but every woman has a moment like this. And it's a *good* sign. Let me take a peep, but I'm guessing we'll be ready to go very soon . . .'

I look at the clock: it's blurry, through the tears. Ten to ten.

'The iPhone said the baby might be here in time for elevenses,' says Toby.

'Whatever next?' says the midwife, winking at me. 'I think it's time to fetch Mr Waverley back again. He might be a bit more use than a fancy phone. Don't go anywhere, will you?'

*

The room feels packed, now there are four of us.

Soon there'll be five . . .

My brain can't process that. Pain and noise and struggle and white light and instructions in my ear . . . finally, Mr Waverley is paying *me* some attention.

His voice is softer than I expected, less bossy, more encouraging. The midwife stands on my other side, so that her whisper sounds like an echo.

Push.

WAIT, now, wait!

Push again. Harder, harder.

Now, *wait. Pant . . . pant. The baby will be crowning soon, let your body do the work for you.*

I do what I'm told, even though every cell is screaming at me to push and push till it's over with . . .

Toby moves from foot to foot. His iPhone lies abandoned on the side table.

I'm trying to stay upright because the midwife says gravity helps. But my legs are as insubstantial as rubber. 'Have to lie down.'

'Come on, then, sweetheart, the hard work's nearly done. Up you get.' And they help me onto the bed, propped up against the raised back.

Toby takes my hand. 'I love you, Brains.'

'Right, Toby, will you be at the sharp end for the big moment, or with Miss Barrow?' asks Mr Waverley. 'We're reaching the point where you need to get in position.'

Toby looks at me. 'It's up to Sandie.'

It's another thing I tried not to think about in that antenatal class. I sat there wondering, for the zillionth time, how I'd got myself into a situation where I had to choose whether to let my boyfriend watch my private parts be pushed to their limits.

He looks so young right now. It's hot in here, so his face is flushed, and his blond hair stands on end where he's been running his fingers through it over and over.

'If you're up to it, then so am I,' I say, and my own voice sounds different, like a growl.

A new contraction comes, and I am allowed to push. I'll explode unless I can get this baby out soon. The pain was one thing, but the pressure is something else. I seem to be floating above us, looking down on my body and the cluster of spectators grouped between my open legs.

Isn't that what's meant to happen just before you die?

I feel awfully sad, suddenly, that I'll never meet my baby if I am dying . . .

'I can see the head. God, Sandie, I can see the head.'

'PANT, Sandie. PANT! Let the baby come in his own time.'

I feel like I am falling through space onto the bed, and the pain is back, but different now: not contractions, but the most ferocious pressure and pulling as the baby travels towards life, millimetre by agonising millimetre.

The midwife said, *his own time.* But how can she know it's a boy from the head?

'Oh, he's got little tiny black curls all over his scalp,' says Toby, astonished.

What was he expecting? Platinum blond?

'FUCK! Fuck! Fuck! Fuck! Fuck!'

Jesus, the pain. I feel the pressure against my skin. Tearing or stretching? I can't tell but it's like I'm burning . . .

'Come on, sweetheart,' the midwife says, from somewhere ten thousand miles away, and then Mr Waverley's voice, 'Easy does it, almost there, my darling girl.'

'I can see his face, Sandie. Oh, my, his face. With eyes and ears and a mouth and the tiniest nose and . . .'

Toby's eyes meet mine, and his are as full of tears as mine are, though for different reasons. I'm still feeling the most forceful pull, as the doctor slides the baby out of me . . .

. . . oh my God, a baby . . .

. . . and moves up towards me and passes the baby up onto my stomach, skin to skin, and he helps me to take hold because I don't have any strength left . . .

I wait for a scream. That's what's supposed to happen, isn't it? Instead I feel Toby's hand on my shoulder as I look at the face for the first time, and the baby blinks, then opens his eyes and for a moment the world stops, as the clear blue wisdom in them knocks me off balance.

'My baby,' I say, half question, half statement.

'*Our* baby,' whispers Toby.

The baby's skin against mine feels warm and familiar, and I can't close my eyes for as long as those are locked onto mine.

'Your baby *girl*,' says Mr Waverley, and I blink, hard, and when I open my eyes again and see her lovely face, I wonder how the midwife could ever have thought she might be a boy . . .

CHAPTER 25

Emily

The text from Toby arrives while I'm waiting for Mickey to show up.

BABY BARROW GARNETT ARRIVED THIS MORNING AT 11.22. SHE WEIGHS 7LB 4 AND IS ADORABLE. SANDIE IS A SUPER-HEROINE, AND DOING WELL TOO. FINDING A NAME TO SUM UP THE BABY'S BEAUTY IS GOING TO BE SO HARD. LOVE A VERY PROUD DADDY.

I stare at it, feeling relieved for them, but sad too. I hadn't even known she'd gone into labour. And the text message is obviously a round-robin, not personalised at all. That's that, then, eh, for our friendship?

If Freddie were here to cuddle, it might be slightly easier, but it's a Duncan weekend. I wonder what surprises will be in store when he returns the Fredster on Sunday. A Millwall tattoo across his shoulders, maybe. Or a pierced eyebrow?

I can't even summon up a smile as Mickey's truck comes tearing round the corner so fast that his bales only just stay on the back. He brakes heavily and stops alongside me, jumping out of the cab and then reaching out to give me an enormous bear hug. I'm so startled that I can't speak.

'You looked like you needed that, gorgeous. Sorry I'm late. I got caught in a pile-up on the old Oxford Road. Pig escape.

You should have seen the buggers run. Trying to save their bacon.'

He is the king of unlikely excuses, but it's almost impossible to stay cross with Mickey. 'Well, your pupils are waiting.'

'I couldn't get a quick drink of water first, could I? I am *parched*.'

I show him into the shop, and up to the flat. As I pour the water into a glass, he stands in the kitchen, his body too large for this tiny space. I feel hot and bothered – God, what a hormonal cliché. I bet he gets this reaction everywhere he goes: desperate housewives falling over themselves to mop his iron-man brow, and all sorts besides. Will mentioned a while back that there's a rumour Mickey has been busy across the shires, with a kid in half the county towns.

By rights that should make him unattractive, and yet . . .

'Fabulous. Exactly what I need.' When he takes the glass from me, he lets his hands brush against mine, 'accidentally', and does this Princess Diana thing with his eyes, all the better to show off his long sandy lashes. He's so obvious that it's almost funny.

'It's not fair to keep your fans waiting any longer, eh, Mickey?'

I don't wait for a response but walk out, and he follows. When we get down to the common again, I see a little group of women, led by Wendy, are already there to 'give their blokes moral support'. Yeah, right.

I could stay and watch myself, but I get the sense that he's targeting me for the Mickey treatment, and it makes me feel uncomfortable. Instead, I leave him to do his thing, and get in the Snowvan to drive to Upper Findlebury, where Abby has promised tea and cake and a pitching practice session, ahead of the Green Goddess final. I wouldn't quite classify her as a mate, but since Will went, I've been spending more time with her, because her husband is hardly ever around either.

'I thought we'd have a picnic,' she says, when I get there.

We walk – or rather, I walk and she waddles – over to the village green. Nuclear families sit at intervals spaced so precisely that I wonder if there's a grid system chalked on the grass. The entire contents of the John Lewis Outdoor Living Collection is on display: parasols and picnic blankets, hampers and sun hats.

Is it very disloyal to Heartsease to admit that I feel rather comfortable here?

We find ourselves a bench because if Abby sits on the grass she'll never get up again, and she lays her melamine pop-up table with a teapot, cups, and a multilayered strawberry shortcake.

'You're keeping busy,' I say.

'You think I *made* it? No, there's a great woman who lives in the village, bakes to order and delivers to your door. And, no, you can't have her number. She's part of the Upper Findlebury female force to be reckoned with!' She laughs, to show she's joking.

'So is your pitch coming along OK?'

Abby sighs. 'I can't focus, with the heat and my weight. Besides I've always been a bit of a deadline junkie. I don't like planning ahead. But I'm still happy to listen to your pitch, if it'd help?'

And so she sits, eyes closed as though she's dreaming, as I try to convince her why Heartsease Common deserves to be as rich, successful and all round lovely as Upper Findlebury . . .

I think I've sent her to sleep. That's not the most promising of signs . . .

'Abby?'

'Uh?' She blinks, then draws her hand across her eyes to wipe them, spreading mascara across her right cheek. Even Abby can't maintain her immaculate grooming in the face of late pregnancy. 'Sorry. I did hear it. Well, most of it. It's very strong. Your passion really comes across.'

I know she's just saying that. 'Thanks.'

'No, seriously, you're doing well, especially with Will away and everything. Not long now till he's back, though, eh?'

I nod. It's not that I haven't missed him – I have – but things have settled down into an easy, please-myself rhythm without him around.

'He's enjoyed it, has he? Doing his own thing?'

'Hmm. I think so. He's been trying to sound tired on the phone, so I don't get the hump about it being one long holiday, but every now and then he starts getting that *I'm going to change the world* tone in his voice.'

She laughs. 'I know all about that. To be honest, it's one of the reasons I was so surprised when I first found out that you'd got together. What with you having Freddie and everything.'

'Oh, yes?' I try not to sound too interested, and bite into another slice of shortcake, to stop myself asking more.

'Hmm. Only you know the way he always insists he never wanted kids? That they'd get in the way of all the stuff he wanted to do in life?'

'Right.' He's *never* said that to me when I've begged him for a baby. Only that the timing's not right, or the business needs to grow first or there's an R in the month.

I try to take it in: *Will never wanted kids!*

'I guess it was all a big fib to save my feelings, though, eh, Emily. I wasn't the girl for him, was I, and all it took was for him to meet you to change his mind?'

Crumbs of the moist, deliciously sweet shortcake stick to the roof of my mouth like bitter coffee grounds. 'Yes. That must be it.'

Either that, or I haven't changed his mind at all, and the whole eco-summer school is his way of taking time out to pluck up the courage to tell me the truth . . .

CHAPTER 26

Sandie

Ruby Lois Madeleine Barrow-Garnett is screaming again.

I don't think she's stopped since we brought her home.

If she could write a diary, it would go something like this:

DAY 1: *Where the hell am I? And who are they? Maybe if I keep quiet no one will notice me.*

DAY 2: *If I scream enough will they let me go back to where I was?*

DAY 3: *Where are they taking me now? Waaaaah.*

DAY 4: *I don't like this. Waaaah.*

DAY 5: *My throat hurts from all this screaming. Waaaaah. It hurts.*

And now it's day six. Maybe she's getting calmer. Or maybe I'm developing more of a tolerance for her amazing range of screams.

'Shall I bring her over?' Toby asks.

I nod. I'm certainly not a natural when it comes to feeding, but even my most ham-fisted efforts do quieten her down for a little while. He picks her up out of her cot and puts her in my arms and I rummage around with my T-shirt and my maternity underwear, too tired to feel embarrassed any more.

She latches on and I wince momentarily, before her face distracts me. Our *daughter*. How strange it still feels to think that. She is so much prettier than she should be. This is not parental bias. We took her out yesterday, only round the block, even though Toby had to talk me into it, because I was terrified that the soft summer rain would feel like a monsoon on her precious face. But she seemed content, and attracted the kind of attention that only beautiful babies can.

Beautiful she may be, but she's brought us to our knees. At the hospital I was on a strung-out high, fuelled by adrenalin and relief at having got through the birth. Oh, and a constant buffet of room service delights, delivered to the hotel-style suite they moved me to immediately after delivery.

On the advice of the midwife, we'd insisted that baby Ruby be presented to the world *before* I came home from hospital, and it worked like a dream – Gramma cooed like a woman possessed while sizing up the hygiene standards, while my mother was threatening to check in herself, 'for a rest cure'. Grazia turned up with a choice of cava and champagne, and held the baby like a natural.

There were two absences. I was surprised that Laetitia didn't show, if only to keep up appearances in front of Mr Waverley. It was harder to pretend I didn't care about Emily not turning up, but nothing could burst my big happy bubble.

But once we came home – not to the Chiswick homestead, of course, but to the rented rabbit hutch – the soreness and exhaustion kicked in. And at exactly the same moment that Ruby got over the stunned-to-silence shock of being born and began to howl like a jackal. Within twenty-four hours, every room looked like the aftermath of an earthquake in Mothercare, and Toby and I have been plunged into a world that no iPhone app can help us navigate.

Funny how he hasn't mentioned the idea of being a house husband since Ruby arrived . . .

Monty barks, and a second later the doorbell rings.

'Ignore it,' I mouth to Toby as he comes in from the kitchen, clutching Monty's jaw together.

The best-case scenario is more flowers, and even that horrifies me: the house smells of sweet decay, thanks to the many neglected bouquets we've been lucky enough to receive. The guilt of watching them wither makes me feel even wearier.

'But what if it's the health visitor doing a spot check?'

Toby and I share this unspoken fear that, sooner or later, the authorities will find out we're barely capable of looking after ourselves, never mind a brand new, defenceless human, and will despatch a SWAT team. Though there've been a couple of times when I've felt so incompetent that I might almost welcome a dawn raid.

Toby puts the dog on the sofa, and then straightens up, heading for the hall with the gait of a grandfather, not a new dad.

Silence. A truly chilling silence.

And then, the worst possible word. 'Mum!'

I freeze, and the baby looks up at my face and shrieks a shriek unlike anything I've heard her make in the last five days.

Laetitia strides into the room, her face the picture of disgust: whether in response to the surroundings, or to me, I can't tell.

'So this is my first grandchild,' she says, her voice curious rather than hostile.

My legs are weak so I can't stand up, but I hold the baby up, and she takes her.

'This is Ruby Lois Madeleine,' I say. 'We chose names with the same initials as the three most important women in our lives: Ruby for my Gramma Rowena and also because it seems to match Garnett, somehow. Then Madeleine for my mother Marnie, and Lois . . .'

She nods, as she scoops up the baby. 'I wouldn't wish the name Laetitia on anyone. But Lois?' She chews over the sound. 'Lois.' Grandmother and granddaughter scrutinise each other's features.

Two extraordinary things happen. First, Mrs Garnett's sour

face changes. Becomes . . . almost softer, with a tiny flicker of recognition. Ruby has stopped shrieking and continues to stare.

'Come on, now, baby Lois,' says Laetitia, heading for the door.

'Mother!' says Toby, standing in her way.

'Oh, I'm not abducting the child, Gannet. Though the authorities might have something to say about the state of this house. No, I'm just taking her outside to meet someone important.'

I find enough strength to rush out after her, and her car is parked right outside. There's someone in the passenger seat.

'Miss Hart?' says Laetitia, knocking on the window till the door opens. 'Miss Hart, it's as I thought, you are *desperately* needed if this infant is going to get through her second week unscathed.'

Miss Hart walks round the car. She is slight, and tidy-looking, with a fierce aura that reminds me of my grandmother, though this woman is only forty or so. And then she sees Ruby, and smiles a smile warmer than the sun.

Laetitia is about to hand the baby over when Toby intervenes, putting his body between the women.

'Mother, you're coming very close to being banned from seeing us ever again. What the hell are you playing at?'

'Oh, Toby,' she says, laughing, but hanging onto Ruby with unmistakable steeliness. 'This is your present. Obviously, I considered flowers and smellies and romper suits or whatever they're called these days, but frankly I thought Miss Hart would be more use. I've hired her for two weeks. I expect she'll have you shipshape within two days.'

I open my mouth, but nothing comes out.

'Oh, do shut your mouth, Sandra. The one thing I've always liked about you is that you come out and say what you think, however unpalatable.'

But before I can answer, Miss Hart is walking towards me.

She puts her hand on my arm. 'You look tired, my dear, which is not surprising, after all your hard work.' She smiles across at Ruby, and then at Toby. 'But if you're willing to share a little of that work now, and the fun of spending time with this special little girl, then I promise you, things are about to get an awful lot easier.'

And she is true to her word.

Miss Hart had already charmed almost a hundred babies before arriving on our doorstep – 'ninety-six, to be precise, and yes, of course I can still name every single one of them, thank you!' – but that doesn't mean Ruby delights her any less.

Everything is *perfect* or *funny* or *adorable* or, often, all three. Even when she saw our spare room, crammed to the fake rafters with the beautiful Beatrix Potter themed items I'd chosen for the huge nursery in the real house, she didn't flinch.

'I have the most comfortable airbed,' she said, and it was only then that Toby and I realised she was going to be living here twenty-four-seven.

Miss Hart is the complete opposite of Laetitia. She gently deposed Ruby from her short but tyrannical reign, and instead introduced rules that made such perfect sense that they barely seemed like rules at all. There are walks, feed times, bed times, bath times, rest times. Not just for the baby, but for all of us.

She has taken over, it's true, but in such a way that I don't feel usurped myself: I watch her, and I learn, and she insists that Ruby comes to me five or six times a day, but the brief absences seem to make my new daughter and me closer, somehow. Miss Hart has *even* conquered the washing machine, possibly the most evilly intentioned household appliance I've ever encountered. Right now it's purring its way through the third load of the day. It's a comforting, purposeful noise.

The rest of the house holds its breath. Monty is sleeping. So is Toby. Miss Hart is doing some shopping.

So why can't I get on with my work?

I've read and reread emails about gluten-free cupcakes, and delays in celebrity endorsement deals, and a national street entertainment strike that might cause pirate-and-parrot supply issues on our opening day, but none of it seems to stick. Perhaps it will be easier when I go back to the office next week, for a few hours at first. Perhaps not, though. Maybe *this* is why women have maternity leave? Because, after the baby comes, they cannot be bothered with the small stuff?

Mss Hart is a darling but I can't ask her about that. She is childless herself, and told me on day one that, at forty-two, she has no plans to go shopping for embryos or designer sperm.

'The trouble is, Sandie, I adore babies, but once they're past twelve weeks, I completely lose interest.'

No. Miss Hart wouldn't know the answer. But I know someone who might . . .

I long to call Emily. Of course, career has never mattered much to her, but she might tell me the truth about the rest of this rollercoaster ride. I do have the numbers of a couple of women from the antenatal class, but I don't want new friends. I want an old one.

But she's made her decision. Toby texted her, as he texted everyone, as soon as Ruby arrived, and we sent her the official announcement card, too. I could almost have forgiven the way she was at the baby shower if she'd replied, but nothing came back.

So I guess that is that.

August

CHAPTER 27

Emily

I could have done without the grand send-off.

'Surprise!' Jean shouts as I come down the stairs, taking tiny steps so as not to split my one smart skirt.

I have a bad feeling as I follow her into the shop.

The great and the good – or should that be the good, the bad and the ugly – of the village are jammed in here. Bob Frobisher, the chair of the Churchwomen's Guild, the vicar and even the monstrous Wendy from playgroup.

Oh.

There's Mickey. He must have made a special trip, and the thought makes me blush. I'll say one thing for him, he's a trier.

'We wanted to say thanks for all you're doing for Heartsease,' says the vicar, and the others begin to applaud.

I try to smile. 'It's an honour. But please, please don't get your hopes up.'

'Too late for that,' says Jean. 'Even the kids are in on it.' She leads me outside, where nine Tiny Tykes, including Freddie, are lined up. The Tyke on the end begins to unfurl a banner that's almost as tall as she is, while the other children sing:

'Good luck, good luck to Emily,
She's always super-friendly,
We know she cannot fail to please
And bring the cash home to Heartsease!'

The banner reads, HEARTSEASE HEARTS EMILY! and features a stick version of me, complete with straggly blondish hair, and a pot belly. I bet Wendy's responsible for that addition, though it's not completely inaccurate. Will's gone on his second summer school, and like last time I find the many temptations of the store impossible to resist. It's like living on top of a giant, inexhaustible biscuit barrel. To think I was only complaining a couple of months ago about my angles.

Freddie breaks ranks and runs over to me. 'Good luck, Mummy,' he says, his arms reaching up to my waist. God, he's so tall now. My big little boy.

I search the faces in this small crowd, even though I know I won't find the only other person I want to see, because he's two hundred miles away in a Welsh valley with the most intermittent of mobile signals. He offered to come back for the pitch, but I could hear the lack of enthusiasm in his voice, and, anyway, what could he do? Even Abby isn't taking her perfect husband with her, because she reckons it'd harm our case to look like we're the little wives fronting up men's ideas.

Even though that's exactly what I was doing at first. Only in the last few weeks have I begun to find the confidence to include my own thoughts in the pitch, to think I might have something to add. The whole idea has grown since I got to the finals, so now it feels too ambitious to be possible.

They're still gathered round me, as though they're expecting a speech. Ah well, in for a penny.

'My friends, my colleagues, my fellow Heartseasers, thank you,' I begin, and they nod approval. Mickey winks. 'Um, I don't quite know what to say except . . . I am very touched by this. Very. Since I arrived here two years ago, I've had so many adventures and been given so much support for our first store, and now the craft store, too. You've been wonderful and we've been so happy here . . .'

And then I realise I'm talking in the past, because I don't think I am happy here any more. I feel trapped and ignored and friendless and, worst of all, I know an awful lot of it is my fault. Heartsease hasn't changed, but I have, and yet I don't have a clue how to snatch back the contentment I felt when I first moved in with Will.

Someone coughs.

'And, er, I will do my best to bring the money back, because I know we deserve it – and we need it – so much more than Upper Findlebury ever would. So, let's hear it for Heartsease! Hip hip, hooray!'

'Hip hip, hooray! Hip hip, hooray!'

My neighbours head back towards their homes and their offices, I kiss Freddie, and he skips back with his Tiny Tykes. Maybe now is the time to go home to Somerset. He's about to start school anyway, so what difference would it make if he starts back at *my* old village school? He'll make friends any-where. Will and the secret shopping girls were my reasons for being here, and right now I seem to have lost them all.

I wonder what Sandie's baby looks like. How they're all coping. It must be a whole month now. Maybe I should have swallowed my pride and called, but I couldn't trust myself not to say something loathsome again. I mean, last time I saw her I meant to be nice as pie, and ended up more or less accusing Sandie of sabotaging her baby's health by working too hard . . . what kind of person have I turned into?

'Hey, gorgeous.'

Mickey is next to me. Too close. Or is it? I can feel warmth coming off him, and it's not unpleasant. 'Surprised to see you here. Shouldn't you be building an eco-house with your bare hands somewhere?'

And I look at his hands and wish I hadn't because I'm imagining what else they can do. Must be hormones. Or the sunshine.

'I was just passing, but Jean called to ask if I'd like to lend my support. I hear I get a mention in your pitch.'

I feel even hotter now. 'Er. Yes. As a . . . case study.'

'I've been called a few things in my time,' he says. Then he whispers, 'Feel free to study me any time you like, Emily.'

'I'm running late.'

He nods. 'Sure. Good luck.' Then he leans across and kisses me on the cheek and when he leans back again, there's the wickedest of smiles on his lips. He keeps waving as he crosses the common.

'It was OK, wasn't it, Emily? To do that?'

Jean is at my side, looking nervous.

'Of course,' I lie. 'Thanks for organising it.'

'I thought you might appreciate the support, you know, with Will being away. Though I have to say, you've surprised me, dear, at how well you've handled it all on your own.'

'Really?'

'Hmm. I thought you'd be a dead loss, actually. Was rather worried what poor Will would come back to.'

'*Poor* Will?'

She looks at me steadily. 'At my age, I don't have time to dress things up. I always thought you were the weak link, Emily. Sweet, yes. Well meaning *most of the time*, but no business sense whatsoever. However, I've been pleasantly surprised. You have more backbone than I expected, even if you are grumpy.'

'Am I?'

When Jean smiles, her face is more rumpled than her stockings. 'I don't think I've heard you laugh for three months now.'

'You're exaggerating.' I feel myself scowling as I try to look back. 'There was that time . . .'

'Oh no there wasn't. You've been hard work, Emily.'

Weird. I thought it was Will who'd lost his sense of humour, but maybe he'd given up making jokes because I never laughed. 'And that's why Will is avoiding me?'

She stops smiling. 'He's on a course. He wants to improve himself. Unless *you* think he's avoiding you?'

'No,' I say. 'Well. Maybe I do. I don't know.' I shake my head, to shake away the thoughts. 'I need to go.'

She reaches out and puts her hand on mine. 'We all know how hard the two of you have worked on this business, and everyone's grateful. But you must remember what's important, eh? Do your best with the pitch, but no one will think any the less of you if it doesn't work out.'

'Will would think less of me.'

'Ah, he can be a bit stubborn and serious at times, but he loves you for what you are, and not because you're some sort of eco-genius.'

But does he love me? There's only one person who can answer that, and it's not Jean. 'I hope you're right, because Katie Price has more chance of being picked as a Green Goddess than I do.'

Abby – more of a Green Goddess than I'll ever be – greets me on the platform at Upper Findlebury station because, of course, we don't deserve our own station in Heartsease.

'Bloody hell, can you actually get any bigger without having to declare yourself a new country?' Abby's been my only confidante when Will's away, though I'm still not completely sure I'd call her a friend. She is from a different planet, and for once I don't just mean the Next Village Along. But she really rates my pitch, and without her I might have chickened out by now.

'Bizarre, isn't it?' Abby says, staring down at her own belly with a kind of benign bewilderment. 'I can't get in the driver's side of the car any more, so it's a good job we're on the train.'

'Are you nervous?'

'About the birth or the pitch?'

I smile. 'Both.'

'The birth, yes, I'm scared to death, though thank goodness having twins and being over thirty-five means I can have a Caesarean, no questions asked, without having to endure Chris cheering me on like a seventies-era football manager.'

'Will would be more into doing it all with Bach flower essences.'

'Yes, well, it's the men who can afford to read up on what they fancy, while the women do the hard work. And now we're expected to find the time to be green goddesses too.'

We step on board the train. 'Is that what you're going to tell the panel?' Abby hasn't been keen on practising her pitch in front of me too many times, in case she loses the spontaneity. But what little I've heard is very slick.

'What do *you* think? No, today, I am all about girl power and the *next* generation,' and she pats her bump. 'My secret weapons. I'm not really that nervous. You?'

'I'd probably rather go through labour again.'

'They'll be pussycats. European Union, women's rights, equal ops. They'll probably offer us stress counselling afterwards. You'll be terrific. You've rehearsed your pitch over and over again. Plus, it's a great project.'

'Is it?'

She nods. 'I don't back losers, Emily Barrow.'

'Even if they're in direct competition?'

Abby laughs. 'Oh, I'm only doing this to keep busy till the twins come. I don't seriously expect to win. It's not like we need the money round here, now, is it?'

We're pulling out of the station: the rails slicing between the whitewashed houses and the long, leafy gardens with their sustainable-wood climbing towers, and their fair-trade hammocks, and their fox-proof coops with rescued chickens.

'No.'

'Well, then. Let's enjoy our day out. Although,' she yawns, 'I'm very sorry about this, but if I am to stand any chance of staying awake through my own pitch, then I'm going to have to take forty winks. Wake me up at Paddington!'

Her eyes are closed before she even finishes her sentence.

The all-female panel might be right-on, but judging from their choice of venue, they also like the high life.

The Lodge is a few streets from King's Cross station: an 'eco-hotel' which, according to the brochure we're given in our conference pack, doesn't compromise on luxury *or* green credentials.

'That'll be why the paintwork is that nasty off-white,' Abby says, 'in case people thought they'd dared to use optical brighteners. And I bet the notes they put on the bed asking you to use the bath towels more than once are printed on recycled paper.'

I nod, though I don't know what she's on about. Most of the hotels I've stayed in, I've wished I'd brought my *own* towels.

The pitching sessions are being held in the first-floor drawing room, which is awesomely grand and gorgeous, with soft blue walls, rich wooden floors and two candelabras the size of dairy cows hanging from the corniced ceiling.

'Bet *they're* not low-energy light bulbs,' whispers my right-hand cynic.

The sun is so dazzling through the floor-to-ceiling windows that the lights don't need to be on. But the refreshment table doesn't look very sustainable: a mountain of exotic fruit salad with its own Air Miles account, plus every kind of bottled water.

I couldn't manage as much as a sliver of kiwi right now.

At one end of the room there's a row of tables for the judges, laden with more water and smoothies, and the candidates' chairs are set out in a semicircle, to make it look informal and relaxed. Ha. As if. Apart from Abby and me, there are four other finalists, cookie-cutter eco-darlings, who combine effortless elegance with clean consciences and flaxen highlights. I try to think positive: at least I will be memorable in my dark suit and my 'Mummy's left me alone with her make-up bag' clown face.

Maeve Topping, she of the ethically sourced household products and the startling red hair, claps her hands together. 'My friends, please take your seats, because it's time to get this show on the road. I'm so pleased to see a tremendous turn-out here: not only the entrants, but also journalists and campaigners. Let me introduce you to my fellow judges: Olivia Gardner is a partner in the Earth Bank, our corporate sponsor, and has an impeccable record in funding both mainstream and development projects.'

The fierce-looking woman to her left nods an acknowledgement. She can't be more than twenty-five.

'And to my right, we have Angelika Boontje, whose genius idea this was in the first place. We're very lucky that she's taken a break from Brussels to join us today. She has set up competitions like this right across Europe, but her plans don't stop there. Oh no. I am secretly confident that before long she will take over the world.'

Angelika smiles broadly. She's the only other person here who reminds me of me: my age, with mad curls instead of the usual ironed hair, and I bet she's only wearing that blotch-patterned wrap dress because it's great for concealing stains.

'So, without further delay, let's hear what our talented short-listees have come up with. We are going the traditional alphabetical route, so our first contender, please, is . . . Abby Capper!'

Abby gets to her feet and heads for the rostrum at the opposite end of the room. Everyone gasps at her size.

'Are you all right to stand?' asks Angelika, already standing and ready to offer her seat.

'Fine, thanks. It'll ensure my pitch stays short and sweet – the twins will start to kick if they think I am going on a bit.'

A fond sigh goes round the room now. *Twins!* For all the strident 'sisters are doing it for themselves' stuff, evidently we're all still suckers for a multiple birth.

'My friends,' says Abby, 'thank you for inviting me to pitch. When I first heard the news, I fired up the PowerPoint on my laptop, and was on the point of putting together an all-singing, all-dancing presentation, as I always did in my old job, as a senior retail operations manager in a large and successful chain of home wear stores.'

Funny, since we've become closer, I'd forgotten Abby was responsible for shutting down Will's branch because it was unprofitable.

Still. Water under the bridge.

'But then I stopped for a moment. I realised that the fancy reports were only one way of getting things done, quite possibly a very *male* way of getting things done. *Ooh, look at my PowerPoint, boys!*' she says in a man's growling voice. '*No, no, mine's bigger and longer than yours.*'

The women laugh obligingly. I've heard this bit before: she's not exactly going out on a limb with an all-female audience.

'And as my initial proposal was all about female empowerment, I realised it was time to do things *my* way. I do have a flashy brochure, which you'll find in your conference packs, but to be honest, since I knew I was in the finals, my idea has just been growing and growing. A bit like me. And now I want to talk from the heart.'

Abby touches her bump, a gesture I've never seen her make before. 'We all have our reasons for wanting to protect our fragile planet. My two reasons are perhaps a little more obvious than usual at the moment . . . but I have always had a deep commitment to green issues. While I worked at Bells & Whistles, I was personally responsible for introducing . . .'

I feel myself drifting off as Abby recites her perfect CV. Funnily enough, I haven't planned to include my own career highlights in my presentation, given that they are limited to organising the bank's Secret Santa five years' running, and winning Smile of the Month in January 2001 (and then only because everyone else had won already).

'. . . ours is a village in need. It may not head the deprivation lists . . .'

You can say that again, Abby.

'But surely, as women, we can recognise that impoverishment comes in many different forms.'

I smile. I know Abby didn't finish her speech until last night – she can't sleep anyway now she's so big – and I wonder what she's come up with. This might just be a project to keep her busy till the twins arrive, but she's not the type to allow herself to look stupid in front of other people.

'The kind of poverty I am talking about is poverty of community, of aspiration.'

I sit up in my chair, wide awake.

'The village of Upper Findlebury, like so much of Britain, and Europe, and the West, is focused on all the wrong things.'

It must be a coincidence. She's been so tired that she hasn't realised that . . .

'Consumerism. Competition. Struggling to keep you and your family on top.'

I run on with the words in my head: *but what those very personal priorities do is cut us off from any sense of community. Any shared responsibility to help each other . . .*

'The trouble with focusing on such personal priorities is that they cut us off from any sense of community. They make us feel we have no shared responsibility to help each other or to make choices that protect the planet.'

I try to catch her eye, I shake my head, and signal for her to stop. But she ignores me completely, her own eyes locked onto the three judges, who are hanging on her every word.

My every word.

I want to stand on a chair, shout at her to stop, tell them that it's my speech she's reading out. But . . . well, is it possible that she might have been so discombobulated by her pregnancy that she thinks these are *her* ideas?

'My proposals are about bringing people together through action and through creativity. And, as in my original proposal, I am concentrating on *women's* creativity. The craft movement has enjoyed the most incredible resurgence in the last three years . . .'

I didn't write *this*.

'And I plan to capitalise on that growth to open Britain's first academy of refound art and crafts, combining women's knowledge and their passion for the environment, to educate both sexes in creative skills to make saving the planet fun as well as fundamental. A treasure trove of knowledge, enthusiasm, beautiful objects *and* complete integrity.'

Complete integrity?

That bitch wants to open her *own* Handmade.

'Though women will be the leaders, we will involve all generations, all communities and backgrounds in the most important skills swap in a generation. I have made links with universities in every continent, to ensure we can take advantage of all the latest research on reuse and recycling, but also so we can feed back our discoveries.'

Not only stolen it but . . . bloody hell, how did I let this happen? Made it bigger. More pretentious. More *wankerish*. But also, though I hate to admit it, more . . . winnable.

'It goes without saying that our new centre will be built to the highest sustainable standards, and our main centre will be constructed from straw bales, using technology developed by a master craftsman, from a neighbouring county. OK, we'd prefer it to be a woman, but right now Mickey Burke is a world leader in this technology. '

Mickey? My *Mickey?*

'You will notice that my funding proposal also includes scope for two international female interns per year, one from Africa, and the other from anywhere else in the world, who will bring the ideas from the science and humanities disciplines to our project. From the granny with her recycled knitting, to the teenage girls building homes made from sustainable sources, the Upper Findlebury Refound Academy takes its lead from women's needs and women's crafts, but, of course, it won't exclude men. It absolutely embodies the spirit of think local, act global. I want my twins to be proud of their mum, their village, their country – and I think this will achieve that.

'Together we *can* recycle the world!'

Recycle the *world*? She's recycled everything Will and I have done, but turned it into something that makes me feel simultaneously sick *and* green with envy.

But apparently I'm the only one to think that way because the entire room has greeted her rousing bloody speech with deafening applause. I stare at my hands, which are clenched into fists in my lap, and I try not to lose control.

I wait for her to come and sit by me, to see what she does, but when I look up, I realise she's been 'promoted' to a seat right by the judges.

Maeve stands up. 'Well, thank you, Abby, for a splendid kick-off. If all the pitches are like this, this afternoon will sail by. And now I'd like to call on Mattie Brown from Kent to outline her project, followed by Emily Cheney, before we take a short tea break.'

'I want to talk to you all about energy . . .'

Mattie seems to be in desperate need of an energy injection. She has a whiny voice, and a half-baked plan to change the world with raw food. I try to zone out of what she's saying, so I can focus on my own pitch, but the hopelessness of the situation chills me. Poor Heartsease, to be represented by a loser like me. It's like that song, 'Always a Bridesmaid'.

I might as well leave now.

But then I think of Jean, then of the little send-off she organised for me this morning, and then her unsubtle pep talk. Dare I go back and face her if I don't at least try?

I don't know who I am any more. Not the sweet, funny Emily everyone loved. No, I'm moody and silly, so self-pitying that I haven't smiled for months, according to Jean. A jealous cow who sent her friends packing with bitchy comments. A loser who can't keep a man because she's got no backbone?

Or could there be *another* Emily? The one who managed, somehow, to survive on her own in London without crawling home for tea and Cheddar and sympathy? The one who tricked her oh-so-sharp-husband into a better deal post-divorce? The one who thought she might just deserve a good life and a good man?

I'm aware of a change in the room. Mattie has stopped after only a few minutes, her face pale with stage fright. Lukewarm applause follows, and as Mattie returns to her seat Maeve stands up again. 'Thank you. Another interesting proposal — and do remember, everyone, the pitch is only part of the process. We are looking for passion, of course, but not always a command performance.'

Mattie manages a brave smile, but I think we all know that for her, it's over.

And for me?

'And next, we welcome Emily Cheney, our second finalist from Berkshire.'

I walk to the front, brushing past Abby, so she knows that I know what she's up to. Perhaps she thought I was too stupid even to realise. She looks away, slightly flushed.

'Hello,' I say. I look at the jury, and I hesitate. I could tell them the truth right now, use this moment to discredit Abby.

OK, so they might not believe me, there's no proof that I wrote my speech before hers, but I could say enough to put doubts in their head about both of us.

And let *Mattie* and her Uncooked Carrot Burgers for Inner City Youth get the dosh? Not an option.

As I stand there, I realise something astonishing. *They don't scare me.* Not even old iron-drawers-banker Olivia. No. What scares me is being without the things that matter to me: Freddie, Will, my family in Somerset, but also my family in London. Grazia and Sandie and Toby and their little baby . . .

To tell the jury about Abby would be another case of Emily pulling the 'poor me' card. It hasn't worked for me, not since I convinced Duncan to marry me – and look what a bloody triumph *that* was. So why do I keep playing the victim?

'You know, I had my speech all worked out,' I say, daring Abby to look up at me. 'Word perfect, it was. Slick, confident, with impressive figures. But I've realised that's not me.'

Angelika has leaned forward in her seat. I can see her beige bra poking over the top of her neckline, and it gives me hope.

'Some of us are corporate beings. You know, what Abby Capper said earlier, about the PowerPoints and the spread-sheets and the macho world of one-upmanship and look at my CV.'

I shrug. 'That's not the person I am. After school, I worked in a bank. It wasn't a career – I didn't much fancy one of those, because it sounded a bit like hard work. So I did my job, went out with my mates, went home again, the way we all did.'

It occurs to me that I might be rambling. Ah well. In for a penny. 'Not the greatest of starts for a female eco-preneur, is it? Except, you know, maybe it is. Because people change. I'd never have dreamed that I'd be standing up here, that I might have got this far.

'See, if I know about anything, it's dreams. I used to dream of a fairy-tale wedding. And then I dreamed, and got a fairy-tale divorce. I moved in with the man of my dreams – yes, a man, sorry, but if we want to change the world, we've got to involve them too – and together we set up home and business in an imperfect village called Heartsease Common, up the road from Upper Findlebury.

'Like Upper Findlebury, we lacked community. But unlike Upper Findlebury, which I urge you to visit, we also lacked basic facilities, decent fresh food, a purpose, a train station, a primary school, a source of employment, a super-fast broadband connection, a beauty salon, hairdresser, post office, chemist, well, we lacked pretty much everything.

'Drive through now, like everyone else does at twenty miles over the speed limit, and you might not see *that* much difference. But it's there, if you slow down. We set up a store selling knick-knacks. Didn't work. Then we started noticing all the brilliant foods made by our neighbours, and we tried to sell those. Cut a long story – and an awful lot of trial and error – short and we've ended up with something a bit like a farmers' market, but with prices that suit Heartsease's credit-crunched pockets rather than Findlebury's more generous salaries.

'Don't get me wrong, it's not a class war. It's simply evolution. Last winter, the lease on the old chemist next door finally came down to a rate we could afford, so we decided to set up a craft workshop and store. I don't know if we'll discover the meaning of life, but we know a great recipe for red velvet cupcakes, and people are having fun and they're visiting the village and suddenly we've got a bit of an identity.'

I realise I'm sounding lame now. Must move on. 'Look, my ideas aren't that different from Abby's.' I bite my lip so that the desire to explain exactly *why* that is doesn't get too much for me. 'I'd even like to share some of them, like the intern thing. That's great. But I'm more into evolution than revolution. I think people need to find out for themselves what matters: whether that is being creative and turning old clothes into new ones, or planting seeds, or riding a bike for the first time since they were ten.'

Maeve looks pointedly at her watch.

'The scheme's in my handout. We're talking about taking over the entire parade of empty shops next to us, and offering them to new businesses with an ecological contribution to make. We want our local nursery to embrace sustainability and a low-carbon future, but in a way that doesn't put the fees up. We want . . . well, it's all there. It could work really well. That's what we think, anyway . . .'

I shrug, aware that I haven't delivered anything like a rousing finish. I smile, and head back towards my seat, and it's a good twenty seconds before the applause comes, and even then it's very much consolation prize applause, the sort you hear when the brave-but-crap person gets thrown out of a talent contest on telly.

Maeve announces the tea break, and I hide in the loos to avoid seeing Abby, because I might punch her bloody lights out, and then I sit through the other pitches without taking in anything more than the same old words . . . sustainable, blah, empowerment, blah, generational change, blah, blah, blah.

At the end there's a glass of organic Gloucestershire wine on offer, but I don't want to 'network' with any of them, and anyway, I need to make sure I get a different train from Abby's because those electrical rails might be that bit too tempting. No one sees me leave, because no one notices me.

I don't care. It's all bollocks anyway. Let them give the money to that bitch if they want to. Some of us think friendship's more important than winning. If this whole thing has 'learned' me anything, it's that. I can't teach a master-class on friendship, but as I travel out of London, back into the 'burbs, I know I *must do better*.

This time I'm going to get an A plus for effort.

*

I arrive back in Heartsease late afternoon, after buying a gin and tonic from the train buffet car, and then taking a taxi from the village *before* the Next Bloody Village Along, because I couldn't stomach passing through Findlebury with its smug station and its stupid hanging baskets.

The store's closed, and Freddie is at a birthday party this evening, so I let myself into the flat, dreaming of a long bath and an even longer drink.

'Hey, gorgeous. How did you get on?'

I jump. For a moment I think it's Will but then I realise it's *Mickey* sitting on our sofa. He makes it look like a doll's armchair.

'What are you doing here?'

'Well, after your send-off this morning, I thought with your chap away, you needed a welcome home party too. Sorry. I really didn't mean to scare you. I can go if you want.'

But he doesn't get up. He looks very much at home.

'I meant . . . *how*?'

'Oh, I came back via the village an hour ago, it's on my way home, and I hoped you might be back by now. I got chatting to your friend. Jean, is it? Then I was thirsty and I came up here to get a glass of water and she locked me in. Must have forgotten about me.'

It's completely implausible, and coming from someone else, it'd be a bit . . . well, stalkerish. But there is something so confident and roguish about Mickey that it's hard to stay cross with him for long.

He gestures at the table, where there are two empty glasses and a bottle of red wine. 'I brought my own booze. As a thank-you for including me in your pitch.'

He's not even bothering to try to sound plausible now. Somehow that makes me more confused. I ought to be angry at the intrusion. But part of me feels flattered that he's gone to all this trouble. When was the last time *Will* surprised me?

'Say something, Emily.'

I stare at him. It's been one of those days.

He stands up. I swear he's going to hit his head on the high ceiling, like Alice in Wonderland. 'Listen. We both know there's something between us, but I'll go if you want me to.'

'I . . .'

'If you *really* want me to.'

Mickey is whispering now, and the question no longer seems to be about whether he's going to leave, but about whether he's going to . . .

Thinking about it makes me tip my head up slightly and that's his cue. I close my eyes, which is the wimp's way out, I know, but I don't want to take any responsibility for any of this.

So I feel, rather than see, him lean towards me and there's what seems like an eternal gap in time before his lips meet mine.

Lips that taste of red wine and green grass and rolling tobacco. Of being a teenager, with no responsibility, no stress . . .

Irresistible.

I'm kissing back. I feel fragile and sweet and girlish with him towering over me.

Kisses from days when there was no one to answer to . . .

'Emily . . .' His huge hands are on the small of my back, and moving down.

Days when there was no one to betray . . .

It's like someone's clicked their fingers and brought me back to the present day.

'No. I can't do this, Mickey. It's not right.'

He keeps kissing me, just for a second or two more, testing my resolve. I force myself to open my eyes to break the spell and his are so close to me that I can see white-gold flecks on his pupils. They seem to dance . . .

I pull away, only slightly, but far enough.

'You sure?' he says.

I nod.

Mickey steps back and smiles, an admiring, slightly wistful smile. The way a connoisseur would appreciate a painting he can't afford. 'Fair enough,' he says. 'Would have been lovely, you know.'

It's difficult to be angry, because he's so straightforward about it all. 'I'm sure it would have been,' I say, and I'm not lying. 'Except for the paralysing guilt.'

He smiles again, then puts his hands behind his back, like a butler, and leans forward to give me the lightest peck on the forehead. 'Guilt is a waste of energy. You know where I am if you change your mind. And enjoy the wine. You deserve it.'

And he's gone before I can say anything else.

I slump onto the sofa, which is still warm from his body. I don't know what to think or feel any more. But I know I'm glad I stopped it before it started. The kiss was lovely and yet . . . it wasn't Will.

Emily Cheney might be many, many things but she isn't a cheat. Though Mickey's helped me in one way. He's made me realise that what I've worked for here means the world to me, and I'm not talking about the store.

If Will doesn't want me, or what I want, then that's one thing.

But to lose him or the other people I care about through neglect or stupidity or stubbornness . . . well, that would be something I'd never forgive myself for.

CHAPTER 28

Grazia

If Barcelona was bliss, then Sitges is stupendous.

All blue-skied days and glowing nights, with an arty crowd rather like Leon's old circle, with one *essential* difference: my new friends do not take themselves seriously. The dress code veers from stunning to silly, and so does the dancing. I feel about fifteen years old, except when Joel and I wake late morning and know that we must find the strength, somehow, to begin partying all over again.

We spend our afternoons alone, reminding ourselves that the passion we feel for one another is not waning, despite our 'parenthood'. When we need to refuel we sip cava on the balcony overlooking the packed beach, and talk about ourselves, instead of about the kids.

However, all good things must come to an end, and so I sit in the car back from the airport, trying not to let the low August clouds and the torrent of text messages from Daisy bring me down to earth too soon.

'What's the latest?' asks Joel, as my phone buzzes again.

'Off. He has not responded to her last two Facebook pokes, and so she has changed her status to single as a last attempt to provoke a reaction.'

'I'm starting to feel sorry for the poor boy. My daughter is seriously high maintenance, isn't she?'

'Who knows? Maybe this is normal behaviour now?'

Joel kisses me. 'Thank goodness we're too bloody old for all that.'

I pull a face. 'Speak for yourself.'

'Shit, you're not on Facebook now, are you?'

'Only to stay in touch with Daisy. Oh, and because Pierre says that I need to use *social networking* to promote my exhibition.'

'Ah, well, if *Pierre* says it, it must be right.'

'Not jealous, are you?'

'Well, he's got plenty to offer. He can put you on the embroidery map. He can tell you your make-up's too strong or your heels are too tarty. But,' he leans over and kisses me on the lips, 'he can't do *that* as well as I can, can he?'

'No,' I admit, noticing in the driver's mirror that my face is flushed, so there is no point denying the effect Joel has on me.

'I'd like to say that the minute we get home I will ravish you on the stairway,' he whispers, 'but I think the kids might object.'

Actually, for all the interest the children show when we do arrive back, we could have worked our way through the entire Kama Sutra in the hall without them noticing. In fact, we have to go up to the landing and call out to get a response.

Daisy's door shifts a few centimetres, and a foot with different coloured nail polish on each toe props it open. 'It's *him*,' she mouths, and then runs back to her laptop, the door closing behind her.

'Her play-hard-to-get strategy worked, then?' I say.

'I'll say hi to Little Lord Fauntleroy, you go and get yourself a coffee,' Joel suggests. I still feel uncomfortable around Alf, so I do not object.

In the kitchen, I set up the coffee machine, enjoying the

familiar ritual. It is the only thing in this place that feels like it belongs to *my* life, because Joel bought it and a small grinder for me when I complained yet again about his appalling instant coffee. Of course, it is as it should be: this is the children's home, not mine. But even as the beans bounce violently against the blades, and begin to release that smell, one of my favourites in the world, I feel the other things about myself become fuzzy around the edges. My passions – and my moods – are deadened as soon as the security gates close behind us.

Perhaps, when the children leave school, he will sell up and move in with me.

How can I possibly think that far ahead?

The super-heated water hits the coffee grounds, and I breathe in the intense vapour. Grazia is all about such extremes. The evenness that parenting requires might be good for steadying me, perhaps, but do I *want* to be evened out? For Sandie, it is different: when I saw her with baby Ruby for the first time, she had a calmness that was certainly more than the all-fall-down exhaustion of a new mother. She will grow as Ruby does, and I have a confidence that however hard the next few months, motherhood will suit her better than she could have dreamed.

Not me, though. The more involved I feel with Joel's kids, the less I feel like snarky, snobbish, *interesting* Grazia, and also the less mental energy I have to sew. Before I went to Sitges I barely touched my embroidery, yet as soon as I spend time only with adults, I am on fire again, full of ideas.

I have forgotten who said that the pram in the hall is an end to creativity – Joel would know – but in my case, it is the line-up of smelly teenagers' trainers, and Primark heels.

'Grazia?' he calls out.

And then there is Joel, who seems to have promoted me to fully fledged stepmother – well, almost to parent-in-chief at times – without ever asking me whether that is what *I* want.

'GRAZIA? Would you come up here please?'

I head up the stairs. What does he want me to do now? Wash behind the boy's ears? The pure light of the Costa Brava seems a world away.

Joel is standing at the top, shaking his head. 'I don't believe what he's bloody well done now. You're *definitely* not going to believe it.'

'Dad, you can't make me.' Alf's voice is sulky, but a little less defiant than normal.

I hesitate on the top step. Perhaps this is the time to draw that line in the sand. 'Joel, I am not sure I feel comfortable getting involved with things that do not involve me personally. Surely this is between you and Alf—'

'But it does involve you.'

'Really?' I think Joel is more of a traditionalist than he likes to pretend: he does seem to believe that children are women's business.

It is the middle of the afternoon, but Alf's bedroom is dark, because he has his blackout blinds drawn. The only light comes from his huge computer monitor. No laptop for Alf – he has built his own system with components ordered from all over the world. Joel cannot seem to decide whether to be proud of the boy's technical acumen, or ashamed that his steamiest encounters occur with a soldering iron.

'Explain to Grazia what I found you doing,' Joel instructs, and Alf cringes.

'Look, if this is about what I think it is about, it is better man to man, surely,' I say. The idea of the poor boy having to confess to looking at pornography in front of his father's middle-aged girlfriend seems guaranteed to add layer upon layer of extra hang-ups.

And then I notice the image on the screen.

'Is that . . . ?'

Joel shakes his head, almost beyond words. 'Like I said. It involves you.'

The image is of a slim, olive-skinned woman, stepping out of the bath. The bath in the main family bedroom . . . *here*.

I am torn between shock and . . . actually, a tiny glimmer of pride. I look in good shape. After last year's brief foray into the dangerous world of cosmetic intervention, all the fillers and injections have disappeared, and yet what I am left with is a stronger face, somehow, and a lean, powerful body.

A body that, against all expectation, still somehow appeals to a teenaged boy.

The weirdness of that hits me now. '*How?*'

'Exactly my question,' says Joel. 'Perhaps the bloody peeping Tom would like to explain?'

Alf does look utterly mortified, and a part of me – the part that is not wondering what else he might have seen, or how long he might have been looking – is almost amused. 'The camera,' he mumbles eventually.

Joel looks confused, but I think I know what Alf means. 'The camera I gave you as a present? The video camera?'

Alf nods, looking down. 'It . . . was an experiment. In remote control devices. I wanted to see whether I could rig it up with a movement sensor and then take a live feed to my computer.' He dares to look up now. 'It's legit technology, same as they use on *Springwatch*.'

'So why didn't you put the camera in a bloody nesting box, you little bastard?' Joel says. 'Hang on. *Movement* sensor? Does that mean you filmed your sister, too?'

'Ugh. No. Gross. She's got her own bathroom, I wouldn't want to see her without her kit on.'

'But I use the main bathroom too, Alf. Have you got *me* on camera?'

A sly smile turns up the sides of the boy's lips. 'Don't worry, Dad, your secrets are safe with me. I deleted them. I don't want to see you taking a crap, thanks.'

I look at the screen. 'But you do want to see *me* on the toilet?'

We're both blushing, but Alf is blushing more deeply than me.

'That's not because I'm a perv, or whatever. It was so I could test the remote focus and movement function. It's got a seriously good lens, too, for such a small unit.'

'Jesus *Christ*,' says Joel. 'You are one weird fucking kid.'

'How long have you been filming?' I ask.

'Took a couple of days for all the parts to arrive, including a bigger hard drive, and a day to put it in. I . . . well, I had it ready for the day before the party.'

'The *party*? So you've got footage of all your sister's friends in the toilet?' Joel is shaking his head, I would guess with 95 per cent outrage and 5 per cent reluctant admiration.

And now I remember something different: the cackling gang of boys that greeted us at the top of the stairs when we returned to the house after the party. 'Did you show your friends the video of me?'

'Um . . .'

'You little bastard,' says Joel. 'If it isn't bad enough – and it really is very seriously bad – that you're filming my girlfriend naked, you're actually *pimping* the pictures around your grubby little friends.'

Alf shrugs, which I am guessing is not a smart thing to do right now.

Joel walks over to his son, takes his shoulders, and begins to shake him. Alf stares him out, with a challenging glint in his eye, which enrages Joel even more.

'You ungrateful brat. Do you think I want to have to wipe your arse and clean the dribble off your chin like a stroppy toddler? I never wanted to be a father anyway and to end up with a devious little shit like you adds insult to injury!'

'Joel—' I put my hand on his arm, but he brushes it off.

'No, he needs to hear this. I have to put up with enough whingeing from him and his sister about how hard their lives are and what they have to deal with. Well, guess what, sunshine, it's not much more fun for me either. I thought you guys might have grown up a bit by now. I dunno, found *real* friends out there in the *real* world, instead of relying on the bloody Internet.

'And by your age I was going out with girls, you know, flesh and blood girls instead of leering over older women on film.' He looks at me, realising what he has said. 'Not that I have any complaints about real women, but what kind of girl is going to want to date a bloody peeping Tom, tell me that, eh, Alf?'

Then suddenly Joel seems to run out of steam, and doubt crosses his face. Even though I know he should not have lost his temper, I feel sorry for both father and son. I remember how my mother tried to get through to me when I was Alf's age, and yet it was as though we were speaking different languages.

For the first time, I begin to see it from her point of view. *Sorry, Mama.*

Alf's face has not changed, despite his father's rant. He remains insolently passive, knowing, as every child does from toddlerhood onwards, that the minute your parent loses control, you have won.

Joel waits for his son to flip. We all stare at the floor. Eventually, Joel sighs, and walks towards the door. I follow, and as we are leaving Alf makes a strange noise, half-laugh, half-groan. We look round.

'Gee, thanks, Dad, always knew I could rely on you for a guiding hand.'

September

CHAPTER 29

Emily

Operation New Emily hasn't got off to the best of starts.

First of all, I called Sandie immediately after the Green Goddess pitch, full of remorse and ideas to help with the first few months of the baby's life.

'I'd love to babysit. Even overnight if you like, so you and Toby can enjoy a little private time together again.'

There was a pause. 'Ruby is four weeks old. What makes you think I'd want any kind of private time with Toby right now?'

Ruby . . .

Another silence. 'I have to go, Emily. Thanks for the kind wishes. I'll be in touch.' And I realised she'd hung up on me.

At the end of that week, Will came home from Wales and I was waiting for him at the station. I hadn't gone crazy and made a banner, but I did have a bunch of flowers with me, because I read in a magazine that men never got flowers.

He didn't expect to be collected: I saw him before he saw me, and he crossed over the footbridge slowly, shoulders hunched under the weight of his rucksack, a weariness on his face despite the touch of sun on his cheeks.

'Surprise!' I said, jumping out from behind the chocolate machine.

He *did* look surprised. Baffled, really. I hadn't exactly been going out of my way to support his studies. In fact, when he left, I'd joked that if he wanted to buy a one-way ticket to Wales, then that was fine by me.

So I guess I can understand his confusion when I pulled the bunch of flowers – yellow gerbera, a reassuringly chirpy and un-girly choice – out from behind my back. He touched one of them, tentatively, like he was expecting it to squirt water into his eyes.

'They didn't come from the joke shop, honest! They're because I wanted to say I'm sorry for the way I've been. I am not going to be that way from now on. I've finally, finally grown up.'

Will's mouth smiled but the top part of his face was a frown, as though there was some kind of tussle going on in his head, but eventually the smile won. 'That's great, Em. Really great.'

I leaned forward to kiss him and we ended up crashing noses, and we both laughed it off, and at the time I blamed the flowers and I thought, well, that'll be OK, because when we get home to Heartsease and he's unpacked and relaxed and caught up and told me about the course, *then* he'll kiss me properly and then . . .

And he hasn't touched me since. Well, not like *that*. Ten days later and he only seems to want to spend time with Freddie, but even then he's distracted, nodding his head at the Fredster's stories without asking questions back. I haven't changed, and I know he can't possibly sense what happened with Mickey because I'm not even sure it happened any more.

What was it that Abby said? *You know the way he always insists he never wanted kids? That they'd just get in the way of all the stuff he wanted to do.*

Of course, she might have been lying, as she was about so many other things. But maybe she wasn't. Either Will is feeling the weight of the world's troubles on his shoulders – or he's already decided he's leaving us, and is looking for the right moment to do it. The thought keeps me awake at night, as I lie there, noticing the distance between us in our tiny bed.

But I'm not giving up. I use the small hours to plan and plot to prove that I am, finally, the woman my friends, my family and my son deserve.

Will drops his bombshell as I am ironing the packet creases out of Freddie's first ever school shirt. It is the Night Before the Big Day, and the feeling of déjà vu – of being my mother, my face hot with steam and my nostrils full of starch – is surreal, but comforting. Until I notice that Will, sitting on the sofa surrounded by coursework, hasn't moved for several minutes, and has that greenish look Freddie used to get before he was about to throw up.

'Hard work?' I ask.

'What? Oh, no. It's not this.' He stares at me. 'I don't think I'll come with you guys tomorrow, if that's OK.'

My stomach lurches, but I don't let it show. 'Hmm?'

'Tomorrow. It's more of a mother–son thing, isn't it? Plus, we wouldn't want him to be bullied for needing two grown-ups there.'

'He's only four, Will. No one will think he's a *wimp*.' I try to sound calm.

'The thing is, I'm a bit uncomfortable about it myself. It seems like something his father should do.'

That stings. 'There are a lot of things his father should have done, though, aren't there? But Duncan's an inadequate shirker who can't cope with responsibility and you're ten times the man he is.'

Aren't you, Will? Please don't give up on us now. Not before I have a chance to prove myself.

'Nobody's perfect, Em,' he says, and opens his mouth to say something else.

I get in first. 'We can ask Freddie,' I say, knowing he's bound to want Will there.

'OK. I suppose that's the best idea.' He stands up. 'I'm off for a breath of air. It feels different here, after Wales. And too much coursework makes me a very dull boy.'

I finish the school shirt. I hold it up and something about it makes my throat tighten: the tiny cuffs, maybe, or the floppy collar, or the slightly shiny easy-care fabric, because there's no point in splashing out on organic cotton when he'll have grown out of it by Christmas, the rate he's shooting up right now.

I want to follow Will out, talk to him about tomorrow and how it'll feel to see my boy – *our* boy, because Freddie is the product of three parents, really, and has spent so much longer with Will than with Duncan – take this huge step. But of course I can't leave the flat with Freddie asleep, and perhaps Will does simply need some space.

I pull myself together, moving the shirt onto its padded blue hanger, and folding up the ironing board.

See, I am a grown-up. I can stop myself bursting into tears at the tiniest provocation, and I can think rationally and sensibly about the future.

Now I simply need to prove it to the people that matter.

None of us sleeps properly, so we end up eating our breakfast at six forty-five in the morning. Freddie has been appointed King for a Day by Will, and has chosen what we all must eat – three Weetabix for energy, with chocolate milk for taste, and two Babybels in a toasted sandwich. But the Weetabix sticks in my throat.

'So, shall we toast the King of Heartsease?' says Will, and we hold up our beakers. 'To the newly grown-up King Frederick Prince!'

'To the King!'

Freddie beams and I want to kiss Will right now for finding such a smart way to stop any last-minute nerves.

'Now, then, King Frederick. Do you want both of your loyal subjects to accompany you to school this morning, or just one?'

I hold my breath. Freddie looks puzzled. 'Wh-hy?'

'Oh, nothing.'

Freddie bangs a little fist on the table. 'Explain!'

'I've heard the Kings and Queens of Findlebury only choose one parent, usually female, to take them.'

'Why?'

'I don't know, Freddie, but perhaps it's to prove that they are brave and grown-up.'

I shoot Will an evil look, which he ignores. Why is he being such a manipulative bastard? Freddie chews this over, as he chews his Weetabix with an open mouth. For once, I don't tell him off.

'OK,' says Freddie. 'Only Mummy, then. But don't be sad, Will. I still love you lots.'

Will has the grace to look shamefaced about his emotional game playing. The old Will would never have behaved like this, so he must have rationalised his behaviour somehow. Maybe this is about being cruel to be kind, as he detaches himself from us, step by tiny step.

In the Snowvan, Freddie and I are singing stupid songs, but as we approach the school, our bravado deserts us. Upper Findlebury Primary might claim to be a village school, but it seems the villagers think it's too dangerous to walk to school, so the streets are gridlocked with shiny 4x4s and we have to park five streets away. At least no one will see the van.

Ahead of us, there's a blur of maroon uniforms, along with little cliques of women with immaculate blonde hair. I pull at my own kinky bits, but feel them springing back into place defiantly.

Ah, well, sod it, I will never belong so why bother to try?

'Mummy, I don't think I want to go to school after all.'

Freddie's voice is terribly young. Too young for the eleven years of playground politics and classroom drama that lie ahead as soon as he crosses the school gates.

Maybe I could home educate? I'm certainly good at story-telling . . .

No. I need to lead by example, show Freddie that life is not something to fear. Even though leading by example in this case means *he* is the one who has to be brave.

'Listen, Fredster, we all feel nervous before we try something new. But school is great, honestly. OK, the lessons can be a bit boring, but the teachers can be lovely, and you'll make friends. New friends who will last you the whole of your life, if you're lucky.'

Is that true? I lost touch with most of my friends when I moved to London, and I've messed up royally with my new ones. But I guess I also know that I might still be able to win them back, now I've realised how much I screwed up. You keep learning into adulthood, and right now I am still hoping this lesson hasn't come too late.

'Don't want *new* friends.'

Poor Freddie. All his friends at Tiny Tykes are younger, so they won't start till next term. He's on his own. I squeeze his hand tighter. I can't imagine any of these mums becoming my best buddies either. As I walk towards the gate, I spot a group wearing the kind of designer clobber that wouldn't look out of place on the catwalk. They assess me quickly and ruthlessly, and then look away. I am dismissed. Well, fine. I don't have time to spend an hour airbrushing away my zillions of flaws before dropping Freddie off, only to be socially excluded for my failure to produce a perfect replica of the Windsor Castle from sugar-free, taste-free jelly.

Another group are all pregnant. For a moment I panic, in case that bitch Abby is one of them, but these have smaller, *designer* bellies, draped in soft stretchy cottons. I feel that familiar craving for another child: it's what women do, isn't it, when they see their first-born taking steps towards independence. With another baby, I'd be too busy to worry about losing Will or Sandie.

Except . . . haven't I spent long enough avoiding the issues?

Freddie has stopped walking. His face is screwed up, like he's trying not to cry, and the sight of it makes me feel wobbly myself. I scan the crowds and finally I see another woman on her own with a small girl clutching her hand. The child's uniform is pristine, her shoes unscuffed, and her Poppy-logoed cotton book-bag slaps against her bare legs in the wind because it is completely empty.

'Let's make a friend right now!'

I stride over to the woman who has a rabbit in the headlights expression that makes me feel like I am looking in the mirror. She's tried a bit with her make-up this morning, but her mascara is gluing her lashes together at the bottom.

'Hello. Are you all new too?'

Suspicion crosses her face, but then she looks me up and down, as all the other mothers have. The difference is that *her* face doesn't wrinkle with distaste, but relaxes a bit. 'Yes. Yes, we are . . .' She doesn't seem to be able to remember quite what to say next.

'I'm Emily. And this is Freddie.' I hold out my hand to the mother, and Freddie copies me, holding out his to the little girl.

'Tina. And this is Maisie. Say hello, Maisie.'

Maisie hides her hand behind her back, but she does mumble, 'Hello,' and Freddie smiles uncertainly and then reaches into his own not-quite-empty bag and pulls out a bag of sweets. 'Would you like one?'

'It's a little early—' Tina starts, but then she censors herself.

'They're sugar-free,' I whisper, 'though I haven't told *him* that,' and we exchange a conspiratorial look.

305

Freddie tears the top off the packet and empties two, three, four fruit-shaped gums into his palm. 'You can choose the colour,' he says. 'The banana ones are yummy.'

Maisie studies them for five . . . ten . . . fifteen seconds, and I feel as though the playground noises have faded away as we all wait.

Finally, she takes the red, strawberry-shaped one.

'Thank you, Freddie,' she says, and my son puts the other three in his own mouth, and they chew, silently.

And I know, somehow, that we're going to be OK.

CHAPTER 30

Sandie

Five a.m.

Just me, three hundred gleaming new dummies, and a couple of security guards: it's enough to make me fall in love with Garnett's all over again.

I couldn't sleep, so I thought I might as well come here. I left our crowded house in a state of grace: Ruby dreaming of whatever she dreams of, still under the mystical baby-whisperer regime, even though Miss Hart left last week and already seems more like a fairy godmother than a real person. Toby and Monty snoring in sync. Gramma on one sofa, scolding someone in her sleep, and Marnie asleep in the chair, dreaming of beautiful men.

But I had to be here. The excitement – and the terror – is too much.

Soon the hit squad of last-minute cleaners will arrive, to mop up anything the evening cleaners missed. Today I'm taking no chances. Babs will be at my side, of course, but she's got her hands full with the Treasure Hunt project, which she's project-managed, concealing a hundred prizes around the store, including the coveted necklace. I've already floor-walked from the bottom to the top, checking price labels and signage and bins and light bulbs and all the other tiny items on my mental list of Things That Have a Tendency to Be Missed.

Toby thought my control-freakery might be reduced by having a baby, but instead I now keep a back-up list, on *actual* paper, in case tiredness makes me forget the essentials. Toby calls it my Battleaxe Plan.

Today mine runs to five separate pages, headed:

BEFORE WE OPEN: *Cleaning, Staff Appearance, PA System Check, Key Scents, Lift and Stairs, Group Photo, Final Stock Check, Walkie-Talkies, Motivational Cheer, GO!*

AT OPENING TIME: *Opening countdown, Ribbon Cutting, Celebrity Assistants, First Customer Awards, Treasure Map Distribution, Pirate Choir sing new Garnett's theme song.*

HANDLING THE MEDIA: *Name Badges, Goodie Bags, Photo Ops, TV Interviews and Set-Up, Behind the Scenes shots.*

EVENTS AND SIDESHOWS: *Live Bands x 3, Pirate Contest & Kids' Shows, Customer of the Hour, Prize Draws, Product Demonstrations x 45, Interactive Web Launch with global podcast and video stream.*

FINANCIAL TARGETS: *Hour by Hour, Dept by Dept, Reporting, Tally Keeper in Staffrooms and Staff Canteen, Grand Total After Store Closing Announcement and Reward Drinks.*

Toby's responsibilities today are to charm the customers, pose for the cameras and repeat the same carefully formulated sound bites about the 'New Garnett's'. It might sound easy, but it's the part I find excruciating – yet another example of why we make a great team. I don't get off entirely scot-free, though. We've agreed to a cringeworthy family shot, featuring Toby, me, Ruby and bloody Laetitia. I almost said no, but the 'three generations of the dynasty' line was our best chance of good publicity so we're going to try our hardest to stay civil for half an hour.

Though, actually, since she awarded us Miss Hart, I have

softened a little towards my former enemy. Or maybe I've softened to the world now I have Ruby.

No. That's not right. I love my daughter with a fierceness I never knew I had, and I love Toby more than ever when I see the two of them together. But in every other way, I am more ruthless than I have been before. Like when Emily called with her half-hearted apology, and I couldn't bear to listen.

Being sweet hasn't got me where I am, and it certainly won't get Garnett's out of the woods.

'TEN . . . NINE . . . EIGHT . . . SEVEN . . . SIX . . . FIVE . . . FOUR . . . THREE . . . TWO . . . ONE . . .'

Toby gives me the briefest of private smiles.

'Open Sesame!'

And then he cuts the garnet-red ribbon that's stretched across the main entrance, and the doormen tip their hats at the people queuing outside, and as the first ten customers push inside, they're handed huge ribboned gift boxes, each containing one of our ten 'signature' products that you won't find anywhere else in Britain, from our Cherry Pie designer handbag, to the exclusive Japanese Cherry Blossom Neck Cream. Of course, no one else knows that our skincare exclusive was *supposed* to be Aguasalisnectarin, the brand new American brand of wrinkle-fixer that only last week was banned by the US Food and Drinks Administration for causing such paralysing acne that the testers wanted their wrinkles back. That was a *very* close shave.

As the lucky ten take their first steps inside and are given the first Treasure Maps, our staff applaud and cheer, and the string quartet begins to play the lively polka that my research suggests is at precisely the right pace to get those spending impulses racing.

Like well-drilled officer cadets, the staff march from their welcoming posts back to their own corners of the store and I allow myself a few glorious seconds to watch the customers flood in. Toby meets and greets them like the star he is, making each one feel like a valued guest at an intimate soiree. If I could only keep him on the door full-time, I suspect the battle would be half-won.

These crowds are better than I could have hoped. Not quite on Harrods sale scale, but people keep coming and coming. Of course, customers aren't much use unless they're buying, and all the conjurors and side-shows and live music in the world won't make that happen. Now I have to hope that all the work we've done together here in this store has created a kind of magic of its own.

But what if it hasn't? What if—

'Sandie?' Toby has disentangled himself from the customers and is taking my hand.

'Sorry. Bit overwhelmed by it all.'

'I think you'll find that's pages one and two of the world's longest to-do list done and dusted, congratulations!'

'Oh yes,' I say, going back to my clipboard and then wishing I hadn't. 'Which means now we're onto the scariest part of all.'

'Facing the press?'

'No. Facing your mother.'

God – and Gramma – please understand that I am trying my very best in the face of almost impossible odds. But if my smile doesn't end up looking altogether genuine in the photos, that's because it really, really isn't.

'I'll take the child, shall I?' says Laetitia, though it's less of a suggestion and more of a demand. 'The matriarch holding the youngest addition to the dynasty.'

'*More like the ugly past and the better future*,' whispers the *Daily Telegraph* photographer, who has had enough of Laetitia's artistic suggestions, including one idea that a few extra lights might 'make the baby's skin look a little paler to highlight the family resemblance'.

Thank goodness Toby didn't hear *that*, or he'd have walked.

Laetitia still hasn't acknowledged me, although she did say to Toby that the store is 'rather too crowded for a pleasurable shopping experience', which makes me so mad I can't speak.

We smile, anyway, for snap after snap, until I am on the verge of snapping myself. Suddenly Laetitia is the world expert on retail reinvention, making quips about 'teaching the younger generation a thing or two about what brings the customers in, and as you can see, I still know my onions'. Toby raises his eyebrows at me. I know he wants to say something, but I made him promise me that he wouldn't disagree with her in front of the journalists. I wish I could rip off my shoes to show the blisters I've earned from walking about a thousand miles up and down these floors in the last few weeks. Toby tells me I've even been marching in my sleep, my sore heels knocking against the mattress.

Still, it's good for shifting the baby weight.

None of the hacks asks me anything once I've retold that same old story about first coming here from the Midlands with my gramma and falling in love with the store even though we could barely afford the little tub of talcum powder. That's what they like, the rags to riches story of the little girl made good, and that's when their attention switches back to the Garnett dynasty. I can't decide if this is racism, classism, or plain lazy journalism. I don't care *that* much about the credit, but I can't wait until this farce is through and I can get back to the shop floor.

Ruby behaves the best out of all of us: taking her grandmother's fake kisses without a shudder, and maintaining that expression that is something near to a grin, even though the baby books insist she's too young to be smiling on purpose.

'I think that's the last one,' says the photographer, and now Ruby is the only one still smiling, as the rest of us let our true feelings show on our faces.

'Need to get back,' I say, already planning my route through the store, via the Sleep-In event in the bed department, via the artisan ice-cream-making masterpiece and then the cheap-and-chic eco-fashion show.

'Actually,' says one of the journalists, 'I have a final question. What does Mrs Garnett have to say about the rumours about your former manager, Edgar Murray, attempting to undermine the store and open the way to a takeover by your brother-in-law, Roland Garnett?'

I stare at him, and Toby gulps, but Laetitia's face stays curiously passive, and I don't think that's entirely because of the cosmetic procedures she's so fond of.

'It's in the hands of our lawyers,' she says, casual as anything.

'Mum?' Toby has gone quite pale. Roland is his *ex*-favourite uncle, a charmer who spent half of the store's profits in the eighties and nineties, before spending several years in prison. His treachery almost certainly caused Toby's father to have a stroke that left him half the man he used to be, until he died last year.

'Oh, it's nothing to get worked up about,' she says, scowling at the journalist. 'Do we look . . . *bovvered*? Now, much as we'd love to spend the afternoon chit-chatting with the lovely media, we all have plenty to do on this busy launch day.'

And the press officer escorts the journalist away before he can ask any more awkward questions.

'Mother?' Toby asks, as soon as we're out of range.

'Shall we talk about this on the sixth floor, Gannet? I wanted a personal word with Miss Barrow anyway.'

I feel sick. The last time she 'wanted a personal word', she offered me a pay-off to take myself and my unborn baby out of her son's life for good.

Gramma has been hovering at the sidelines, as she's more willing to cope with the messy end of baby care than Laetitia, so I hand Ruby over with a kiss. Toby and I follow his mother to her den on the management floor. As I walk in, I realised she's had it redecorated and kitted out with all the latest technology. I think of my own broom cupboard, with the laptop that crashes every time I open my email, and the chair that won't adjust and the air vent that deafens me every fifteen minutes.

'I spotted some of the workmen at a loose end last week,' she explains, as we gawp at the fancy new wallpaper, 'and they were awfully helpful.'

Toby grips my hand more tightly, more to stop himself lashing out than to keep me calm, I suspect.

'Now then, I have some important things to say. Number one, this business with odious Edgar and that little shit Roland. I know you're both going to ask why I didn't keep you "in the loop" or whatever the current phrase is—'

'Yes, we are both meant to be directors,' I say, but she talks over me.

'The point is that the two of you had quite enough on your plates already, what with babies and relaunches and suchlike. I decided it would be better to keep it to myself. I might not be awfully hands-on, but there are times when only the sharpest of fingernails will do.' She looks at my broken nails, and stretches out her own scarily long talons.

'So it's true?' Toby asks.

'Roland was absolutely nutty to think he could endanger the grand dame of Oxford Street,' she says.

But that's where she's wrong. If Roland was behind the rumours, then he came terrifyingly close to destabilising us. 'What was Edgar playing at?'

'Roland offered him the world, even though I am sure he would have sacked him the moment he got his hands on the store. Anyway. We've hit Roland with a suitably intimidating libel suit, and Edgar is skulking around, hoping we don't sue him for breach of confidentiality. Nothing to fret about.'

I'm about to argue, when I look at her desk and see a photograph of Ruby that I've never seen before.

'Where did that come from?'

'Oh,' she says, looking a little embarrassed. 'Oh, I asked Miss Hart if she'd mind taking a few snaps. She has many gifts, doesn't she? I was planning to get them enlarged for you, too, but somehow . . . well, we've been busy.'

Miss Hart really is gifted. The picture is stunning. Ruby is so beautiful, far more beautiful than I had a right to expect. Even though it's been just minutes since I handed her to Gramma, I feel my milk prickling in. I am awed by what we've created, Toby and I.

My walkie-talkie squawks. 'Second floor to Launch Director, can you come in, please, we have the winner of the On the Hour Competition?'

I press TALK. 'Be with you as soon as I can.'

'What was it you were saying?' Laetitia asks.

'I . . .' I pick up the photo. 'I'm surprised.'

'Ah. Well. I suppose that is connected to why I invited you up here. I wanted you to know that, if I am honest, I have had something of a change of heart in recent weeks about *family*.'

Toby and I gawp at her. My walkie-talkie crackles.

'I know it's a busy day so I will be brief. The birth of little Ruby has awakened my inner grandmother in a way I honestly hadn't quite expected. She looks so much like you when you were a baby, Gannet, which was such a lovely surprise!'

'You mean, she wasn't as black as you expected?' Toby says, and I scowl at him.

'I have to admit, I was never the most maternal of women, and when friends have spoken of the joy of grandchildren, I was sceptical, but you know, they were right. All the cuddles and none of the troubles.'

She laughs that twinkly little laugh, the one she's never bothered to use for my benefit before.

'And, once Miss Hart had got you all into a nice routine,

you've surprised me too, Sandra. I'd always thought of you as quite a cold fish. Nothing like a Garnett. But I can see you are trying your hardest with Ruby, and, well . . .' She pauses, and sighs, and then smiles like the Queen. 'I think perhaps it is time to welcome you into the fold.'

My jaw drops. 'I beg your pardon?'

'I have no further objections if you and my son wish to . . . make your relationship more permanent. Although do please give me some warning beforehand, so that I can ensure I am looking my best. Maintenance is so important for we women, isn't it? I can recommend someone delightful on Harley Street if you'd like to perk yourself up, too. Wedding photographs are with you for a lifetime.'

If Laetitia has noticed the expressions on my face, or Toby's, she's doing a great job of ploughing on regardless. Like Toby, I didn't think the woman could do anything to surprise me any more, and yet here she is, bestowing the grandest prize she can imagine in her warped little universe, and neither of us has a clue how to respond. It's like she thinks that the only reason we haven't married is that we were waiting for *her* say-so.

And I can't help wondering what she'd say if she knew that her alpha-male son has gone back to talking about becoming a house husband, now that Ruby's on her best behaviour.

'I do think family is the most wonderful thing, don't you?'

I stare at the walkie-talkie, trying to will it into life, so I can escape back to the shop floor. But it stays silent.

'Mother, you are absolutely incredible,' Toby says, after a long, long while.

Her hands are all aflutter. 'Oh, well, you know what they say. To err is human, to forgive divine.'

Does she seriously think she needs to forgive us for anything? But when I look at Toby, I decide it is not worth asking. And she did, after all, give us Miss Hart.

'I ought to get back to the battlefield,' I say.

'And me,' Toby agrees.

For a moment, Laetitia's regal composure slips and her face sags in something like disappointment. What was she expecting? Champagne and hugs?

'Far be it from me to keep you two from your work. It's been a triumph, it really has. Quite marvellous. Good to know that the old guard will still come to your father's corner shop when it counts, eh, Toby?'

And we leave her there, smiling benevolently to the empty room, and I know that however much I'd love to own Garnett's, or have an office like hers, I'd never swap places with that lonely old woman.

Home.

Funny how this mean, scruffy house has been transformed into a home by Ruby's presence.

She's unsettled tonight, and Marnie and my grandmother are pleased to hand her back when Toby and I finally return from the store, exhausted, yet way too buzzy to contemplate sleep.

As soon as they leave, we head up to the nursery with Ruby. Toby looks even wearier than I do.

'Go downstairs, Toby, and get the champagne. I'll get Ruby to settle down, and then I need a celebratory thimbleful of fizz. I've been on my feet for nineteen hours.'

'It's me, me, me with you, isn't it, Sandie?' And he ducks out of the way before I can hit him.

At first, I think Ruby is as wired as we are, her huge eyes assessing me. Countless times now, I've stood in this tiny box room, watching and waiting.

'Sleepy time now, Ruby,' I say, conscious that Miss Hart's regime has been interrupted, and knowing that it's not my daughter's fault if she is restless. I slow down my own breathing, hoping to calm us both.

And she seems to tune in, and her eyes grow heavy and then

– it's like a miracle – she sleeps. As I gaze at her face, it runs through a thousand tiny changes of expression, as though she is practising for when she is bigger: the sweet smile that will get her what she wants, the scowl that might prove she has her mother's temper, the dreamy gaze where her eyes are half-open that makes me think of her daddy . . .

It's almost midnight by the time I come downstairs. Toby is bolt upright on the sofa, a champagne flute in his hand, fast asleep.

I take my glass and consider waking him up with the sound of the champagne cork popping, but perhaps that should wait for a few days. Though I am cautiously optimistic. Today's takings were twenty times as much as normal, which is obviously not sustainable, but I hope the buzz I felt will last. Perhaps that's the real reason that Laetitia is trying to call a truce. She always wants to be on the winning side.

Which means . . . I think we did it.

I allow a quiet, but unmistakable, feeling of triumph to spread through me, more pleasurable than champagne. *I* did it.

I snuggle up to Toby, leaning against his body gently, so I don't wake him, and closing my eyes so I can focus on how deliciously quiet it is here, nothing but the sound of his breathing and of Ruby's, via the baby monitor. My *family*.

CHAPTER 31

Emily

I didn't mean to come here, but somehow I can't be in London without Garnett's pulling me back.

Sandie's done a brilliant job. The place sparkles in the morning sunlight, and even though the leaves are turning brown on the trees outside, there's always something so spring-like about fresh paintwork. The new colour scheme reminds me of red velvet cupcakes: the soft white of cream cheese frosting, and the deep ruby of the soft cake inside.

It's working, too. People are stopping outside the windows, pointing, smiling, and, most important, going in. I am green with customer envy. The temptation to join them inside the store is strong, but definitely resistible. I don't want to risk it all by rushing in.

Instead, I take a photo of the new Garnett's on my phone, and then jump onto the number 94, back to the first – and only – home I've ever had here in London. I have things to do, people to see, life-changing decisions to see through. Today is the final stage of Operation New Emily, and I cannot afford to be late. It won't start without me.

Shepherd's Bush looks different, now they've dumped an enormous shopping centre behind the tube station. To me, this great palace of steel and glass lacks the romance of a store like Garnett's, but I guess I'm biased.

The bus carries on, towards the authentically rough and ready part of the neighbourhood, and I get off halfway up the Goldhawk Road. I consider taking a detour to look at our old house, but I decide against it. Even though I know I wouldn't have been happy there, I'm not sure I can bear someone else being happy there either.

The office is between a kebab store and an off-licence, up three flights of stairs, above a dentist. It smells familiar, of fat and mouthwash, but somehow the smell makes me feel perky. It's not till I get to the top of the steps that I realise why: this is where I cooked up the plot to get my revenge on Duncan. But that was clear-cut. He was in the wrong, I was in the right.

With Will, it couldn't be more confusing.

'Emily, hello!'

My solicitor is currently 'between' receptionists, or that's what he told me on the phone. He's . . . a bit slapdash, I guess, but he worked bloody hard on my behalf last time. Geoffrey got a serious kick out of kicking Duncan where it hurt, and his fees weren't excessive, though the customer service leaves something to be desired.

'Coffee machine still not working, Geoffrey?'

'Ah, well. No. Boiled over once too often. Why don't I lock up here and we'll get one in Starbucks?'

We don't go to Starbucks in the end – too jammed with buggies – but find a tiny Middle Eastern café full of steam and brass ornaments. It makes me feel like I am in an episode of *Spooks*.

'So, are you sure you want to leave this latest guy too? You don't want to make a habit of it.'

'God, no,' I say. 'But I need to know if it's a possibility. What my options are.'

'You're a funny one, aren't you, Emily? Last time you

didn't want to know any of the details, so long as I could make it work.'

I stir the mint leaves in my tea cup, so they spin round and round like a tornado. 'I think I might have grown up.'

'As your lawyer, I'd advise against ever doing that.' Then he laughs. 'OK, as far as the stores are concerned, there's no legal reason why you couldn't take over the leases from Will, with his agreement, of course. But, well, as your friend, do you seriously think that you can run both of them, on your own, with your son to take care of, too?'

I shrug. 'I did while Will was away in Wales studying.'

'For a few weeks. But is it sustainable long-term? Then there's the money. Right now the craft centre hasn't even had a full year of operation, so how do you know it's profitable long-term? So you could work like a maniac to keep both going, and then find one sinks the other.'

'That's my business, isn't it?'

'Sure. I'm only qualified to advise you on the contracts. But if I were your dad, say, I'd be asking if you'd gone mad to think you can do it all on your own.'

I smile. 'Yeah, well, that's why I haven't mentioned it to my dad, isn't it?'

Geoffrey shrugs. 'You know, I think I preferred the old days, when young women listened to their menfolk.'

'Some human rights lawyer you'd have made. Look, Geoffrey, I don't know whether I'll end up on my own, or whether Will wants to be with me, or . . .' For the first time, it occurs to me that I actually have a choice about whether I want to be with *Will*, just as much as he has a choice about being with me. 'It's about planning ahead. I used to count on luck to make things turn out right. Now I want to keep my options open.'

I take a folder full of leases from Geoffrey, and walk towards Chiswick. The fresh air helps me think.

'EMILY! My most favourite girl in the whole of England!'

Kaspar runs towards me, followed by Big Janis and Little Janis. 'My heroes!' I say, hugging them in turn.

To the outside world, the three might look like any other gang of Latvian builders, but to me they were lifesavers. Back when I was living up the road in a dingy flat, they were my downstairs neighbours and between them they fixed my boiler, fixed up the apartment and fixed my faith in humanity. Oh, and also hand-carved the most wonderful Noah's ark for Freddie: an heirloom piece I will keep for the next baby, just in case.

'No little Freddie today?' asks Big Janis, his blond porn star 'tache more bushy than ever.

'I have another pair of animals for his ark,' says Little Janis, reaching into his pocket to pull out a small parcel, wrapped in Latvian newspaper and tied with string. Without realising it, he's replicated the current 'designer eco gift-wrapping' look that Will has decided to insist on in the shop.

I take the parcel and tuck it in my bag. 'He'll be thrilled. Now, then, shall we see what needs to be done?'

We walk from the corner of the street, down the middle of the road, like we're the hit squad in a Tarantino movie.

Stop it, Emily. Stop living in the movies, pretending you're someone else. You're you, and that's good enough, isn't it?

Toby is waiting outside. When he sees me, he doesn't smile. OK, well, I can cope without smiles. All I need is for him to believe in *me*.

'Hi, Toby.'

'Hello, Emily.' He doesn't kiss me. When I called him first of all, he almost hung up on me because he thought I was calling to get him to take sides. I had to talk at a million miles an hour to keep him on the line.

'How are things going?'

'Good, thanks.'

This is obviously a whopping great lie. Even in the

flattering lunchtime sun, the house is a dark, hulking lump. Overloaded skips are scattered around it, like giant ducklings. And there is complete silence where there should be productive clattering to catch up with long-passed deadlines.

'These are the boys. Kaspar, plus Janis and Janis.'

'Welcome,' he says, switching on the famous Garnett's charm as he shakes hands with each one in turn. 'I have heard such brilliant things about you three. Did you really build the earth in seven days?'

They look at one another, bemused.

'English sense of humour,' I say, and they nod as though this explains everything. 'Shall we look around?'

The boys instantly take their hard hats and fluorescent jackets from their workbags, and follow Toby up the overgrown path.

'Can't say I am exactly looking forward to this,' he says.

'It'll be a doddle.'

Right. Only one job remains on my London to-do list, and it's the one I am least looking forward to. But it's also the whole reason I came in today, and I don't take the easy way out any more.

The prize reception is at the same hotel as before, with everyone invited to celebrate the winner. I bet I'm not the only one who has been rehearsing the loser's smile. The best I can hope for – and I know this is not in keeping with the new can-do me – is that Abby the Double-Crossing Bitch from Hell doesn't win either.

But I have the most horrible hunch she might . . .

I focus on the stuff that's right with my life. Freddie is *loving* school, even though he's only two days in, and he's head over heels in love with Maisie. The weather's holding. The boys are miracle workers.

I wait until the last possible moment to go inside. The less time for small talk, the better, and I plan to rush off the instant it's all over, to pick Freddie up. Only when it's precisely one minute to two do I step into the hotel, and up the stairs to the OTT ballroom where I watched in horror while my ideas were stolen by a scheming cow.

A scheming cow who, at this very moment, is in deepest conversation with *Will*.

I didn't even tell him the announcement was happening today.

She sees me before he does, and looks guilty as hell. I haven't mentioned to Will what she did. No point.

As I get closer, I realise she is no longer pregnant, and she's lost not only most of that impossible bump, but also the bloom on her face. She looks harsh, and the thick make-up doesn't disguise her cold features. Or maybe it's that I am seeing her as she is for the first time.

I summon up a smile, and march over to them.

'Abby! Will!' I air-kiss Abby, trying not to choke on her horrible perfume, and then I put my arm around Will. 'How did you manage to get here? I thought you said you were too busy to be spared from the shop?'

He gives me a strange look and then realises I'm pretending I did tell him, to save face in front of her. 'Wouldn't have missed this moment, you know me.'

Then I have a horrible thought: that something might have gone wrong with Abby and the babies at the last moment. Otherwise they'd be here, wouldn't they? 'Everything's OK, isn't it?' I say, nodding towards her stomach.

'Oh, yes. Fine. Lucius and Saskia. They're nineteen days old. Arrived on schedule, and I'm nicely zipped up again. Honeymoon fresh, and not allowed to lift a finger, which is a terrible hardship, as you can imagine.'

I look at her. 'And the babies?'

'They're *very* noisy. I suppose that's to be expected, at least the nanny says so. I decided to leave them at home. Too late to play the baby card, now, isn't it, and it'd have been hell for

Federica to get a double buggy across London.' And she laughs: I can't tell whether she thinks she's genuinely funny, or whether she's being herself now that I know what she's like.

'If you put it like that, then I suppose you're right. Do you have a picture of them?'

Abby looks surprised. 'Um. Er, no, I don't think I have one in this handbag.' Then she looks over my shoulder. 'Time for the big news.'

She sits down and I see her wince and, despite knowing what a nightmare she is, I feel a certain twisted admiration for her, showing up all guns blazing with a barely healed Caesarean scar.

I manage to steer Will to the row behind Abby. 'You didn't have to come to watch me lose.'

'I got you into it. Least I could do was to see it through. Though there were plenty of times when I didn't think you'd get to this stage.'

'*Charming.*'

'But you did. I'm so proud of you, Em.'

I stare at him. I can't remember the last time someone said that to me. Probably my dad when I passed my driving test on the fifth attempt?

'Better make the most of that feeling, because I reckon it'll be over in about two minutes.'

Maeve Topping walks to the podium and is careful to smile at every single one of us: Abby, me, the pale raw food pioneer, and three others I barely recognise because I was in such a state after Abby's double-crossing pitch. 'Well, thanks so much for coming, my friends. I see we even have a few men here today, for a change. They're welcome, so long as they remember where the power lies. Because one thing we've felt so strongly, as judges, while we've been trying to make one of the toughest decisions of our lives, is the power of women.'

She pauses, and we know we're meant to applaud the sentiment, so we do.

'I'm not joking about how tough it's been. We've worn a hole in the meeting room carpet with pacing. But in the end we had to follow our instincts.

'I won't keep you in suspense for much longer, but I did want to say that, however bad it might feel to lose, everyone who got to this stage is a winner, and we intend to offer you all business mentoring, because in an ideal world we'd like everyone to make their plans work.'

I'm about to pull a face at Will at this attempt to make the losers feel better, but then I realise mentoring might not be a bad idea. So long as we're not mentored by the winner, because I'd put what little dosh I have got on it being Abby.

'Enough consolation prizes. We are about to piss five of you off, and make one of you pretty bloody ecstatic. Except, well, we've decided to break the rules a little, so determined are we to add to the sum of human happiness.

'In fact, our decision is in the spirit of the whole award. We want to share the love, and, in this case, the money.'

Maeve looks round the room.

'It won't be too difficult to share, given that our two winners are almost neighbours.'

Oh, God.

'Do any of the other contestants live in the same area?' Will whispers.

'Not that I know of.'

The same thought has occurred to Abby, who looks round at me nervously.

'We felt that the two women we've chosen were both on the same wavelength, yet also displayed complementary skills – homespun *and* sophisticated, ambitious yet simple.'

If it *is* the two of us, then no prizes for guessing who the homespun, simple one is. They might as well call me the village idiot.

Will gives me a little thumbs-up, but I don't know whether to laugh or cry. Two minutes ago I would have laughed off the idea that I might be taking the money back to Heartsease, but if the price is having to work with *her*, then I'm not sure it's worth paying.

'So I would now like to invite up Abby Capper and Emily Cheney, joint winners of Green Goddess UK!'

For a second there's silence as our fellow competitors absorb the bad news. My own name sounds wrong, coming in the same sentence as the word *winner*. Then I hear the applause and Will kisses me – briefly, but properly, the way he hasn't for months – and I stumble to my feet, and almost collide with Abby, and then we do a ridiculous *after you – no, after you* dance, before she shrugs and pushes to the front.

'Well done, you two!' Maeve says. 'I hope it won't be too much of a trial to pool your resources.'

A look passes between Abby and me, and I *wish* I could tell whether she's simply happy to be herself in all her hideous glory now that I know what she's really like.

'It's the best news I've heard all year,' says Abby.

'Absolutely,' I say, and then the photographer holds his camera in front of us as Maeve gives us each a bunch of flowers, and we grin as broadly as we can as the flash goes off.

Being a winner is harder than it looks. People keep *looking* at me, so I can't let my guard drop until an hour later, when Will and I are safely in a taxi back to Paddington.

'I suppose the eco-thing would have been to offer to share a cab with Abby,' he says, kissing me again. 'But I wanted you all to myself.'

I sit upright, feeling oddly deflated. Now is not the right time to tell him what she did. And definitely not to mention what I almost did. Maybe it'll never be the right time. Maybe, for once, Emily the gabbler needs to keep her gob shut. Besides, there are bigger concerns right now.

'All to yourself? It's funny, because for the last couple of months, you've been going out of your way to avoid me.'

'That's not true. I've been busy with the shop and the course.'

I shake my head. 'I don't believe you.'

He looks away. 'I . . . OK. All right, yes. I suppose I have been keeping out of your way.'

'What did I do to deserve that, Will?'

'I needed to do some thinking. We didn't seem to be making each other happy. Correction. I wasn't willing to do what you wanted to make you happy, i.e. agree to a baby. And I felt that was all you wanted me for. A substitute for Duncan.'

'Seriously? You thought I was such a glutton for punishment that I wanted *another* Duncan in my life?'

'Well, no. But a husband, yes. We rushed into everything, didn't we, Em? Duncan threatening us pushed us into things that we might not have chosen immediately.'

I bite my lip. That's the first time he's said that. 'What *things*?'

'Like moving in together. Opening the store.'

'*You* asked *me* to run the shop with you, Will.'

He examines the taxi floor. 'Yeah, I know. I know. But maybe I wasn't ready for commitment, and that's why I've been such a bloody disappointment to you.'

'When did I say you were a disappointment?'

'You didn't have to *say* it for me to know it.'

'What are you trying to say, Will?'

'Look, it wasn't only about me, the going to Wales stuff. I also thought you needed to know you could do stuff on your own. That both of us needed to know that we could survive on our own, so that then we could decide whether we still wanted to be together.'

I won't look at him now. I stare at the taxi meter, going up and up. 'So you're saying that the eco-money thing was some kind of secret test you were putting me through, to see if I'm worthy of you? That you did it for my own *good*?'

'No.' He puts his hand on my cheek, to make me look at him. He is looking very, very sincere. But possibly not guilty enough for my liking. 'No. If anything, it was more about my proving to myself that *I* am worthy of you and Freddie.'

'Shouldn't I be the one who decides that one?'

He opens up his hands. 'Yep. You should. But for what it's worth, you've changed while I've been away, Em. For the better, I mean. Not only because you've won this award, but also because for the first time ever, I feel you could manage perfectly well without me.'

'You think?' I snap back.

'Don't you?'

I see my reflection in the taxi window. He's only saying what I worked out for myself before I went to the solicitors: I have hidden resources, more than I ever appreciated before Will left me alone. There's a steeliness in my eyes now.

'So if I can cope without you, have you worked out if you can manage without me, then, Will?'

He sighs. 'Shit, this isn't how I planned this, but it's coming out all wrong. Yes, I can manage without you, and Freddie. But I'd rather not.'

'Glad you've sorted out a plan for him too.' I know I sound sneery, but he bloody deserves it, playing with our lives.

'That was another reason I had to get away. Freddie and me are so close already, and the longer I'm around, the less I'd be able to live with myself if I wanted to leave. I had to decide.'

'And have you?'

He nods. 'I want to be with you, and Freddie.'

'Because you know we can cope without you? God, that is so predictably *male*. And you know another thing that's predictably male? The fact you're always bloody running away. You did it at Christmas, too.'

Will looks uncertain. 'I—'

'And you did it to Abby. You see, it's all very well giving me time on my own, but didn't you think it might backfire? That

I might decide that no man is better than one who can't make up his own mind?'

'No. No. Wait. It's not like that. I don't . . .' He looks around him, slightly wild-eyed. 'I didn't want to talk about it here. Now. But I have something very important to say. I don't only want you. I want what *you* want, too. A proper family. You, me, Freddie and . . . someone new. Someone brand new.'

I gawp. 'A baby?'

He nods.

'Another . . . another mouth to feed? The patter of little carbon footprints?'

He nods again.

'I don't believe you.' And I don't. I feel confused and angry and, OK, yes, a tiny bit excited. But mainly I feel manipulated.

'That's it, guv. We're here.'

We look up, and we're outside Paddington Station.

'You pay,' I say, flinging the door open. 'I'm getting the next train. I don't care what you do. Except someone needs to pick up Freddie from school, and given that you couldn't be bothered to take him for his first day, perhaps you'd like to fetch him today.'

'Of course. I'd love to.'

I climb out.

'You need time,' Will calls out, but it sounds more like a question than a statement.

'Yes. I do. My turn,' and I leave him behind and lose myself in the crowd of passengers. Now I have what I wanted so much, for so long, do I still want it?

CHAPTER 32

Grazia

I must have been to a thousand exhibitions in my life, but *never* my own.

What does one *wear*?

'Anything at all will look wonderful, Grazia,' Joel says. 'Something embroidered, perhaps?'

I reach back into my wardrobe and pull out the red Russian jacket I bought for Emily's craft day in the spring. The weather is right for it – I felt a distinct chill when we went for a walk in St James's Park this morning – but somehow the colour and design are too showy. 'No. I will distract people from the images themselves.'

We visited this morning, to make certain the exhibition was picture perfect. Joel was thrilled by my work, and, specifically, by how it reflects on his prowess as a lover. Something about the scatterings of cross-stitches in the sky suggests star-studded orgasms, according to Pierre. I try not to think about their little liaison, way back when . . .

I stay silent on what my pieces mean. It is one of the tactics I picked up from my late husband. The less you say, the greater your reputation grows.

I am also staying silent about Alf. It seems rich for me to complain too vocally about his dirty little videos when I am parading dirty little images of myself and his father on public view. But Joel has stayed angry, banning his son from the exhibition.

As if the boy would want to attend something so acutely embarrassing.

However, Daisy has demanded a place on the guest list. I think she is planning to find an artist to fall for, and then wants to spend the summer posing in the nude. I will do everything in my power to prevent that happening because being a muse is not something I would recommend as a career option.

'Why don't I choose for you?' Joel suggests.

I hesitate. Trust is, of course, essential in any relationship.

'What's the matter, Grazia? Don't want to give up control?'

'Are you saying I am a control freak?'

Joel laughs. 'Obviously. But I like a woman to take control now and again. Remember?' And he winks.

'I remember. OK. OK. I will take a shower while you choose. So long as you swear you will not choose something hideous. It could be a deal breaker if you get this wrong.'

He pretends to quake. 'Faint heart never won fair lady.' He gets up off the bed and pokes his head into the wardrobe. 'This is not so much a wardrobe as an entire *wing*, you know.'

I shrug. 'What can I say? I am an artist. I am a woman. I like clothes.'

'All right, then. I accept the mission. And now . . .' he takes a very deep breath, 'I'm going in. Send out the search party if I am gone for more than thirty minutes.'

I emerge to find he has selected a scarlet dress I had forgotten all about. I am on the point of rejecting it as too young for me, but he insists I try it on, and I realise that the cut is more flattering now I have filled out a little, and the colour takes away any sallowness from my skin.

'And these shoes,' he says, holding up my favourite black

platforms, 'and of course, this bag,' an antique silk clutch we bought in Barcelona.

They are perfect together. Leon would never have taken the time to choose for me, though he did not hesitate to ask me to change if he didn't think I looked right. But then I was the fool for letting him be so bossy.

'A good effort,' I say, determined not to allow him to become too big for his boots.

My mobile rings. *Emily.*

I would prefer to let it go to answerphone, but I still feel guilty about the rift between her and Sandie, because it happened right here, in my apartment.

'Hello, Emily. How are you?'

A pause. 'I think I'm well. Actually I'm not sure.'

I suppress a sigh. I do not have time for someone else's existential crisis right now.

'Anyway, sorry. That's not why I'm calling. I wondered if I could still come along tonight? To the launch?'

'Oh. Of course. But . . . you know Sandie is coming.'

Another pause. 'Yes. I hoped she was.'

'Fine. Good. I would love to see you there.'

'Don't worry, Grazia. I won't make a scene.'

The fact that a scene has even crossed her mind makes me shudder, but I can hardly refuse her. I only hope that tonight, for once, I stay the centre of attention. And that my work is worthy of the limelight.

I arrive a full hour before the doors open, and immediately wish I had been late.

Pierre tries to ply me with wine and compliments, but neither help. Suddenly the whole idea seems the height of crazy egotism, and my pieces look amateur in this spare, brightly lit gallery space. I even begin to wonder whether the exhibition is nothing more than a vanity project that Joel has secretly funded, to make me feel . . . what? More than his accessory?

'Is this going to be all right?' I ask Pierre. 'They will not laugh at my doodles with a needle and thread?'

'Some might. Or some might say that your work is a bunch of smutty old samplers.'

'Is that what you think?'

'You know I think they're brilliant. But people are entitled to their opinions, even when they're horribly wrong. You must remember that from your life with Leon.'

'Yes.' Leon would disappear into his studio for weeks on end after a bad review, and though I held the fort, I struggled not to see the response as childish. Now I am about to get a taste of that medicine. Nowhere left to hide . . .

'Anyway, the fizz is cold, the canapés are warming. The exhibition is happening with or without you.'

Joel arrives twenty minutes beforehand, with the delicious Daisy, who is almost dwarfed by the bouquet she is carrying.

'For you, with all our love,' she says, kissing me.

'All of it? Even Alf's?'

She smiles – oh, where did she get that self-possession? – and whispers in my ear, '*Especially* Alf's!' And she giggles.

Then time veers off in a new direction, pulling me with it, so hours become minutes. My whole life seems to pass through this gallery in two hours. First, a few of Leon's old friends, who would normally never be seen in such an off-centre place, step inside with strained smiles, preparing themselves for inevitable disappointment. But then they surprise me with the warmth of their compliments.

Original, technically sophisticated, passionate, intelligent, inspired . . .

If they mean just half of it, then I am doing well. Selina, who organised the auction sale of Leon's final works, even slips me her card. 'Not that you don't know my number off by heart already, you wicked girl, Grazia. I can't believe you

333

didn't call me first, I know plenty of places where you'd make so much more than you're asking here.'

Then there are Pierre and Joel's friends, a more motley collection of people who are already determined to love what I do, but seem to love me even more once they've actually seen it.

And then there are Sandie and Emily, at opposite sides of the room. I keep trying to cut through the crowd to drag them face to face, to tell them there should be an end to this, because they have more in common than they have keeping them apart.

But each time I try, someone else stops me: Joel, for a kiss; Daisy, for the lowdown on some callow youth she has spotted; Pierre, to tell me another collector has been attempting to negotiate to 'snap up' one of my pieces, even though I am still far from convinced I want them sold. The erotic ones are, apparently, creating an incredible stir.

Then Pierre claps his hands, and when this does not silence people, he wolf-whistles like a builder, and that works.

'If I could trouble you to stop drinking and gossiping and speculating on the work for one moment, I would like to say a very few words about this exhibition.'

The guests mumble towards silence and when they've got there, Pierre smiles. 'Before I stumbled on Grazia's work, I thought I'd seen it all. And now I think right here, tonight, we're seeing the birth of a new career. A new vision. In most artistic spheres, of course, the novelty and energy of youth is irresistible. Yet in the case of Grazia, maturity adds to the visceral appeal of her work.'

'Are you saying that I am old, Pierre?'

Everyone laughs. 'I must look braver than I am,' he says, and they laugh louder.

My mobile buzzes, and a moment later, so does Joel's. Pierre ignores it, but as people refill their glasses to toast me, Joel shoots me a worried glance.

'To Grazia and her X-rated future!'

'To Grazia!'

When they've cheered, Joel sidles up to me. 'You need to see this. In private.'

I slip out into the tiny office at the back of the gallery and he follows. I open up my phone to find a text from Alf, with a video attached. 'I cannot open it, my phone's too old,' I say.

'I can, unfortunately.' He passes me his smart phone, and I see myself. Naked. A different shot from the one I saw over Alf's shoulder, but taken from the same angle, in the family bathroom. I touch the screen and the picture comes to life, as I towel myself from head to toe, with a final shake of the body that makes my breasts jiggle.

'Why send the clip to me now?'

Joel sighs. 'Because he's an evil little fucker. It's not *just* a clip, Grazia. It's . . . it's online. *Public.*'

'*Anyone* can see it?'

He scrolls upwards on the phone. 'Anyone who likes to go onto the . . . um, *Magnificent Mature Moments* website. He's headed it: *My Wicked Stepmother.*'

I'm trying to process this when Pierre comes in. 'What's with the hiding? Your public want you.'

'They've got more of me than anyone could want,' I say, giving him the phone. Pierre gawps as he realises what he's seeing.

'Who?'

'Fucking Alf,' says Joel. 'When I get my hands on him—'

Pierre shakes his head. 'You do realise he's done us the most amazing favour, don't you? I mean, used the right way, this will get us the kind of PR that a new artist can normally only dream about. Of course, it'd be different if you were looking rough, Grazia. But as it is, well, Joel, you're going to be the envy of an awful lot of men.'

'I'm going to get a taxi home right now and force the little sod to take it down.'

'Joel, it's too late for that,' says Pierre. 'Once it's gone up, it's up. Everything's for ever, now, on the web.'

I still cannot make sense of this: do I want to be known for my body of work, or my body? And is it really too late?

'I'll strangle him, then,' says Joel.

Now I feel angry – with Alf, yes, but with his father too. 'No, you will not. But you know this is not aimed at me. I am nothing more than the . . . porn pawn. It is aimed at you.'

'I'll send him away to a tough school or something. Somewhere that they don't have the bloody internet. Borstal.'

'And fob him off on someone else yet again?' I shake my head. 'You are really not listening to me, are you?'

'Of course I am.'

'Joel, can you not see what is happening? You are making the mistakes your parents made. Choosing not to get involved. The difference is that you know the damage that will cause, so you have no excuse for passing the buck.'

He shakes his head. 'I'm not. I'm talking about getting him the help he needs.'

'Perhaps you could start by apologising to him for saying you never wanted to be a father. What he needs is to know you love him, no matter what.'

'Maybe I'm too selfish to love anyone. That's what Faith always said.'

I shake my head. 'Look, I never knew Faith. I am sure she was a good mother. And of course it was a tragedy that she was taken from Daisy and Alf so early. But that was not *your* fault, Joel. You have to stop feeling guilty and start taking action.'

He says nothing.

I sigh. 'And you wonder why your *son* is not behaving like an adult?'

I walk back into the gallery, numb but oddly determined. If there is really nothing I can do about this, then I will enjoy my night. Perhaps now it is time to knock together the heads of my secret shopping friends, to tell them to start behaving like adults too.

And then I see him.

'Grazia.' He mouths my name and the crowd seems to part as I walk towards him, and then we are out on the street.

'You,' I say.

'Me,' says Nigel. 'I heard about the exhibition. I was due back anyway, for meetings, and I thought . . . well, I wanted to see you again.'

I think about the embroideries, and I know I do not want him to see them. 'Do not go in there. It is . . . private.'

He smiles that crooked, boyish smile. 'Oh yes. Very private. So private that you've invited a hundred of your closest friends.'

'Not like that. It would be strange. Some of the things I have depicted . . .'

Nigel nods. 'I know. I looked at the catalogue online. Only a few, but enough. My granny's handicrafts never looked like those.' He coughs. 'They, um, they did make me realise I missed you. Have you missed me, or . . . ? Well, I guess from the pictures, you might have moved on.'

'I, er . . .' It is my turn to stumble over my words. 'This is almost finished, you know. Wait for me to say my goodbyes and then, well, would you have time for a drink?'

He smiles. 'A drink with an up-and-coming artist? I think that would be my pleasure.'

Three o'clock in the morning.

I have been sitting in the same spot since midnight. What next? I see three paths, where once, not so long ago, I only saw a dead end.

Nigel.

Joel.

No one.

The options spin round and round in my head, and

337

perhaps the champagne is playing its part, too. Do I choose a toyboy rollercoaster, a maze of stepmotherhood, or a gloriously selfish life as an artist?

Or something else altogether?

Nigel has not even said he wants me back – he insisted to me over our drink that he was only in London for bonus discussions with his bosses – but I have a feeling he would not object if I suddenly booked a one-way ticket to Hong Kong. And imagine the embroidery that place might inspire . . .

Strange how at twenty my life was closed off and here, pushing fifty, it is all so open again.

And then something occurs to me. Something so obvious that really, it should have occurred to me before now. If I stay here, I could be to Daisy and to Alf what Edith was to me. Edith, the tweed-and-chiffon-dressed Englishwoman who brought the world to my godforsaken Ligurian village. Edith, who taught me to sew, but also taught me so much more: that widowhood can be the start, not the end. That as long as you are living, you keep learning.

But is that what I want? Is caring the only way for a woman to define herself?

My hands are as restless as my thoughts, and I cast around for a piece of fabric and my sewing box. The ritual of stretching the fabric taut between the two wooden hoops and choosing a colour to capture my mood soothes me, but also gives me an idea.

I will see if I can stitch my way to an answer . . .

CHAPTER 33

Sandie

If the Muppets are surprised as Laetitia leads them in a standing ovation when I enter the boardroom, then they keep it under their toupees.

When the applause has died down, she holds up her hand. 'Let me be the first to congratulate both Miss Barrow, and also my son on his *excellent* choice of right-hand woman. Really, we could not have expected better from the first three days of the new, improved Garnett's.'

Toby and I take our seats. He's in an odd mood today, though it might be because he's been up with Ruby half the night. Being manhandled by 'Granny Garnett' for half of Tuesday put her in a grouchy mood, and then I had my first baby-free night out at Grazia's exhibition, already feeling pissed off with myself and with Emily and the fact we didn't even *speak*. I returned to find Daddy and Ruby both borderline hysterical. I'd have given them *both* Calpol if I'd had enough.

Laetitia continues. 'It is so hard to find people you can trust these days, isn't it? The situation with Edgar was . . . so regrettable. Which is why I am so pleased that we are now in a position to put the stewardship of our much-loved store back into the hands of the family again!'

She beams at me expectantly and it takes me several seconds to realise what she means.

'Me?'

She nods. 'We want you to be the Executive Store Director. Of course some might call us rather rash to invite you to join us on the board on the evidence of only a few days' trading but these are days when delay is more dangerous than rashness, I feel.'

The board. They want to make me a director.

She pauses. I think she's waiting for me to jump in and beg, but I'm too astonished. And there's also the small point that I've given Garnett's many years of loyal service, so to reduce that to 'a few days' trading' doesn't exactly count as giving credit where credit's due.

'But we like to think we can be modern and responsive. Perhaps, even, to admit that by hanging on to Edgar for too long, we made a mistake.'

Toby grabs my hand. 'Oh, say yes, will you, Brains? We can't do it without you.'

'You were in on the plan?'

He shrugs. 'No. Not at all. But I think it's a marvellous one. It's what you always dreamed of, isn't it, Sandie? From the day you arrived as a trainee . . .'

I think of it, then, how it felt to go behind the staff-only doors for the first time, and how overawed I was by the history and the scale and, especially, by the management floor. Of how I longed for this to be *my* empire. How when that happened I would feel I had truly arrived.

Now it's here, I wonder. I have my own business already, and I don't know whether throwing in my lot with Garnett's after all that's happened is the right thing to do.

But who am I kidding? I've let my secret shopping consultancy slip horribly since being given the contract here, and the only work I have outstanding is the impossible wedding shop, which I have failed at completely.

'I . . .'

And aren't I already in up to my neck with the Garnett family? Plus, for all my doubts about Laetitia, I am perversely impressed at how efficiently – and ruthlessly – she dealt with Roland, Edgar and the threat to the store.

'A decision sometime this week would be nice, and I should warn that refusal often offends,' says Laetitia.

I close my eyes. What would the girls say? Grazia would point out that to do anything other than to stand by my man would be asking for trouble.

And Emily? Emily is silly and frivolous and irritating and thoughtless and everything else. But she's also a dreamer – and if she was standing here now, could I honestly tell her that this *isn't* what I want?

Before I open my eyes, they're clapping again, and I realise it's because I've been nodding, and Laetitia has taken that as my yes.

'Yes,' I say, even though they can't hear me above the clapping. 'Yes.'

Now it feels as I thought it would. I deserve this. No one could ever say I didn't earn it the hard way.

We're in a taxi on the way to our poor house, to see the latest carnage the builders have inflicted, and the fizzy feeling is still there, even though I am dreading the site visit.

'Look, I don't want to burst your bubble, Brains, but I wonder whether we should give up on the house as a bad job.'

'How would we do that?'

Toby shrugs. 'We could . . . well, sell it to someone else? As a work-in-progress? Then buy a brand new place.'

'Yes, that'll work, with the housing market in the state it is at the moment.' I am bone-tired, but I need to find the energy to shout at the builders again. 'Leave it to me, I'll give them—'

My phone rings. Lisabet, the wedding shop girl. I've avoided her all week, so I ought to answer. 'Hello.'

'Sandie? God, I thought you'd disappeared. I just wondered . . . well, how that report was coming along. The report you said would be with me weeks ago.'

I sigh. I *hate* letting people down. 'I'm sorry. Really, I'm so sorry. Things caught up with me, and I was hoping I might have a sudden insight into what's going wrong, but you're doing everything right from what I can see. Perhaps it might be better to try someone else. I certainly won't charge you anything, but it might be for the best—'

She hesitates but then I think I can hear sniffing. 'I need your help.'

I sigh. I owe her more than this. 'Hold on a moment.' I cover the microphone and whisper to Toby, 'It's the wedding store. I ought to go over there. Talk to her face to face. It's the least I can do. Could you bear to take a detour after we've been to the house?'

He sighs. 'I suppose. If we must.'

I uncover the microphone. 'I'm on my way to a meeting, but I can come by straight after that. I honestly don't know how much use I can be, but I will try my best.'

'OK,' she says, her voice subdued, and she rings off.

The fizz is definitely fading now. The taxi turns into 'our' street, towards the house that I've believed for so long now would be the one where we'd raise our family. But maybe Toby's right and we would be better off buying something off the shelf. We can't be distracted from saving Garnett's, not if we want to stay financially secure.

The clouds above us are grey and heavy with the possibility of thunder. At least when I shout at the builders the neighbours might not hear me. I open the taxi door. 'Wait, please,' I tell the driver. 'This won't take too long.'

I step down from the car and turn towards the house.

This isn't right.

The house has a weird *glow*, and it takes me a few seconds to realise that's because it now has windows reflecting the clouds, and bright white window frames. There is even – how? – a gorgeous, shiny, bright red front door that makes me think of phone booths and postboxes and new starts.

And for the very first time the turret doesn't look as though it's about to tumble down onto our heads . . .

I walk towards it. Am I so knackered that I've started hallucinating?

Weirder still, instead of the builders, I'm seeing my mum and my gramma on the front drive . . . and Marnie's holding Ruby. I race towards her, taking the baby in my arms and feeling her warmth. It's only now that I see Grazia next to them.

'What the hell are you guys doing here?' I ask my gramma, and she frowns at 'hell'.

Now Emily steps out of the front door. I definitely *am* hallucinating. Except, as she takes my hand, I can feel the squeeze.

I hand Ruby to my grandmother and follow Em – well, what else am I supposed to do? – and the paint fumes make me feel even dizzier. But what freaks me out completely is the fact that our hallway, well . . .

'It's finished!'

'Hey, hold on. The boys are miracle workers, but we haven't had *that* long, yet. There's at least . . . oh, another fortnight to go.'

The boys. It triggers a memory of Emily's squalid little flat in Shepherd's Bush, which was transformed into an airy apartment with the help of three Latvian builders.

I follow her. It's still a mess, but it's a productive mess. I can imagine that, under the dustsheets, and the small scaffolding towers, our forever house is about to burst out of its chrysalis.

We walk into the living room, where the three miracle workers are covered in paint and dust. Big Janis, with hair as blond as Toby's, Little Janis with a darker moustache, and Kaspar, the father figure: they're busy painting the walls a wonderful shade of dove grey.

'How?'

'Oh, they were only working on a stupid office conversion, so I managed to persuade them it'd be worth their while.'

'And the other builders?'

Emily laughs. 'I think that they saw these three boys as a threat to their masculinity, so they've buggered right off with talks of lawsuits and all sorts.'

'Ah, we'll bury them under solicitor's letters,' says Toby. He's right behind me.

'You *knew* and you didn't tell me?'

'Didn't want to spoil the surprise,' he says, before ducking out of my way as I reach out to hit him. 'But they've done more in the last two days than the other wasters have managed in months.'

And as we go from top to bottom, from the garden room to the turret, I realise it's true. We're not ready to move in yet, but we will be, and soon. This is home.

Now the fizzy feeling is back again, and I hug Toby and then I turn back to Emily. 'You sorted this for me?'

She nods. 'I . . . I wanted to do something good. To do the right thing. Even I got bored with being selfish in the end, eh?'

'Shh . . .'

I'm about to tell her that she's not selfish, but I decide that there's another way of doing it. Even though it feels awkward, I pull her towards me and I hug her: to thank her for everything, to tell her it's all right and it'll always be all right between us, because whatever our many, many differences, we're friends.

Weird. Even going to meet Lisabet isn't enough to make me feel down now that I know I've got the baby, the job, the man . . . and, almost, the house.

But I do feel sad for her. I know what it means to put yourself into a business – your ideas, your beliefs, your faith. I will tell her to be brave, to keep trying. That courage is needed for a happy ending.

The taxi stops at the entrance to the cobbled mews.

'Shall I wait here, too, then?' the driver asks hopefully, but Toby hands Ruby to me while he pays him.

I kiss Ruby – she's been very good – and hand her back. 'You don't have to come in with me,' I tell him. 'It might look, well, unprofessional, I guess.'

He takes my hand. 'No. I better had. You never know how these bridezilla women can get . . .'.

Lisabet answers the door, frowning. 'I wasn't sure you'd show up, to be honest.'

She turns around and goes inside, and I follow her into Your Perfect Day, wanting to be anywhere but here because I feel so useless. I want to be at home, planning for our big move, but that makes me feel even guiltier about failing her.

She shows us into the drawing room, which has a fresh bunch of flowers right in the centre, and a bottle of champagne on ice in a silver bucket in the corner. This is what I don't understand. They have everything taken care of here, so why on earth are they not getting any work?

'This is all for my next lady,' says Lisabet, gesturing to the flowers. 'Let me go and get my papers so I can make notes.'

'I hope she's going to take it OK, because I honestly don't know what to say to her.'

'It does seem a pretty smart set-up here. Every girl's dream, eh?' Toby laughs.

I look around. 'It is good, yeah. I mean, the funny thing is, on my recce, I almost started to think that weddings could be fun, even though you know how I feel—' I turn round, and then I stop. 'What are you doing?'

Toby is on the floor. Well. On his knees. He's reaching into his pocket and pulling a small, square, purple box out of his pocket. 'Sandie . . .'

'Wha-at?'

'Um. I know it's something I've asked before, well, more than a few times before, but this time I've gone to a bit of extra trouble, so please promise not to dismiss it, because I do think—'

'Toby? Did you set all this up?'

'What?'

'My assignment. The contract. Was it all . . . a ruse?'

'Well. They do offer a *bespoke* service. You know. Wedding needs catered for, including proposals. I thought getting you in here might help sell the idea a bit.'

I'm backing away slightly, and he's moving along the floor towards me on his knees, like Pingu, and then he stops and holds out the box, which is still shut, and says, 'Please stand still, Sandie, so that I can actually ASK YOU TO MARRY ME.'

I stop. 'Was that *it*?' I try to stop myself smiling.

'The proposal?'

'Yes. Because it doesn't seem very well planned.'

'Oh. Um. Well, now you've stopped moving, perhaps I can have another go. Sandra Anne Barrow, mother of my beautiful daughter, right-hand woman, brainiest girl I've ever known and certainly the brainiest I've ever been to bed with, *please, please* will you agree to marry me this time? Because I really am getting quite bored with asking now, especially when I happen to think that it's actually a bloody good idea for us to spend the rest of our lives together.'

He looks down at the box. 'Whoops. I think I'm meant to have opened this, eh?' And he does, and I see the ring, with the deepest, darkest red stone at its heart. 'It's inspired by the antique pendant I gave you, way back, to say thanks for all your help with the spreadsheets. Well, that's what I said it was for. I reckon we already knew we loved each other, but hadn't *quite* been able to admit it to ourselves, never mind each other.'

I reach for the ring, but then I realise what that would signify, so I hold back. 'A garnet?'

'I promise you it's not about egomania, or the name, exactly. I can afford a diamond if that's what you want. It's just that a garnet is the warmest stone I know. I think it's probably . . . well, um, the colour of my heart.'

'You big soppy man, you . . .'

'Come on, Sandie. This is the last time I will ask you, I swear. I won't bother you again if you say no this time. A guy does get the hint in the end.'

I close my eyes and I see Emily's face, and she winks – and then I open my eyes again and I reach out and I take the box.

'Is that . . . ?' Toby says.

'That'll be a yes. It's turned into, well . . . one of those days when I don't think no is an option.'

April 23rd

St George's Day

CHAPTER 34

Sandie

'Are you ready, girls?'

The crowd cheers, and the American actor smiles, his tombstone teeth crowding out of his mouth. 'Are you *sure* you're ready?'

A bigger cheer. I catch Emily's eye and she grins. '*Still can't believe you got him*,' I mouth to her, because she'd never hear me above this racket.

'*It's all about contacts*,' she mouths back.

The truth is, without this famously short A-lister, none of us would be here right now. He's the same guy who made his chauffeur take a thirty-mile detour after hearing about the Heartsease chutney. Without him, Emily would never have thought of selling home-made groceries. Sometimes, life's about luck.

'*OK, you guys.* You asked for it. The inaugural Green Goddess Findlebury to Heartsease Race is about to begin.'

Findlebury is the ideal place for a St George's Day fete. Half of the UK's bunting supplies are hanging up across the village green, and there are red-and-white flags flying, alongside the flags of fifty more nations of people who've made their home locally.

All right, so the attempt at baking the world's biggest scone did fail, but every one of this afternoon's competitors got a chunky slice to give them energy, and the local TV news people are here to film the race.

'On your marks, paws, tyres and trainers?'

Ruby, Monty and I are the Garnett's Gadabouts, all dressed in deepest red. Across the green I can see Grazia, aka the Scarlet Woman. She refused to stand next to me because she said two shades of red can only clash horribly, but actually I think she's been in training for the run and doesn't want to be held back by us.

Babs has come too, running in white, with a veil, as Always the Bridesmaid. I felt a bit awkward when she showed up, but she laughed it off and turned round. On her back there's a sign saying Suits Me Just Fine.

'Get set?'

Emily is the Handmade Rainbow, dressed in a hot-and-sticky-looking outfit made up of craft taught in the workshop area: violet crocheted hat, indigo knitted singlet with blue embroidered number, green silk shorts, with yellow, orange and red screen-printed trainers. The boys are waiting for us in Heartsease, because this is a goddess-only race. Monty is going to have to keep his tail firmly between his legs.

'GOOOOOOOO!'

The starting pistol sounds, and we really are off!

As the two hundred women and girls surge forward, Monty pulls away sharply and I almost let go of the lead, but as I cling on, I feel myself being dragged along. Ruby is laughing like a drain as I pant and trip and try to keep hold of both of them.

I always knew I wasn't cut out for the multi-tasking of motherhood.

'Come back, Monty! Here, boy . . . um, girl!'

He's still racing and howling excitedly, like the Hound of the Baskervilles' younger brother. Perhaps one of the other dogs has caught his fancy. Toby might have given up his bachelor habits, but Monty is still playing the field . . .

There's Grazia, overtaking me already, and at her side there is Daisy, barely puffing as she keeps up easily with her glamorous stepmother. Not that Joel and Grazia plan to marry. 'I will not make that mistake again, Sandie. Anyway, keeping him on his toes also ensures he goes to family therapy, which seems to be doing wonders for the frightful Alf, too.'

It wasn't the easy option: that would have been to go with Nigel. I could have imagined Grazia in Hong Kong, sewing up a storm and hosting marvellous expat soirees at luxury hotels. But she told me that her embroidery gave her the answer. She stitched through the night after her exhibition launch, not stopping to look at what she was doing until her fingers were so tired that they froze in position, and her eyes were blurry.

'The dark blue fabric was all bunched up and I straightened it out, not knowing what was there. And then I realised that the image I had sewn was a house. Not a designer house like mine and Leon's, but a regular, cartoonish house with a chimney and square windows and a pitched roof. And then I realised: it was Joel's. Not a house I would ever have bought for myself. I had chosen a white floss with flecks of silver, so that the shape was like a house lit up against the night sky. And I knew immediately that this was the place I could call home.'

Daisy waves as the two of them disappear into the distance. Up ahead, I see the surgically enhanced buttocks of Abby, encased in a cream velour number. What are the odds that she's already worked out a short cut, or that her husband is waiting down a side road with the Porsche? From what Emily's told me, she's a total fraud, from her 'homemade' boxed dinners to her plagiarised pitch.

On the plus side, Emily has Abby exactly where she wants her. She doesn't like to call it blackmail, but there's a good reason why Heartsease has ended up with the biggest share of the European funding pot. Emily reckons Abby's more worried about the Findlebury mummy mafia discovering she doesn't make her own soufflés than she is about them learning she's a back-stabbing cheat.

In fact, Emily thinks Abby lost interest in the whole Green Goddess prize the moment she'd won, and now has her sights set on becoming an MEP.

All in all, I can't help thinking that Heartsease is a much nicer place to be.

I definitely wish I was there right now. *Six miles.* I really should have taken the bike.

Emily is next to me now. 'How . . . are . . . you . . . doing?'

She's out of breath, but glowing, and not just with sweat. I know she's not pregnant yet – I'm expecting to have a ringside seat on the other side of the bathroom door when she embarks on the test – but she has the aura of a woman who is having a lot of fun trying . . .

I'm glad she forgave Will, though I am also glad she stood up to him. Public schoolboys always need a feisty woman to keep them in check. I've learned that much from my time with Toby.

'I am so out of condition,' I reply, but I'm surprised that I can say it without huffing and puffing too badly.

'Rubbish, Sandie . . .' Emily says, sounding like she's about to collapse any minute now. 'We all know . . . you've been having . . . extra sessions . . . with your personal trainer . . . for the wedding!'

The wedding. *My* wedding. That still sounds even less real than *my* daughter.

'No, but I have been taking the stairs at work.' And given that I go from the top to the bottom of Garnett's about fifty times a day, that must be helping.

Monty howls again and I feel the pull on the lead get

stronger. 'I think I'm going to have to leave you now,' I shout out, as he drags me forward. 'See you in Heartsease . . .'

By the time we get to the edge of the village the pain has stopped and the adrenalin has taken over. Monty has abandoned the heavy breathing, and keeps turning his head to give me little looks as if to say, *are you serious about keeping going?* And Ruby, unbelievably, has fallen asleep. Even now, nine months on, Miss Hart's magic has made ours the most laidback of babies.

The cheering is getting louder as, ahead of us, the first runners make it across the finishing line. I can see the shops and the common in the distance. Half of Berkshire's scaffolding is holding up the old parade, as it's being transformed into little studios for artists and crafters, and there are striped refreshment tents lined up on the grass. The idea of carrot cake and pink lemonade helps me to keep going despite the pain.

A cluster of our finest menfolk are by the finishing line. Monty picks up the pace, which makes Ruby wake up, in time to see Daddy leaping up and down like a loon.

'Come on, BRAINS!' he's shouting. 'COME ON, RUBY!'

It's enough to give me energy for a final push, despite the cramp in my legs and the stitch in my side, and the blisters forming under my fingers from clutching the buggy handles. There's Will, too, with Freddie on his shoulders, and Grazia and Daisy glugging down energy drinks, with Joel next to them, and Alf taking photographs for the Heartsease Common website that his dad has press-ganged him into building, to divert him from less . . . savoury projects.

The finishing line has been knitted by Jean's crafting class, in the shape of hundreds of tiny hearts all linked together, and it's raised as I approach, and there's a cheer, and Toby is hugging me, and lifting Ruby out of the buggy to hold her too, while Monty nips impatiently at our heels.

'My two best girls!' he says.

'What did we come?' I ask, leaning on him for support.

'Forty-seventh, I think. But you're always number one to me.'

Later, we lounge around on Heartsease Common. Normally it'd be that bit too chilly in the April breeze, but after the run, we're warmed up. As well as carrot cake and lemonade, there's champagne to keep us going.

I do love this place. It's not as chichi as Upper Findlebury, of course, but the Green Goddess grant is already making a difference. The artists' studios will be finished by early summer, and the brand new resource centre, built from straw bales, is taking shape at the far end of the grass. Babs seems to have developed an intense interest in eco-construction techniques, judging from the amount of time she's spent with the hairy blond giant who is giving her a demonstration. Though maybe it's not his building skills she's entranced by . . .

I lie down on the picnic blanket, with Ruby beside me. I've earned my rest. Garnett's had a great winter, and the signs for spring are even better. Toby's excelling as a house husband, though his mother definitely doesn't approve. And while the preparations for our midsummer wedding have been almost as time-consuming as the entire store relaunch, I think I've finally got it under control.

'Look, sweet pea,' I say, pointing towards Grazia and Emily, who are whispering and giggling as they circle the common handing out free samples of Heartsease's finest produce and leaflets about the Handmade workshops. Emily is a born eco-preneur, even though it's taken her a while to realise it. 'Who are they?'

'Gnnnnnnurrrrgh,' she says, with complete confidence.

'That's right. Your two, very magical godmothers. Who also happen to be Mummy's best friends.'

I relish the words, knowing that happy ever after means

nothing if you can't share it with the people who'll always come good in the end. I think of Grazia's gift to my daughter: the dream quilt, embroidered with so much love and hope. Every time I put her to bed, I notice something new, and I wonder which of those dreams will come true.

Ruby opens her eyes wide. I recognise the look: it means she wants a story, even though I've no idea if she understands a word of what I say yet.

'OK, Ruby, you win. Are you lying comfortably? Then I'll begin.'

And she closes her eyes, her lips curving into a smile when she hears my voice. As I begin my first ever fairy story, I have no idea what will happen next but I have a feeling it will be good.

'Once upon a time, there were three girls called Sandie, Emily and Grazia . . .'

ACKNOWLEDGEMENTS

Writing *The Secret Shopper Affair* has been a labour of love – I've come a long way with Emily, Sandie and Grazia, and I hope I leave them (for now!) in a happier place. Meanwhile, I move on knowing my French knots from my granny squares, and an awful lot more besides.

Crafty teacher Catherine Hirst was both inspirational and technically spot-on, while Jennifer Pirtle at The Make Lounge in London is doing terrific things to spread the word about hand-made. If you're inspired by Grazia or Emily, then feelingstitchy.com is a wonderful place to discover more about contemporary embroidery, while stitchnbitch.org will point you in the direction of places you can learn to knit (hey, they might even let you crochet too). There are more of my favourite sites and blogs on my website. I'd also like to thank Benita Brown, Antonella Morga and Tansy Hawksley for helping me get to the bottom of what an Italian woman would know about embroidery.

As usual, the people at Orion have done a smashing job stitching together a rough and ready manuscript into a book. Loulou Clark really worked hard to get the right look for the fabulous new cover. Angela McMahon and Sophie Mitchell endeavour as always to get books to make headlines, while

Jade Chandler has ensured that I hit my deadlines. Thanks to Juliet Ewers, Susan Lamb, Lisa Milton, Genevieve Pegg and Jon Wood for all the enthusiasm and support for this book – and the previous ones. Particular thanks to the wonderfully thorough and observant copy editor, Liz Hatherell, for keeping me on track and out of trouble, an especially tricky job with a sequel. And, of course, thanks to Kate Mills for knowing what's best for the book, whether it's subtle tweaking or the odd bit of slash and burn . . . !

Thanks to Peta, Harry and everyone at LAW, but especially Araminta, for brilliant advice, and unfailing kindness mixed with common sense.

Writer mates understand the pleasure and the pain along the way. So thanks to members of the Romantic Novelists' Association, and the Girly Writers – I've missed you, it's not the same online! The People of the Board are always a welcome distraction. Special thanks to Linda Buckley-Archer, Sarah Duncan, Giselle Green, Meg Sanders, Stephanie Zia and especially to Sue Mongredien for reading excerpts, and to Matt Dunn for advice and Americanos.

Lots of love to chums, old (well, not *old*, but you know what I mean) and new. Thanks especially to the many fab people who gave us such a warm welcome in Barcelona! Ah, the research for Grazia's time in the city was tough, I'll admit . . .

Love to David and Diana Carter, Jenny, Geri, Toni, my parents Barbara and Michael, and Rich. Profound apologies to anyone I've forgotten. You know what my memory is like.

Finally, and most importantly, many thanks to you for reading. Honestly, it wouldn't be the same without you! If you'd like to get in touch about crochet, books or anything else, I'd love to hear from you via my website, www.kate-harrison.com.

Kate Harrison
November 2010